SHADOW TALK

A MILITARY SPACE OPERA TALE

P. R. ADAMS

PROMETHEAN TALES

This is a work of fiction. Names, characters, places and incidents are used fictitiously. Any resemblance to actual events, or persons, living or dead, is coincidental. All rights reserved. No part of this publication may be reproduced, or transmitted in any form or by any means, electronic or otherwise, without written permission from the author.

SHADOW TALK

Copyright © 2019 P R Adams

All rights reserved, including the right to reproduce this book, or portions thereof, in any form.

Illustration © Tom Edwards
TomEdwardsDesign.com

❀ Created with Vellum

ALSO BY P. R. ADAMS

For updates on new releases and news on other series, visit my website and sign up for my mailing list at:

http://www.p-r-adams.com

The War in Shadow

Shadow Moves

Shadow Play

Shadow Strike

Shadow Talk

Shadow Pawn

Shadow Fall

Books in the On The Brink Universe

The Stefan Mendoza Trilogy

Into Twilight

Gone Dark

End State

Stefan Mendoza: The Human Deception Trilogy

Split Image

Hard Burn

Null Point

The Rimes Trilogy

Momentary Stasis

Transition of Order

Awakening to Judgment

The ERF Series

Turning Point

Valley of Death

Jungle Dark

Chariot Bright

Dawn Fire

The Lancers Series

Deep Descent

Deadly Game

Dire Straits

Dark Secrets

The Burning Sands Trilogy

Beneath Burning Sands

Across Burning Sands

Beyond Burning Sands

The Second Burning Sands Trilogy

Inside Burning Sands

Over Burning Sands

War for Burning Sands

Books in The Chain Series

The Chain: Shattered

The Journey Home

Rock of Salvation

From the Depths

Ever Shining

DEDICATION

For those lost during Operation Eagle Claw.

1

The *Valor*'s general quarters alarms dug into Captain Faith Benson's nerves like icy daggers, and the flashing red light alert seemed specifically designed to blind her. Her dress whites had gone from a comfortable fit to a hugging, restrictive bind. The bridge crew had to be feeling the same way, hunched over their stations at the broad console that held helm, weapons, and communications controls. She'd only taken the command station because of her duties as task force commander readying for a diplomatic mission with the Gulmar. Now she was stuck there when it should have been her XO running things.

Benson checked the clasp holding her long, brown hair in place. She squinted her jade eyes at Commander Dinesh Chopra's back. Her XO was too absorbed in managing the bridge crew to show any sign of concern over her inexperience with a ship the size of the *Valor*, the biggest and deadliest in the Kedraalian fleet, maybe in known space.

Chopra turned from his place behind the helm station and strode to her side. He stood on his tiptoes, a habit born from compensating for his height. Flashing lights reflected from the deep gold of his bald head. "Not good, Captain."

It felt to Benson like the bridge had grown hotter. "No ships still?"

"Nothing so far but debris."

"Distress signals? Transponders?"

"We're still scanning." But the way his soft cheeks bunched up—they weren't going to find anything.

"It's too much debris spread too wide to be one ship."

"Yes."

"That rules out an accident."

Chopra chewed on his bottom lip. "This definitely wasn't an accident."

"We need to get out in front of this. Have Lieutenant Nuñez contact the Gulmar to inform them of the situation. Emphasize that we're searching for survivors."

"What should we say about possible causes?"

Benson had been wondering about that herself. "Tell them what we know: No ships appear to have survived, and we're receiving no emergency signals."

Her XO hurried over to Nuñez's station and the two huddled. The communications officer seemed to tower over Chopra, but that was mostly thanks to her lean, dancer's physique and the curly brown hair piled on top of her head. She was taller, definitely, but the crown of her square face was only slightly higher than the XO's bald head.

While they worked through the particulars of the message, Benson studied the sensor data coming in from the weapons station. Lieutenant Mahama—the chunky young man on duty—was still hunched over the console, head slowly swiveling left and right, then up and down as he ran through the assorted displays available to him.

Benson tapped a curious signal on her own command station and sent that to him. "Lieutenant Mahama?"

He turned, his round, dusky cheeks slick where sweat trickled down. "Yes, ma'am?"

"This signal I've identified—what is it?"

"I can't tell, Captain. It's on the extreme edge of the debris field."

"It looks pretty large. Could it be a ship section?"

"We'd need something to move closer. Would you like one of the signals ships to redeploy away from the task force?"

"What I'd like is to have gunships out, scouting the debris fields and—"

Chopra's head came up from where he'd been working with Nuñez at her station. The XO glanced from the weapons officer to Benson. "You'll…want to run any deployment changes through Commander Tuleyev, Captain. Wouldn't you?"

Benson did her best not to clench her jaw. "Thank you, Commander Chopra."

Tuleyev was her second-in-command and her first-in-pain-in-the-ass. He was another officer who had suffered during all the budget cuts and promotion delays, and he should technically have outranked her, except for his promotion to captain being delayed again. Although it seemed likely he would receive the promotion next cycle, he had made it quite clear that he wasn't thrilled at the idea of serving under someone junior to him. All his years of experience on the command staff of larger ships held value, but it was nullified by his bitterness.

She sent the call through private communications rather than through Mahama's console.

Tuleyev didn't respond.

This time, Benson couldn't prevent herself from grinding her teeth. "Lieutenant Nuñez, please open a call to the *Lyon* and inform your counterpart I would like to speak to Commander Tuleyev."

The young woman nodded, then covered her mouth and blunt nose with a hand. No one seemed to enjoy dealing with the *Lyon* crew, especially when it meant involving its captain.

Chopra drifted over to the command station, hands clasped in front of him. "You think the Azoren got wind of this meeting?" He was barely audible over the siren.

Despite the whispering, Lieutenant Konrath—the navigation officer—flinched. His sharp profile took on more color than could be explained away by the alarm light. Like a lot of people in the Kedraalian military, the young man carried a badge of shame that extended beyond his pale features. Part of his family had been in the Azoren movement before the War of Separation, and a distant uncle had conducted terrorist operations before taking his family into Azoren space. Konrath had undergone extensive background investigations just to enter the Navy. Benson could only imagine what had been necessary to get assigned to the *Valor*.

She lowered her voice. "We know they have spies in high places."

"Have? Weren't most rooted out?"

"I doubt it. You think it could be something else?"

"The Gulmar are known to have rival factions. I was actually surprised to learn the Gulmar Conglomerate still held power after all these years."

That knowledge about the Gulmar came from the XO's economic and political studies, of course. "The GSA and SAID both list the old power structures as unchanged. Wasn't the Conglomerate significantly larger than its next closest competitor?"

"Probably close to twice the size, but that was decades ago."

"They're pretty bloodthirsty, right?"

Chopra frowned. "By our standards. It *is* the objective of a corporation to keep the business entity alive and profitable at all costs."

"At the expense of everyone and everything else, yes."

Nuñez twisted around, making the move look graceful regardless of the cramped quarters. "Captain? Transferring Commander Tuleyev to you."

Benson and Chopra exchanged pained smiles, then he stepped away. She took in a cleansing breath, then activated the channel. Video—choppy at first—revealed a thick man with jowls and saggy flesh that almost looked like it was melting. Gray eyes stared from under craggy lids. Flashing lights reflected off thick, steel-gray hair that must have been formed in a mold.

"Commander Tuleyev. Thank you for taking—"

"*Captain* Benson, good morning to you."

Without meaning to, she let her eyes drift to the clock that tracked the time at Varudin, the Kedraalian capital. It was nearly noon. "We have a curious signal on the outer edge of the debris field and need to redeploy a signals ship to see if it might be an emergency beacon."

Tuleyev hunched slightly and let out a grunt. "You have set your mind to this already, and still you come to me with the premise of… What is it, exactly, you wish to appear to be doing—consultation?"

"Yes, Alexander, consultation."

"Well, *Captain*, my position would be that we face a mystery, yes? We have yet to understand what this debris is, yes?"

"That's correct. I think there might be more data—"

"Does the *consultation* continue? I ask, because you seem to have arrived already at an answer, and this before my input has actually been fully heard."

"Time *is* important, don't you think?"

"So many questions, and yet I haven't answered the first. You would hear my advice, yes?"

Benson squeezed her lips tight and nodded.

"Ah! That is much more like consultation! So, to my point: You wish to redeploy the task force, and yet we have no idea what we have stumbled upon here. Could this be the remnants of the Gulmar ships? This we do not know, and it seems unlikely."

"Why is that?"

"Very few weapons exist that could render ships of sufficient mass and size into such small pieces that…" He nodded toward what she imagined was the *Lyon*'s main display, where the debris field most likely occupied his attention.

"It could have been an accident. If they carried nuclear warheads—"

The older man's bushy eyebrows raised. "Once again, before I can speak, I am interrupted."

"I'm sorry." It was past noon now. Benson figured her second-in-command might make his point before 10 p.m. Maybe.

He nodded, lips puckered and brow creased somberly. "Yes, I see."

"Commander Tuleyev, may I ask you a question?"

"Another one? So soon?"

"Regarding your assessment so far."

"Ah! Yes, this is still in my mind a matter of consultation."

"Do you believe the Gulmar sent the promised ships or not?"

"The Gulmar, you ask? Did they send their Fleet One as promised? Well, Captain, are they known for doing as promised, or are they known for—how would you say it?—hoping to work angles to maximum advantage?"

Mahama stiffened, then glanced over his shoulder at her. "Captain, we've got a pretty good reading from the *Ganges*: That's a sizable piece of a ship."

Benson muted her connection to Tuleyev, who was still rattling on. "How big?"

"It could be a major compartment. And there are three others of similar size in that area."

Benson turned to Chopra. "Have Chief Parkinson ready drones. Tell Lieutenant Halliwell to have his Marines prepare to launch in ten minutes. Pull teams from the *Ganges* to supplement our forces. We'll need Commander Dietrich to send a medical team along with the Marines. At this moment, we have to hope for survivors."

Chopra closed his eyes and stepped away from the helm station; he understood.

"*Captain?*" It was Tuleyev. "Have you abandoned my *consultation?*"

"No—" Benson remembered she was on mute and with a sigh undid that. "No."

"Yet you have not answered questions that I pose."

"I'm sorry. We've just had an update."

"An update? This is possible without redeploying ships?"

"The *Ganges* was better positioned to get a scan in."

"The *Ganges?* I see." Disappointment oozed from the older man's voice.

"I'm sending Marines and medical units to investigate."

"Because the *Ganges* managed a better scan?"

"Yes. There are larger ship segments, possibly intact compartments."

"Is it acceptable for a moment of bold observation, *Captain?* Because it seems to me this discovery has led to the behavior of a search-and-rescue officer. This task force, it is still intended for diplomatic purposes, yes?"

Search-and-rescue. He said it as if SAR was something despicable, as if she should be ashamed of her years aboard the *Pandora* and the lives she'd helped save. "We're also here for strength projection."

"Yet here we are, risking Marines for a possible rescue?"

"Only the strong can manage humanitarian behavior in the face of adversity."

"Yes. But, for the sake of clarity, the mission objective is intact?"

"We are still on a diplomatic mission, if that's what you mean."

"I see, I see. Hm."

"Do you have something you want to note for the record, Commander?"

"We are not search-and-rescue. This is all."

"Noted."

"Without change to your course, yes?"

"No change to my course, no."

"I see."

"Commander Tuleyev, until we see proof otherwise, we're going to have to assume this was the promised Gulmar task force."

"Proof? What proof? You mean the radio signals and emergency beacons?"

"The task force could have faced an event before it could react."

"Event. This is a word meaning what?"

"I'll leave it to you to decide, Alexander. We're going to check out these potential compartments to see if we can determine that. Please have the *Lyon* maintain a secure posture."

"Yes, a security posture. As would be advisable for a task force in hostile space, you see."

Benson disconnected. There was too much going on to put up with Tuleyev's hurt feelings and borderline histrionics. The task force was operating without any meaningful data, and the large chunks of debris they'd located might hold answers.

Chopra drifted past the command stations, then settled beside her. "That didn't sound like it went well."

"It didn't. He thinks we should just sit here and wait for...I don't know."

"We have yet to hear back from the Gulmar."

"But we've transmitted an update. How close is their nearest station?"

"That we know of?" The XO pinched his bottom lip. "It could take days before we hear anything back. Weeks if they have to send back to Radetta for approval to respond. And that assumes they have a Fold Space transmitter."

Of course, things couldn't be simple. She was on a diplomatic mission to a government that had been formed by corporate interests after breaking off during the War of Separation. She was seeking an alliance with the blessing of a prime minister who very likely was facing a no-confidence vote in the next few months, and the maneuver that brought about the vote was her mother's doing. If the debris were all that remained of the Gulmar's main naval force, and the Azoren had been behind the attack, it meant that the Azoren still had spies deeply embedded in the Kedraalian government. It also meant the Azoren military was capable of sustaining its ongoing war against the Moskav Alliance and overcoming the loss of the task force sent to attack Kedraal.

Benson had only ever wanted to captain the *Valor*. She'd only ever wanted to see peace and prosperity return to her people. Now she wasn't sure what was a realistic hope.

Low-scale war? A cold war where the intelligence agencies played their dirty tricks against each other, operating beyond the sight of the citizens they supposedly protected?

A hot war, the sort of thing the Azoren seemed ready to embrace…

They had come close. They had probably been hours from firing nuclear missiles on Kedraal or possibly simply hurling asteroids into the atmosphere.

Benson's communicator buzzed. She knew before checking the display that it was Halliwell. "Lieutenant Halliwell?"

"We're ready to launch, Captain." In the background, muffled voices mixed with the clatter of gear being secured and engines powering up. He lowered his voice. "What's going on?"

"We don't know. Maybe we've found some intact compartments."

"Dietrich assigned Kohn to run the medical teams."

"Ensign Kohn is experienced with these sorts of operations, and he's way ahead of schedule in his training."

"That's nice, Faith. He's also sitting right next to Parkinson."

"Can't you put them on separate shuttles?"

"We're only taking three from the *Valor*, and Toni wants two of those ready for rapid response."

Meaning no non-essential personnel. "We don't have any enemy signals."

"You want to just assume this was some sort of accident?"

"No." Benson turned away from the bridge crew at the forward console. "Clive, we don't have time for me to hash this out with Dietrich. I'm already fighting with Tuleyev."

The Marine commander sighed. "Can't we just for once get a functional team?"

"What would that look like?" Benson studied her bridge crew.

"I don't know. Different."

"People are always going to have problems. We have to make do with what we have."

"Sure." Halliwell disconnected.

He'd been brittle since taking command of the task force's Marines. It wasn't the stress of it. He knew what he was doing and didn't have secrets to keep like Gadreau had. She would work things out with Halliwell. Later. Maybe a quiet meal in her cabin. Maybe something…more.

At the moment, what mattered was getting eyes on the spinning wreckage floating through space, twisting away from the area where the Gulmar ship or ships should have been waiting for the prearranged meeting.

Something told her those pieces of debris held the answers she needed.

That same intuition told her the answers were going to change things forever.

2

Against the infinite, black backdrop of space, Benson had trouble picking out the six Marine shuttles. She jumped from the gunship escort cameras to shuttle cameras, then back to the *Valor* sensor feed. Chopra managed the bridge crew while she focused on what Tuleyev would dismissively call a search-and-rescue operation.

And what if it was? Even in combat, lives mattered.

Still, she caught the concern on her XO's face—the tight-pressed lips and the fine web of wrinkles around his eyes. This was more fodder for Tuleyev to agitate for her removal as commander of the task force once they returned to Kedraal.

She shook out her arms, letting the tension ease out from her shoulders and neck. Although she'd turned the siren off, the warning light continued to pulse. Even that wouldn't keep the crew sharp if she couldn't stay on top of them. Chatter would fill the silence. Distraction would settle in.

Chopra eased back to the command station. Perspiration had activated his cologne, which gave off an idealized sense of the sea: pleasantly briny and sweet. He swallowed. "Almost to the first debris chunk."

On the command station display, the camera of the lead gunship revealed a roughly cube-shaped piece of blackened material. Sensors said the shape was ten meters to a side, excluding the pieces that poked out here and there. "If there's a hatch to it, it's melted."

"It could be a sealed compartment—weapons capacitors or some sort of storage module."

"The spin on it, the rate it's moving out from where the Gulmar were supposed to be waiting for us…"

"We can't jump to conclusions." The bald XO sighed.

"You have."

"I have?"

"Jumped to conclusions. You think it's part of a ship."

He ran a knuckle under an eye, wiping away sweat. "This is dead space."

"I know." Nothing should have been here, so what else could they be looking at but the remnants of the Gulmar fleet? The thought ate at her.

Nuñez's head came around. "Captain, Lieutenant Halliwell's requesting a connection."

Benson stiffened. The formality was necessary, but it never grew easier to deal with, especially with so much on the line and so many watching. She put the communicator headset over her ear. "Put him through, please, Lieutenant."

Halliwell's voice was in Benson's ear—deep and even. "Captain Benson?"

"Go ahead." She tried for something close to his level of calm and failed.

"Who's on the call with us?"

"It's just us."

"Good. You getting the video feeds okay?"

"I am."

"Three large chunks of wreckage, two smaller ones. The biggest is out at the edge and moving away the fastest." He highlighted the pieces he was referring to with bright green lines on her display.

"They look like sections of ships."

"Yeah. I think we're going to need to ask for more Gulmar ships."

"Fleet One was supposed to be their largest formal security force."

"If it was, they aren't really much of an ally, are they?"

"They—" Benson caught a look from Mahama, who quickly returned his attention to the main display screen. She turned slightly and tried to lower her voice even more. "They rely on mercenaries and privateers more than fleets."

"But this was supposedly going to be their biggest fleet, right?"

"Yes. They only have two, officially."

"Any idea how big?"

"Big. Several destroyers and frigates. Maybe a light cruiser."

"Are we ready to fight the Azoren if they're still in the area? It had to be a decent-sized force to take out the biggest Gulmar fleet."

The confidence had to come from the captain, even if Benson couldn't feel it in her bones. "We're ready."

"If you say so. This is a *lot* of debris."

"Shadow technology could have gotten them in close undetected."

"If this is all that's left—"

"We've got the latest countermeasure systems and weapons. If we can't handle them, the Republic's in trouble."

Halliwell snorted. It would be years before he got over his cynicism toward the parliament for all the reckless cuts they'd made to defense spending. "We're setting down on the next piece. We'll leave a team on this one to see if they can figure out what's inside."

"What about that larger chunk?"

"Parkinson's launching his drones once we get a little closer."

"That outer piece is moving on a different vector. They'll be out of range—"

"He's got three drones, so he can set up a relay to extend comms range. The second they show signal loss, he'll pull them out."

"All right." She should've known better than to underestimate Parkinson.

Raised voices cut into Halliwell's audio. She recognized Kohn, then Parkinson. The two were talking over each other, getting louder and louder.

Halliwell whistled. "Hold it down!"

One of the shuttles peeled off from the group and headed for the closest of the three large debris chunks. A gunship took position far enough out to keep the shuttle and blackened cube in view. The shuttle matched velocity and rotation with the wreckage, then latched on with extended claws.

Nausea teased Benson's nerves as the shuttle fired navigation rockets to stabilize the connected objects.

When the shuttle airlock opened to release a couple Marines, Benson turned her attention to the other shuttles. They were swarming toward the second charred object, which was easily three times the size of the first and looked even more damaged. Rather than a simple shape of a cube, this actually had the appearance of a full compartment—longer and with a more complex shape to it. If she had to guess, she thought it might be a reactor.

There it was: acceptance of the inevitable. This was the Gulmar fleet.

As the shuttles maneuvered, three small shapes launched from Halliwell's.

Parkinson's drones.

They were riding on a propulsion wing, what amounted to a rocket pack with fuel tanks spread across the length. It was designed for hull repair teams and some of the heavier components they had to move around. The drones relied on internal air tanks and small maneuvering systems meant for finer navigation. They wouldn't be able to close on the distant chunk by themselves.

Halliwell grunted softly. "We're latched on."

Benson switched to the closest gunship camera to get a clearer look at the shuttle, which was just now firing its thrusters to slow the rotation. "That looks like it could be a reactor."

"Kohn said the same thing."

"What's the radiation look like?"

"No worse than background levels. Our suits can handle it."

"I'm drilling down using the gunship cameras." She squinted. "I don't see any hatches on this one, either."

"There's a lot of fire damage. Hey, Kohn wants to talk to you."

"All right."

"Um, are you sure?" The way Halliwell's voice drifted toward a challenge wasn't a promising sign.

"Why? What's going on?"

"Well, he wants to take a medical team out."

"We need eyes on. If this was the Gulmar fleet—"

"You know it was. Parkinson says we need to take some readings, capture some video, then send that off to the Gulmar and head home."

"And you agree?"

"I don't much care for him, but the chief's right this time around."

"That wouldn't be much of a start to diplomatic negotiations."

"It's not our mess to clean up for once."

"We have a mission. Go ahead and have the ensign join the call."

Halliwell sighed. "Parkinson's going to want to join, too."

Benson winced. She'd hoped Kohn entering the medical program and tutoring under Dietrich would be enough to kill the bickering with Parkinson, but Kohn's commission and transfer had only made it a little more difficult for the two to squabble. Anytime their paths crossed, though, they didn't hesitate to give each other grief.

She leaned against the ring that surrounded most of the command station. "Put them both on, please."

Kohn's youthful voice came through immediately. "Captain Benson, I'm pretty sure this is a reactor."

"I agree. You're planning to take a medical team out?"

"Petty Officer Oliphant and Lieutenant Yueh. I want to look for a hatch."

"The odds of finding a functional system—"

Parkinson guffawed. "He thinks there're survivors in there. Like someone's going to live through a blast that tore a ship apart!"

Benson cleared her throat. "It looks like an intact section—"

"Intact? You see those lateral panels at the far end? That's probably what used to be the access to the drive systems. That's reinforced composites, probably ten times stronger than the best alloys available. Whatever tore this thing apart produced enough force and heat to break that."

"Thank you, Chief. I understand that the odds are slim anyone survived."

Kohn's readout showed he was requesting a private connection. When she declined, he mumbled something over the shared link.

The young man was going to have to build up some self-confidence one day. Benson took a calming breath. "What was that, Ensign Kohn?"

"I said the one place where anyone would have a chance of surviving would be in the reactor."

Parkinson laughed. "This had to have been a nuclear blast!"

"And the reactor has the heaviest shielding."

"What are the odds someone's going to be in there, huh? Zero. And if they are, they're radioactive paste."

"Technicians wear the same sort of environment suits we do."

"You're not thinking clearly, Chuck! That compartment's been spinning—"

Benson rubbed her forehead. "Chief Parkinson, how can you be so sure it's a nuclear blast?"

"The damage we're seeing, the way these pieces have been blown so far out… Nothing else makes sense. I put together a simulation based on some pretty simple assumptions: typical fleet positioning, what we know about Gulmar ships, how long they've been spinning around. You want to see it?"

"Please. For now, let's give Ensign Kohn a chance to explain his position."

On the display, the shuttle finally had managed to kill the hulk's rotation. External floodlights lit up even more of the blackened wreck, but there wasn't much detail to make out.

Her communicator vibrated when the engineer's simulation file arrived.

Kohn made a smacking sound. "Someone in an environment suit could survive the blast. The force wouldn't breach the hatch. If they weren't thrown around too badly by the sudden loss of gravity and the introduction of spin, there would be plenty of surfaces to latch onto. Then it's just a question of air supply in their suit."

"What about radiation?"

"Actually, the biggest problem would be the released steam, but the coolant materials would be the most radioactive. U-unless they built the reactors with lower-grade components, then there might be some activated elements. I'm assuming their ships are like ours."

Benson stifled a groan. The Gulmar had always skimped on safety measures. Regulations of any sort had been key pain points for the corporations that ended up revolting against the Kedraalian government. Regulations that focused on the safety and well-being of personnel? Those had been considered criminally intrusive. All that mattered was profits. Labor was an endless and cheap commodity.

She rubbed a thumb across the support ring. "Take your team out there. Keep an eye on radiation levels. I don't want to lose a single person. Is that clear?"

Parkinson growled, but he was cut off by Kohn's voice. "I was hoping we might recall one of the drones if we found a hatch."

Now she understood what the two had been fighting about. She could almost imagine the engineering chief stewing, his little body tensing into a ball, and his bright eyes bugging out.

In fact, before she could respond, Parkinson's growl rose in volume. "No!"

Benson held her breath.

Kohn's voice dropped to a whisper. "There could be radiation—"

"We are *not* a SAR team anymore, Chuck!"

"It could mean saving lives!"

Halliwell texted her: *Stop them, or I'm clubbing them both unconscious.*

He was right.

Benson muted the two of them. "Chief, Ensign Kohn, I think that's enough. The chief's correct here: We're not on a rescue mission. Ensign Kohn, if we can save lives, obviously let's do that. But for the moment, the drone assets have been committed to that third compartment. Maybe it holds the answers we need. Let's get your team out there and see if we can find an entry. We'll proceed from there. Okay?" She unmuted them.

Kohn's breathing was heavy, as if he'd just finished a sprint. "Okay."

She disconnected the two of them and made sure no one else could hear her talking with Halliwell. "Those drones are nearly on target. If they can't find something fast, I want them recalled."

The Marine sucked in a breath. "You don't want to appear to have favorites."

"I think I'm doing a pretty good job of that. Or am I not?"

It sounded like harnesses unsnapping and boots clomping in the background. She could imagine Halliwell tucking his long legs back to allow Kohn and his team to get out. Even among the other Marines, Halliwell was imposing. He was tall and had the sort of muscular frame that still allowed for speed. If she'd let him, he probably would have swatted the other two men around to get them to settle down.

Finally, the background noise ended in the hiss of an airlock door, and her Marine contingent commander seemed to settle down. "Kohn's out with his team, and Parkinson's got his control helmet on."

Meaning that the chief was now in his own world, running the drones through the augmented reality system. When he was like that, he wasn't concerned with anything else. In fact, the only time Benson had ever seen Parkinson happy was when he was interfacing through AR with machines.

She switched the command station display view to Kohn's suit camera. He and his team were moving across the blasted ship compartment with an ease that came from training and experience. There were only so many designs and layouts to existing spacecraft, which made it easier for operations like they were on.

Halliwell's connection flashed blue. "Hey! We've got something from the drones."

Benson leaned closer to the command station display. "What?"

"Parkinson thinks he's found a reinforced section that would be just aft of the bridge."

"Black box?"

"That's what he's thinking, yeah."

"It should've been transmitting."

"He says it's really messed up, but he thinks he can get into it. He, um, he wants to have a couple shuttles and a gunship head out to lengthen the relay."

"It's your mission team." Benson realized Chopra was staring at her, jaw thrust forward. He wanted to talk to her. She waved him over and muted Halliwell. "Problem?"

"Commander Tuleyev has been in contact with the rest of the task force."

"He has?"

"It's all aboveboard: signals checkout, confirmation of scans. Safe."

"But he's operating outside his assigned area."

The bald XO nodded.

"All right." Benson adjusted her coat. "Let's get a clear message out to the task force: We have a possible black box discovery. If this is the Gulmar fleet, we…"

"Yes?"

We what? Send an apology over the loss of life and fly back to Kedraal? Abort the mission? "We head for Radetta at full speed."

"The mission continues?"

"We came here to discuss an alliance against the Azoren. I would think after losing their primary fleet to an unprovoked attack, the Gulmar leadership would be even more desperate for allies."

Chopra pinched his bottom lip. "You led the fleet against the Azoren fleet that attacked Kedraal."

"Only at the end."

"Do we have sufficient firepower to face a fleet like that?"

"We'll do fine. We've never had a ship as powerful as the *Valor*. No one has. Please pass along the message. And make sure Commander Tuleyev sees it."

The XO did a sharp heel-turn and huddled with Nuñez.

Benson almost laughed at the absurdity of her confidence. The *Valor* could hold its own in almost any battle, but it had been months since the engagement with the Azoren shadow tech fleet. If another such fleet existed in the Azoren military, it would almost certainly would have seen upgrades by now.

Of course, that assumed that the Azoren had the resources to put another fleet like that into space…

Halliwell's connection flashed to blue again; she unmuted him. "Sorry, Clive, I—" She winced, but no one seemed to have heard her. "We're dealing with problems here."

"I can only imagine. That potential black box?"

"Chief Parkinson found it?"

"It's a Gulmar ship. The *Welch*. That was a destroyer, right?"

"Yes. Their flagship." She had her proof now. "Can he retrieve the box?"

"He's working on it. And Ensign Kohn radioed in. They've found a hatch. It's a mess, but they've nearly got it open. I sent a couple of my Marines to support."

"Radiation?"

"Safe, so long as they don't linger."

"If this was another Azoren fleet, they could be in hiding somewhere."

"I thought our sensors could pick them up?"

"I did, too. But if they've upgraded, maybe it's not possible."

"You want me to pull everyone back?"

It wasn't a good idea having the task force spread out so far, but if there might be a survivor... "Have everyone ready to bug out."

"Trust me, we are."

Benson turned back to the display on her command station console, now flipping from the shuttles and gunships to the command and control interface. She had her task force in a standard defensive configuration, with the signal ships forward, aft, and on the flanks. The more vulnerable ships were in the center of the formation, surrounded by an imaginary bubble of frigates, destroyers, cruisers...

And the *Valor*.

But that was probably what the Gulmar had done, wasn't it? They were supposed to have been ten destroyers of varying capability along with half as many support ships and several frigates. They had been warned about Azoren stealth technology and given the means to detect it for now.

Yet all the evidence pointed to a sneak attack.

How—?

Just as Chopra turned toward the command station, Halliwell's signal flashed blue again. "Survivor!"

Benson signaled for her XO to wait. "A survivor? One?"

"Yeah." The Marine commander sounded annoyed. "And she's a mess, apparently. Broken bones, some serious radiation exposure."

"I thought they would be in environment suits?"

"Kohn says these were cheap suits. Multiple breaches that were patched over, but it was probably after the worst of the exposure."

But they had their survivor! Benson muted the connection to Halliwell. "Commander Chopra, please send a message to the Gulmar that we've recovered a survivor and have confirmed the loss of the *Welch*."

The XO's eyes widened, then he returned to the communications console. He and Nuñez began whispering immediately.

Benson relaxed—only a little, a drop from full-on panic to partial panic. She took Halliwell off mute.

He was talking. "—get her back to the *Valor* or not?"

"Could you repeat that?"

"I said Kohn's worried about her condition. He wants to stabilize her before moving her. That seems risky, but so is moving her."

"We need her alive."

"She's not going to last long. He said the only way she'll survive is with a transfusion, radiation treatment, and going into cold sleep."

"I-I think what we can learn from her is more important than her survival." Benson nearly gagged at the words. It must have been the way Martinez had felt when faced with the SAID's orders to take the *Pandora* into the Azoren DMZ. *I wanted command. This is command.* "Bring her back to the *Valor*. We'll treat her here."

"He's not going to like that."

"I know. I'll talk to him. And Dietrich."

"We'll be back in twenty minutes."

"Hurry."

Benson stepped down from the command station. "Commander Chopra, we have a Gulmar sailor on her way to the *Valor*. I intend to see her escorted to the infirmary. Please inform Commander Dietrich."

Chopra's tongue flicked across his lips, and his mouth opened, but rather than protest, he turned back to the communications station.

Good. There would be plenty of time to argue over how she'd dealt with the situation. What mattered now was getting the survivor aboard and finding out how the Gulmar fleet had been ambushed.

As Benson rushed through the passageways to get to the lift that would take her down to the hangar bay, she fought back doubt and loathing. Her knees were ready to buckle, and her body trembled.

She was committing murder, killing a service member of a potential ally's navy.

I'm saving lives, dammit!

There was some reassurance in that, wasn't there? Or hadn't the same justification been used to defend heinous acts throughout history?

It was a troubling question she didn't have answers to.

3

———————

It felt wrong to Benson—the *Valor*'s pristine bulkheads and decks, its bright lights, the precision and perfection of the multibillion-credit ship. Rushing through that on a whispering gurney: a broken human, ruined face twisted, ruptured lips bloody, shattered throat rasping an inadequate protest.

Kohn jogged alongside the gurney that had been waiting for the shuttle in the hangar bay, studying the computing tablet hooked to the shiny rail holding the body in place. "Her name's Farouk. Twenty-five. Chief Nuclear Technician."

Benson breathed hard, nearly gagging at the stench coming off the injured woman. The captain felt clumsy in her dress uniform, which clung to her damply. "She talked to you?"

The ensign shot a stunned look back over his shoulder. "No."

"How'd you find out who she was? Is?"

"Her computer tablet was still operational. You realize she's in so much pain, she couldn't possibly put together a coherent thought, don't you?"

"I—"

The Gulmar technician's right hand raised up: blood-caked, blistered. Benson reached out instinctively, but the nurse pushed the gory hand back down.

Kohn tapped the tablet dangling from the rail. "She's been stuck in that compartment for nearly eight hours."

Eight hours! "That's from her tablet, too?"

"Yes. There's a little video on it. I guess it was the moment after the explosion."

"Were you able to pull it off the tablet?"

"I've been a little busy, ma'am."

"Perhaps Chief Parkinson could give it a look."

"When he's done with his drones, I guess." Kohn scowled. "It looks like she tried to save her team. In the video, I mean. She was pushing them toward the airlock."

"Thank you."

Kohn and the medical team squeezed into the main lift; his glare uninvited Benson. She joined Halliwell and Grier in the smaller lift.

Grier seemed pale. "Five corpses. I think they were lucky."

Halliwell's brow knotted. "Maybe they'd argue that."

The lift door closed, and they began to rise. Benson gulped at the air, which seemed compromised. Maybe it was the smell coming off the Marines' environment suits after riding in the shuttle with…that.

"Parkinson…?" Benson closed her eyes, but the nuclear technician's melted face wouldn't go away.

Halliwell sighed. "Going back out to bring the drones in."

"We'll need that black box if we want to make our case to the Gulmar."

"I think the Azoren did that for you."

Grier sniffled. "Won't they just play innocent?"

Before Benson could answer, the lift came to a stop, and the hatch opened. Kohn and the nurses were already rushing the gurney toward the medical center, where Dietrich and his senior staff awaited. The captain rushed after them, barely noticing the Marines in her wake.

Inside the infirmary, Kohn was stripping out of his environment suit while talking with Dietrich. The chief medical officer was a little taller than his protégé but sagged from the strain of a life of bad decisions. A face that might once have been almost handsome was now puffy, the pockmarks of a youthful illness now pronounced. But the older man's eyes were still animated, bright, and clear. The two men were throwing medical data back and forth in a clipped exchange that bordered on robotic: vital signs, medicine and procedures that had already administered, medicine and procedures that needed to be started. They were quibbling over the next steps: what had priority between pain treatment and stabilization efforts.

Benson stepped forward. "Commander Dietrich—"

The chief medical officer shot her a warning look: *Not now!*

She crossed her arms, realizing for the first time there was a smear of blood on her left cuff from the Farouk woman. "Commander, I'm afraid fleet business overrides the concerns of a single woman's life."

That brought Dietrich fully around, bright eyes alive with righteous anger. "You think I didn't hear the discussions running around about us not being SAR?"

"We aren't."

"There's never anything wrong with saving lives, Faith!"

"Our mission is to hopefully do that, and on a scale that dwarfs the lives lost here, if this was the Gulmar fleet."

Dietrich pointed to the surgical bay glass wall separating him from the nuclear technician. Beyond that wall, nurses were cutting away remnants of the environment suit, careful to peel away as little skin as possible when they did so. "That young woman still has a slim chance at life, and I intend to see—"

"I need to talk to her."

"If I do my job properly, you'll have your chance in a few months."

"I need to talk to her *now*."

"Now?" The chief medical officer seemed torn between a laugh and a scream—lips and brow quivering. "You're talking murder."

"I'm talking about the possibility of saving millions of lives."

"And exactly how do you see that? How does she have anything to offer—?"

"She's the only survivor of a potential ally's fleet, Ernie. Maybe she heard something. Maybe she saw something. We *have* to know."

"No. I refuse. This is my staff. This is my operation. My oath is to do no harm and to ease the ills of my patients. What you're asking for is an abrogation—a repudiation—of my duty. You want an execution, turn to one of your gun-toting enforcers."

Benson felt movement behind her and noted the way Dietrich's eyebrows went up. Halliwell and Grier were still there, and they probably weren't keen on being described as enforcers. "Ensign Kohn, what's the best-case scenario for this technician?"

Kohn hesitated halfway toward the sanitization basin. He glanced at Dietrich, then looked away. "Assuming no internal injuries, the transfusion should take her up as high as a ten percent chance of living. Once we can treat the pain—"

"Ten percent chance of living how long and with what quality of life?"

"Well, she…"

"Her legs looked like jelly."

"Um, her suit was breached. She was thrown around a bit before she could secure herself—"

"So she'd lose both legs. Her eyes? Her face?"

"She'll need reconstructive surgery. The legs could be replaced. And—"

"Cancer? How much radiation was she exposed to?"

"Actually, not that much. Certainly, she'll have a hard life, but if we can get her through the worst of this, she *will* have a life."

Benson gulped. She wasn't going to call the two men liars, but she was sure they were being overly optimistic. "I have to talk to her."

Dietrich stepped between Benson and Kohn. "Prep yourself, Chuck."

Kohn remained frozen for a moment, then he hurried to the basin and turned the water on. A slender, dark-haired nurse carried a set of scrubs toward him as he soaped up.

Benson stepped closer to Dietrich. "Ernie, this is an order."

"Captain, I'm afraid you can't order me to kill someone."

"I'm not. I'm ordering you to do everything you can to save her life *after* I'm done interrogating her."

The older man's face reddened and shook. "You don't have the right."

"I have the obligation, and that—" She fought back shakes of her own. "That's what matters."

Dietrich twisted away, still trembling. "Prep yourself."

Benson peeled off her coat, barely noting the way it came away with a hushed wet sound. The pink of her skin showed through the thin white shirt where it stuck to her.

Kohn slipped into his scrubs, attention focused on the surgical bay. "Captain, we could pull more from her computing tablet."

"We'll try. It could take time."

"I-I know."

"What if it didn't capture something critical? What if she's the only way we'll ever know what caused this?"

The ensign bowed his head as he pulled his gloves on, then he headed into the surgical bay, leaving Benson to soap up at the basin. It took her a moment to realize Halliwell was beside her, breathing heavily through his nose.

"It's not murder." He seemed ready to charge the glass wall.

"They know that. They're doing their job, nothing more."

"Yeah, well, they're the same sort of people who get outraged when I do mine."

"No they don't. They understand the role of the military."

"You heard them. They think we're assassins." Halliwell's hands bunched into fists.

"Commander Dietrich gets sloppy when he's mad."

"Or when he's drunk."

Benson stuck her hands under the faucet, letting the hot water wash away the foam. "He's got it under control."

"Sure he does." The Marine commander scratched the back of his neck.

"What's the matter?"

"Nothing. It's just...war. It's not the time when you want to look too close at ethics is all."

The air dryer finished, and Benson turned to the dark-haired nurse, who held out the open set of scrubs. "We can talk about this later."

"I know."

Benson wanted to hug him just then, to explain to him that he was fine, and they'd get through all this. "You understand why I have to do this?"

"Sure. You want proof."

"There's more. Tactics."

"Tactics?" He screwed up his eyes.

"We know how the Azoren fleet operated in our space. Who's to say they did the same here? They could still be out there. There's every chance that our task force is their actual target."

"I understand." Halliwell shuffled back to Grier, who looked equally miserable.

Cold air blasted Benson as she pushed through the airlock that led into the brightly lit surgical room. The *Valor*'s facilities were larger than the *Pandora*'s but not much more sophisticated. There were three stainless steel surgical platforms, although they were polished and showed no sign of use. Farouk rested on the leftmost of the platforms, now completely removed from her suit. A nurse pulled a mask from the nuclear technician's face, peeling away skin.

Dietrich waved Benson in. "Captain. We've administered enough pain medication to allow the patient to speak. We've also given her stimulants to bring her around any moment now. Of course, I advise against all of this. The mix of drugs would be dangerous to someone in perfect health. As you know, her condition is tenuous at best."

"Thank you. Is this being recorded?"

The chief medical officer pointed toward the dome of lights overhead. "Crystal clear audio and video."

To be used against you in a court martial. "Thank you."

Looking into the young woman's face, Benson felt all the questions that came when faced with death or imminent death: Where did this Farouk woman come from? Did she have family? Who was she in life? Did she have a loved one? Did she have children? Was she happy? Sad?

Farouk's milky eyes shifted, and she made a weak, gurgling sound.

Dietrich waved a nurse in. "She's—"

The nurse squeezed in close to the young woman, metal basin in hand. Farouk moaned, then she turned her head and vomited. Without missing a beat, another nurse wiped the patient's face gently, once again coming away with bits of bloody flesh.

Dietrich's mouth was hidden by his surgical mask, but his hostility came through in his eyes. "Please proceed, Captain."

Benson waited until the vomit-covered nurse had backed away, then moved closer. "Chief Farouk?"

The young woman turned. "Wha'am'i?"

Where am I? "You're aboard the Kedraalian Republic battleship *Valor*. You were the only survivor of the *Welch*?"

"Ugga."

"Were you part of Gulmar Fleet One?"

"Yegs."

"You were on shift when the attack came?"

"Yegs." She struggled to get that out; one of the nurses gently inserted a tube into the young woman's ruined mouth, and water slurped for a moment.

"Chief Farouk, the Azoren hit you nearly eight hours ago. Did your fleet detect the attack? Did you get a sense of how many ships they had? Was it a superior force?"

Farouk shook her head, or at least she seemed to.

Too many questions. "Did your fleet detect the attack, Chief?"

"No."

"Did you get a sense of how many ships they had?"

Another shake of the head. The young woman was having difficulty breathing, making strained, sucking sounds.

Dietrich rattled off a string of directions, and the nurse with the sucking tube moved in while another prepared a hypodermic. Kohn said something that brought his superior around. "Ensign Kohn, if I feel that you could add value to the diagnosis, rest assured that I would seek your opinion."

The ensign bowed his head and backed away.

Many aboard the *Pandora* had been fragile or high-strung. It was the nature of the job and a reflection of the low standing that search-and-rescue had attained over the years that people with fractured personalities were squeezed into inadequate facilities to perform probably the most stressful and thankless job in the military.

Aboard the *Valor*, things were different. It was a ship of war. The stress was directly related to the mission. One moment, they were projecting strength to remind the Azoren that the Kedraalian military had teeth. The next moment, the ship might be showing those teeth. When things cooled down again, Benson would need to remind everyone of the value of professionalism and courtesy.

Dietrich waved her back in.

"Chief Farouk?" Benson wanted to hold the young woman's hand, but it was a raw, ruined mess. "Do you have any idea how the Azoren were able to destroy your fleet so completely?"

Farouk shook her head again. "No. Not…" She hacked, and the nurse with the suction tube moved back in. This time, bloody saliva discolored the device.

Dietrich's eyes narrowed. "The percentage is diminishing rapidly, Captain."

Benson clenched her jaw. "Was your fleet able to get off a shot at the Azoren? Were you able to get a recording of the attack force? Did you hear anything on the communications channels before the *Welch* was destroyed?"

The nuclear technician shook her head, then she stopped and nodded.

"You got off a shot?"

A head shake.

"Someone managed a recording?"

Another head shake.

"There was something on the comms about the Azoren fleet?"

Farouk nodded then shook her head. "No."

"I…I don't understand. There was nothing on the comms?"

"Something on the comms. Bombs detonated."

"Bombs detonated on your ships?"

The technician nodded, then hacked again. The nurse sucked more bloody saliva away.

Bombs. That didn't seem very likely. That would require teams getting up to their targets and planting explosives. Her Marines could do that, but it was bloody, desperate work. The Gulmar ships should have been able to detect the Azoren Marines approaching.

Unless there was a new ship or new technology in play.

The nurse stepped back, but Dietrich's bright eyes bore into Benson's. "One minute, Captain."

It didn't seem like the young woman would even last that long. "Chief Farouk? The bombs? The Azoren Marines got past your sensors to plant them on your hulls?"

Farouk shook her head. "Already onboard."

"Saboteurs? They had saboteurs?"

The technician nodded. "Spies. Saboteurs. Systems failed."

"So the Azoren ships got up on you because your systems were knocked offline?"

"No. Some ships…intact. Killed saboteurs and spies. Not Azoren."

"What? I'm sorry, Chief. These saboteurs and spies weren't Azoren?"

"Not Azoren. Our people."

Traitors. Like the privateers from the *Rakshasa*. "But the Azoren fleet—"

Sirens sounded: General Quarters.

Benson hurried to the intercom station on the wall beside the airlock entry. "Commander Chopra, what's going on?"

"Incoming ships, Captain." There was a hint of panic to her XO's voice.

"Gulmar?"

"We can't tell. They're just…flickers on our sensors."

New technology. It had to be. "I'm on my way."

Benson tapped the button to open the airlock inner door and tugged a surgical glove off.

"Captain!" Kohn sped toward her.

"Yes?"

"Chief Farouk asked for you."

Halliwell stared at Benson through the glass; he was ready to go. *Right now.* "I need to get back to the bridge, Ensign."

"You've put her life at risk. You don't owe her another few seconds?"

Heat rushed through Benson's cheeks. She followed the young doctor-in-training back to the surgical platform, where the gory technician wheezed.

Benson delicately touched the other woman's shoulder with a gloved hand. "I'm here, Chief. You wanted to tell me something?"

The Gulmar technician nodded. "The fleet."

"The attack fleet?"

Another nod. "Not Azoren."

The monitoring equipment pinged. Signals spiked, then flattened. Dietrich rattled off more medical jargon at the nurses.

Benson squeezed the young technician's shoulder. "Not…Azoren? Then who?"

"Khan." The word was a raspy whisper that faded into nothing.

But it was enough to make Benson's guts turn to ice. Con? Khan? The Khanate? Could it be? After so many years, and with so many sure they'd been broken?

She sprinted to the airlock and out of the infirmary. The Khanate! If that was true, the task force's tactics would need to change. They'd spent the past months training for the wrong enemy.

And there was a very good chance they were vulnerable to the tactics that had wiped out the Gulmar fleet.

4

Chopra was standing on the raised command station when Benson reached the bridge. He was bent at the hip, eyes squeezed shut, face creased in pain. It was the look of someone stuck in a…discussion with Tuleyev.

He's a good XO. Benson sucked in the cool air and touched Chopra's hand.

Relief washed over the bald man. "Commander Tuleyev, excuse me, please?" Silence. Chopra nodded. "Yes, she's just returned to the bridge. Just now. Yes, of course, I'll transfer you."

She waited for her XO to step down, then took his place at the station. Her communicator vibrated, and a moment later, Tuleyev's voice was in her ear.

"Captain?"

"Commander Tuleyev. Thank you for your patience."

"Eh, what?"

She powered up the display panel and loaded the latest intelligence data: number of ships, size, identifiable profiles and signatures, vector and velocity. Updates were coming in on a live stream. "I'm still assessing the threat, but I would appreciate your thoughts, Alexander." As if he could have kept them to himself.

"Ah! Yes! Already, I have ordered ships into a modified defensive formation."

"Modified? I had everyone positioned per standard—"

"The numbers continue to fluctuate, as do the readouts. Our ships, they were spread too thin for such a large force."

Thirty-two unique signatures so far. That was twice the size of her task force. "Do we know where they came from?"

"A Fold Space opening, according to the *Sinclair*."

The best signals ship in the task force. How hard had she fought for the upgrades to the sensors packages and almost been denied? "Any idea which direction?"

"Their vector is consistent with a launch originating from coreward."

A quick glance at the updated data on her display confirmed that. "They came in from behind us."

"Not directly, no. Space is vast, you see. It is possible they came from anywhere."

"Thank you, Alexander. Anywhere *behind us*."

"But—"

"If they attacked the Gulmar from the same or a similar point in space, they could have appeared to *be* us."

"No such signals have been detected, *Captain*."

How does someone so unimaginative and rigid make it so far? "It wouldn't do much good to send us false signals, would it? We know where *our* ships are, and we know the Gulmar fleet was wiped out."

"Ah, yes—now your meaning is clear. If they were to be among us—"

Oh! The saboteurs! "Alexander, we're going to need to institute two-person integrity going forward."

"Two-person integrity? What is wrong?"

"The Gulmar ships had saboteurs aboard. They were damaged even before the attack happened."

"Saboteurs? Our crews are the most reliable available!"

Benson turned away from the bridge crew and lowered her voice. "Do you want to risk this entire task force on the possibility that whatever intelligence leaks alerted the Khanate to this meeting were purely on the Gulmar side?"

"Khanate, you say? This attack force is Khanate?"

"Yes. I'm sorry. The situation is fluid, but that's the intelligence we have right now. Lieutenant Halliwell will be updating your Marine detachment momentarily. I'll want all critical systems under constant guard."

"My Marines are prepared to repel boarders, *Captain*."

"Your Marines will follow the orders of Lieutenant Halliwell. We're one task force with one mission. If you need some time to come to grips with that, please step aside and allow your XO to take command while you work that out."

As Tuleyev considered her words, the red symbols drew closer. With each second, the data became clearer: thirty-five ships now; two were of an unfamiliar configuration—long and tall; four were nearly as big as the *Lyon*. She assumed those were cruisers. The rest were smaller, not even destroyer size. Maybe frigates.

And they were all showing signs of stealth technology that wasn't quite on par with what the Azoren fleet had used to slip into Kedraalian space but was still giving the signals ships fits. The Khanate ships were maybe ten minutes out from extreme range and lock-on was uncertain.

And now *another* ship appeared on the scan.

Tuleyev finally cleared his throat. "I have been in contact with my Marine commander."

"Good. Does Lieutenant Kong understand the situation?"

"She does. I made a point of sharing all information immediately rather than risk confusion, you see."

"Thank you, Commander Tuleyev."

She disconnected. The rest of the task force needed to be caught up. "Commander Chopra?"

The XO stepped back from the bridge console and came to her side. "You managed to keep your sanity."

"Barely. We're up against a situation."

"With Alexander?"

"With the enemy fleet."

"Thirty-six ships is a bit much."

"Thirty-six *Khanate* ships."

"Not Azoren?"

"Our Gulmar survivor said it was definitely Khanate."

"We haven't trained for their tactics. Do they even have tactics?"

"That's the situation. When I was going through the academy, everything they taught about the Khanate was already ancient history. They didn't even have a capital ship when they declared independence."

Chopra pinched his bottom lip. "Heavily armed merchant ships and tankers, much like our Commander Tuleyev's grandfather piloted in defense of Kedraal."

"Exactly. I believe most of those were lost within the first ten years."

"They were switching to short-range fighters, I thought?"

"Fighter-bombers. Suicide craft, like the old Japanese Zeroes." She tapped the two strange-looking ships, filling her display with their profiles. "If you were to try to modernize a fleet built around that sort of philosophy, you'd want what amounts to an aircraft carrier."

"Suicide craft don't seem terribly practical against ships capable of the sorts of speed and maneuvering we can manage."

"They don't." She shrank the size of the long ships and brought up the other profiles. "Four cruisers and thirty frigate-sized ships. It's potentially a good deal more firepower than I would have expected, but if we can manage lock-on, I think we can handle the threat."

"You don't sound convinced."

"Because I'm not. What if those aren't frigates? What if they're troop carriers? What if they're tenders? What if everything comes down to those two big ships or those four cruisers and those two big ships combined?"

The XO stood on his tiptoes. "We could head deeper into Gulmar space."

"I think we have an obligation to test the enemy, don't we?"

Chopra's lips parted, but his words were lost when the hatch opened, and two Marines stepped onto the bridge. They wore their dark gray combat gear, covered by black armor. Their carbines were at low ready as they took up position on either side of the hatch.

The three junior bridge officers stared for a moment, then looked toward Chopra and Benson.

She tried to smile reassuringly but didn't have the heart for it. She nodded at the main display screen in front of the bridge station, where the enemy ships were still nothing more than red triangles. "Those ships aren't Azoren but Khanate. Our Gulmar survivor warned us that their fleet was damaged by saboteurs prior to the attack."

Instead of reassuring the officers, the explanation caused them to straighten their backs and glance at each other.

Benson finally managed a smile. "While we obviously believe our crew are trustworthy, we want to ensure our ships don't suffer the same fate. Lieutenant Nuñez, you'll need to work with Commander Chopra to communicate this to the rest of the fleet. Lieutenant Mahama, please coordinate with our signals ships to crack the electronic countermeasures and stealth technology that fleet is using. The Khanate is supposed to be decades behind us technologically. Figure out what's going on." The young man bowed his head. "Lieutenant Konrath, please coordinate with the task force to return to the defensive dispersal I had established previously."

Konrath's pale eyes became slits. "Commander Tuleyev ordered—"

"The commander was operating from old intelligence." Benson leaned forward and squeezed the material of the support ring surrounding her station. "Please inform your counterparts that going forward, tactical command including maneuvers will come through the *Valor*."

"Yes, ma'am." The young man spun around and focused on his station.

Chopra's attention remained focused on the Marines. "You have ideas for tactics?"

On the command station display, the enemy ships still appeared to be coming straight for Benson's smaller task force. Lock-on didn't seem any more likely, and the enemy hadn't apparently managed lock-on, either. It was possible they had the same weapons systems or—hopefully—even older systems. Benson was having a hard time believing anyone could have a ship to match the *Valor*. It had only been launched a couple months ago. Its systems, software, armor, and weapons were all the latest designs.

Once again, she drilled down on the two large ships. "Our training tells us to stay tight when we're unfamiliar with the enemy."

"Yes."

"Rely on concentrated defense systems to limit incoming weapons effectiveness. Read the data and react."

"The doctrine kept the fleet intact during the War of Separation."

"Things have changed. These people shouldn't even be in space."

Chopra craned his neck to get a better look at the big display. "But they are."

"Which tells me they had help."

"Help?"

"Someone smuggled those ships to them. Or they smuggled the technology to make them."

"There are DMZs separating—"

"Like Alexander said, space is vast. I've been through the tightest part of the Azoren DMZ. There's no way to completely block people off. You just can't do it."

"And these people who gave the Khanate technology?"

"It makes sense they'd share tactics, doesn't it?"

"I suppose." Light bounced off the XO's bald scalp as he turned back to the Marines. "That means following our doctrine would leave us vulnerable."

"It would. Perhaps they've been given weapons that would capitalize on our formations. Or maybe they have the means of taking our systems offline."

"We have shielding capable of withstanding significant EMP attacks."

"Think outside the box, Dinesh. These people just wiped out a capable fleet."

"Yes…" The XO clasped his hands behind his back. "I'll leave you to your tactics and get this message out to the other ships."

"Thank you."

Benson turned away from the Marines and the bridge crew and connected to Halliwell. He took a moment to accept. "Clive?"

"I'm busy, Faith." There was heat to his voice.

"You're still mad I made you split your forces up?"

"I've been butting heads with my 'subordinates.'"

"You're in a captain's billet. You've got a line to captain. Remind them of that if you have to."

He grunted. "Won't matter. They're academy grads; I'm a grunt."

"You're *my* grunt. Remember that."

"Yeah, well, I don't think that'll make it any better. If anyone ever figures out—"

"I didn't put you in charge of the Marines because I…" *Because what? Because I love you? Do I?* "You're one of the few people I can trust, okay? You don't have a crazy agenda. You're not some curmudgeon who has a commission because your grandfather was a war hero."

"I get it."

"Good, because I'm going to need your support. The possibility of spies and saboteurs is terrifying. Your Marines are going to be the key to protecting our most important assets."

"Do you really think it's a threat? Seriously? We all went through background checks—"

"After what happened on Kedraal, this whole Owls and Ravens thing within the GSA, the SAID coup, do *you* trust anyone?"

"I trust you and Toni."

"That's my point exactly. I trust *my* crew, warts and all. Everyone else, we have to keep an eye on." Benson glanced at the bridge crew.

What did she know about them? Just what was in their records. Konrath had family in the Azoren movement but wasn't himself involved in anything radical or dangerous. His mother had broken off communication with her brother and spoke out against him as a traitor and ideological monster.

Mahama's family descended from sailors and had been in the space tourism trade since before their arrival in Kedraalian space. He had lost far-removed cousins to Khanate followers when they'd hijacked one such cruise ship. As with everything the Khanate did, the deaths had been brutal and had been sent back for broadcast over Kedraalian networks. During her first year at the Academy, Benson had seen one of the archived videos of a woman being spaced by Khanate followers.

She shivered.

All she knew about Nuñez was that her family were entertainers: artists, actors, dancers. The communications officer was the first to enter the military. She'd been a ballerina as a child and still had the wiry physique.

And Chopra. He was more than competent. He had recommendations and decorations. His scores were good. He'd actually seen combat early in his career, albeit against pirates. Still, he knew how to kill. He'd seen people on his ship die.

This was the crew she needed. She would keep them on the bridge until the engagement was over.

Konrath straightened and turned slightly. "Maneuvers have been coordinated among the task force, Captain. Request permission to begin combat maneuvers."

"Proceed, Lieutenant."

Benson squeezed tighter on the support ring as G-forces pressed against her. It would begin with maneuvering thrusters to push the ships farther apart, but they would soon be accelerating, moving in somewhat random patterns coordinated and controlled through the task force's interconnected computer systems. Space might be vast, but for a task force to bring concentrated firepower against an enemy, ships needed to be within reasonable distances of their targets. The actual controls—vector, thrust, firing—were all automated, but humans selected the patterns and modified them.

Now came the wait. At some point, a system would fail, or a sailor would make a mistake, and someone would manage lock-on. Weapons would fire across the immense distances separating the vessels. Maybe a missile would detonate in the path of a maneuvering ship. Maybe a shield would go down just as a hail of railgun rounds arrived and the outer hull of a ship would twist and rupture.

And people would die.

It was how naval combat went.

Except...

Benson brought up the data that had been collected on the Gulmar fleet. Unofficially, it probably had eighteen ships. Officially, the *Welch* had been the flagship. It was supposedly on par with a Kedraalian destroyer.

And all that remained of the fleet was an expanding field of debris and three floating chunks that together couldn't qualify as a gunboat.

The Khanate had done that.

Backwards. Hate-filled. Anti-education. Murderous. Barbaric.

They followed a ridiculous code, men swearing themselves to war in the service of the Khan and his satraps, women accepting roles as child bearers and parents. A small number of each were put into some sort of priesthood. And everyone made treks to one holy site or another. The greatest was a building in the middle of a heavily wooded island that held the final resting place of the first Khan and the seven icons he had taken from Earth to form his religion.

She could remember the greatest of the icons: gold tablets found by the khan in the heart of the radioactive desert on Earth, a place once known as the Middle East. And there was the compass taken from the ship the original Khan had been born on. That supposedly always pointed toward their final resting place: the Guiding Star. Then there were the weapons that had belonged to the Khan, the most important being the saber he'd used to kill ten enemies.

In one swing. These people believe anything.

Among the other relics were "the Khan Kabal"—the scripture—the words of the first Khan captured over the course of his life.

She'd tried to read the writings once. It was ramblings, mostly. Absurd tales, prayers, parables, and commandments.

And that was apparently what some people needed.

How many millions had fled to the Khanate after it had declared itself during the rebellion? Three? Five? They had joined easily ten times as many who had been gathering on those planets for years, taking pilgrimages and disappearing, slipping from sight of those who were actually happy to see them go. After all, who had the stomach for people who felt they had the right to tell everyone else how to live?

That was the way of the zealots.

Now those zealots had a fleet. They had mystery and technology and fanaticism.

It was a terrifying mixture.

Maybe they had studied Kedraalian tactics. Maybe they knew what to expect. But it seemed more likely they had something more helping them. How else could they suddenly reappear as a threat after decades of isolation?

She would only know once the ships engaged, which seemed inevitable.

5

About ten kilometers north of the Grand Assembly Plaza and a few blocks west of the Avenue of the Founders, the Cornwell building occupied the center of a large lot. Surrounded by thick, slate stone walls topped with matching spikes, the grounds were a mix of beautifully manicured botanical spaces and peaceful marble headstones. From the hotel room where Group for Strategic Assessment agent Lieutenant Brianna Stiles surveilled the building, it was hard to reconcile the inviting appearance with the security measures she'd detected so far.

Long shadows merged and faded into the gray of twilight, but the man she was waiting for remained ensconced inside the distant building. She leaned back from her long-range scope and powered on her tablet. Soft blue lines formed into a simple interface, which prompted her for a code before scanning her eyes and taking a thumbprint. Once through the login, she pulled up the file on Kusno Saripado.

Senior Manager of Analysis & Reporting, Counter-Espionage Directorate.

Twenty-two years of service with the CED.

Salary at the highest grade available to non-elected officials.

A twenty-five hundred square foot house on the edge of Varudin in

Morocco Heights, a nice but not insanely posh neighborhood mostly occupied by people with generations in civil service and elected office.

Forty-four years old. Short. Round-faced. A mole as big as the tip of her pinky rested at the outer corner of his beady, right eye.

It would be a kindness to describe him as average looking.

His position was as senior as someone could get inside the intelligence community without appointment or election. There were only two layers between him and Prime Minister Mengitsu Zenawi, and those layers were career politicians. When it came to *real* influence—the person with authority through acceptance of expertise—Saripado was one of the most powerful men in the capital.

And many trails led to him as a problem.

Family ties to the Patels. Family ties to the leaders of the independence movement on Dramora. Greater financial wherewithal than should have been possible from his pay.

Brilliantly, none of the red flags were enough to trigger concerns during background investigations.

The Patel family had a long history in government. They were "respected."

Dramoran independence was safely hidden behind a firewall of claims of patriotism.

Legitimate investments paid out *almost* enough to explain away financial curiosities.

But a dedicated agent—someone with unlimited access and time—could see through shadow and deceit. It was something Stiles had a particular knack for. And now she had the authority to unravel the twisted mess that was the Owls and Ravens.

Saripado was the most promising thread.

Her surveillance gear beeped: Saripado was leaving the building.

The little man stuck to the main sidewalk until he was about twenty meters out from the building, then he cut north and disappeared behind a hedgerow. Stiles switched to a camera mounted on the wall beyond the hedgerow, capturing the civil servant without a meaningful break in coverage. He strolled into a broad parking lot that was mostly empty at such a late hour. Even dedicated intelligence analysts maintained a healthy work-life balance. After all, the Kedraalian Republic wasn't at war at the moment.

Six cars were all that remained in the lot, and Saripado's was fairly obvious among them: only a year or two old; a high-end luxury model without all the trappings; occupying a designated space just beside the often-empty spots provided for the senior leadership.

From the angle of the camera, minor details popped out.

Saripado had a barely noticeable limp, which mapped to a boating accident during college.

On his left side, opposite the large mole, was a deep scar from a cyst that had required surgery to drain. He'd been nine at the time, and his doctor had advised treatment with medicine, not understanding the true nature of the problem. His left eyelid had the slightest deformation as a result, never fully opening. This enhanced the appearance of being beady eyed.

When he slipped into the car, he did so awkwardly, favoring his left hip. That was the result of a hard fall in a game of polo at university, which left him in the hospital for nearly two weeks.

All the minor medical scars were correctable, and the costs would have been fully covered, but Saripado was a practical man without the sort of ego to see the imperfections as relevant. His wife was cute, her family wealthy, and the pain was inconsequential.

It all mapped to a complicated profile. This wasn't the sort of man who couldn't be compromised easily. His interests were aligned with those of the Republic.

To a point.

It was the narrow fork where things diverged that interested Stiles.

She checked that her equipment had sufficient storage to continue recording for several hours, confirmed the connection to her tablet, then shoved that into a small travel bag on the end of her bed, slung the bag over a firm shoulder, and let herself out into the hallway. The hotel had thirty floors; she was on the twenty-eighth.

Once in the elevator, she released a cyberattack to offline cameras on the top four floors, then opened the elevator door and stepped back out. The stairwell with roof access was just down the hall.

Although the floor was mostly empty, she hurried, hoping to minimize the odds of running into anyone. The unfortunate truth was that no matter what she wore or did to her hair or didn't do for makeup, she stood out. Athletically slender, pretty, with golden-brown skin that always had a healthy glow—she was meant to catch eyes by design.

A door opened farther down the hallway as she slipped into the stairwell. She closed the door softly behind her, then she stripped off the loose shirt and pants she'd been wearing. She could have been a tourist in the outfit, a fan proud to wear the colors and logo of the Varudin soccer team. But what she wore beneath…

Absent power, it was simply a skintight suit that might be worn by a scuba diver or even a swimmer. But once she slid the mask on and activated the power, the circuitry embedded in the charcoal gray material gave her shadowsuit the same sort of chameleon capabilities as the most advanced ships.

She stuffed her clothes into the bag and powered the suit on, then skipped up the stairs to the roof.

It was cool now, the sun completely gone and night settling in. Vehicle lights traced the transport network of the city, moving with quiet efficiency. A few flyers danced around the outer edges of the metropolitan sprawl.

No one watched her. No one was aware of her.

She ran to the far side of the roof, away from the walled compound, then sprinted back toward the wall facing the CED headquarters. Centimeters short of the short wall around the roof edge, she jumped.

The chameleon stealth circuitry put a load on the suit's limited battery life. Its power-assisted wings had demands of their own.

Transparent, micrometer-thick membranes provided the gliding lift. Cameras and other sensors, though, provided constant feedback and adjustment to keep her on-course. There were a thousand variables that had to be accounted for, some of them more critical than wind.

Arms held out, legs pinned together, she dove, whipping along at speeds greater than most of the vehicles below her. After a moment, she banked left, sliding along less than a meter out from a building side. Then she leveled off, then banked again.

Her suit flashed a warning about thermals, and she adjusted.

The building was still five kilometers away when her surveillance gear notified her that Saripado was on the highway home.

Another alarm flashed, this one warning about a significant drop in the wind. Stiles adjusted again, but her altitude dropped.

Sensors fed data to the suit's processors, and a course advisory popped up.

She had to change her landing target.

Based on her optimal adjustments, she could clear the outer wall on the east side of the compound, maybe reaching an area shielded by mounds of flowers and shade trees. It wasn't ideal, but...

Stiles adjusted and tensed, fighting to keep altitude. When her sensors detected a thermal ahead, she adjusted course and fought to regain altitude.

It wasn't enough to reach her original target, but she would clear the wall.

Barely.

She dropped, always searching for but never finding more opportunities to climb, until the wall was in sight. Floodlights were on now, reflecting off the slate and the broad, gray gate that was fashioned after the wrought iron barriers used elsewhere. But the gate, like the spikes atop the wall, was made from a composite that was much stronger than iron or steel.

Those spikes were a concern now. The suit still guaranteed that she would clear the wall, but it was going to be close, and she kept dropping.

And dropping.

It looked uncertain enough that she nearly aborted. She could clear the wall and the spikes atop it with effort if she landed on the outside, but the suit said she was safe.

Then it was too late. She was coming up on the wall fast, with no real opportunity to adjust. Everything showed a sickly yellow-green: suboptimal.

She passed over just as the sensors flashed red.

All she could do was suck in her gut and arch slightly. Her ribs cleared, her belly, her groin—

A spike slashed across her left thigh.

Fire shot through her leg. She gritted her teeth.

Ahead, the raised mound filled the optics, which displayed a green approach that quickly dipped toward yellow. She was slowing, but it was hard to keep her wounded leg completely straight. The yellow line turned orange, and she banked slightly to compensate.

It wasn't enough.

The suit did what it could to kill velocity, but she was an imperfect aerodynamic object now. She collapsed the wings and tucked into a tumble, rolling hard and angling as much as she could for the mound.

Stiles skipped along the ground, grimacing as the energy from her flight bled off. On the upside, the impacts were recharging batteries she would need to launch herself over the wall when she was ready to get back out. On the downside, everything hurt. The suit wasn't meant to provide protection against such a rough landing.

Finally, she was rolling uphill, and the momentum died until she came to a stop against the sturdy base of a thick, green shrub.

She pushed up and immediately tested her limbs.

There was still pain everywhere, but nothing refused to work. A few tentative squats, a handful of jumping jacks—she would be a network of bruises for a few days, but she could move.

A pinprick in her left thigh caught her attention: The suit was dispensing an anti-inflammation and pain suppression injection.

Things were a little worse than she'd realized.

Blood darkened her thigh where the spike had sliced a shallow finger-length gouge into her. The suit was built to contend with such wounds, closing not only the material but her own flesh when she pressed the cut together. The circuitry was still fully functional, even if she wasn't.

She shook her limbs out and rolled her neck while the drugs worked their way through her.

Nearly six minutes had passed since she'd left her room. The connection to her surveillance gear was still solid, and there were no indications she'd been detected.

Time to go.

Stiles stuck to the bushes and other cover as she hurried to the building. There were four entries on the bottom floor, but each was swathed in security devices. Her work inside the building required a minimal footprint, so she headed for the west wall, where a small gap in the security apparatus gave her the best approach.

She climbed.

Once again, the suit provided more than her own exceptional training and athleticism could accomplish. Micro-fiber and suction devices worked together to give her an almost spider-like clinging ability where the surface was otherwise too smooth or lacking in obvious finger or toeholds.

When she reached the rooftop, the suit was well below half power. She'd relied too much on the clinging to compensate for her aching limbs. She would have to recharge while inside the building.

Her sensors indicated the rooftop entry was monitoring on only a few circuits: pressure, a camera, and a simple infrared beam that bisected the entryway.

She captured the standard feed signal to the pressure sensor and fed a continuation of that to it.

The camera was a live, continuous feed. It would have a constant timestamp overlay. Fortunately, it was set to a fixed position. Stiles hooked into the feed, duplicated the static image, then generated a timestamp to match the existing one. Once she was satisfied with the video, she fed it to the system as an overlay on top of the actual camera feed.

That left the infrared beam. There were no easy solutions for it. Whoever had designed the intrusion detection system had probably intended that as the main protection.

Stiles pulled a cable from the integrated belt resting on her hip. When she depressed a stud, the cable stiffened. With a little effort, she shaped it into a "u," then she pulled two more thumbtip-sized devices from her belt and worked those onto the ends. Those devices were specialized mirrors.

Now came the tough part.

She pulled a thin, long pouch from the fabric on the outside of her wounded thigh and slid lock picks out to deal with the physical lock on the door. It took nearly a minute to overcome that, putting her at nine minutes since departing her room.

Once she had the door lifted, she slid the U-shaped device onto the frame, waiting until the mirrors were perfectly aligned with the infrared beam, rerouting it to give her enough room to squeeze in, then activating the magnetic elements within the device to hold it steady against the frame.

No alarms sounded.

But they would if she wasn't quick about it. Something as simple as temperature changes inside the stairwell below would register and trigger an alarm.

She sucked in a breath, drove away thoughts about her twitching thigh muscles, and slid through the opening to the stairs below. Once through, she pulled the door closed. Her exit was still going to require the false camera feed and beam realignment tool.

Saripado's office was on the top floor, looking down on the parking lot. Stiles brought up an overlay for her optics to guide her to that destination.

A single guard patrolled the building's three stories while another monitored the security station. It was easy enough moving through the halls without running into anyone. The cameras inside weren't going to register the flicker of her suit as a problem, not like the one on the rooftop door would have.

At Saripado's office, she overcame the biometric scanner easily enough with duplicated data, then once again turned to the lock-picking tools.

Once she closed the door, the office was dark. Her night-vision optics amplified what little light came in from the windows. To help, she turned on an ultraviolet flashlight.

Her objective was simple: the civil servant's desktop had a computer system built in.

She grunted softly when she reached back to pull her small tablet from a sleeve on her right shoulder blade. The device held aggressive and highly illegal hacking software. It was one of the few means to overcome the sort of security used by the CED. Stiles hesitated a moment before turning the device on. Her intrusion was already illegal enough, but using the software...

I'm committed.

Saripado's computer terminal flashed to life, and symbols flitted across the device display. The biometric security was easy to bypass thanks to what she'd used on the entry. Overcoming the encrypted authentication keys would take time.

Stiles tried to relax while the device cut through security layer after security layer. There was a power outlet on the wall behind her; she pulled the suit's power transmitter module from a sleeve on top of her right foot and plugged into the outlet. The suit's battery registered the slow pulse of energy coming in.

All she needed was a few minutes of transfer, less time than she would need to pull from the terminal.

The authentication system flashed on the desktop, and Saripado's interface glowed in front of her. His wife's face smiled in the background, then she mouthed something. Video of the two of them at a beach played after that.

Distractions.

Stiles flipped the hacking device over to retrieval functions, confirmed she had a high-speed connection, then began the download from the civil servant's system. Any databases he had access to, any data stored on his system or remotely—anything he had touched in the last two years—she was pulling down.

As she'd expected, it was a *lot* of data.

Her timer indicated fifteen minutes and twelve seconds had passed.

She'd hoped to be on the roof seconds ago. The wounded leg had thrown everything off. It was sloppy, taking too many risks.

The download was at seventy-five percent.

Stiles pushed up and wandered around the office, recording everything—diplomas, certifications, photos, awards.

All of it was in her research already, but it was different seeing things in person. Even the way the furniture was arranged, the patterns worn into the carpet, the contents of desk drawers…

She checked those next, searching for anything that might add to the imperfect impressions she had of the man.

The bottom right drawer didn't open when she tried it.

Out came the lock-picking tools. A minute later, the drawer opened.

Printouts stored in hanging folders. Antiquated, but it was probably more secure than keeping things in the system.

One at a time, the folders came out, and she flipped through them while her suit recorded the contents. Everything would be digitized and sorted later, allowing her to better analyze what she'd found.

As she restored the last folder, she spotted something at the back of the drawer: a small, wooden box.

She pulled it out and opened it.

Inside, a ring sat on a felt mound. On the face of the ring was a black, avian head in profile.

Raven.

She put the box back away and locked the drawer.

The download was nearly complete, so she pulled the power transmitter from the outlet and put that back into place.

Seconds later, the download finished. Just ahead of the twenty-one minute mark, she disconnected everything and powered the desktop down. A final scan of the room confirmed she'd left it as she'd found it. All of her gear was stashed away. Her job was done, and she'd left no impression of her intrusion.

Stiles smiled, let herself out of the door, and took a step toward the stairwell.

Then she froze.

Someone had moved off to her right, down the hall, but she couldn't see anything now.

A quick check confirmed the guard on duty was a floor below.

How—?

Something pricked the small of her back, then ice coursed through her.

She collapsed.

6

The *Valor*'s giant display felt like a sun, giving off enough light to almost wash out the flashing warning light. Pressure like a migraine rapidly built behind Benson's ears as the general quarters alarm shrieked its alert. She struggled against the urge to run back to her quarters to slip into her flight suit. How ridiculous would it be if the *Valor* were blown to pieces by whatever secret weapon the Khanate had, but her body survived? Someone might find her frozen form and wonder at the ridiculous dress uniform and the makeup she'd put on for a diplomatic mission that never took place.

Then again, did it really matter how ridiculous she looked if she lost her task force?

An obvious solution presented itself: Blow the Khanate ships from the sky!

Except they still couldn't get lock-on.

Lieutenant Konrath turned enough so that his face was in sharp profile against the display. "Beginning advanced maneuvers, Captain!"

Benson braced herself as the floor shifted slightly beneath her. They were accelerating for combat now, beginning the crazy zigzagging that would make anything but clean lock-on with an energy weapon almost useless.

Unless the Khanate had something revolutionary in their inventory.

It was Mahama's turn next. "Enemy ships within extreme weapons range. No lock-on, Captain."

Benson glanced at her own display, drilling down on the closest of the enemy ships. The oblong twins were at the front, while the bulk of the smaller ships flanked out. Several of the smaller ships held to the rear, protected by the cruisers.

It was an odd formation, but it almost confirmed her suspicion that the fleet had a sizable support complement. She counted ten of the smaller ships hiding behind the cruisers.

Tenders? Transports? Something.

And the cruisers. Why wouldn't they be forward? They should have the best shields, armor, and weaponry.

She connected to Halliwell. "Clive, do we have all our shuttles back in?"

"No." He sounded winded, as if he were running. "We have two out for Parkinson to reclaim his drones."

It took a second to find the ships, which were being escorted by Gunship-81. "Get them back."

"He said they're almost there."

"We can build new drones."

"They've got the black box and some other systems from that ship."

Dammit! "We're getting no lock-on. I can't tell if they're picking us up or not. If they can get lock-on, those ships will be prime targets."

Halliwell grunted, and it sounded like gear rattled near his mic. "I want two of you positioned here. Sergeant, anyone carrying crates, kits, even handbags—search them." Another voice came over Halliwell's communicator, acknowledging the order.

He was positioning his Marines.

Benson went back to the display, trying to puzzle out the Khanate formation and how they could have possibly overwhelmed the Gulmar so completely. There were no obvious design advantages in what she was seeing, other than the annoying stealth technology. Then again, the fleet itself was a troubling technological oddity. Getting worked up over just one—

"Faith?" Halliwell sounded calmer.

"Sorry. I didn't realize you were still positioning your Marines."

"I put a second team at the intersection where the lifts open onto deck three. Too many access points open up just beyond that area."

"The *Valor* wasn't designed to deal with saboteurs."

"You can say that again. It's going to be a mess if we're ever boarded."

"Can you still put a force together?"

"For what? I've got half my people on guard duty."

"I don't know yet. Something about this Khanate fleet is bugging—"

Mahama straightened. "Vessels deploying, Captain."

On the giant display, dozens of smaller craft were splitting off from the twin elongated ships. The smaller craft had about the same profile as a standard shuttle.

Benson waited a moment for an update. "No lock-on?"

"No lock-on, ma'am."

The smaller the vessel, the harder to acquire a meaningful lock-on, especially at range and with the targets moving at the velocity these were. She queried the *Valor* sensors for an estimate. It put their numbers at fifty with a better than seventy-five percent confidence.

Fifty.

"Lieutenant Nuñez, Lieutenant Konrath." Benson waited until the two officers were looking at her. "Please alert the task force to implement coordinated point defense fire the second those smaller craft close. Alter planned maneuvering to bring ships closer together the instant those smaller craft indicate they've selected a target. I want sufficient point defense fire to discourage those pilots."

The officers nodded, then turned back to their stations.

Commander Chopra drifted closer to the command station. "You suspect these are fighter craft?"

"That would be preferable to what I mentioned."

"The Zeroes?"

It seemed impractical. For a smaller craft to both outmaneuver and manage lock-on against a larger ship… Where would they have room for the sensors? How could they stuff a big enough engine in? Life support, ammunition—small attack craft just weren't viable.

Yet there they were: fifty ships spiraling around, heading toward…

Chopra saw it at the same time she did. "They're going after the *Amazon*."

Benson couldn't believe her eyes. The small craft were flying ahead of the destroyer, somehow anticipating its path. That couldn't be possible. Their courses were random, controlled and coordinated by the computer systems across the task force.

"Lieutenant Konrath, those small craft—"

"I see it, Captain. I'm programming in a new set of paths, but the *Amazon* isn't responding."

"Not respond—?" Benson glanced at Chopra. "How is that possible?"

Konrath shook his head. "Something must be blocking system signals, ma'am. We can't implement the changes until the *Amazon* acknowledges its changes."

Creases furrowed Nuñez's brow. "The *Amazon*'s reporting systems failures, Captain. They can't make adjustments and can't manually override. Commander Velez is requesting that we eject her ship from the coordinated maneuvering package."

"We eject them from the package, and we leave them on their own."

"She understands that, Captain. She thinks it might be the only way to regain control of their systems."

The flashing lights reflected off Chopra's head when he bowed it. "Without changing course, they're going to be headed straight toward those fighters."

Benson's guts twisted. There were no good options for the *Amazon*, and Velez knew that. "Eject them from the package."

Konrath hunched over his console. "Ejected."

"How long before we know if they've regained control?"

Nuñez shook her head. "They're still working on the systems, ma'am."

And the small craft were still swarming toward where the ship was headed.

Benson reconnected to Halliwell. "They've got fifty small craft out there, headed toward the *Amazon*."

"Fighters? That seems pretty impractical."

"These seem to know our maneuver patterns."

"So, change them."

"We tried. The *Amazon*'s systems are locked out."

"How—?" The Marine groaned. "The same way they knew we were coming here?"

"They must have access to a lot of our critical systems configurations."

"Not good."

"Not at all. Their spy network must run deep."

"Can a fighter craft carry advanced enough systems to pull that off?"

"Locking up systems?" Benson caught a skeptical frown on Chopra's face. "I think it's highly unlikely, and it looks like Commander Chopra agrees."

The bald XO frowned. "I can't see how they would have effective fighters."

Benson muted her connection. "We're maybe a minute from finding out."

"Hm." Chopra scooted over to Nuñez's post, and the two began chatting.

Benson unmuted. "Clive, I don't think those fighters are the problem."

"Um, okay. Have we seen what they can do yet?"

"No, and I'm hoping we won't. If the *Amazon* can reset its systems and get away from them, we can rejoin it to our package. But that's not the problem."

The tall Marine sighed. "Sounds like a problem to me."

"Those little craft can't carry much aboard them. Weapons systems are going to take up most of the space for them to be effective. They're not outmaneuvering us."

"Okay. So what's the threat?"

"They've got four big ships that are just hanging back in reserve. There's a large wall of frigates, but those seem to be positioning themselves to attack the *Amazon*, too."

"You think the big ships are running the show?"

On her command station display, the big ships were still sitting at extreme range. The occasional attempts to get lock-on seemed especially ineffective against them. "I think they're command-and-control platforms of some sort. Probably full to the brim with electronic countermeasures and counter-countermeasures."

"Oversized signals ships?"

"They're not doing anything obvious to support their fleet."

Chopra twisted around and leaned toward Benson, as if he'd caught part of the conversation. He edged over to Mahama's station and engaged the heavyset young lieutenant in fast chatter.

Halliwell exhaled. "There's not much I can do about that, Faith."

"Actually, I think there might be."

"Like what?"

"Like take two of our stealth shuttles out with the Marines you have available to you and see if you can get up on one of those big signals ships."

"*What?*"

"They're not engaging in the battle. The frigates aren't hanging back to protect them."

"And you expect our rail guns to tear them up?"

"Maybe they could. We don't know if they have shields up. But I think you could do more by getting aboard them and showing them that we can do sabotage, too."

Chopra raised a hand. "Those large ships have significant EM footprints."

Benson smiled. Big electromagnetic footprints meant they were at least partially involved in the operation.

Stealth technology could only go so far.

Then Mahama groaned—a soft sound that seemed inadequate as the main display focused on the *Amazon*. It had changed course, but the smaller craft were now a swarm around it, speeding right at it.

Impacting.

No weapons, just tons of metal and composites accelerating into it. And almost immediately after the impacts, fire plumes marked where the ships must have detonated, burning away escaping atmosphere and tearing even greater holes in the hull. The nearest frigates piled on, firing into the crippled ship.

Mahama bowed his head. "The *Amazon* is effectively dead, Captain."

That settled it for Benson. If she was right, and their systems were compromised, they were all going to be in the same condition soon. "Clive, take two shuttles. Load them with explosives. Mount breach modules and shield disruptors to the hulls."

"Two shuttles? I can barely get two squads in with all that gear."

"That's all you'll need. If you can get onto their hull and cut through, plant your charges and get out."

Halliwell was silent for a moment. "If you think it'll work."

"I think it's our only chance. We can't just flee, not without testing out tactics."

"They'll just follow us."

"Or head into Kedraalian space."

"I understand. We'll do what we can."

"I'll have the *Sinclair* escort you and Gunship-99." She pointed to Chopra, who huddled with the bridge officers. They nodded. It would be their responsibility to coordinate the ships leaving the package and adjust maneuvers again to give them a wide berth. "I think this is our best chance."

"Keep me updated." The big Marine disconnected.

He obviously wasn't happy, and he had every right not to be. Even if the *Sinclair*'s electronic countermeasures were effective and kept the shuttles and gunship hidden from the enemy sensors, they were still heading into the heart of trouble. The cruiser-sized ships almost certainly had armaments of some sort, regardless of their roles. If the assignment were more certain to have a meaningful outcome, he would have embraced it, but it was high risk with little chance of reward.

That's how desperate the battle had already become. They needed something, and they needed it *now*, or they were going to have to make a run for it, and that would mean abandoning Gulmar space and any chance of an accord.

The remaining fighter craft were wheeling around now, heading toward her ships. They would choose a target soon, and the pattern would be repeated.

Benson wasn't about to let that happen. "Lieutenant Konrath!"

"Yes, ma'am?"

"Change evasive pattern. Generate something random. All ships need to operate in threes, and I want this initial pattern to draw the attack force away from the other ships. Keep the *Valor* closest to those enemy cruisers until Lieutenant Halliwell's force is away, then position us between the Khanate frigates and those cruisers."

The young man's eyes squinted in concentration as he bent over his console. "Generating new patterns, Captain."

"Lieutenant Nuñez, contact the shuttle and gunship returning from the wreckage. Have them join Lieutenant Halliwell's force when it launches."

The communications officer was already on a call but nodded confirmation.

Chopra eyed the Marines at the entry hatch, then slid back to the command station. "You think those cruisers are going to hang back?"

"No. Any form of ECM has a limited effective range."

"Are you inviting them to come after us?"

"Better us than some of the other ships."

The XO gulped, then he squinted. "You don't think they'll attack the *Valor*."

"Not initially. We're too big a nut to chew. For now."

They leaned against the acceleration as Konrath's new maneuvers kicked in. On the huge display, the *Valor* was closest to the cruisers, with the *Castro* signals ship and the *Ganges* taking roughly parallel courses. Benson's cruisers—the *Lyon*, *Seattle*, and *Cairo*—each headed away from the *Amazon* and the enemy craft maneuvering away from it.

As Benson had expected, the four cruisers adjusted course as well. They headed toward the *Cairo*'s cluster of ships. "Lieutenant Nuñez, notify the *Cairo* that one of her ships is the next target. Lieutenant Mahama, the second we know which one, have the *Lyon* and *Seattle* move into support positions. I want those frigates to know what they're up against."

Nuñez shouted out, "Yes, ma'am!"

Mahama's response was more subdued as he worked his way through the weapons interface.

Lieutenant Konrath looked back over his shoulder at Benson. "Shuttles are away, Captain. Course changed to come up on the frigate group flank."

Benson switched her station display to a split screen, with Halliwell's group on the right and the Khanate frigates and attack craft on the left. There were still nearly forty of the smaller vessels. From a completely cold, calculating perspective, that meant her task force was probably more than could be destroyed in one attack. That knowledge didn't offer much comfort, but it was something to file away.

Konrath glanced up from his console to study the giant display. "Captain, they're going after the *Montgomery*."

"The *Cairo*'s signals ship?"

"It's not responding."

Chopra's face pinched tight. "They can overwhelm our ECM and ECCM?"

A twinge of regret settled into Benson's gut. She should have brought Parkinson back aboard and have him dig into the data. "Get everyone into position. *Now*. And be sure to capture all data available—"

Mahama spun around. "Enemy cruisers have launched missiles!"

"They detected our shuttles?" Benson didn't care about the panic in her voice. The shuttles weren't meant to go against high-end missiles.

"At the *Amazon*. Four missiles."

There were survivors aboard the ship, but there wouldn't be if those missiles hit. "Change course. Intercept those missiles. Open fire the second we're in range."

Even before Konrath acknowledged, the *Valor* lurched from the abrupt maneuvering. "Course changed, Captain."

The tug of acceleration increased, forcing Benson to widen her stance and bend her knees. Although the missiles had been fired from far away, they were on a relatively straight line, while the *Valor* had to manage a slow pivot. They could manage more thrust than the missiles over time, but the rockets were part of a dedicated weapons system with no fragile humans aboard. As a result, the weapons could perform more aggressive acceleration and maneuvers.

Benson split her display into three, bringing up the rest of the task force in the third window. The other ships were doing exactly what she needed them to do: closing on the frigates. Perhaps more importantly, the *Cairo* and the gunship that had been part of its group were already laying down fire on the fighter craft. Despite their size and the lack of lock-on, the point defense systems were making an impact. One of the fighters was falling back from the pack, engines dead. Another exploded, trailing fire for a long breath before blowing apart.

Fire. That had to mean atmosphere. Were there pilots aboard?

Seconds dragged as the fighter craft drew closer to the signals ship. The rest of the task force was now near enough to open fire on the frigates, which had either missed the closing maneuvers or were simply unprepared to break from their establish tactics. The first shots connected, and debris blew out from sections of one of the enemy ships.

Mahama flashed a relieved smile at Chopra, then Benson. "The *Mao* reports lock-on. They're concentrating on two frigates right now."

Chopra sank in on himself a little. "So we *can* get through."

Benson crossed her arms over her chest and drove a knuckle into her chin. "Distance? Are those frigates operating without the same protection they had earlier? Is it because those cruisers launched their missiles?"

The bald XO sighed. "We'll have to analyze the data. If we survive."

"We're going to survive. The question is how long before we drive them off." *And who we lose before they go.*

Halliwell connected to her. "Captain Benson, do you read me?"

He was calling through the shuttle's open channel. "Go ahead."

"We're feeding video now through the *Sinclair*."

As he spoke, Mahama opened a window on the giant display. The enemy cruisers were off to the left, weapons bristling along the dorsal and ventral spine. Missile launchers ran along the port side facing the cameras. On the sloping hull between the dorsal center peak and the visible missile launchers array, clumps of antennae were mounted on what appeared to be turrets.

There were symbols on the hull: the Khanate's swirly alphabet.

She ran a translation. "*True Light of the Way.*"

"What?" Halliwell sounded distracted.

"The name of the cruiser."

"Okay." A red square marked a relatively flat section of hull forward of the antenna arrays. Halliwell typed something in: *Entry point.* "We're going in here."

Benson pulled the image to her own display and tapped what looked like point defense turrets. "What about these guns?"

"If we can get in close enough, they'll be useless." He highlighted a bulge in the skin forward of the intended landing spot. "This is a design flaw. See this bulge? The forward point defense guns can't get past that."

"If you can get in that close undetected."

"It's a well-built ship. There's no getting in without risk."

The video flickered, and the angle changed dramatically. "What was that?"

"Shield disruptor. We're going in. The *Sinclair* tracked the bulk of the signals to this ship. It's—"

Turrets spun around on the cruiser hull, and the signal winked out.

Benson stiffened. "Mahama! Nuñez—what just happened?"

Nuñez glanced up at the dead window on the main display. "Signal lost, Captain."

Mahama bowed his head. "They...could be directing ECCM at the shuttles, ma'am."

Except a quick check of the situation with the *Cairo* showed its gunship was still operating without guidance. The enemy cruiser's point defense systems had turned around, as if they'd managed lock-on. Had the *Sinclair* lost its stealth and signal-scrambling capability when the shield disruptor fired? Had the Khanate guns destroyed the shuttles?

Benson's heart pounded. "Range to missiles?"

"Extreme range in..." Mahama brushed a hand across his brow. "One minute."

A minute. The cruiser's defense systems could have turned her people into floating bits of gristle and bone by then.

Chopra clasped his hands behind his back. "There is always a chance it was a system malfunction."

Benson swallowed. "We need to solve this puzzle." Did she sound convincing?

Her XO nodded. "We do."

Mahama drilled in on the missile tracking symbols. "Weapons hot, Captain."

Lines traced across the gap between her ships and the missiles, indicating where lasers had fired. Other lines drew out cones to represent the anti-missile railguns that were setting up an expanding cloud of small-caliber rounds that would shred missile systems on impact.

Beam after beam fired from the *Valor* and the *Ganges*, but nothing connected with the missiles.

Mahama sighed. "Closing to effective range. Ten seconds. Lock-on!"

One of the missiles exploded. The other three immediately began evasive maneuvers.

The *Valor* matched, and once again Benson found herself bending her knees to adjust to the tug.

After a second, Mahama seemed to brighten. "Lock-on! Two missiles!"

One of the missiles exploded. The other took a strange course, an apparent continuation of an evasive maneuver. It must have lost a control system.

The fourth missile continued on.

How many survivors would there be in the *Amazon*? A hundred? Seventy-five? There was no justifying the thoughts in Benson's head—let the missile hit, adjust course to go after the cruisers. Halliwell and Grier's team plus the gunship and the *Sinclair*? That was barely a hundred hands.

Chopra seemed to sense her anxiety. "One missile will not destroy the *Amazon*."

It was what she needed to hear. "We're not going to take that chance."

Mahama leaned over his console. "Missile impact in one minute."

The *Amazon* tumbled in space. There were no defense signals coming off of it. No weapons systems operational.

Benson squeezed the support ring. "We need that missile destroyed, Lieutenant."

"Yes, ma'am. We'll—" His head came up. "Lock-on!"

Lines flashed across the display. Cones showed a precise targeting for the railguns that slowly pinched across the missile's possible path, then—

"Direct hit!" Mahama raised a fist in celebration. "Missile destroyed!"

Benson let out a breath. Her task force was giving the enemy frigates fits. Already, three of those ships were out of action, and a fourth was maneuvering away. The fighter craft were still headed for the *Montgomery*. Did she have the right to redirect the *Valor* away from the frigates?

Nuñez pointed to the giant display, where the dead window now showed a completely different video feed. It looked like an airlock—a shuttle airlock—was latched onto something: an umbilical. At the end of the hard frame, bright light flashed from a circular device.

It was a hull-breaching module.

The Marines were getting ready to breach the cruiser hull!

Audio buzzed over the connection. "Captain Benson?" It was Grier.

"Yes, Sergeant Grier? We lost your signal."

"The lieutenant's shuttle was hit by defensive fire."

"Is he— Are they okay?"

"He's alive, but he lost about half his team. The rest are cutting in about fifteen meters forward of our position. Um, Clive's hurt. I thought you should know."

Benson blushed. "Thank you." Did Chopra cock an eyebrow? "What's it look like for the hull?"

"Not too long. Another minute. The other team's maybe a minute behind. They've been dealing with things."

"I understand. How's the *Sinclair*?"

"Hiding. The gunship's right in its shadow. Did you mean to send Parkinson out here?"

"The… Yes. I thought he might be able to help."

"Ugh. Thanks. Would you mind passing whatever it is you want from him on for me, ma'am? I'm about ready to blast the fuck out of some Khanate sailors."

Mahama flashed a toothy smile—a *vengeful* smile.

Nuñez held a hand up. "I'm connected to Chief Parkinson, ma'am."

Benson could almost imagine the little man's demands for an explanation. "Please let the chief know that we need an analysis of those ships: role, operational methodology, vulnerabilities."

"He's…asking why he couldn't conduct that analysis from the *Valor*."

"Tell Chief Parkinson the *Valor* wants him to be our eyes."

"Yes, ma'am." The young woman made a pained face, then turned away.

One thing that could always be counted on was Parkinson's winning charm.

On Grier's video feed, the glow from the hull-breaching module dimmed. A Marine moved down the umbilical and dragged the device back, then another one moved forward and kicked the hull section clear. It rattled as it fell inside the ship, revealing an inner hull. Once more, the module was dragged forward and attached.

Grier waved the Marine back. "Inner hull. Shouldn't take long for this one."

Benson's mouth felt dry. "Do you have any idea where you are?"

"Well, we've never seen this model ship, but the systems estimated this would be a deck, maybe just above it. The engines are probably too far aft to get to, but power lines, control systems—we've got enough explosives to make this a really nice party."

"They'll probably have Marines of their own."

Grier's camera turned to one of her Marines, and she smacked a pouch on his hip. "Look at that, ma'am! We brought extra ammo! Oorah!"

The light on the breach module went out, and the Marine Grier had smacked rushed down the umbilical. She squeezed past as he pulled the module back into the shuttle, then looked back at the squad of Marines behind her. "Ready, boys?"

They roared.

She kicked the hull segment in, and it fell to the deck about a meter below. "Nice piloting!"

Grier dropped through the opening and rolled away, creating a crazy, tumbling image on the display. She and her squad were near an intersection. Bright lights embedded in the walls revealed more of the Khanate's strange symbols. One of the Marines slid a satchel across to Grier.

The Khanate had insisted on its own language long ago. Its people spoke that language primarily and sometimes exclusively. Why fit in, after all?

Benson checked on the *Montgomery*. The fighter craft were seconds out.

"Sergeant Grier, if you and your team could find a target—"

Gunfire roared, and rounds hammered the deck near the satchel. Grier's camera view twisted around, catching several men in what appeared to be relatively light armor. They had assault weapons that looked familiar—old.

The Kedraalian Marines moved to the best cover they could find and returned fire. A moment later, one of them howled and fell to the deck. Blood pooled under him.

Grier hissed. "They've got us caught in a crossfire, Captain!"

Benson turned back to the video of the *Montgomery*. One of the fighter craft crashed into the larger vessel, and almost immediately fire erupted.

An explosion.

Another of the smaller vessels slammed into the signals ship.

Another explosion.

The fighters continued slamming into the ship, until Nuñez bowed her head. "*Cairo* reports the *Montgomery* is lost."

Lost! The odds of survivors on a ship that small… Benson sagged. "Tell the *Cairo* to get out of there."

Chopra cleared his throat. "Commander Tuleyev is going to demand we change tactics, Captain. Perhaps it's time to break the engagement and flee?"

Benson clenched her jaw. "We need to figure this out."

"I understand. Maybe we could regroup? The Gulmar might have some ideas?"

The Gulmar? Their only ideas would be to bribe the Khanate, but the Khanate didn't take bribes. You were either joined the Khanate or put to the sword. What they needed was to cripple the cruiser. "Sergeant Grier, any updates?"

"Still pinned down, ma'am!" The Marine's camera showed a second member of her team down but moving.

"Do you have any ideas?"

"To get out of this? Not really. We could use our grenades and maybe make a run for it, but that wouldn't go well."

"You don't think the grenades would get to the enemy?"

"I'd rather save them, if possible. I sent a probe out to get a look at the layout. I—I guess we could blow ourselves up with the explosives?"

Blow themselves up. Like the Khanate pilots, if there were pilots inside the fighters. It would do *something*. But was that just the temptation of eliminating a competitor for Halliwell's attention?

Grier grunted and looked down at her arm, where smoke rose from a segment of armor. "Son of a bitch! Those are some nasty guns. Captain? What's the call? We can rig these charges with a dead man's switch."

Benson saw the way her XO frowned. "Do you have an idea, Commander?"

"I'm afraid not. We'll have to do something, though. The fighter craft seem to be headed for the *Lyon*, and Commander Tuleyev won't let his ship be destroyed in pursuit of something so pointless."

The word stung, but it was true. Looking back on it, the tactics had been flawed. They hadn't figured the Khanate forces out. Two ships were gone, one of them a complete loss. And Halliwell was wounded, maybe dead by now. There were no obvious weaknesses in the Khanate force.

Grier's weapon chattered. "Captain?"

Chopra's eyebrows arched. "Captain?"

They were waiting on her. All of them. And she had no idea what to do.

7

———

Hazy light. Burning but cold. Everything was cold.

Stiles pulled her head up from where it had been anchored. Not anchored. Her head weighed twenty kilos, easy. It left her neck a throbbing ache. Cracked lips that tasted like blood. Another pain in the intense chill. Squeezed into a gray room with ice on the walls.

She tried to sit upright but couldn't. A chair—hard, smooth, slick.

Urine. She'd peed herself at some point.

Closing her eyelids was a risk. Would she open them again? She had to.

Her brain was mush. Not just the cold, but the way she shivered, the lethargy—hypothermia wasn't far off.

Shake it off. Don't give in. You were sloppy. Don't accept failure.

They'd put her through worse as a kid. A couple years after the pool.

She'd woken early in the morning, sitting upright in her bunk. A thin sheet was all she had to cover a hard mattress. Her roommate was gone—dead.

Stiles spun on her butt and leveled her feet on the cold floor. Her arms stuck out like sticks from a black, sleeveless top. Her legs were thicker in black shorts, less wiry and more powerful. Even with accelerated aging, she was a couple years from puberty, but she was taking well to training, gaining strength and agility.

Her door opened, and her twin stood there. Darien Caville. "You hear it?"

She pushed off the bunk. "Yes. Someone broke in?"

"The power's out. I couldn't find anyone else."

He'd come for her last. That hurt. Or he was lying. He liked to test her that way. "We should run."

"That's not the mission."

"The mission is meant for us to figure out."

"There's no figuring out: Protect our people."

"We don't even know the people we're supposed to die protecting."

"We will when the time comes."

She skated across the floor, the soles of her bare feet whispering. Beyond him, the hallway was dark and empty. "I'm going to test the exit."

He stepped aside. Their last two sparring sessions, they'd proven to be equals in combat, and he didn't seem to be in the mood to test her right then. "Go ahead."

There was a small flashlight hidden beneath her mattress. She checked the beam, then hurried out.

Her passage through the building was too loud, but he'd said it was empty. If it wasn't, the noise she made wasn't going to be as important as where she went. That was a path she'd mapped over the years, a series of hallways and doors, a stairwell with a keypad she'd figured out the code for, four flights of stairs, then more hallways and doors.

The last door opened onto the outside world. There was a parking lot, and sitting in that lot was always a vehicle: an ambulance. No matter what, that vehicle would be there, waiting at the bottom of a flight of metal stairs.

She'd nearly made a run for it a year prior, after one of her instructors had gotten rough in a training session. She'd struck the woman with a solid round-house kick, catching her off-guard. The blow had drawn blood.

No matter how well-trained, no matter how disciplined, you weren't going to beat someone with enough training who was bigger and stronger.

Stiles had been immobile on her bunk for two nights after the beating.

Aching. Plotting. Waiting.

The wait was over.

She punched the code into the keypad and sprinted up the stairs. Part of her hoped Darien would change his mind and come with her, while another part liked the idea of being alone, not having to protect or rely on anyone else.

At the door to the outside, she paused.

There really hadn't been anyone else in the halls. The power really was out except for emergency lights and whatever circuit the keypad was on.

All that stood between her and the outside world was the final door.

And fear. Discipline, as Darien called it. That was his belief, not hers.

She darted to the door and shoved it open, threw a foot out onto the steel landing that would give her access to the steps, which would take her to the ambulance.

But the staircase wasn't there. The ambulance wasn't there.

Just a pool, black in the night. Its surface was uneven, strange.

When she impacted, she understood: ice. Ice and freezing water.

She went under, blew out her breath screaming, swam for the surface.

It was gone. The night sky was starless, moonless.

Her fingernails scraped across a cover that was flush against the water: hard, plastic. No air. No way out. Freezing.

Don't give in.

Metal clanged heavily—a door being thrown open.

Her eyelids came up reluctantly. A couple in their mid-thirties dressed in matching jackets and slacks stepped in, him with dark, slicked-back hair; her with long, winter-gold hair bunched in a knot at the back of her head. They were pale, but his was the result of bleaching or a condition, because he had Southeast Asian features. Her paleness matched her Nordic look.

Asian Man frowned and shifted the bundle pinched between his left arm and ribs: clothing. He wrinkled his nose and averted his eyes just a little. "Is this really necessary?" Steam slithered from his mouth.

Nordic Lady rolled her eyes. She kicked something at Stiles's feet: a plastic tub filled with ice water. "She's not complaining."

It hit Stiles at that moment: She was naked. Bloodied. Bruised. "Where…am I?"

"That's what they always ask." Nordic Lady smirked. "You're dead."

Dead. The meaning was clear to Stiles: Someone had faked her death already. No help was coming. "GSA? SAID? CED?"

"You can't remember? Doesn't matter, really."

"How long?"

Asian Man turned back just enough to look Stiles in the eyes. "A couple weeks. I-I've never seen someone last so long."

Nordic Lady snorted. "A human couldn't. She's a Genesis."

"Genesis are humans."

"Not like *us*."

He studied the clothes bundle pinned to his ribs. "She has human DNA, doesn't she?"

"Cooked up in a machine, sure."

"We could use someone like her."

"I don't think so. They're a travesty."

Stiles tested the bonds pinning her arms behind her: solid. It was probably too much to break free of even when she wasn't broken. And she was *very* broken at that moment. "Ravens."

The man's head came up, his eyes running up and down her body, lingering on the tub. He wasn't affected by her other than to feel pity. Maybe he had other interests, but it seemed more likely he'd simply been immunized or altered. That was a problem. "Why did you break into Kusno Saripado's office?"

"He's a Raven. Like you."

Nordic Lady slapped Stiles. It wasn't a full swing with everything behind it, but it stung. "Where's the leak?"

"The leak?"

"I told you last time, drop the act. You know where you go if you don't cooperate?"

"No."

"Deletion."

Silence Center. A site dedicated to scrubbing all evidence. Acid vats, meat grinders, furnaces. There were options to get rid of bodies. Stiles spat blood onto the floor. "There isn't a leak."

"You just found Saripado's name in the bottom of a bag."

"There were connections. His family and the Patel family go back years."

Nordic Lady sneered at Asian Man. "You see? Even a Genesis can break."

He circled the room. "What's your obsession with the Patels?"

Stiles tested her bonds again. "They're at the heart of this conspiracy."

"Conspiracy?"

"Pirate operations. They're shipping illegal technology to the Gulmar Union."

Asian Man scuffed to a stop behind her. "How did you discover that?"

"Records. Research."

Nordic Lady slapped Stiles again. "You need to do better than that. You remember what we did last session? You screamed. I can turn the current up high enough to stop your genetically engineered heart. We can revive you."

Asian Man cleared his throat. "I like that we're making progress." He came back around to look Stiles in the face and held up the clothing bundle. "I have approval. You cooperate, you agree to join us, and I walk you down the hall. There's an apartment—comfortable bed, hot shower, decent food. You're hungry, right?"

Stiles was famished, but she only realized it when she concentrated on that. Her stomach felt small. There was acid at the back of her throat. They'd done a job on her. "What does Saripado do for you?"

Nordic Lady chuckled. "Didn't get to look at the data you stole, hm?"

"He's providing cover for the pirates. He's taking money from the Patels."

The Ravens glanced at each other. The woman's cheeks reddened.

They hadn't expected that.

Nordic Lady crossed her arms, burying her hands in her jacket. "Messing with the Patels is a death sentence. You might want to consider that."

Asian Man tucked the clothes under his arm again. "She's right. They serve a purpose—a valuable purpose. So does Saripado."

Stiles shivered. Her training, the mental and physical conditioning, her design: She could only go so far. Despite what the gold-haired woman said, a Genesis was human, and even an optimized human could be broken. "Why are you doing this? Why betray the Republic?"

That brought a frown to the Asian Man's face. "It's part of the deal."

"Deal?"

Nordic Lady's thin lips twisted into a smirk. "Everything's a deal. See? This is why we can't work with her. She's too naive."

The Asian man started pacing again. "We have to change things, Agent Stiles. Or do you prefer Brianna? Lieutenant Stiles? Do you really even know who you are?"

"I'm a Genesis 3. Genetic Simulacrum System."

"That's who you are? You don't even pretend to have parents?"

"I was artificially created by Martgun GenCorps specifically for this role at the GSA. I couldn't have parents."

Once again, the Asian man stopped behind Stiles. "That seems like a sad answer. Is…" He huffed. "Is that who you *want* to be? I mean, do you have an identity of your own?"

It was a question that would haunt Stiles until she died. She was third generation in a line of genetic research that she still wasn't sure about. She knew *her* purpose but not the original purpose. She wasn't sure *anyone* knew the original purpose. Did that first-generation Genesis creation know who it was before it died? Did the second generation? "I know who I am."

Asian Man came around to her left shoulder, his polished shoes millimeters shy of the blood she'd spit out. "You're loyal to the Republic, aren't you?"

"As loyal as anyone can be. If I have a parent, it's the Republic."

"Yes. Exactly! They paid for you. They trained you."

"They did."

"And you understand that the War of Separation that tore us apart was illegal?"

"Not by the terms of the treaties."

"Objectively. The acts of violence, the betrayal and sabotage—those were crimes that would have led to life sentences for the actors if not for all that happened."

"We signed the peace treaties. We can't change that."

"Under duress! Millions died. Millions more would have died without accepting peace."

"Is that what the Ravens are for? You want to reverse the war?"

Nordic Lady shook her head. "She doesn't get it."

"Help me understand."

"The war left us vulnerable, but it gave us an opportunity. So long as the brave were willing to do whatever it took, we could make these terrorists pay."

"You don't want to reverse the war."

"Reverse the war? Bring those people back into the Republic?" Nordic Lady squinted. "We rooted out the cancer. Well, it rooted itself out. Now all we have to do is destroy it."

"You…want to destroy the people who broke off from the Republic."

The Asian man stepped behind Stiles's chair. "When we fled Earth, we tried to bring along only the best and brightest. You understand? Our home world was destroyed through greed and hatred. Somehow, we let damaged people through. Now they've self-identified."

It sank in for Stiles. "War. The war gives you a chance to—"

"To purge. To cleanse. These are the people who should never have been brought from Earth in the first place."

"Not all of them. Millions were forced to remain on the planets we gave up in the peace treaties."

Nordic Lady shrugged. "Every war has collateral damage."

"And giving the Gulmar technology? It's not in order to secure an alliance?"

Nordic Lady's eyes narrowed. "She doesn't understand."

Asian Man sighed. "I know. I had hoped—"

"It's her design and training. She can't see the big picture."

Stiles swallowed. "I'm trying. It's hard to understand. You want war to force change."

Asian Man's lips compressed. "The galaxy is larger than we would ever be able to fill in a thousand lifetimes, but those people can't see that. They want a species of a very specific type: a genetic ideal; people who follow an economic doctrine that strips away freedom and independence; people who worship some strange deity dreamed up by a psychopath. Before we can have freedom to become what we're destined to be, we have to eliminate the threats to that freedom."

"And the Owls? They agree with this?"

"The Owls have their own agenda. And they've become inconsequential." Asian Man dropped the clothes to the floor and reached inside his jacket, pulling out a small weapon barely larger than his hand. "I'm afraid we now have all we need from you, Agent Stiles."

She stared at the barrel, noting the strange design. It didn't seem big enough for a deadly projectile unless he aimed for her head, and then it would have to get through her reinforced skull. But he was pointing to her chest. "Did you break me?"

"Earlier? No. But we know enough now. Your design was too complete. You'll die before we can convert you."

"Deletion, then?"

"It's better than a lifetime stuck in a cage, isn't it?"

Stiles thought back to her childhood, to the training that had broken her and removed any sense of identity. It had been a life in a cage. Who—what—she was came from that. "They'll stop you."

Nordic Lady nudged the clothes bundle with the tip of her shoe. "Will they?"

"I won't be the last they send after you."

"The GSA is fresh out of Genesis 3s now, and they've never made any progress using regular agents to infiltrate."

Asian Man didn't seem to be taking any pleasure from the moment. "Ask yourself this, Agent Stiles: How did we know you were breaking into the CED? Our influence runs throughout the government. We will always be one step ahead of everyone. Now, I'm afraid you have an appointment with some very...brutal technicians."

The gun popped, and there was a pressure in Stiles's chest. She had a moment to glance down, where a small, shiny metal cap protruded from the flesh covering her sternum, then an icy sensation coursed through her.

Shake it off. Don't give in.

But she had no choice. She was human. And she had reached her end.

8

In the cabin of Satrap Karno, lights twisted and flashed, seemingly dancing to the constant chatter of the captains of the Glorious Fleet of Conquest. His breathing was shallow, his skin damp with sweat. It wasn't just the lights on the display spread across three of the walls of his room that seemed to hammer him. Electricity jumped from one nerve ending at the base of his back to another, one of many chronic reminders of the brutal treatment his body had been given.

He breathed in the thick, soothing cloud of incense and massaged the atrophied muscles of his thighs to no avail.

This is your gift.

The pain, the ruin of his body, had been the blessing of the Holy Khan, part of the crippling blows that now confined Satrap to the pillows arranged around his bed. He consoled himself that he didn't need his legs to command the fleet. He had a mind like no other in the Khanate, an uncanny and deep understanding of the weave and shift of starship tactics. That mind had saved his life but also cost him his freedom.

Born Sutan Karno, he was the child of a minor administrator on Iberia, which was now known as Azh Kali in the language dreamed up by the first Khan. Excellent scores at school and a soft, perhaps pretty face had gained the attention of the priesthood, and that attention had led to selection for service in the palace of the current Holy Khan on Azh Shivan.

Satrap squeezed his eyes shut at the memories of that service.

If the Guiding Star had meant for us to know absolute power, it would have stricken from us all corruption and bedevilment.

Now, though, Satrap's concerns were greater than the horrors of a childhood destroyed by a vile, old man. The Glorious Fleet of Conquest was minutes away from the stroke that would shatter the Kedraalian fleet, yet his captains were bickering. Family names were being besmirched. Threats were being leveled. Were they an army instead of a fleet, he would have been forced to delay the engagement so that his pigheaded nobles could draw their sabers and darken the ground with blood, all in the name of honor.

A bell sounded: Someone was at the hatch to his room. Ikhama.

"Enter!" Satrap covered his bony legs with a silky blanket and leaned against the pillows.

The hatch opened, admitting an elderly woman in long, white robe before closing again. Her braided hair was silvery and thick where his was black and thinning. The belt cinched at her waist hung off the jut of pelvic bones, while his blue satin robe bulged over the potbelly that had developed since the paralysis caused by the Holy Khan's final strike.

She bowed, then settled on the rug at the bottom of his bunk, knees bent and eyes closed. "Our Satrap brings glory to the fleet."

"You are plagued with an excess of kindness, Ikhama."

"You summoned me."

"I would talk with you."

After another bow, the old woman pushed back onto her butt and crossed her legs in front of her, eyes still closed. "Two enemy ships have fallen. So says the captain of the *Desert Sands.*"

"They have. These were easy strikes for his fighters."

"Irritation? In the voice of Satrap?"

"Ikhama, when you listen to the words of my brilliant captains, what do you hear?" He waved a hand through the air, and the chatter from the speakers grew louder.

"Confusion and chaos are the strongest voices in war."

"They can be, yes. But this is more than confusion and chaos. It is a conspiracy of fools. Hear them? They challenge not just each other—which is wasteful enough—but me. They challenge the doctrine we spent the last two years codifying and training against."

"*Anxiousness clouds the mind of the stallion.* They wish to run free and strike down the enemy with their mighty thews."

Satrap stared into the glowing images of the battle. "How long have you been an Ikhama?"

"Since birth, Satrap."

"Did the Holy Khan ever bless you with his attention?"

The old woman's dark eyes opened, stopping short of a wide flare. "Our Holy Khan does not indulge in the pleasures of the flesh. The Ikhama are never directly in his presence alone."

"The shahs and moqad would contest that claim."

"What the Holy Khan does with his generals and governors is in the name of the Guiding Star. He gains no pleasure from it."

Satrap snorted. "My captains should experience such a void of pleasure."

"Captains are the arms of the satrap. They are the means with which you strike for our Holy Khan."

"They should burn in the fires of the Guiding Star!"

"Has the Holy Khan failed to give his greatest leader the blades and horses to strike down the enemy?"

"You tell me, Ikhama. We should already be looking upon the burning husk of the great flagship the Kedraalians have invested all their hopes in. Instead, we maneuver yet to draw it in."

Bony fingers settled on the old woman's brow. "Spies and saboteurs."

"Perhaps that is the problem. As well, our own have failed to perform as expected."

"Cowardice and treachery."

"I can't know—" Something in the display caught his attention: red circles. They flashed along the green oblong of the *True Light of the Way*. "Enemy craft?"

The old woman's hand fell away from her face. "Trouble haunts the satrap?"

"It haunts our fleet!" Satrap tapped the middle fingers of his right hand against the palm three times, activating the private communicator embedded in his skull. "Captain Zohar, what is this I see on my display?"

After a moment, Zohar's features materialized, ghostly on top of the images of battle. The man was younger than Satrap and fit. Brown hair swept back from a hooked nose and protruding chin. Rather than fear or surprise, the captain's green eyes flashed annoyance. "What is it you see, Satrap?"

"Ships! Among the fleet!"

"We have engaged the enemy. There will be ships among—"

"Look at the tactical display! There are ships on top of the *True Light of the Way*!" The idiot had been paying attention only to the attack instead of the entire battle space.

And, indeed, surprise finally did cause the captain's lips to squeeze tight. "A small force. Already, defenses fire against the attackers."

"The problem is greater than that, Zohar. How did they get so close? How did they know to attack the *True Light of the Way*?"

"A question in need of answer."

"I would have that answer, please."

The connection died.

Ikhama massaged the knobby joints of her fingers. "Concern ever flies alongside ambition. Which strikes down the other, only the Holy Khan knows."

Satrap tugged his silk robe free where it had bunched under his arm. "You know this war is not my ambition."

"Yet the strings of command wrap around your fingers."

"And the strings of my life stretch back to the throne on Azh Shivan."

"The candle that burns brightest ever catches the clever eye."

He waved the woman's nonsense away. "In a realm where everyone has their nose stuck in the ramblings of a senile fool, it takes nothing to stand out."

Ikhama's fingers pressed against her wrinkled brow. *"Blasphemy knows no title, and justice cares not the purpose or blessing of the blasphemer."*

"How great a prisoner are you, Ikhama? Can you remember your true name?"

"My name is my title. My title is my service to our Holy Khan."

"Our Holy Khan brings annihilation to us in his mad thirst for purity."

"There is only what has been blessed by our Holy Khan. All else is falseness and—"

"—*and deception.* Yes, yes, I know the writings of the Khan Kabal."

The old woman shivered. "It was the father of all Khans who conceived of us, Satrap. In his dreaming of the Ikhama, though we are many, we are one."

So what she knows, they all know, and thus Holy Khan knows. "Praise our Holy Khan."

"All praise to the light of the Guiding Star." She relaxed.

It might have been that her concerns were legitimate. Satrap had read manuals about cybernetic surgery in his youth, when his mind had been insatiable and his role as a simple candle lighter in the quiet shadows of the palace had left him hours to connect to the sealed-off library underground. There had been nights where the pain of abuse had been too great to sleep, and he had found the only solace in mint tea and the electronic volumes still accessible to the clever and determined.

Yet even cybernetics had its limits, and if the Kedraalians had managed to get close to the *True Light of the Way*, the fleet could be destroyed long before any message of blasphemy sent by Ikhama reached the Holy Khan.

Satrap's jaw itched—a connection request. A glance up and to the right revealed it was Captain Zohar. Satrap accepted, taking some solace from the annoyed sneer on the younger man's face. "You have news, Captain?"

"The infidels have sent a handful of vessels."

"How did we miss them?"

"They are small. If not for shutting down the shields of the *True Light of the Way*, they would not have been detected at all."

"And why do they send these small vessels to our active control ship?"

"Insertion of boarders."

Marines? That seemed a desperate move. "And these boarders have been dispatched?"

"They are pinned down shy of any critical systems. They will be dead in moments. Our Holy Khan guides the weapons of the security teams."

"Do they require assistance?"

A smirk curled the captain's lip. "You question the guidance of our Holy Khan?"

"I question anything that could allow for our single most important ship at the moment to be boarded by Kedraalian Marines!"

"*Strength comes through determination.* These are the words from the Khan Kabal."

"Determination can't stop a bullet or disarm a bomb."

"These are the words from the Khan Kabal!"

"Shouting the same words makes them no more wise or applicable than before, Captain. Ready teams from your own security forces and send them to assist the *True Light of the Way*."

The younger man drew up to his impressive height. "Weakening my security forces leaves me and the *Might of the Khan* vulnerable!"

"And since I am aboard your ship, it leaves me vulnerable, yet I order it."

"I will not give my rivals advantage."

"Your contemporaries have no means of dispatching you while my Jakkara protect me… Unless you give me reason to replace you."

Zohar glowered. "I will send two squads."

Satrap barely noticed the disconnection this time. He was already running through the security and communications logs to get access to the *True Light of the Way*'s systems. "Has it ever troubled you, Ikhama, how inefficient we are?"

Cloth hissed as the old woman bowed slightly. "*Cream rises to the top, but only through churning do we produce—*"

"*—do we produce butter.* Thank you. Do you have only platitudes in your head?"

She pressed the fingers harder against her brow. "You would have what change about our inefficiency?"

"Less of an obsession with promotion and elimination seems a good start."

"Securing your position."

"My position is safe until the fleet completes its mission or is destroyed." The *True Light of the Way*'s security systems were accessible now. Satrap scanned through the video cameras until he found the enemy Marines. "Our enemy is more clever than desperate, I think."

"What Satrap's eyes see only Satrap knows."

He transferred the video to the wall display. "My mind is open. You should give it a try, Ikhama."

The old woman gasped softly. "Infidel soldiers aboard holy ships!"

"Yes. If you look closely, those are not soldiers but Marines. Those pouches they carry would be explosives. And they seem to have quite a lot. They came prepared to deal quite the blow."

"What strike may leave a bruise will not slay, and from where I have fallen I shall rise again to strike with even greater ferocity!"

"The original intent of that was to invoke a brave defense, you know."

"When the unbeliever takes—"

"Ikhama, I asked you to visit me to share my thoughts, not to drown in rhetoric and dogma."

She bowed once more, this time with an audible creak of bones. "I listen."

"You heard my interaction with Captain Zohar."

"Your disdain for the captains of your fleet is clear as the bonfire in the black of night."

"These Kedraalians worry me, especially now with—" Satrap glared at the ongoing gun battle aboard the *True Light of the Way.* "We should have come upon them embroiled in panicked acts to salvage critical systems. We should have found them unable to hide and unable to see us. Instead, they have implemented tactics unfamiliar to me. They seem to know us and to hide from us."

"Technology dulls the blade of the sword, and that is the true test of strength."

"Yes. Swords in space make all the sense in the world."

"Our Holy Khan speaks—"

"When he wrote his crazed manifesto, he was dying from radiation poisoning. I don't think it's the place to go for true insight, and it's certainly not terribly applicable to what we find ourselves up against. Please. I need the mind of someone who isn't bedazzled by the idea that we can conquer our enemies by killing each other, and that leaves my Jakkara bodyguards

—who are quite deadly but not intended for this sort of thinking—and you. Will you set aside your obsession with all the trappings and nonsense and speak with me as an educated and clear-minded person?"

There was anxiety in the woman's dark eyes, a promising sign of at least consideration. Yellow teeth bit into a thin lip, then she nodded. "What we say here remains within your walls."

"Our Holy Khan is misguided in this war."

"It is the word of the Khan Kabal, Satrap."

"No. As deranged as our Great and Holy Khan was when he wrote that, he still had a better understanding of our situation than any who have followed. There is a purity to simple thought. There is a beauty in fanatical unity. You can find strength in the subversion of the individual to the ideal. But when the cause is defined as the purification of the universe, the slaughter of all unbelievers—it was never the design."

"Our Great and Holy Khan was a warrior. He fought against the infidels."

"He was a trickster. I've seen the records he couldn't destroy—arrests for grifting; thievery; forgery. He wandered through radioactive waste-lands on Earth for a year."

"To find the golden tablets. It was the Guiding Star—"

"Ikhama, no. He was no warrior. And that's the point we face now. His teachings were not the wisdom of a seasoned general. He actually spoke of peace, even if he did a poor job of articulating his intent."

She shook her head, and a tear trickled down her cheek. "You were not the right choice for this holy quest."

"I am the *only* choice. This fleet would be broken into many warring groups if any of these idiots were in charge. Captain Rouhani would kill every other captain."

"His ambition is great."

"He's an idiot. When have we ever seen sustained peace amongst our people?"

"When the infidel attacked."

"No. The reason we lost everything all those years ago was because we couldn't stop all the infighting long enough to unite to defend ourselves."

"And now, with the satraps, that has changed."

"Has it? When you talked to the captain of the *Desert Sands*, did he speak of the glory of the fleet or the glory of his pilots and his ship?" Satrap tapped his ear. "Remember that I listen to my captains all the time."

"It is your fleet. My duty is in your service, to see that you have all that you need to implement the will of our Holy Khan. Speak, and I listen."

"We struck down the Gulmar force as easily as we expected to. Our training, our capabilities, our spies—everything was as we expected. I have no doubt that were we to turn our attention to them now, they would be struck down fully, just as our Holy Khan desires. But the Kedraalians—"

"They are every bit as unholy, Satrap."

"Leave out unholy. Judgment doesn't win wars. We've spent decades inserting spies and recruiting adherents to our cause. Our reach is everywhere."

"As our Great and Holy Khan said it would be."

A shuttle exited the *Might of Khan*'s belly, followed by a second.

Zohar's people were finally headed to the *True Light of the Way*. On the security video aboard that ship, the Marines fought on, now pressed tight against bulkheads and decks. They might not be able to reach vital control areas with their explosives, but if they were detonated, they could tear through the deck and hull. The damage would be substantial.

Satrap pointed to the video. "You see? They do to us what we were supposed to do to them."

"Cowardice can seize even the convert's heart."

"Our people are willing to die for the cause, remember? If they didn't strike, it was for a reason." Satrap picked at the folds of his robe. "You were an Ikhama when the Kedraalians offered to rebuild our military for us."

"In the palace, yes. Their representatives brought gifts and spoke with admiration about our Holy Khan and the brilliant defense of Azh Shivan."

The old woman had no idea of the lopsided losses suffered before the Moskav fleet departed. That, or her need for complete acceptance of the words of her Holy Khan made it impossible for her to retain the truth.

"What did the Kedraalians ask for in return for these weapons and technologies they gifted?"

"Nothing. They admired us, and they reminded us that it was the Moskav who had struck the final blow in a war the Kedraalians never wanted."

"No gift is given without expectation of something in return."

"Some might see the Guiding Light and understand—"

"Ikhama. We are speaking openly."

She shrugged. "There were a few hundred people with influential families still within the old Republic. Those families refused to believe their relatives had willingly accepted our Holy Khan as their master."

"Our Holy Khan surrendered prisoners to our enemies? In exchange for weapons?"

"When the merchant opens his hand to offer gold, demand also his wife and child. Offer him a bed for the night, then ask for gold in the morning, for he is a merchant and knows nothing else."

Satrap nodded absently as Zohar's shuttles neared the *True Light of the Way*. They were flying under the cruiser, staying close to the hull, hidden. "What other gold was demanded of the Kedraalians?"

"They..."

"Yes?"

"They also wished for access to a useless planet."

"A useless planet? We exacted— We gave them access to one of the worlds we had claimed after the Holy Rebellion?" That hadn't been in the library.

"They offered money on top of the weapons and technology."

"I see."

That was something to consider. He would have to search the data he'd hoarded over the years to see what planet might match the description. More curious was the unrecorded transfer of prisoners back to the Kedraalian Republic. Who had truly suffered more in such a transaction? The Republic had already lost hundreds of thousands—millions—of lives during the rebellion. Their puppet administrators and governors who hadn't escaped before the fall had been hanged ingloriously. But any prisoners who hadn't been converted should have been executed. That was the scripture. To have such people alive to trade away...

Ikhama clasped her bony hands in front of her. "Has our conversation that is meant for no other ears concluded, Satrap?"

"Almost. There are two more things I would ask of you."

She bowed. "I listen."

"I need you to set aside your belief in the sanctity of infighting and backstabbing, at least for the duration of this war against the infidels."

Her wrinkles deepened as she winced. "In the service of our Holy Khan."

"Exactly."

"And the other?"

"I want you to keep an open mind to the possibility that the Kedraalians have as much to gain from this war as we do. Perhaps more."

Her eyes narrowed. "That is heresy, Satrap. It diminishes our Holy Khan."

"Sometimes things are not as we understand them. Consider the possibility our Holy Khan anticipated this."

She pushed up from the floor, bowed again, then exited, leaving Satrap with his display showing the Kedraalian Marines fighting the *True Light of the Way*'s security forces and the two shuttles carrying Zohar's reinforcements. The chatter of the captains blended into the background as the fleet commander pondered the strange turn in expectations and the odd tactics of his opponent.

What had come from the trade of weapons for hostages? What had been on the planet the Holy Khan had no interest in?

Those answers might hold the key to defeating the Kedraalians, and that was something that galled Satrap.

9

————

"Captain Benson?"

It was a loop, playing endlessly in Benson's head, blotting out the quiet hum of activity that was always present, even in the chaos of battle.

She pushed herself up until she was at her full height, legs quivering, hands shaking. The battle wasn't lost—not yet. She had a chance to salvage it, to save lives, to save ships.

Her throat was parched, the saliva like cotton on her tongue. On the giant display, the focus was now on the situation playing out aboard the Khanate cruiser.

Halliwell was wounded.

Grier was pinned down.

Red triangles closed from one of the other cruisers: reinforcements.

Chopra was at the command station, a scent like cloves rolling off of him. "We could disengage. At this stage, it would be a stalemate."

The Marines guarding the entry sneaked peeks at the battle, at her. Would she abandon their commander and his chief NCO?

Benson couldn't abandon anyone. She couldn't surrender the battlefield.

She had a plan.

"Lieutenant Nuñez, please inform the *Ganges* that she will be joining the *Cairo*'s group."

The square-faced communications officer nodded.

But Benson's XO wasn't as ready to accept the command. "Our destroyer—?"

"One moment." Benson fought to stay calm. "Lieutenant Konrath, adjust course."

The helmsman's pale eyes sparkled. "New course, Captain?"

"Intercept those enemy cruisers. Maximum maneuvering acceleration."

"Yes, ma'am."

Chopra coughed. "The *Valor* is an impressive ship—"

"But—" Benson smiled as confidently as she could. "—it can't take on four cruisers all alone."

Her XO bowed his head. "Once we know their capabilities, maybe…"

"I only want to get their attention. They haven't sent their fighters after anything larger than a destroyer, and their numbers have been diminished." She leaned against the tug of maneuvering thrusters and bent her knees to prepare for the acceleration.

It came quickly, nearly taking Chopra down. He grabbed at the poles holding up the command station's supporting ring. He seemed paler as he regained his balance. "If the fighters do come at us, and we're engaged with their largest ships, it could be *sticky*."

"Until we crack their tactics, everything is going to be sticky. Lieutenant Mahama, the instant we have anything resembling lock-on, fire missiles on those cruisers."

Mahama blinked. "Understood, Captain."

"Preferably, not at the ship our people are aboard."

The bald XO glanced at the Marines guarding the bridge. "Those missiles could be the difference between victory and defeat."

Benson swallowed. "It's only one volley. We can produce more."

"The battle has barely begun."

"Dinesh—" She squatted so that her head was close to his. "We have a chance to strike a blow here. We actually have Marines aboard one of their cruisers."

"But they're pinned down." He was barely loud enough to be heard.

"The odds of us getting Marines onto an enemy ship… Do you know what this opportunity represents?"

"I do. My concern is that we might be risking too much in search of a payoff."

On the giant display, Gunship-99—the escort for Halliwell's shuttles—skimmed along the enemy cruiser's hull, slowly moving toward the closing enemy shuttles. The cruiser's weapons weren't reacting to the gunship, and the shuttles continued on their course beneath the cruiser.

Benson nodded at the display. "If we can get their attention and buy the Marines just a moment of respite, we have a chance to turn the tide of battle."

Chopra blinked rapidly, then thumbed sweat from the corner of his eye. "I have a hard time imagining myself supporting Commander Tuleyev, but in this case, I do wonder if his caution might not be advisable over riskier and more aggressive tactics."

"Noted." She straightened.

The XO's chin came up as if he might be offended, then he worked his way over to the helm station. It wasn't as if Chopra was wrong. Benson was wrestling with uncertainty that intensified with each passing second. But she had more than Halliwell and his Marines on her mind. Even if it meant losing them, if a blow could be struck against the cruisers—even just disabling the signals of the one her people had boarded—it seemed likely that would force a change in tactics. Or it might simply be enough to identify the foundation of those tactics. Either way, abandoning the Marines so that the task force could flee with its tail between its legs didn't serve any purpose.

Mahama turned around suddenly. "Fighter craft have changed course, Captain."

Benson searched the section of display dedicated to the main battlefield but had a hard time spotting the small craft. "New target?"

"It…looks like us?"

She spotted them at that point. More than thirty of the red triangles remained. Now the frigates were pulling away from the elements of her task force that had been committed to engaging them.

She had the enemy's attention.

"Ready a second wave of missiles, Lieutenant."

The weapons control officer turned back to his station. "Readying missiles, ma'am. Still no lock-on."

"The *Sinclair* has lock-on, doesn't it?"

Mahama's head came up. "Yes, ma'am."

"Pass missile control on to their targeting and launch, please."

A heartbeat, a sharp intake of breath, and— "Missiles away, Captain."

Benson switched her attention to the battle inside the enemy cruiser. "Sergeant Grier?"

Gunfire crackled across the Marine NCO's connection. "Yes, ma'am?"

"How are you holding up?"

"Well, it's just me and Patrone uninjured, but we're holding our position." Grier's camera played across the passageway. Of the other seven on her team, only one seemed completely out of action, but blood was smeared across the deck near other Marines.

"They have reinforcements incoming."

"Oh, that's good. I think we can beat them by clogging up the corridors with their bodies."

"Your gunship escort is moving to intercept. I have the *Valor* moving toward you as well."

"The *Valor*? Captain, I don't mean to sound ungrateful, but the task force—"

"I don't intend to sacrifice this ship or the task force, Sergeant."

"Okay. We—" Grier's words were drowned out by gunfire.

"Sergeant Grier, has Lieutenant Halliwell's team breached yet?"

"No, ma'am. Their breaching module was damaged. It's taking a lot longer than they expected."

"Are they going to be able to breach?"

"Last report was they're nearly through the inner hull."

"Will they be better located than you to go after vital systems?"

"They should be, but it's only Clive and four others."

"He's up?"

Grier snorted. "You know him, ma'am. He'd have to take one in the head to stay down."

Benson relaxed slightly. "Did your probe make it deeper into the ship?"

"Hold on."

Gunfire roared, then abruptly died. For a second, Benson thought the sergeant might have been hit, then a file came through. The captain loaded it onto her display. A light pulsed in a long corridor: Grier's Marines. Another light pulsed farther down the corridor: Halliwell's breaching point. Between the two Marine signals, there was an intersecting corridor that ran to a corridor that paralleled the one Grier was in. Markers indicated hatches and lifts, which had low resolution imagery attached to them. Two of the hatches were highlighted in green and had small squads of lightly armored defenders standing outside them.

Grier reconnected. "Clive's through the inner hull."

Benson smiled. "The probe did a good job."

"Yeah. I think we've got a pretty good idea of the layout now. We're actually not far from some critical positions."

"Any idea what they are?"

Gunfire filled the channel, then Grier's voice roared even louder. Finally, she seemed to regain control. "Sorry. They made a run at us."

"Are you okay?"

"My armor's holding up, but my environment helmet's a mess."

"Did you say if you knew what those defended positions were?"

"It's all crazy symbols, ma'am. We'll have to see if we can get inside."

"If you can capture the symbols, we can get a translation."

"All right."

On the main display, the missiles sped toward the cruisers, which apparently were still unaware that they'd been locked onto. That probably meant the gunship still hadn't been detected. If it opened fire on the approaching enemy shuttles, that stealth would be compromised.

Benson muted. "Lieutenant Nuñez, could you contact the pilot of Chief Parkinson's shuttle?"

Nuñez tugged on the hem of her uniform jacket. "Yes, ma'am."

Seconds dragged by. Soon, the enemy shuttles would have visual on Gunship-99 as it maneuvered for a shot. If Benson let it fire, the missile lock-on might be compromised. If she didn't, reinforcements would arrive just when Halliwell's small team was breaking through.

"Captain?" Some of the tension left Nuñez's face. "They're maneuvering at the moment. They'll be close to the *Sinclair* in one minute."

One minute. Even the fastest docking would require time. A minute? "Have them work with Gunship-99. They need to take the task of attacking the enemy shuttles. Have Gunship-99 pull back and provide cover over our own shuttles."

"Yes, ma'am."

Benson caught Chopra's disapproving look. Was she really putting the mission at risk? The enemy fighters were still at least a minute out; the frigates weren't even at extreme range. It seemed unlikely they could do significant damage to the *Valor* if she could just buy the Marines enough time to disrupt the Khanate signals ship.

Mahama waved the XO over, and the two conferred, then Chopra studied the weapons control station. That wasn't a promising sight.

Grier was in Benson's ear. "Hey, Captain? Guess who's in the ship now?"

"He's in contact?"

"His suit radio can handle the short-range comms. You're just going to have to let him go through me for now, ma'am. Check this out."

A grainy, choppy video replaced Grier's already grainy video. The signal indicated it was Halliwell's camera. He was looking on a cluster of at least ten enemy security personnel. They were apparently oblivious to his threat. Fortunately, their armor seemed as light as the other force Grier's cameras had caught. Ruby dots indicated where Halliwell's team had targeted.

Hissing filled the channel.

Not hissing—gunfire.

Half of the Khanate security team dropped before they realized they were being attacked from behind. The survivors spun around, but they fired wildly and failed to shift to better cover.

And then they were down.

Benson's fingers ached from squeezing the support rail too tightly. She pulled her hands free and sneaked a look at the closing Khanate fighters, then checked on Gunship-81, which was escorting Parkinson's shuttle. The gunship and shuttle would arrive on target mere seconds before the fighters could close on the *Valor*; the Khanate frigates would be within extreme range at about the same time.

Where was the rest of her task force? They should be harassing the frigates!

As if sensing her surprise, Chopra scuffed up to the command station. "Commander Tuleyev has prioritized rescue and repair operations."

Benson choked back a curse. "Have him assign two destroyers. I want those frigates lit up—"

"He refused to talk to me. You've endangered the entire mission. *He* says."

After all she'd done to keep the crew limited to people who had a history of operating as expected, someone had stuck Tuleyev into the mix. Argumentative, unimaginative, difficult— "Lieutenant Nuñez, connect me with Commander Tuleyev *immediately*."

The communications officer nodded. She was already talking with someone.

Her counterpart aboard the Lyon.

Benson turned her attention back to the Khanate cruisers. Gunship-99 had already moved back to provide cover. The missiles were closing...

Nuñez tapped her ear, then pointed at Benson. "Commander Tuleyev, ma'am."

Without waiting for the acknowledgement tone, Benson turned away from the bridge crew and the Marines. When the tone sounded, she sucked in a deep breath. "Commander Tuleyev, you will—"

"*Captain* Benson, your tactics have put the task force in danger—"

"*Commander* Tuleyev! I am not interested in your assessment of my decisions at this moment. Do you understand? I want the task force firing on the Khanate frigates, and I want the attack to involve all weapons."

"There is too much risk—"

"Commander, these are your orders. Follow them. Now."

She disconnected. There was no misinterpreting what she had said. Either Tuleyev would attack the frigates, or...

There were replacement options, assuming the *Valor* pulled through.

Grier switched the video back to her feed. She was hustling down a corridor, running just behind three Marines. "Captain! Clive's going to hold this position. I'm taking everyone mobile enough to—"

Movement down the passageway preceded gunfire.

The Marines pressed against the walls; they'd found the Khanate forces. From the video, it appeared the enemy team had moved from their position outside one of the guarded hatches.

Benson squinted at the video. "How many defenders did you see?"

"I think that's all of them. Nice and bunched up." Grier held up a grenade. "Glad I hung on to these." She activated the weapon, then tossed it down the passageway, where the small explosive bounced.

Then it detonated with a bright flash followed by wisps of white smoke.

Grier's team moved forward, slowing to finish off any defenders that were still moving.

The sergeant stopped in front of one of the hatches the probe had identified. In her video feed, the strange symbols were overlaid by the more familiar Humana alphabet, labeling the area: *Munitions*.

"Oh, now isn't that enough to make a girl wet? You seeing this, Captain?"

Benson smiled. "How long to get through the hatch?"

Grier waved one of the Marines forward, watching over the shoulder as a small device—a thin, palm-sized slab of clear plastic—was pressed against the security panel mounted to the bulkhead. The device drew a more familiar control panel over the embedded one, then numbers flashed on that pseudo-panel. After a few seconds, the numbers blinked rapidly and turned into asterisks.

"Damn." The sergeant waved the other Marine back, then pounded on the hatch with the butt of her weapon. "That sounds pretty thick, Captain."

"We don't have time for finesse."

"I'm more about the blunt force, anyway." Grier opened a satchel and pulled out a clear box of what looked like putty. It was maybe two hundred centimeters on a side and about twenty centimeters deep: a shaped charge. "Everybody back! Captain, how long before those reinforcements arrive?"

Benson turned back to the external sensor feed, which showed Gunship-81 now positioned beneath the cruiser and the shuttles. Because of the defensive weapons running along the bottom of the Khanate ship, the gunship would only get one chance to strafe the two shuttles before making a run for it. The feed coming from Gunship-99 showed green from Gunship-81: They were ready to fire.

A quick glance at the other part of the display showed the Khanate fighter group mere seconds away from the *Valor*. At least Tuleyev had brought the rest of the task force around to harass the enemy frigates again.

Gunship-81 opened fire, tearing the enemy shuttles apart with ease. Almost immediately, the weapons mounts beneath the cruiser came to life, whipping around, seeking a target.

But Gunship-81 was already accelerating away, twisting and juking.

Get out of there! "Sergeant Grier, the current wave of reinforcements shouldn't be a concern."

"Okay." Grier was backing down the corridor, out of sight of the hatch.

A much louder explosion rumbled through the corridor. Debris clattered off the walls.

The Marines didn't wait for things to settle down but charged through the smoke, taking care when moving through the jagged ruin of the hatchway. Grier's camera feed showed a compartment filled with crates secured to bulkheads. Once she was close enough to one that her video could clearly pick out details, Benson's heart skipped a beat.

It was clearly labeled in Humana: Explosives.

Grier whistled. "You seeing this, Captain?"

"I am. Get as much imagery as you can, then blow it. Blow all of it."

"On it."

Benson tried to keep up with the video feed, but the *Valor*'s evasive maneuvers and Chopra's pacing behind the helm crew made that impossible. "Status?"

The XO turned, sweat glistening on the top of his head. "We won't be able to evade the fighter craft for long."

Mahama offered a grim smile. "Our guns have destroyed three so far, ma'am."

The smaller craft were swarming, moving around in clumps of four. They weren't packed in tight enough that point-defense weapons could spray an area and wipe out the entire group. That presented a challenge to the targeting systems, which were programmed to seek out optimal firing solutions.

But the distance separating them wasn't so great that other weapons couldn't be effective.

"Lieutenant, if we were to launch a volley of missiles between us and the fighters…"

The young man's grim smile twisted into something more devilish. "That could work, Captain."

Chopra frowned but this time didn't complain about their weapons supply.

A sudden maneuvering change nearly threw the bald XO to the deck. He smashed against Nuñez with a grunt, knocking her against the console. Konrath wasn't so lucky, actually falling and sliding.

Benson kept her balance thanks to the support ring of the command station, but the Marines tumbled from their positions. She glanced around to be sure people were still moving, then hopped down to help Konrath up. "Very aggressive maneuvering, Lieutenant." Another lurch nearly sent the two of them down again. "Is everyone okay?"

The Marines hurried back to their posts. Chopra muttered an apology to Nuñez, then he straightened his crumpled uniform. "It seems—"

As soon as Konrath got back to his station, his features twisted. "Captain?"

"Yes?"

"That wasn't a normal maneuver. Some of our shields have been disrupted. The systems are trying to get functional shields between us and the fighters."

The fighters! Three of them were closing, maneuvering so that the odds were improved that one of them would hit. Such maneuvers should have required advanced sensor systems at the very least to keep up with the complex work the *Valor*'s evasive maneuvers and electronic counter-measure systems were executing. It didn't make sense with a craft so small.

And yet the edges of the giant display flashed yellow, and the previously quieted general quarters alarm sounded again.

They'd been struck!

Mahama turned. "We've lost missile control, Captain!"

Not just a hit but either the luckiest strike possible or a precise one.

When Benson regained her station, her eyes were drawn to Grier's video feed. She was helping Marines back through the hole that had been cut by the breaching module. Her camera just barely caught another Marine in a patched-up suit, who was firing at something outside the range of the camera.

The damaged suit, the size of the Marine...

Halliwell. It had to be.

Benson scanned the *Valor*'s damage control report: The only serious damage was to the missile launch system. Some of the launch tubes were completely gone. That was bad, but the *Valor* had plenty of weapons, and they could fabricate replacements for any system with time.

But her Marines were under fire again. "Sergeant Grier, what's going on?"

"I guess they had more security people." The NCO grunted as another Marine climbed up and into the hole. "Clive's holding them off here, and Corporal Fandi's putting heat down the other corridor."

"Were you able to plant charges?"

"Oh, we planted charges, ma'am. This ship's about to have a whole new experience."

"Can you get out of there?"

Grier's camera panned around. There were just two Marines visible: Halliwell and a smaller, bloody, armored suit a little farther away, lying prone. "It's just the three of us."

"Can you get out?"

"If we leave, they could get into that munitions compartment."

And disarm the explosives. "It's a risk we'll have to take."

"Well, my shuttle's sealing off the entry and pulling away."

"Is the other shuttle still functional?"

"Mostly. I guess."

Konrath shook his head. "They're changing their tactics, Captain. The frigates are putting fire up now, limiting our maneuvering. We can't evade them for much longer."

On the giant display, glowing indicators created a web of beams and projectiles that were funneling the *Valor* into a tighter space. Benson swallowed. "Sergeant, you need to get out of there now and blow that ship."

"All right, ma'am. We've got a couple grenades left."

"Hurry."

Grier dashed across the passageway, hurling a grenade past the prone Marine, then grabbing the back of the Marine's armor. "Clive! Give 'em a dose of shrapnel!"

Halliwell stopped firing and pulled a grenade out as Grier and the wounded Marine headed away. He'd barely gotten the grenade away when a distant explosion came through Grier's connection. Halliwell fell back, helping her with the bloody Marine.

They stopped beneath a smooth, glossy hole. Grier cupped her hands, and Halliwell went up without argument. His arms and head dangled down, waiting for the wounded Marine, who she handed up.

Gunfire cracked against the passageway deck and bulkheads, then against her armor.

Grier grunted and staggered. "Fucking guns!"

Halliwell's hand reached down and she took hold.

They were in the space between the hulls, moving awkwardly and—to Benson's eyes—as slow as turtles.

And then they were in the shuttle.

Grier's camera showed her at the umbilical controls. "Don't care about atmosphere evacuation, so…"

She pressed a red button, and the airlock closed just ahead of the umbilical detaching from the shuttle. Her camera feed shifted to the shuttle's camera, as the damaged vessel pulled away from the cruiser.

Benson's fingers pressed hard against the support ring. "Sergeant Grier—?"

"Demolition charges triggered."

Gunship-99 and the Gunship-81 fell in behind the wounded shuttle. Grier's and Parkinson's shuttles were ahead, already speeding back toward the *Valor*.

Mahama wiped the back of his hand across his face. "Captain, we can't get a clear shot on those fighters."

Konrath nodded. "Five fighters closing. We can't maneuver—"

On the shuttle's camera, fire gushed from the enemy cruiser, probably from the hole in its hull. A second later, more fire erupted, this from farther back.

Nuñez's head came around. "EM signals from that cruiser have stopped, Captain!"

The fighters swarming around the *Valor* flew off, following strange vectors, as if they'd lost guidance. Seconds later, the Khanate frigates broke off, accelerating toward the enemy cruisers.

They'd broken the attack!

For the moment.

Relieved sighs slipped out from everyone, then Benson shook out her shoulders. "Lieutenant Mahama, I want those fighters swept from the sky. If we can capture one, do so. The rest need to be turned into harmless pieces of metal in the next twenty seconds."

"Aye, Captain!" The heavyset officer almost giggled as he bent over his console.

The moment of levity was fine—necessary.

Because everything had changed. They were now at war not just with the Azoren but with the Khanate, and Benson knew in her gut that the combined forces would be enough to crush everything in their paths.

10

———

With all the modifications that had been inflicted upon Satrap's body since his appointment as the great admiral who would purge the galaxy of all enemies, sleep never truly came. But there were times where the chatter of his officers and the data stream took on sufficient sameness that he could almost float in the relative calm.

Only in the sweet, pungent haze of incense that permeated his cabin was there a feeling of calm. To overcome his Jakkara bodyguards, Zohar would have to expend the last of his own security forces, which would be suicide.

So, with the battle sliding toward its inevitable finish, Satrap rubbed at the aches left by Holy Khan and sought what peace there was in digital rest.

In such a state, the battle became soothing colors and sounds: magenta updates in a sea of cobalt laced with gold symbols draped across curtains of deep drones that represented filtered words.

Damage to the *Valor*. Enemy Marines pinned down. Success. Imminent victory.

Satrap's eyes opened. The drone was gone, replaced by the staccato roar of angry officers. Gone with the comforting sound was the magenta bitstream. Prickly green and white bursts overlaid with bright red alarm updates.

True Light of the Way was in trouble.

"Captain Zohar?" Satrap's connection to the captain came to life, and the other man glared back.

"You have roused yourself from slumber then."

Data continued to update—all bad. "Fires and explosions aboard the *True Light of the Way*. What has happened?"

"The Kedraalian Marines broke through the defenders. They set explosives in the munitions compartment."

"Marines? There were too few to be a concern. Your squads—"

"My squads were killed as they entered the airlocks."

"How?"

Zohar sagged, and a twitch flashed across his face. "A small craft our sensors failed to detect until it fired."

The updates were like little, heated needles being driven into Satrap's scalp. "What can we do to help? The fires rage. Many are dead."

"We can do nothing. The munitions explosions tore through decks. Secondary explosions ruptured life support systems and a reactor wall."

A compromise in design to cut costs. Yet another decision Satrap had been silenced on when he'd challenged it. Munitions should be spread across multiple sections of the vessel, each sealed behind reinforced bulkheads and with concussion and fire venting to direct the worst of the force away from vital areas of the ship.

Had it been greed, pride, or impatience that had led Holy Khan to compromise? Or maybe Satrap's protest of the decision had been enough to push the old fool into settling on something he'd only been toying with.

Satrap rubbed the crease where his right thigh and hip met. Throbbing pain had returned. "Their ships come toward us. Who has taken control of the fighters?"

"We discuss the matter even now."

That had been the agitated chatter. There were only three captains of signals control cruisers remaining with the *True Light of the Way* in its death throes, but that was no help. The captains would argue every point, probably even after only one remained.

The *True Light of the Way* gasped its last meaningful data burst as more systems failed and fire consumed precious oxygen. There would be survivors, brave souls sealed off in compartments or who had located environment suits. They were as good as dead, though. Whether the Kedraalians took them captive or—more likely—blasted the hulk to bits and killed them.

Satrap transferred control to the *Might of the Khan*. "Captain Zohar, you are now in command of the fighters. Have them return to the fleet."

A smile flashed across the other man's face, then transformed into a frown. "Only a few remain."

"Then save those few."

"Their pilots have already sworn their souls to our Holy Khan. They await the joy of the light of the stars."

"Which they will never see unless they die as warriors. Recall them."

"We must strike while we—"

Satrap groaned. The man was such an imbecile. A handful of fighters weren't going to change the course of the engagement. At this point, what mattered was salvaging resources. Rather than argue with the captain, Satrap signaled the return at full burn.

Zohar rocked back. "You have taken control—"

"I have done what I ordered you to do."

"Your captains control the battle space. The satrap provides strategy and guidance, nothing more."

More reports were coming in: the frigates were suffering significant attacks, and the enemy seemed to be heading for the carriers, if only indirectly. That and the attack on the *True Light of the Way* were clear indications that the stealth systems that he had been assured would stand up to the most advanced sensors in use anywhere in known space were in fact failing.

"Zohar, we must flee this space."

"Flee? Our fleet is vastly superior to the enemy!"

"It won't be if we stay and fight them. The situation has undergone a complete reversal. Our advantage is lost. We must end this engagement and find a place to effect repairs and build more fighters."

"A retreat shows weakness."

"It shows wisdom."

Zohar rose to his full height and puffed out his chest. "Your captains will not agree to this!"

The connection died.

And immediately, the tenor of the chatter among the officers changed. Zohar was stirring them up. With the fleet facing an enemy that now had the initiative, Satrap's officers were talking about…mutiny.

He connected to Ikhama. "Can you come to my cabin again?"

"The winds sing in calm and whine in—"

"Ikhama, there is a very real chance that the fleet could be destroyed."

"I will come."

After a moment, the connection was closed.

What would it take for these people to understand the stakes? To Satrap, it was obvious that they had underestimated the enemy or at least had overestimated their own capabilities. He could see in the ebb and flow of the last hour the potential for deception in those who had created the mighty fleet he now commanded. Always, their motivation had seemed an odd thing, shrouded in mystery and lies.

If the Ikhama had no true understanding of the motivation, then perhaps no such thing existed.

Still…

The *Might of the Khan* had more computational power than any ship ever built. Part of that was the command and control systems required of the flagship of the fleet. Another part was the systems required for the fighter guidance, something he had argued should have been installed in the carriers themselves. But another part of all the computing power was for him, for the role of the fleet commander.

Current tickled his spine as he bowed his head in concentration. It had taken days of extreme exertion to transfer the vast library buried beneath the palace on Azh Shivan. There had been times Satrap had questioned why he had bothered with so much dangerous work. Now…

Previous searches for data on the fleet and the people who had pitched the design and construction had always been direct: who, when, where?

Satrap tried connecting threads this time.

What did he know of the Holy Rebellion Against the Infidel?

Dates. Places. People. At least the information promoted by Holy Khan and his Ikhama. But the library hidden beneath the palace had more.

Going back to the times where Holy Khan had traveled to Earth and illegally walked its fouled lands in search of answers to the questions that had been burning his soul, the data was exhaustive.

Humans had fled the Earth for its colony worlds. They had done so in the millions, turning pleasure cruises into migration opportunities. Pollution of all sorts had left the planet a miserable place that killed its occupants with a broad assortment of weapons: storms, cancers, earthquakes, tidal waves.

Billions stayed behind to face the coming apocalypse, many because they were too poor or too uneducated or too stuck in their ways to leave the world they had weaponized.

Fleeing to the stars didn't leave behind the flaws etched in DNA. Stubbornness, intolerance, irrationality—it all came to their new home.

That had been the genesis of the new utopia's end.

Eighteen colony worlds spread across as many systems had proven inadequate for the varied and broken species, and adding new colony worlds hadn't been enough to make things work.

When the grievances of the people who hadn't been able to toe the Republic's demanding line grew too great, revolution had come.

The Azoren movement: eugenics and the elimination of "inferiority," which was anything that didn't match an odd physical "ideal."

The Moskav movement: the embrace of an old, failed ideology that also suborned citizens to the state.

The Gulmar Union: the oligarchic collection of billionaires who refused the tyranny of regulation and taxation.

And the Holy Khan. The Great Khan. The bearer of golden plaques etched with the words delivered by ascendant beings from beyond the stars. They had chosen a failed and troubled man as their prophet and gifted him with an alphabet and language and an ideology he spent his life committing to books that were now every bit as holy as his entombed, tumor-riddled corpse.

With each faction, with the way the war had forced them to claim planets and systems rather than sweep the stars clear of their enemies, it was clear the revolt against the Kedraalian Republic hadn't been coordinated.

How many millions had been abandoned behind the bloody borders hurriedly hacked into shape? It was a question that was personal and painful to Satrap.

More importantly, it had somehow drawn the Kedraalians out for compromise.

With each file touched, little bits of knowledge revealed themselves.

It wasn't a singular flashpoint that triggered the devastating war but a series of events that had somehow slipped past the attention of government leaders. Protests and counter-protests. Small acts of violence that should have sounded alarms, which were silenced in the name of protecting freedoms.

And then the violence escalated, birthing the rebellion.

When the borders were finally established, people found themselves redesignated Azoren, Gulmar, Moskav, or Khanate, simply by the misfortune of the draw.

Without a doubt, some of those people were more important than others. Satrap's own family had suffered terribly before converting. But these people the Kedraalians had negotiated for, offering weapons and more in exchange...

The cabin door chimed: Ikhama.

"Come!"

She slid past after the hatch opened, the material of her gown rasping softly until she went through the ridiculous bowing ceremony that caused her knees and back to pop. *"Whispers carry on the winds as dark as the temptations offered from the abyss."*

"You mean that my captains conspire to bring about a mutiny."

Her head bowed until he couldn't see her face. "You tell them our Holy Khan has failed and all is lost."

"I've said no such thing. The fleet is in a perilous position now."

"As leaves falling in the autumn breeze, the enemy is numerous but dead."

Satrap groaned inwardly. How could people allow themselves to drift so far from facts in pursuit of ideology? "Our fighters are all but destroyed. The enemy has seen through our current tactics and has forced us to reassess."

"*A mighty sword shone brilliant in the black of space, ready to strike—*"

"Ikhama, the failure here extends beyond the competence of a single officer, including the satrap. Do you understand?"

Her head shook slightly. "I don't. Your officers—"

"Are wrong. They believe numbers are the only thing that matters. They believe too readily in this technology."

"Our numbers are inadequate?"

"Only if we stay here and allow the enemy to destroy us."

"And that enemy has seen through our ability to hide like the vengeful djinn who protected the Holy Khan?"

"Somehow. For now. That means that maintaining this ridiculous posture of engagement will see us all destroyed. You see?"

Now she nodded. Hesitantly. "I had committed myself to prayer for guidance."

"And I'm sorry I had to ask you to come to me again so soon. Without your intervention, though, Zohar and his rivals will set aside their hatred for each other until they have the power to cut me down."

"*The stallion might ride to victory with the champion in its saddle, but—*"

"*—an arrow through his heart leaves the majestic beast to stomp and preen without significance.*" The pain in Satrap's hip flared. He shifted until it passed. "This is the problem we face. Our fleet without the commander appointed by Holy Khan can do nothing more than stomp and preen."

Ikhama scratched at the small patch of white whiskers growing from the tip of her chin. "One does not need the words of our Guiding Star to see the flaw in this."

"You would think not. The insistence on setting us all at each other's throats makes rational thinking a rare and precious thing."

"*What guile might the fox show in the face of the bear?*"

Satrap cringed at the common allegory. Like many of the Great and Holy Khan's writings, it was unlikely there was any sort of direct observation of what he'd written for his followers. It seemed more likely a coyote had been the intended trickster in the comparison. A fox would do. "You find my words sacrilegious."

"Your soul faces the perdition of the dark between the stars."

"Possibly. Yet I was the one chosen by the Holy Khan to lead this fleet."

"Satrap is your name, and it is the title granted for your holy conquest."

"Can one question the will of the Holy Khan and not be accused of heresy and sacrilege?"

The old woman rocked back and forth. "This is the clever wit of the fox."

It was more like using the twisty and irrational thinking of a religion against its adherents, but Ikhama didn't need to have the point made. "Speak to them. Provide them the words of divinity."

She nodded again, this time with a little more confidence. "This is wise."

"Time matters." Satrap waved to the display, which showed the Kedraalian ships closing. Weapons fire was taking a terrible toll on the carriers and frigates.

"Zohar presents a problem."

"I can't have my Jakkara eliminate him without proving his point to the others."

"He speaks of your family being heathens."

"The Great and Holy Khan's family was heathens before he crafted the wisdom of his holy texts. Does that text not offer that a heathen is forgiven the moment he converts?"

"Caution must be taken in reference to the father of our movement, Satrap. It is heresy to see fault in the way you have."

"Do we not admire logic, Ikhama?"

"When the fox slips into the henhouse, the farmer does not marvel at his cleverness while cleaning the destruction."

Satrap sighed. "I am not the enemy here."

The old woman's head came up until she was looking deep into his eyes. "What matters isn't truth but belief."

"I will practice caution in my dealings with Zohar."

"Unless the opportunity presents itself to practice a deft strike." That was whispered so softly Satrap wasn't sure he'd actually heard the words.

If he'd needed a blessing to kill Zohar, the blessing had been given.

The old woman pushed up from the floor, bowed once more, than shuffled to the hatch. She stopped there, head down. "If we flee, it will be to end the struggle or continue it."

"The struggle is far from over. We need time to fabricate new fighters and to repair damage inflicted."

"And after this?"

"We move on to our second objective."

"Completing the assigned tasks given by our Holy Khan requires persistence and determination."

"Our second objective is achievable. If our intelligence proves correct, this should allow us to return to our primary objective before we move on to the rest."

Once again, the old woman seemed to bow her head. She was working through what amounted to her own logic and problem solving but within the confines of the convoluted labyrinth of thinking imposed by her upbringing. Would she have escaped the limitation of doctrine had she been given access to the data contained in the library beneath the palace? Did her age provide a limitation of its own, a sort of calcification that made radical heresies impossible to grasp?

No. It was the mind of the individual that mattered most. The indoctrination Satrap had undergone had been agonizing and extensive, yet he had been inquisitive and agile. One had to want to see beyond the wall in front of them.

And now that lack of curiosity and nimbleness of thought had everyone's fate hanging in the balance. The Kedraalian ships were closing—

Finally, Ikhama straightened. "The solution is in the petals of the flower. *When the bee seeks the pollen, it must wait until the flower opens.*"

Satrap smiled. "Yes! I hadn't thought of this."

One of the Jakkara poked his armored head through the hatchway, saying nothing yet signaling everything: There was concern for the satrap's safety. The situation was deteriorating.

Ikhama squared her bony shoulders and passed through. *"The winds carry messages of the singing bird and burning fire. Only by paying attention are we aware of the words spoken."*

"Thank you." Satrap's stomach gurgled, and he activated the pump that would slowly discharge nutrients through the tubes attached to his chest.

Tasting food was a distraction. Knowing pleasure was a terrible risk. The leader of the greatest power ever known had to remain focused and loyal to the cause. Seconds passed, and the complaints coming from his gut quieted. A soft whirring was the only change, as his body was awakened to process what he'd put inside it.

He was the creation of the Holy Khan. The old man's will would be done.

If that led to the end of the Khanate, was that really such a terrible thing?

11

—————

On the *Valor*'s giant display, it appeared as if the Khanate fleet began a new set of maneuvers rather than retreating. Yet...

Benson checked her command station display, wishing the deafening general quarters alarm could be silenced for even a moment. Red triangles and diamonds split off, some flickering while others completely disappeared. Against the black of space, her own ships' weapons were brilliant lines traced by the computers just long enough to give her an idea of where weapons fire had gone.

She looked up from the display. "Lieutenant Mahama, what's going on?"

The young weapons officer sucked in his gut. "I...don't know, Captain. They haven't done this before. They're not firing anything other than missiles now."

Chopra stepped back from the main bridge console and rose up on the balls of his feet. "If I were to guess, I would say they might be retreating."

There. Someone else had said it, meaning Benson could believe it. The enemy ships were definitely accelerating away and had broken into multiple groups. It seemed as if their stealth systems were becoming more capable again. All of that was consistent with retreat, and the notion seemed to suck the heat from the bridge air, which had grown thick with sweat.

And yet…

"Let's dispose of these missiles." Benson's toes uncurled. "But stay alert."

Chopra also seemed to relax. "Yes, Captain."

She stepped down, eyes locked on the display. "Lieutenant Nuñez, let the task force know they can come off full alert once the last of the Khanate ships have gone. We'll want rescue operations to begin at full intensity immediately."

Nuñez checked the clips holding her curly, brown hair in place. "Yes, ma'am."

Chopra sidled up to Benson's side. "It might be prudent to perform at least a short shift transition."

Benson squinted at the disappearing red symbols. "Once we're clear."

"They do seem to be running."

"Regrouping. Or maybe trying to draw us into smaller engagements that take away our advantages."

"Advantages?"

"That fleet demolished a Gulmar force that should have been able to stand up to…" She had no idea if the Gulmar fleet really was as capable as advertised. "We stood up to their attack. Our sensors and stealth technology gave us the edge, wouldn't you agree?"

Her XO glanced down. "Something frightened them off."

"We gave them a bloody nose."

"They *did* lose some ships."

"It's quite possible they were counting on sabotage for victory."

"And that would seem to diminish their threat, wouldn't it?"

"Only if you don't consider espionage and sabotage as vital components in the overall military force. Unfortunately, modern warfare has never been about standing in tight formations and killing what you see in front of you."

Chopra glanced toward the corner away from the bridge officers and Marines, then edged over, rubbing his hands together anxiously. When

Benson followed him, the XO bowed his head. "This is going to expose us to contention with Tuleyev."

"The idea that we might have saboteurs among us?"

"His family history… I believe he'll demand that we return to Kedraal for investigations immediately."

"Investigations? Into the crews? No one reported any attempted acts."

"Because you locked down security before anyone could act."

A chill bloomed in Benson's gut. The precaution had seemed a safe reaction to the data gained from the Gulmar survivor. Had it actually stopped saboteurs? That presupposed the Khanate had some sort of sleepers embedded deep within the Kedraalian military and government. She pressed a knuckle against her forehead. "We'll need to maintain a rotation for the Marines."

"How do we know the Marines can be relied upon?"

"We don't, but at least these are people Lieutenant Halliwell and Sergeant Grier know. We'll keep them operating in pairs."

"Spies are trained in deception and guile. Gaining trust is one of the first things they master."

Benson thought back to the way Stiles had been so disarming when she came aboard the *Pandora*. She acted like a vacuous flirt, erasing any chance of being considered a serious person. "We'll need to have a discussion with Commander Tuleyev before we take our next step."

"After we all take a breather?" Chopra's brows arched as he nodded toward the bridge officers.

"Ideally."

"You think he can be reasoned with?"

"We can consult him for his thoughts on tactics and strategy."

"That could engage him. I worry he'll still insist upon returning to Kedraal."

"Then we need to ask him how his grandfather would have handled this sort of situation. Would he have fled?"

Chopra licked his lips. "There is a chance that might get through, yes."

"Let's—"

Nuñez turned slightly to look at the command station, then twisted fully around until she spotted the captain in the back corner. "Captain Benson?"

"Yes?"

"There's a message coming through a Fold Space transmitter. It's for you."

"I'll take it at my station." Benson patted Chopra's arm. "Reach out to Alexander. Try to gauge his mood before the call."

The XO managed a pained smile. "I'll do what I can."

The message Nuñez had mentioned was queued up when Benson climbed back up to stand behind the command station display. From the timestamp, it was easy to see that the message was already weeks old. That meant it wasn't from anywhere near the Gulmar border.

Benson synchronized her command station with her communicator, unencrypted the message, then played it.

Lieutenant Stiles's face appeared on the display, and her calm, confident voice sounded in Benson's ear. "Captain Benson, I hope this message finds you well and in good spirits. I know this isn't likely to reach you until you're deep in Gulmar space, but maybe it can still help you. With everything that happened, I've been given clearance to conduct extensive investigations into this Ravens and Owls conspiracy. Apparently, things run deep, and the infrastructure doesn't really exist to crack the groups open."

Of course, there wasn't an infrastructure in place to stop runaway spies either. Samir Patel had been conducting rogue operations in plain sight, and no one had noticed.

Stiles blinked, and a frown twisted her lips. "While I was doing research, I managed to crack the recording I'd taken from Agent Penn. You probably don't have all the details on that, but he was part of Agent Patel's operation. What's important is what I discovered in that recording. Agent Penn had been deep undercover within the Gulmar privateers and also had been planted inside the Azoren intelligence community. He killed Dev Rai aboard the *Rakshasa* after you and your crew were killed."

For some reason, the news made Benson's throat tighten. Rai had seemed to be a noble and decent man among Chung's cutthroat privateers. There had been a sense of connection between her and the fast-draw expert.

A sigh escaped the GSA agent. "The last words Rai uttered were about the great con. At first when I played back that audio, I thought he was admiring Agent Penn's ability to fool everyone. Then I found this."

The GSA agent split her video input to reveal an image of a necklace with a medallion on it. The image slowly spun to provide a full look at the object.

What...? Benson had never seen anything like it.

Stiles killed the video of the medallion. "It's a symbol of the Khanate. Apparently, their spies carry them. I'm guessing it's to identify each other."

Benson froze the video and scanned the bridge. No one was watching her. She sped the video backwards and drilled in on the image of the medallion as it slowly spun around, then made a copy of that video and sent it to the 3D printer in her cabin. Now they had something to help with hunting for potential saboteurs.

She resumed Stile's video. The youthful agent seemed anxious. "I wish I could give you something more to help you, but my investigation hasn't really uncovered enough to make arrests or anything so useful." The young woman seemed angry for a moment, then shrugged. "I'll let you go. I hope this can at least alert you. Maybe it could provide you with some leverage in your negotiations with the Gulmar. I seriously doubt they have any idea of this threat. Oh! Before I go, please say hi to Chuck for me. I heard he's nearly through medical school. I knew he could do it!"

Benson froze the video again, then replayed it to capture the moment where Stiles said hi to Chuck and recorded that for the medical officer trainee. The young woman's smile left Benson jealous.

Which was stupid, of course. Stiles was a Genesis. It was ridiculous to be jealous of someone engineered for perfection. Benson's life had been much more haphazard and chaotic. If she'd been engineered, there was no telling how far she could have gone in life.

She chuckled. If she was honest with herself, she was already doing far better in life than most.

Chopra craned his neck and gave Benson a hopeful smile. "The last of the Khanate signals are gone. It would appear they've made the jump to Fold Space."

"Let's start the crew rotation, then. Keep everyone on alert."

"And the general quarters alert?"

"Take the task force to ready."

Benson scanned the empty display one more time before allowing herself to really relax. "Commander Chopra, you have the conn."

She smiled at the Marines as she passed. They would need rest, too. Or maybe they would need to be supplemented. The *Valor* had already lost part of its complement, and it didn't seem likely things would get better. If anything, things seemed likely to grow worse.

The passageways were mostly empty as she headed for the medical center. Halliwell had been brought back aboard. He would be another patient under Dietrich's care now. That was something, at least.

Marines acknowledged her as she passed them and entered the lift. Perhaps it would be a good idea to have the crew shift to jumpsuits and to have the zippers low enough that necklaces with medallions would be visible.

Except, what if Chopra was right and the Marines were compromised?

When Benson reached the medical bay, she found Grier standing at parade rest, hands clasped behind her back, legs shoulder width apart, eyes locked on one of the surgical beds beyond the glass wall. After the thick musk of tension from the bridge, the smell of alcohol and medicine was welcome. Benson felt cold, and she was sure the bright lights were showing through her uniform jacket, revealing her pounding heart.

Clive. She stopped a meter back from the other woman. "How is he?"

Grier stiffened. "Commander Dietrich said he lost a lot of blood."

"Is he...stable?"

"Sort of. The injury apparently lodged a piece of his helmet in his skull. Another centimeter, and he'd be like Corporal Ekman."

Ekman. She was a Nordic giant of a woman, as tall as Benson but with a muscular physique closer to Grier's. "What happened to her?"

"Well, she won't need to worry about the latest hat fashions, I guess."

"Oh."

Inside the surgical bay, two of the people in scrubs seemed to be arguing. Even with the surgical masks on, it was obvious who they were when they straightened and their profiles became more apparent: Dietrich and Kohn.

Grier bowed her head. "I don't know if I could train under Commander Dietrich. He seems so nice when he's not in his office, but he's an asshole on duty."

"He's considered one of the best surgeons around."

"Yeah, well he rides Chuck like a show pony."

"They're trying to arrive at the best treatment option—"

The Marine sergeant spun around, almost snarling. "I get it!" She blinked, and a blush ran through her face. "Ma'am. Um. Sorry."

A trembling smile was the best Benson could do. Grier's feelings for Halliwell were no secret, and his commission hadn't changed the matter anymore than his accepting a position as the task force's Marine contingent commander had changed Benson's feelings for him. It was messy, the sort of inappropriate relationship that could destroy careers.

But Halliwell wasn't just a warm, caring lover. He was the sort of Marine Benson needed—a reliable leader who could engender loyalty from anyone. Grier had shaped up into the same sort of Marine, although she was still plagued by demons of her own.

Benson patted the other woman on the shoulder, noting the knotted muscles barely hidden by her uniform. "We're going to be okay."

"I-I know. Thanks."

Dietrich stopped yelling at Kohn long enough to turn to Grier, then considered Benson. The look in the surgeon's eyes wasn't quite one of defeat, but there was plenty of anger.

In the surgeon's view, all war—all violence—was foolish and unnecessary.

But he had the determination to save lives, and he always did everything he could to that end.

Benson cleared her throat softly. "I have to make the rounds. Would you...?"

"I'll let you know the second I do. Ma'am."

"Thank you."

Outside the medical facility, Benson connected to Parkinson. "Chief?"

"Don't even start on me!" The engineer's voice was strained.

"I'm coming to the engineering bay. We need to chat."

"You sent me into the middle of battle again!"

"We're at war. If we didn't take out that signals ship, you might not have had the opportunity to return to the *Valor*."

Her entire ride down in the lift, he didn't say anything, although he left his connection open, maybe so that she could hear his angry breathing.

She closed it when she exited the lift.

He met her at the hatch into engineering. His eyes were bloodshot, and there was the slightest quiver to his face before he turned to escort her back to his office. When the hatch closed, he dropped into his seat, becoming lost in his domain, smothered by the smell of burned circuitry and lit by the glow of test equipment. The act didn't seem to be one of defiance of decorum as much as fear he might collapse. "I'm sorry." He ran a shaking hand over his face.

"From the video I saw, your shuttle wasn't in danger."

"Did you see Halliwell's shuttle? Did you see how close my gunship escort came to getting turned into slag?"

"Our stealth systems seemed to be working."

"Pfft! Not. As. Advertised." He jabbed a forefinger at a clear, blue plastic brick that had video and data streams flashing across the surface. "I assume that's why you came down into the bowels of the ship?"

She leaned past him, noting the way he didn't pull back. His eyes were always hungry when he thought he could sneak a glance at her. "What are the odds the Khanate stealth technology is its own unique line of research?"

"Is that a joke?"

"Dead serious."

"Well, unless you think they could pray technology into existence, I'd say as close to zero as is imaginable."

"You saw the capabilities of their ships."

"Yeah, well, that's not *their* doing. These guys have never been anything more than wackos. I knew a Khanate adherent when I was in college."

"You did?"

"Yup." Parkinson rubbed his sternum. "She spent the day in class and the night reading this book—a physical book!—of this Khan's poems and stories. Crazy. And she was pretty hot, but…" He clenched his jaw.

"Lieutenant Stiles sent a message."

"A message? From Kedraal? Why?" He smiled. "Did she ask about me?"

"It was a warning."

"About what?"

"Apparently, she found evidence of this Khanate problem through investigations of her own."

"Great. Just great. The Azoren, the Moskav, the Gulmar: They'd all take someone like me prisoner and probably try to bribe me to join them. These guys?" He slashed his index finger across his throat.

"You're a good engineer, Chief."

"Good?" He snorted. "More like one in a million."

She picked up the data brick. "What have you found so far?"

"Well, for starters, that black box we retrieved? I think I can salvage it."

"I thought it was fried?"

"The memory modules are stored in their own hardened container. That's all that matters, really. These Gulmar ships aren't a big jump away from Kedraalian design." He tugged at his small patch of beard and twisted his chair around to give her a glimpse at the charred device that must have been the remnant he'd rescued. Wires ran from the blackened casing.

"What do you think you could pull from it?"

His eyes ran up from her chest to her face. "If I told you I could probably put together the Gulmar fleet numbers and location at the time of attack, what would you think of…that?"

"That would be impressive."

"I know, right?"

Benson stepped back. "You know, if you maybe took a little time off from your fan club, it could probably do wonders for your career."

Parkinson crossed his arms over his chest. "I'm already in line for grade five next year."

"There's more to a career than attaining the highest rank."

"Really?"

"And there's more to being a good member of a crew than showing off."

"It's not showing off if you really are that good, is it?"

She handed the brick to him. "I value you, Will."

He brushed her hand with his fingers, frowning when she pulled back. "You don't really show it. I've done everything you've asked of me, but you never visit me down here unless you need something."

"We're in a professional relationship."

"Oh? Like you and Clive?" An ugly sneer flashed across the engineer's face, then was gone. He studied the brick. "I really have tried. To fit in."

"I've had complaints."

"From who?"

"Petty Officer Snell. Petty Officer Lohman. Petty Officer Davitz."

He shook his head dismissively. "They don't work for me, and when they said no, I dropped it."

"You showed them inappropriate images."

Parkinson froze. "I… It wasn't anything explicit."

"When a young woman says she's interested, maybe then you could ask her if she's interested in seeing some of your past exploits. But I can save you the trouble: Most won't. And if it's a fellow crew member, having a recording could get you into serious trouble." Benson tried her best to keep the heat out of her voice. She had no tolerance for crew members exploiting each other, especially after what had happened to her.

The engineer slammed the computing device onto his desk. "You know, I spent my entire life having people tell me I wasn't good enough. You're too short. You're too slow. You're too smart. Why can't people like me for who I am?"

Benson bowed her head. A headache threatened. She needed a workout, maybe a nap. "We have a counselor aboard the *Valor* if you don't want to use the automated systems."

"I don't need someone to analyze me."

"It sounds to me like you might learn something about yourself."

"I already know me pretty well, thanks."

"Maybe you do. But the one thing I can tell you is that the first person you need to worry about liking you? That's you. And right now, I don't think that's happening."

Parkinson reddened. His eyes moistened.

Benson's communicator buzzed. "Excuse me." She exited the cramped office, leaving behind Parkinson and the smell of burned circuits and frustrated anger. "Lieutenant Nuñez?"

Nuñez's face was stretched tight. "Captain! Another call for you!"

Could Stiles have sent an update? "I'll be on the bridge in a moment."

Benson hurried back to the command station, arriving in the middle of shift turnover chaos. She got the communications officer's attention. "I'll take it now, Lieutenant."

The transmission wasn't encrypted or sent through Kedraalian Navy channels. Instead, it was a message from a Gulmar source. "Captain Faith Benson, commander of the Kedraalian task force that has entered Gulmar space. We have received your message. Please do not move from your position. Gunships are en route."

The message ended there: *Gunships are en route.*

Were they coming to assist or to exact revenge?

12

———————

Beneath the shuttle, gently rolling grasslands passed, bending in a late afternoon breeze. The vessel's rockets and engines were a steady vibration that ran through the vehicle frame, creating a rattling drone that was almost peaceful enough to lull Stiles to sleep. She tested her restraints, careful to hide her exertion with a stoic stare out the front window. Rubber-coated steel cable pinched her wrists and ankles, joining them to metal bars. It was too strong to snap, too well designed to break free from.

On either side of her, two brutes in skintight black bodysuits watched her out of the corners of their eyes. Unfortunately, they had the same cold, distant appreciation for her as the women in the front of the vehicle. There would be no escaping captivity this time.

The gold-haired Nordic Lady interrogator twisted around in the co-pilot seat, smirking at the bruisers. "They're immunized, in case you haven't figured that out already."

Stiles bowed her head, nearly gagging on the strong scent of detergent coming off the gray jumpsuit they'd given her. "It wouldn't matter."

"Oh? Giving up?" Nordic Lady snickered. "I know you better than that."

"I can't remember anything from my imprisonment."

"No. I mean I know your kind: Genesis. You don't give up."

A growl bubbled up from Stiles's stomach, and something bitter gushed against the back of her throat. *Bile.* "I haven't given up. I meant that I'm too tired to be able to do anything."

"That's not true, either. You go a day without food, and your body starts to hoard calories."

"Human bodies do that."

"Sure. You do it with a thousand times the efficiency. I've researched you."

"I'm just as human as you."

"I don't think so. You know what separates you from the genetic monsters the Azoren have created?" Nordic Lady looked Stiles up and down. "Blond hair and blue eyes."

"And millions of kilometers of space."

"Distance is meaningless. You might as well be one of them."

One of the bruisers sneered, then he looked away. He was nearly as blond as Nordic Lady, but he had an almost bronze tint to his skin, and his eyes were dark. His nose was broad and flat. "Why'd we have to haul her out here? She's not going to talk."

Nordic Lady turned to the front. "It's just a clean-up operation."

"So toss her into the ocean. Weight her down, and no one ever sees her again."

"We need to be absolutely sure on this. She's the last of them."

Flat Nose considered Stiles again. "Too bad you couldn't turn her."

Nordic Lady spun around. "Are you having a reaction to her?"

"Are you?"

The tall woman's eyes squinted. "When we land, I want you away from the vehicle. Immediately."

"Sure. But I'm not affected by her. I was only saying that we could use someone who's a thousand times more efficient than us."

Nordic Lady turned back around. "They can't be turned."

Flat Nose leaned closer to Stiles. "Don't let her get to you. It's all painless. You'll be unconscious, then they hit you with fast-acting poison. I've actually seen it on an Azoren spy. No suffering."

Stiles swallowed. "Poisons are never painless."

"The knock-out gas—" Flat Nose snapped his fingers. "—takes you out instantly."

"Thanks."

"We don't have to be monsters just because the job is." He shrugged.

"You've killed Azoren spies?"

"Azoren. Gulmar. A Moskav operative. They flipped someone inside the Defense Ministry. That was ugly. She was just a bureaucrat, you know? Mother of three, Employee of the Quarter. Twice. You get those nice, gourmet lunches for three months. Free."

The other big bruiser was a black man—slightly smaller, with razor stubble and a twitch in the right side of his face. "I remember her."

Flat Nose winced. "She sang like a bird."

"Biggest haul we ever had." Razor Stubble scratched his chin. "How many people did we disappear after her? Twelve?"

"Fourteen."

"That was a big victory."

Flat Nose stared into the distance. "Those people… It wasn't painless for them."

"Nope."

The shuttle banked, and they began their descent. In the long shadows of a deep valley, a section of the ground grew darker. They moved closer, and lights outlined a rectangular opening. Once inside the valley, the shuttle slowed, then went into a hover before descending underground.

Engine whine became audible—high and shrill—then dropped into a deep frequency that sank into the bones. Lights flared along the skin of the craft, revealing a big, cavernous space with dull gray walls and floors. There were small, circular hatches clustered in fours all across the floor: recharge and refueling stations.

They settled with a jolt beside one of those hatch sets, and the smaller woman piloting the shuttle pulled her headset off. "All clear."

Nordic Lady stretched around as she unbuckled. "Lopez. Out of the vehicle. Now."

Flat Nose held his hands up, then he unbuckled too and opened the door at his side. "I'll be in the break room on level two."

He hustled away, shaking his head.

After several seconds, Nordic Lady climbed out, pistol drawn. "Get her out of there, Bester."

Twitch Face unclasped Stiles's ankle brace, then reached behind her, muttering as he unclasped the restraints. When he had the bar connecting her wrists firmly grasped, he moved her arms around. "You feel that?"

Stiles hissed. "Yes. My shoulders—"

"That's right. I could dislocate them easily, okay? So don't try anything. You get me?"

"I won't try anything."

He pressed the bar against her back, pushing up until his threat to dislocate her shoulders seemed close to truth. His left hand shoved her knees up, until her feet and the ankle restraining bar were on the seat, then he pushed her toward the open door. Stiles cooperated, even though each exertion left her more drained. Somewhere on the far end of the cavernous room, a metal door clanked shut.

Once Stiles was standing outside the vehicle, Nordic Lady waved the pilot over. "Weapon out."

The other woman—not even Stiles's size—screwed up her face. "She's restrained."

"*Weapon out.* She killed the last group who took her captive."

"Oh." The pilot drew her sidearm. "Why move her when she's conscious?"

"We were running out of time. Holding anyone in a facility for two weeks is risky. Don't worry. If we follow protocol, we'll be out of here in an hour, and she'll be at the bottom of an acid tub, dissolving."

Stiles shuddered. "You don't have to do this."

"Actually, we do."

"We're on the same side."

Bester pressed the metal bar against her back. "Shut up."

Nordic Lady jerked her head in the direction Lopez had gone. "Let's move."

Stiles nearly lost her footing when the big man shoved her forward. "All I want is to stop the Patels from putting the Republic at risk."

"If you believe that, we're obviously not on the same side."

"You want them to sell weapons and technology to the Gulmar?"

Nordic Lady shot an annoyed look at Stiles. "You can't be idealistic in this job, kid. Everything's about the long term, even the disgusting parts."

"Helping our enemies is good for the long term? How?"

"You don't understand."

Ahead of them, the far wall took on clarity: a metal rolling door that was partway open, revealing crates and canisters; and a bright red metal door with a small, thick window on it. Soft, amber lights glowed above the two doors. A giant "1" was painted on the wall to the right.

Level 1. There was a Level 2, and there was a break room there.

Stiles tried to crane her neck to see more, maybe to give Bester a hopeful look, but the big man pulled up on her restraining bar until she gasped. "Please..."

Nordic Lady glared at the big man. "Keep her under control."

Bester growled. "Let me dislocate her shoulders. That'll control her."

"If she keeps this up, I might." Nordic Lady glowered at Stiles. "None of us enjoy this."

"Then don't do it."

"We have to. It's the messy part of the job, but if we want to be vigilant against our enemies, we accept it."

"Let me help—"

"Stop it. No one's going to complain if I let Bester snap your neck."

The big man pressed a hand against Stiles's jaw. "I'll do it, too."

She sagged. "I'm not the enemy."

Nordic Lady's features softened. "I know. You're a tool that got caught in the middle of a fight you don't understand. So, just be quiet and let us get this over with."

The pilot pressed a hand against a section of the wall beside the red door, and a second later, a loud clank signaled the lock was open. She pulled the door open, and Nordic Lady led everyone through.

It was a surprisingly plain and simple concrete room. There were a couple chairs, a low table, and at the other end, a guard station in front of a glass door. A pale-faced young man with a crew cut stepped out of the station. He wore a generic rent-a-cop security guard uniform, which seemed wildly unlikely given the remoteness of the facility and its nature, but Nordic Lady and the other Ravens didn't react with surprise.

The stern look on the guard's pimply face softened as Nordic Lady led her group closer. "ID, please." His gray eyes ran up and down Stiles's jumpsuit.

Nordic Lady dug a card out of a hip pocket. "We called ahead—" Her eyes narrowed. "Did you not get the briefing?"

"What?" The guard's eyes were wide as he stared at Stiles. "What briefing?"

Nordic Lady leveled her gun on the young man. "Immunization. You should have taken a pill this morning."

"Hey—" He backed away, but his attention was split between Stiles and the gun.

"Get back into your station. Now."

Stiles couldn't control herself. She sobbed and shook her head. "Please don't kill him."

The guard's eyes grew even wider. "What?"

Bester reached for her throat. "I told you I'd—"

"Stop!" The guard reached for his own pistol.

Nordic Lady fired, catching the young man in the throat. He staggered back, shocked, dropping his weapon, then reaching for the wound.

It was all Stiles needed.

She pinned Bester's hand against her clavicle with her chin, locked her arms against the tug of the restraining bar, then brought her legs up in a swinging kick that caught the pilot in the face.

The woman collapsed, stunned and moaning.

Nordic Lady spun around, leveled her pistol at Stiles.

But Stiles had already brought her legs back around and swung them into Bester's shins with bone-shattering force.

He howled and released his grip on the wrist restraining bar…

Just as Nordic Lady fired.

Stiles didn't need to see the big man to know he'd been hit. Instead, she dropped to the floor, twisted around onto her butt, and brought her feet up into Nordic Lady's knees.

The Raven dodged back from the worst of the blow but was still off-balance. She fired, this time missing wildly before stumbling over the dying security guard.

Stiles rolled across the floor, coming to a stop beside Nordic Lady as she tried to disentangle herself from the guard, who had grabbed her with bloody hands.

Nordic Lady shrieked. "You are not—!" She tried to point her gun at Stiles but couldn't free it from the guard's grip.

That gave Stiles enough time to bend her back and tuck her legs up, then to bring her arms under her butt and along the back of her legs.

Another gunshot exploded, and the security guard's head jerked backward in a bloody spray.

Nordic Lady brought the pistol around.

Stiles grabbed the weapon and twisted the gun up and back, snapping the other woman's trigger finger as she fired.

The bullet ricocheted off the ceiling and cracked against the floor nearby.

But Stiles had the weapon by then. She twisted it around and aimed it at Nordic Lady. "You were right to say I'm not as human as you."

Terror filled the other woman's blue eyes. "I—"

Stiles put a round through the woman's forehead, then turned and finished off the pilot and Bester.

Nordic Lady had kept the keys to the restraints in a breast pocket. Stiles dug those out and freed herself. She dragged the dead guard over to his station and used his thumb to gain access. It was like a small office: a desk with a built-in terminal, a chair, a wall of displays showing the corridors of the facility.

Since the guard was already logged in, it was easy for Stiles to get into the security system to locate what she was looking for: Systems Support.

According to the logs, there were eight people on duty, plus Lopez. Once she located them all on surveillance video, she locked down the rooms they were in, then locked down the lifts and stairwell doors.

Stiles tore open drawers, searched through logbooks, and felt around under the desk until she found a slip of paper with eight digits scribbled on it: the master PIN. She made sure that was good enough to get her into every room in the facility, then erased the codes for everyone else within the facility.

She slipped back out of the guard station and took magazines and another pistol from the dead, then unclipped the guard's security card from his belt and tore his left thumb off.

There were four levels to the facility.

The top level consisted of the hangar bay, the storage area, and the welcome center.

The second level had the break room, lockers, and a gym.

The third level had the systems support area and the server room. The electrical, communications, and mechanical rooms were also there.

They had been taking her to the bottom floor, where all the dirty work took place.

Stiles took the stairs down, stopping to clear each floor before heading to the Systems Support room. There were two computer support people working there, completely oblivious to everything she'd done. If they hadn't been Ravens, she would have let them be.

She held up her pistol and cleared her throat. "Please raise your hands and move away from your terminals."

The tech support duo did as ordered. They were middle-aged men, one pale and soft, the other dusky and fat. The pale man had liver spots and a couple days of silvery beard growth. The other seemed bent beneath the weight of work, with skin tags prominent on his mahogany flesh.

It only took her a moment to see that they were logged in with elevated privileges. She took a stylus from one of their desks and set the device on top of the input device, to keep the system from screen locking.

When she turned back to the men, she wasn't surprised to find them staring at her, fascinated.

The white one cracked a yellow smile. "We just work on the computing systems."

They wouldn't have been involved in the butchery, so they hadn't been immunized. She returned the smile. "I'm not going to kill you."

Instead, she escorted them into the server room and locked them in a storage closet.

Then she settled at the unlocked terminal and began downloading data.

While everything downloaded, she stretched and tested the limits of her body. The Ravens really had pushed her near to the point of breaking.

She was tired and sore and hungry, and the ventilation system couldn't suck away enough of the smells for her to not realize what she must have suffered: burns, cuts, soiling herself.

She cleaned up in the locker room and changed into a fresh maintenance jumpsuit, then she stopped by the break room to grab some snacks.

Lopez didn't even try to draw a weapon. "I thought you might escape."

"Put your gun on the floor and kick it to me." When he did so, she collected the weapon. "You cooperate, you'll come out of this okay."

He snorted. "I'm not stupid."

"Then you know what's ahead."

"Yeah."

"At least it isn't an acid vat."

She locked the door behind her and returned to the systems support room, drinking an energy drink and chomping on a mouthful of salty chips. There were no portable storage media devices or output ports at the desk terminal, so she directed everything to a specific storage array, then she headed up again.

When she reached the hangar, her body shook from the post-adrenalin rush. She had to search around for the switch to activate the rooftop panel. It might have been something she could control from the shuttle, but she needed to be sure. With the rooftop open, she could make out the last of the afternoon sunlight.

Stiles settled into the pilot seat, powered the vehicle up, and rose out of the underground facility. She settled about twenty meters from the opening and sat back, wishing she'd grabbed more snacks from the break room.

A yellow flash from the console preceded an alarm. She powered the alarm off and exited the vehicle.

Black shuttles with GSA markings on their side descended into the valley.

She waited until they had landed, then headed toward the largest one, stopping when a ramp dropped and Colonel McLeod stepped out. Other agents in their gray uniforms rushed past, headed for the shadowy opening to the facility below.

McLeod waited until the bulk of the force had exited the GSA craft, then ambled toward her stiffly. "I had my doubts you'd make it, Lieutenant."

"So did I. I wasn't sure you were tracking me."

"They didn't destroy the shadowsuit until it was already in their systems."

She shoved her shaking hands into the jumpsuit pockets. "I can't remember everything they did to me."

"Good. Your brain spared you some terrible moments."

"But we have one of their Silence Centers."

"I'm not sure it was worth what you went through. You played it close."

"I needed to be sure I got inside."

He frowned. "You flatlined during their interrogations."

"It's the best way to deal with that sort of thing, right?"

"We conducted a raid on that facility an hour ago. Empty, of course."

"This was the important one." She glanced at the dark rectangle. "Was that guard one of yours?"

"Guard?"

"There was a guard who hadn't been immunized against my pheromones."

"Not ours." The colonel glanced at the darkening sky. "I don't suppose you took any prisoners?"

"A few. There are two technical support people in a storage closet and an agent. Lopez. I think you might be able to turn him."

"I suppose even a small victory is a victory."

Her legs trembled, and he reached for her. "I'm fine."

"No, you're not." McLeod waved her toward his shuttle. "I'm concerned about how hard you're pushing yourself."

"I was designed for this, wasn't I?"

"You're a GSA agent, just like the rest of us. We can't have you taking too many risks."

"I'll be okay."

He pulled her weight against him. "Please come with me. The work we have ahead of us isn't going anywhere, and you're long past due for some rest."

She followed him, stomach growling demands. They'd landed a blow against the Ravens, but more importantly, they'd gained access to sensitive systems full of data vital in the struggle to root the traitors out. Now there was a real chance they might find what she needed to continue her effort to bring down the Patels and their weapons smuggling operations.

Still, it was only the beginning. The shadow organization's roots ran deep. And dark.

13

It was a rare thing for Satrap to leave his quarters. There were numerous reasons for him to remain within its confines: the unmatched connectivity to the ships and networks of his fleet; the central location with armor and shielding that protected him from anything short of a nuclear blast; and the prestige and sanctity associated with the cabin. It was officially sacrilege to attack a sultan, and he was the highest of the high, the Satrap of the Glorious Fleet of Conquest, the favorite of the Holy Khan.

But today, Satrap Khan had broken with tradition. He had to, if he wanted to prevent a mutiny that would tear apart his fleet.

He leaned back as his Jakkara captain guided the holy wheelchair down the dully lit passageways of the *Might of the Khan*. The captain was a slender man, although his armor hid that fact. His boots thudded on the deck as loudly as any warrior's would. Like his fellow soldiers marching in a tight square around the captain, he gave off a strange mix of odors—sweat from the uniform, a metallic polish oil from the armor and weapons, and a combination of cinnamon and anise. The last two were apparently a crucial part of the concoction they drank for power and purity.

What mattered to Satrap was that the Jakkara were alert, their heads swiveled and eyes darted.

There would be no ambush.

The procession came to a stop outside the officers' banquet room. Zohar had two members of his security detachment standing there—angry-eyed men in light armor of a soft blue jacket and deeper brown pants. The Zohar family emblem of a lightning strike enclosed in a circle stood out in black on the left breast of the jacket. Polished brass helmets covered most of the men's heads, including the chin and mouth.

Angry eyed or not, they stepped aside without a word for Satrap and his protectors.

This was a good sign.

Respect for the hallowed warriors was necessary to maintain structure and discipline.

The banquet room had been decorated with flowers and green and orange bunting—the colors of the Holy Khan. A single, large table occupied cabin center. Silver trays of meats, fruits, and breads covered the gold tablecloth.

Zohar sat at the head of the table, impeccable in his dress uniform. Light reflected from the ornamental helmet at his left. To his right sat Ikhama, now wearing an even heavier and more ornate version of the robes she normally wore. To her right sat Captain Ho, of the *Blessed Saber of Xenu*, the second aircraft carrier. Shorter than most, his round face was a deep gold from years beneath the burning sun of Azh Choak, commanding the planetary cavalry. Across from him sat Captain Rouhani, the willowy old man with scars from numerous engagements in his youth with Moskav and Azoren raiders. Now Rouhani commanded the *Divine Wind*, one of the other cruisers. His was the loudest voice in the chatter calling for mutiny.

The Jakkara captain waited until Satrap signaled, then rolled him up to the empty section of table to Zohar's left.

Zohar and the priestess rose as Satrap approached, followed by Ho and Rouhani. The captain of the *Might of the Khan* bowed slightly. "Satrap—your presence is an honor and blessing."

Ikhama bowed her head. *"What river is mightier than the one fed by great streams and brooks?"*

Ho and Rouhani mumbled approval of her choice of scripture.

The hearty and rich aroma of the feast hammered Satrap, who felt in no way mighty. "Thank you."

It was meant both for his host and his guests, but mostly it was a signal to the Jakkara captain that he was free to find a place to watch over the meeting.

That was exactly what the slender bodyguard did.

As the others took their seats, Satrap adjusted the feed from the portable life support system to fill his input tubes with nutrients and painkillers. His body was confused by the proximity to such enticing offerings. There had been a time not so long ago when he would have indulged in the simple pleasures of the flesh: eating and drinking, perhaps the warmth of a dancer for the night.

Such intemperance was unacceptable in critical roles, so even the basic capacity was removed.

Not through surgery or chemicals but beatings.

Pain flared in Satrap's joints where the Holy Khan's blows had shattered bone and torn muscle. Before the old man was done, ruptured organs were already failing. Only then had surgeons been allowed to go to work to create the leader of the conquering fleet.

All praise the Great and Holy Khan.

Ikhama filled a crystal glass with a honey-colored drink, sniffing the fluid before lifting the glass. *"While the farmer of weak and uncertain faith might see danger in the rain that falls for days, he who is strong and steadfast in his belief in the Khan sees only the blessing of water."*

Once again, Ho and Rouhani's heads bobbed up and down in approval.

Zohar barely managed to cover the scowl twisting his face, then turned away from the old woman. "We've begun the recording."

Satrap nodded—just the slightest bow of the head, really. He had sensed the cameras in the corridor, wondering if they might capture how enfeebled the most powerful leader in the khan's service truly was. But the recordings were necessary. They were the signal to the other captains and their officers of the strength in unity between the satrap and his senior officers.

The *Might of the Khan*'s captain snapped a finger, and a trio of slim and youthful officers dressed in all black traced with gold rushed forward to serve food and drink. Zohar and the captains' plates were piled high, mostly with glistening meat, while Ikhama was given only a small slice that was surrounded by olives, carrots, apricots, and figs. A decorative plate was set before Satrap, then the serving officers retreated.

Grease dripped down Zohar's chin as he shoveled bright pink meat into his mouth. "You have heard already that repairs are nearing completion."

Satrap fought back the urge to lick his lips. The meat looked juicy and smelled fresh despite coming from frozen stores. "I've heard, yes. Thank you."

"Ikhama has acted on your behalf not only to convince your captains to flee the battlefield with the Kedraalians but to effect repairs rather than to press the advantage."

The old woman cut a slice of apricot and considered it. "*Winds batter the trees no matter the strength of their trunks; the vines joined together merely bend in the face of the same threat.*"

More of the Holy Khan's wince-inducing allegories. Satrap waved one of the black-suited officers over and pointed at the honey-colored drink. "A sip, please."

"Yes, my Satrap." The officer filled the bottom of a crystal glass, which he set before Satrap, then retreated.

Satrap lifted the drink and sniffed it: sweet, fruity, with a hint of alcohol.

He took a sip, letting the heat roll down his tongue.

Zohar dabbed at his chin with a napkin. "The question remains: Do we pursue the Kedraalian force or not?"

It was meant to sound casual. Since fleeing the battlefield, the chatter among the captains had been evasive, circuitous, abstruse. But Satrap had an understanding of subtext. The same officers had been more forward—even angry—when Ikhama had visited their ships.

To a man, they wanted to destroy the Kedraalian force. Now.

Satrap set the crystal glass back on the table. "We turn our attention now to the secondary objective."

Muscles stood out on Zohar's jaw. He glanced at the other two captains, then thrust his chin forward. "Assurances were given."

"Assurances that we would destroy the Kedraalian task force, yes."

Ho set his knife down loudly, splashing grease onto the dull brown jacket of his relatively plain uniform. "Satrap, we have already fabricated a full complement of fighters for our pilots. They pray each morning for the opportunity to give their lives for the glory of our Holy Khan."

"Good." Satrap caught the subtle nod given by Ikhama that said she had both Ho and Rouhani corralled. "The opportunity to strike is imminent."

"Yes, but the Kedraalians—"

"We will have the chance to finish them soon enough."

Rouhani cleared his throat—not out of deference but to demand attention. "The *Divine Wind* has a single purpose. How can the glory of our Khan be extolled to the universe if we scurry away with our tails between our legs from these Kedraalians?"

Satrap's stomach griped, no doubt protesting being so near the feast. "Captains, I have no need to remind each of you of our singular purpose."

Zohar straightened. "Perhaps there is confusion troubling us. In my memory, our Great and Holy Khan sent us forth to strike down the heathen and crush their militaries."

"That is our purpose."

"It would seem that Captain Rouhani is correct and that running away makes destroying the enemy impossible."

Cool sweat dripped down Satrap's ribs. "The fleet is like a warrior— best capable of striking down its enemies when in prime condition. Captain Ho, your pilots require fighters if they wish to seek the glory of victory in battle."

The round-faced man bowed his head. "It is so, Satrap. Now that we have those fighters—"

"We will proceed to the next objective."

Zohar sighed. "The infidel was close to collapse."

"As were we. I've studied the data since the battle ended. My assumptions were correct: This *Valor* has undergone changes we were not informed of. The task force was able to identify our ships if not to target them."

"Targeting is all that matters."

"Unfortunately, no. With clever enough use, missiles and other weapons do not need direct targeting. They had no lock-on, yet they established sufficient fire that we couldn't reach a target."

Rouhani scowled. "Losses are a part of war."

"A commander doesn't willingly expend soldiers. To risk lives and weapons, the objective must be obtainable, or there must be some purpose served."

Zohar stabbed another piece of meat and chomped on it. "Each day we rebuild is a day the infidels draw breath."

Satrap smiled. "The universe has breath aplenty for us to draw in."

"Yet they mock us with their continued existence."

Ikhama scraped a fork over her plate. *"Time is eternal, yet so is the will and love of the light of the sun. The river doesn't question the rainstorm. Either rain falls and the river continues, or the waters run dry. The light of the sun burns on."*

Zohar thumbed meat from between his teeth. "Words of love?"

"The Great and Holy Khan did not speak only of war." The old woman took a deep breath. "Enemies do not wear only flesh and carry swords. They hide in the darkness of the throat when words are spoken against the great plan. They remain unseen in the dark hearts of those who conspire and deceive."

Ho and Rouhani glanced at each other, then Ho pushed his chair back and bowed his head. "We understand the wisdom of seeking the optimal objective. My pilots will be ready when the target is selected."

Satrap relaxed. "Good. Thank you, Captain Ho. Tell them to study their scriptures until then."

Rouhani stood. "We stand ready to guide the next attack."

"Soon enough, Captain."

The captains did an about-face, then headed for the hatch with Rouhani leading.

The cameras died when the hatch closed. Satrap reached out for any hint of recording devices and found nothing.

He relaxed. "The chatter has already renewed."

Zohar tore a piece of bread and sopped up meat juice. "That is to be expected. Is it talk of mutiny or acceptance of the new target?"

"Acceptance. Reluctant acceptance."

"This is the way for many in service to the Holy Khan." Zohar chewed on the bread distractedly.

"The time will come to fight this Kedraalian captain again."

"Never soon enough."

Aches throbbed through Satrap's ruined body. "Why must we seek our ends so quickly, Captain?"

"Is it not in the Kabal that we have but one purpose? What else is there in life but service to the will of our Khan?"

"You sound as if you've changed your mind about cooperating with me."

Zohar stared at his plate. "The strategy is sound."

"This is the best plan we could hope for. And I assure you, there will be plenty of opportunities to die."

The captain of the *Might of the Khan* emptied his crystal cup. "My wife worries the war will cost us our most precious possessions."

Ikhama lifted her head and closed her eyes. "*The universe has wealth beyond comprehension. Stars hold the light and warmth to give us life. Oceans encase rock rich with mineral. Long after we have returned to Xenu, the universe will carry on until it is time for a rebirth.*"

Satrap fought back a snort. The priestess had chosen one of the Great and Holy Khan's more rambling and incomprehensible writings. The man had stolen concepts and even quotes from so many sources and tried to put the pieces together into a consistent and positive philosophy smarter men had never managed to puzzle out. But there was no arguing the concept with people like Ikhama. She was fully invested and would die that way.

Still, there were times where even she seemed troubled. Satrap massaged his aching thighs. "We have an infinite source for raw materials in space, Captain. There is no need for our precious possession to be imperiled."

Zohar turned the crystal in his hand. "She spoke of our children."

"Ah." Satrap winced. "I have no experience with that."

"The cost of being the favorite of our Holy Khan."

"One cost of many, yes. Are your children at risk for a particular reason?"

The captain set his glass back on the table. "My son has shown signs of interest in piloting."

"A suicide pilot? Those are drawn from the uneducated and simple."

"Yet there is pride in it, and the path is easy."

"Easy, yes. The pilot does nothing more than provide the heartbeat whose failure detonates the explosives."

"You see the simplicity? That is the allure."

"Death? That is all he seeks?"

Zohar frowned. "The glory and fame that comes with choosing that fate."

Ikhama wiped a tear from her eye. "Children are but wheat to be harvested in the service to our lord, the Holy Khan." Her voice dropped to a whisper. "*What treachery, the scythe. What destruction, the war.*"

The captain's frown deepened. "This sounds like blasphemy, Ikhama."

"They are words spoken by the Great and Holy Khan himself, shortly after his followers were slaughtered in droves."

"My apologies. The words—"

"Context holds power to equal content."

Zohar nodded. "A lesson my son could profit from."

Satrap scanned for recording devices again. The words being spoken between them could be used against them far too easily. It was alarming enough for the words to reach his own ears. "At the very least, Zohar, your son should lead warriors in defense of the homeland."

"He should. Unfortunately, that takes effort and time."

"Do you have other sons?"

"None who lived. Our younger daughter—" Zohar sighed. "She has problems in school."

"Most children have problems with one thing or another."

"Not this sort. She challenges the teachings."

"Who has not at one point or another?"

Zohar's eyes narrowed. "This is not impetuous rebellion to be broken by ten lashes. She recites the doctrine back to the Ikhama and explains her logic and how the widely accepted interpretations are flawed."

Ikhama's brow trembled. "*The tree that survives eons of flooding and lightning, fire and pestilence, does so through purity and strength. The heretic dies through a misguided belief in superior understanding of the universe or by allowing a dark spirit into their hearts so that chaos and disaster might replace order and harmony.*"

"We have warned her of this. My wife has spoken this verse many times."

"Wisdom comes with age and the acceptance that no mind is greater than the Great Khan." The trembling reached Ikhama's hands, which she pushed under the table, out of sight.

"The school has issued a warning. With war, tolerance will be reduced."

The sound of leather slapping against skin echoed in Satrap's mind. The pain came soon after. "You—" He coughed and activated an injector to calm his nerves. "You are a captain. Surely, you can speak for her."

"Even a captain might disappear." Zohar's eyes flashed to the Jakkara.

He was right. The blessed warriors had no children and never would. They knew as little of the needs of the flesh as Satrap. Less, even. They were taken from the elite of the various shahs and captains and had been castrated, chemically and mentally conditioned. Satrap could speak a word, and they would kill Zohar and even Ikhama.

And there were thousands like them in the service of the Holy Khan. Tens of thousands more followed the teachings and showed equal loyalty without the conditioning.

No one was safe in the Khanate. Ever.

Satrap leaned back in his seat. "It is best we focus on the war, then."

Zohar squeezed his eyes shut, then nodded. "Objective two."

"It will not go unspoken how important your support was in securing the continuity of the fleet, Zohar."

"Should we survive to return to our homes, I will give my thanks."

"Our fleet is yet the mightiest ever to launch. Reinforcements will restore us."

"Can we say this after our failure to dispatch the Kedraalians?"

"As we discussed, treachery explains much of this. Let the fleet see the value of our operatives when we strike our second objective. Their faith will be restored, and with that, victory shall come easier."

A smile softly curled Ikhama's lips. *"Where waters are still, a true reflection may be easier to see."*

Satrap caught the look of confusion in the captain's eyes before he looked away. It was reassuring to see rationality and vulnerability in a rival. If that ultimately translated into greater cooperation, then the chances of success for the fleet were vastly improved.

Would success be enough to satisfy Khan's hunger for a pure and holy universe? The idea was laughable. Crushing the obvious enemies would provide nothing but a short respite before the need for blood and slaughter would rise again.

And when that happened, Satrap had no doubt he would know the bite of the executioner's blade.

14

———————

Gulmar gunships bracketed the *Valor* as it approached Radetta. Benson swallowed, once more feeling like a prisoner in her dress whites, especially in the presence of the bridge crew, which had reverted to jumpsuits once maintenance operations had become everyone's primary concern. If she were being honest with herself, she had no reason to feel so anxious. Her task force was as close to full strength as she could have hoped after the ambush. Many survivors had already been integrated into the crews of other ships. Weapons systems were almost fully replenished, leaving only the *Valor*'s damaged missile launch system to repair.

And yet, the anxiety had lingered over the days that it took to reach the Gulmar Union capital world. A nagging voice kept at her day in and day out: There were traitors in her crew. The thought had pushed aside even her worries for Halliwell, who wasn't responding to treatment as well as he should.

Benson lost herself in the gentle hum of the air recycling system and the murmur of her bridge officers.

Chopra apparently caught the distraction in her stance. He drifted from the helm station to her side, trailing the faint scent of cloves. "You could always send someone else down to meet this Executive Director Trang."

A tight smile spread across Benson's pinched face. "You volunteering?"

"No. I couldn't drink enough to be relaxed for that sort of work."

"I wouldn't mind a drink myself. Something smoky and sharp."

"Once your meeting with this executive committee concludes."

"When I dreamed of captaining a warship, I never thought I would have to play diplomat. War talks, peace talks—that's not something you leave to a military officer."

"In the distant past, it happened quite frequently."

"I think we've refined the roles of diplomat and combatant since then."

"Isn't negotiation something your mother made a career of?"

"Thank you for making it hurt even more."

The bald XO chuckled. "Will you ever have a reconciliation with her?"

"That's up to her."

Nuñez's head came around. "Message from the escorts, Captain: You are cleared to proceed to the Gulmar Capital Spaceport."

"Thank you, Lieutenant." Benson stepped down from the elevated command station. "Commander Chopra, you have the conn. Keep the task force back from the planet."

Chopra took her place. "Will you reconsider taking Marines?"

"No. Diplomats don't maintain a security detail, and that's my assignment."

She acknowledged the Marines guarding the hatch when she passed. They were all becoming comfortable with having security posted throughout the ships, and that was probably the best reason not to take a detail with her: The Marines were stretched too thin as it was.

Anyway, she was flying down to discuss a military alliance with the Gulmar leadership. Marines might send the wrong message.

Shuttle-138 was waiting for her, a pilot and co-pilot standing at the ramp. They were young and sharp-looking in their flight suits. The pilot was a head shorter than Benson, fuller-bodied and seemingly half as old, brown eyes twinkling and round cheeks full and soft. Lieutenant Aidid. The co-pilot's eyes were level with Benson's. He was an even younger man with a square jaw and broad shoulders; he reminded her of Halliwell.

It was a reminder she didn't need at the moment.

Benson took the ramp quickly, feeling awkward and old. She strapped in as the pilots brought the shuttle online. There was plenty to keep her busy on the trip planet side. She connected her command device to the shuttle system and filled the display mounted to her seat with data she'd been provided by the Gulmar diplomatic liaison.

In the last day, it had been a constant onslaught of information, some of it contradictory to what she'd been briefed with just a few months prior.

The executive committee was still the same: a group of twelve corporate directors "elected" to oversee the union's strategic and tactical goals. Their main job seemed to be crafting slogans and massaging budgets to present a rosy picture for the general populace about the progress being made toward…

That was the part Benson still hadn't managed to put together.

With the Kedraalian Republic, the definition of government was easy to comprehend: Government served its populace by providing security, stability, and safety. The bodies that provided the functions were straightforward: military, police, medical, infrastructure, education, resources, and labor. Of course, each had multiple divisions within, but the core operations were transparent to the electorate.

With the Gulmar, everything seemed to be designed with an eye toward obscurity and deception, starting with the voting.

Not all citizens had a vote, and not all votes counted equally. Most votes were actually merely made to inform appointed bodies of representatives of a general desire from the populace. Those appointed bodies had no requirement to act on the desires. They had no obligation to ensure there was a sanctity of office. Even the most fundamental structure of a democratic electoral system was a lie, as the executive committee and the executive director had final determination on everything.

It was all bewildering. Who could possibly accept a system where the voice of the people was actually meaningless? One person, one vote. It was a simple concept, yet it wasn't universal.

Benson dove through the labyrinth of hierarchies that made up the union.

"Captain?" It was the pilot, her smoky voice smooth and calm. "We're approaching the spaceport. We have an escort."

Outside the starboard porthole, three fighter craft flew alongside the shuttle. The smaller vessels bristled with missiles.

Benson powered down the display. "Thank you, Lieutenant."

Below, an ugly sprawl of ratty-looking, squat buildings followed the contours of a muddy river that curled around red hills on its way to the ocean. Ant-sized shapes crawled through a network of winding streets as red as the hills. Wispy columns of smoke rose from some of the buildings.

The shuttle banked and headed for their destination: a flat, asterisk-shaped compound of black strips. Shiny aircraft sat outside long, low buildings. The compound was surrounded by a high fence, and insect-like vehicles sped along the inside.

Between the sprawl and their destination, there was a clearing at least twenty kilometers wide. More vehicles patrolled in the distance.

Not maintenance and transport vehicles but security.

Did the Gulmar have the same problems with traitors on their home world?

Benson's shuttle dropped lower as they neared the starport, and she made out more of the fighter craft parked on the tarmac. There had to be thirty or more counting their escort.

That seemed a significant security force for a starport.

Aidid set them down with a crisp landing, then she and her co-pilot unbuckled as the engines wound down. They didn't wait for Benson before opening the ramp and taking position at the bottom at parade rest.

She sucked in a breath, coughed at the dusty tanginess of the air, then followed.

It was hot outside, the sunlight a hazy burn on the tarmac. Two of the bug-like security vehicles raced toward the shuttle. There were soldiers or police personnel with their heads sticking out of cupolas and hatches. As the vehicles drew closer, the bug-like appearance resolved into segmented armor and weapons modules. The designs were old, reminding Benson of defense systems from a time before the rebellion, yet these vehicles looked relatively new. The thick, heavy tires were caked with mud.

The security vehicles came to a stop about ten meters away, and personnel hopped out: not soldiers but paramilitary units based on the grayish-blue uniforms with accents and cuts that were closer to civilian than military. It was almost as if style had been chosen over functionality.

One of the men separated from the rest, neck craning as he looked skyward. A sparkling shape seemed to be arcing toward them from a huge wall to the west, nearly hidden by an ochre haze and afternoon sunlight.

The leader of the paramilitary group held his assault weapon at a sloppy angle. He was short and thin, with sunken cheeks and eyes. "You Benson?" His accent was…crude.

"Captain Faith Benson, representative of the Kedraalian Repub—"

"Benson." The man nodded toward the arcing shiny object. "Escort's coming. Want protection?"

The other members of the paramilitary group showed teeth. Most of them had gaps, and all of them were yellow. Some of them could have been women but were so thin that no curves stood out in their uniforms.

"Um." Benson searched around. "Are you our escort?"

The gaunt-faced man snorted. "Security for the starport. Fifty credits, we'll hold this position. Protect your pilots. Ship, too."

If the shiny object in the sky was her escort, it was still at least a minute out. She dug in her pocket for her command tablet. "Do you have a banking system I—?"

"Everyone got an account. Just empty is all."

"Well, I—"

"Easy payment." He pulled a device from his hip pocket.

Her command tablet vibrated at a funds transfer request: fifty credits. She authorized the transfer. It seemed a small price to pay for "protection."

The gaunt-faced man smiled. "Safe now."

He and the others headed back to their bug-like vehicles and climbed inside. When the shiny speck in the sky grew to the size of a small, polished shuttle—part chrome, part blue—the security vehicle engines rumbled, and they sped away.

Benson didn't have time to protest, as the shuttle rocketed to the point where the vehicles had been just a moment before. A side hatch opened, and a tall, handsome man poked his head out. He scowled as he stroked his dark, close-trimmed beard and mustache. "Did they threaten you?"

"Not…directly."

The handsome man relaxed. "Good. Captain Benson?"

"Yes. Do I need my shuttle to return to the *Valor*?"

"That might be a good idea. Are you ready?"

She took a step, then turned back to Aidid. "I'll call you when I'm ready to return."

The lieutenant frowned, then nodded. She led her co-pilot up the ramp, which closed as Benson climbed aboard the chrome-and-blue Gulmar shuttle. It sealed shut behind her as the pilot smiled. "Sorry for the trouble. I'm Floyd."

"Floyd?"

"Floyd Thiessen. I'm sort of the commander of the Second Gulmar Security Fleet. Right now, though, I'm just a pilot playing escort for a visiting dignitary."

"Oh."

"Buckle in. We don't want those bastards asking for a launching fee."

"They don't work for you?"

Thiessen chuckled. "No one works for me right now. They're just trying to make enough money to buy food."

"They looked military. Well, paramilitary."

The shuttle's engines spun up, loud in the small cockpit. "They are, in a way. Same as me. You'll see."

As he spoke, the same armored vehicles accelerated toward the shuttle. Thiessen got it into the air before the security team could hop out, and he pushed the engines hard until they were high above the starport. A moment later, he changed course, heading toward the towering walls nearly hidden in the ochre haze.

Once Aidid's shuttle blasted skyward, tension eased from Benson's body. She turned to Thiessen, who seemed similarly relaxed. "Would you mind telling me what that was all about?"

"The starport?"

"Yes."

He shrugged. "Like I said, they're looking to make enough money to—"

"—buy food. Yes, I caught that. You also said they're military, like you."

A blush spread across Thiessen's bronze cheeks. "Things are different here."

"I gathered as much."

"You might best appreciate the differences in the military."

"All right."

"Well, we don't have one, not like yours. Full-time professionals are expensive. Instead, we're contractors. Right now, a lot of us are between contracts. So, people like that security unit make what they can offering protection. And me…" The pilot nodded at the flight control panel.

"Wait—you're not working for Leona Trang?" Benson gazed at the barren ground speeding past maybe a hundred meters below. Jumping out would be suicide.

"Well, sure—under contract. I've worked for the Gulmar or the Haidakura in one capacity or another since I was fourteen."

"And…you're a…captain?"

"Not like you, but I command the Second Security Fleet, when it's activated."

Benson knuckled her forehead. "Your people—"

"It's different, right?"

"You know about Kedraalian culture?"

"What I was able to learn about when I bought history vids. You can't believe half of what you see in those, though. Do you people still kill traitors by firing squad? Do you still eat them?"

"What?"

"I didn't believe the eating part, but the firing squad seems pretty barbaric."

"I can't recall an execution by firing squad in years."

"And no eating?"

Benson glared at the man, unsure if he was teasing her or not. "Why this huge wall?"

"Because there are people down there in the slums who *would* eat you."

"You have food shortages?"

"Well, those of us who live out there do. The people inside these walls?"

As they passed over the massive defensive structure, the imposing level of work and material involved in the construction became more apparent. It must have been fifteen meters high and a good three meters deep, stretching far beyond her sight in the haze. Weapon stations poked out like thorns at regular intervals, and in the shadows of the lower levels, vehicles rumbled across walkways.

But the imposing wall was soon forgotten as Benson got her first clear look at the interior of the city. Vehicles darted down broad streets of gray, cutting among towering buildings that spewed heavy black and orange smoke that slowly drifted toward the wall and the slums beyond. Deeper past the walled entry point, the buildings looked less industrial and more commercial. Made of steel and glass, they managed a dull sparkle in the haze. And beyond those towers, the *real* towers rose.

Thiessen squinted at the three tallest buildings as the shuttle drew closer. "Gulmar Towers. You want to understand the Union, you have to understand the base of its power."

"The old Gulmar corporation?"

"Conglomerate. Gulmar Conglomerate. Leona Trang is only the twenty-third chief executive officer of the current business, and she's the fourth CEO to rise to executive director."

"So, she's powerful."

"And the sun is a little warm."

Air traffic grew thicker as they moved closer to the towers. It felt claustrophobic, even dangerous to Benson. "How many people live inside the walls?"

"Three million, give or take."

"And how many live in those slums?"

"Ten? Twelve?"

"Million."

"Those aren't the worst ones. I've lived in worse." The pilot snorted.

The shuttle descended, settling on a pristine white rooftop pad. Gimbal-mounted machine-guns popped from the rooftop and pivoted around to target the shuttle doors.

"Automated security?" The concept seemed misplaced to the Kedraalian captain.

"It saves a good deal of money. I doubt you could land an assault force here."

"Is that a real concern?"

"The Azoren have tried. Not here, but on Karkos."

Thiessen worked his way through a few screens on his console, then he whispered something into his headset. A moment later, the machine guns dropped back out of sight.

They didn't encounter anyone until exiting the elevator a few floors down, and that was a smartly dressed young man with slicked-back, blond-streaked brown hair. He had an executive tablet, glossy and black to the outside viewer, a device that could just as easily be part of the decor: flat black metal, shiny black plastic, polished black-and-gray marble, charcoal tinted glass, deep silver carpeting. A matching black stylus moved like a magic wand in the young man's pale grip. "This is Captain Benson?"

The way he assessed her—taking her in head to toe with a tilt of his head—seemed less an evaluation of her appearance than of how she projected authority, which was every bit as annoying. She realized she was straightening her posture under his gaze.

Thiessen looked past the young man, to a dark glass wall at the far end of the hall. "Is Leona around?"

The young man scowled. "The executive director is waiting."

"Best we not keep her waiting, right?"

"Correct." The young man spun around and clomped away.

The pilot leaned in to Benson. "Part of the bloodline. Never knew a day of need in his life."

"Shouldn't we follow?"

"No. You have to make someone like him suffer, even a little bit."

The young man scraped to a stop short of the glass wall and turned around with a groan. "Captain Benson?"

Thiessen arched an eyebrow at her. "Now we follow."

The glass wall parted, two doors sliding aside to reveal a glass-walled conference room that looked out onto the city. A long, dark wooden table was surrounded by black chairs covered in synthetic leather. Four people —two men and two women—were huddled at the far end of the table, looking over something on a display embedded in the surface. They wore the same sort of dark, stylish suit as the young man with the executive tablet, but they were older, their perfect looks showing the touch of wisdom or at least experience. Benson felt ancient in their presence, even though she had no doubt they had twenty or more years on her.

At the other end of the room, a younger woman in skirt and jacket stared out at the bronze streaks of light piercing the haze. Against that backdrop, the woman's gold skin had an unnatural glow, and her hair seemed cut from obsidian. The tailoring of her suit emphasized a fit, hourglass shape consistent with muscular calves. She turned, took a sip from a tumbler with a clear fluid in it, then her full, youthful lips split into a smile. "You're late."

Benson nearly staggered. The woman couldn't be older than her mid-thirties but was definitely Trang. "Executive Director Trang. It's nice to meet you."

"You were late reaching my fleet, too."

"I—" Benson caught herself swaying. "No. We arrived at the appointed time."

"Too late to save them. That's what matters, Captain."

"We weren't sent to save your fleet, Ms. Trang."

The woman took another sip of the drink. "You weren't, were you?"

"The discussions we had hoped for still need to take place."

"You think so?" Trang set her glass down on the tabletop, beside a pair of pink-colored sunglasses that she slipped on. "I've been reviewing the cost of that fleet since the report came in, and I must tell you, I simply cannot see a justification for that expense. And now you want me to talk to you about a treaty?"

"A mutual defense treaty. We actually have many—"

"Where would you propose I come up with the billions of credits to rebuild those ships? The Gulmar Union operates on a budget. We have an obligation to our constituents and customers."

"The ones living in those slums?"

Trang's smile flashed again. "Were you sent to stir up trouble, Captain?"

"No. I think you have enough on your own."

"Do you mean our fleet or our citizens who choose to live like animals?"

"Choose?" Benson strolled toward the window the executive director had been looking out. "How many of the fleet were made up of people from places like that?"

"Most of those who serve in low-level jobs such as security come from lesser means. Those are the ones who choose to rise above. Isn't that right, Floyd?"

The pilot joined Benson at the window. "It's a choice, certainly."

"There, you see? The Kedraalian obsession with opportunity and egalitarianism proves once again misguided."

Benson's legs locked. "We...feel—the prime minister feels—that both powers coming together would benefit. There have always been commonalities between our people, and the differences separating us are almost inconsequential." The words rang hollow at the sight of the dirty river winding its way through the millions so far below.

Trang joined the two at the window, pulling off her sunglasses and offering them to her Kedraalian guest. "Did they bother to coach you, dear?"

"I went through extensive briefing—" Benson took the glasses and glanced through the lenses. Soft amber numbers and letters danced along the inside: Profits and Losses; Popularity and Job Approval; Farming Futures; a market ticker.

"Then you know that our differences are actually more significant than our commonalities." The executive held her hand out for the glasses.

When Benson took them off, she realized how old the other woman's hands looked. Wrinkles, veins, the thin skin—she hadn't received treatment to push back her age everywhere. Not yet. "You accepted the prime minister's request for a meeting."

"Before my fleet was destroyed, I did."

"The only thing that's changed, Madam Executive Director, is that your enemy now holds to a different religion than racial purity."

"And like any enemy, when the time comes, money will resolve the problem."

"Resolve—" Benson caught a smirk flash across Thiessen's face. "You think you can bribe your enemies to leave you alone?"

"Of course we can. Who doesn't value money?"

Benson's heart pounded. "Did you see my evaluation of this fleet?"

"I did. I'm sure it would be impressive. I'm also sure it's not our problem."

"They wiped out your fleet! How many thousands—?"

"Reason enough to stay out of this. We have hundreds of initiatives where money could be better spent. Did you realize we've been ten years without updating our strategic goals? The windfall from goals that align properly to contemporary dynamics… We could realize as much as a ten percent increase in revenues in the first two years alone."

Benson couldn't tell if the executive director was engaging in a bizarre form of negotiating or if something else was at play. "War is imminent. You've lost thousands of security personnel in an unprovoked sneak attack, and you're worried about strategic goals?"

The older woman settled the augmented reality sunglasses on her button nose. "Have you ever heard just how entitled you sound, Captain?"

"En—" There had to be sarcasm behind that. "Perhaps I should come back—"

"Your mother is a politician, correct?" Trang snapped her fingers.

A woman at the other end of the table sat up straight. "Representative Sargota Benson. Never held a senior position in the parliament. Never served in a cabinet position. Never negotiated a coalition. Paid for private tutoring and private schooling for her only child."

Trang nodded. "And she managed to get you into the academy."

Benson hadn't been prepared for negotiating tactics that made things personal. She'd been briefed that Trang was ruthless, that she would do anything to get the best deal, that she would try to knock her opponent off her feet. To call Benson *entitled*? "Maybe tomorrow—"

"How many people did you displace going into the academy, Captain? There are a fixed number of seats each year, right? Seats that are highly competitive?"

"My scores were in the top ninety-fifth percentile."

"A good start but hardly enough to get you into the academy alone, is it?"

"Excuse me." Benson sucked in a breath and took a step toward the conference room door.

"You represent the great Kedraalian experiment, yet here you are, come to the *evil* Gulmar on hands and knees, begging us to be your allies."

"Tomorrow…" The door seemed so far away. How had the prime minister's people done so poorly preparing for this woman?

"War is an unnecessary risk and expense. My people won't accept it."

Benson came to a stop in front of the doors, which refused to slide open. She pushed against the wall to be sure she was in the right place. She was. "I'll be in touch." Why wouldn't the door open?

Trang's reflection was at Benson's side. "Unless you want to buy our services."

"Buy?" Benson spun around. "You're the wealthiest people in the galaxy."

"And we're not interested in spending that money on war."

The glass doors whispered open. A small army of young-looking elderly folk stood in the hallway, faces drained of emotion and life.

Trang waved them in. "Thank you for the visit, Captain. The executive committee has work to do. Floyd, if you could see her out?"

Thiessen swept past, taking Benson by the elbow and escorting her through the cold, lifeless, youthful faces of the Gulmar executive leadership. He whispered in her ear: assurances everything was going to be okay; compliments about the way she'd handled Trang's ambush; tales of people who had fainted during negotiations with the old woman.

Then they were in the air, headed away from the towers, Benson's head spinning and heart pounding. She had come to negotiate for the future of the Republic.

And she had failed.

15

They were nearing the outer edges of the city, where the exhaust hunkered down like clay dust. Thiessen turned toward a squat building and descended, and their shuttle was swallowed by the smoke. Benson's throat itched, even though the air inside the shuttle was recirculated.

She did her best to remain calm. "I know it's my imagination, but it feels like there's grit in my mouth."

"I know." The shuttle decelerated; the descent slowed. His eyes were fixed on the heads-up display lighting the opaque windshield. "It's your imagination. Trust me. When you walk through it, you'll know. It's sort of sulfuric. If you get a lot on your skin, it can burn over time."

"And people *live* here?"

"It's affordable. Winds blow in most nights, carrying everything out to sea. Or over the slums."

The shuttle came to a jarring stop, and Benson's harness tightened. "What are we doing here?"

Thiessen's fingers danced over the console. "We've got some time to kill."

"All right. So we came here why?"

"Well, it's my apartment."

She tensed. "I'm not—"

The pilot blushed. "Whoa! Wait! No offense, but I'm not coming onto you, Captain. Pretty women are a commodity here. Anyway, you're not really my type."

Benson clenched her jaw tight. "Thank you?"

"Oh. Yeah. That came out wrong." He slumped. "Let me try that again from the beginning."

"Please."

He tried on a charming smile. "Hey, we've got some time to kill before the executive committee calls us back—would you like to see Voelker?"

"That's better. Unfortunately, I'm not really interested in your city."

"I don't mean within the walls. I mean the real city."

"The slums?"

"It's where I came from. You want to understand the people of the Union, you start with someplace like this."

"So we just go out to the slums?"

"Well, not dressed like this. Dressed appropriately, you'll be fine."

"And you just so happen to have clothes that will fit me in your apartment?"

He looked at the ceiling. "What I said about women being readily available? I wasn't kidding. You're perfectly safe."

Benson was in Gulmar space as a diplomat. She was protected. In theory, she was respected. But above all, she was expected to make a deal with the people in power, to secure an alliance that would improve the odds of survival against the Azoren threat. And now the Khanate threat seemed even graver.

She unbuckled her harness. "All right."

Thiessen popped the side hatch, and the sulfuric tang he'd described hit. Her throat burned, and her eyes teared up. She stumbled getting out, hacking uncontrollably.

He put an arm around her. "It's the first time. Sorry about that. It gets better. The roof access is just over here."

Coughing and nearly blind, she didn't really have much choice but to let him guide her. After an eternity in the orange haze, a stained door resolved; he opened it. There were steps down: black and rusty. She gripped the rail, and the rust came away.

Not rust: the smoke. It was a heavy particulate sediment on the steps.

There was a door at the bottom of the steps and more stairs down. He took the door, and after a quick turn had them at an elevator. The air inside was easier to breathe, and her tears dried up as the car arrived.

The pilot's apartment was three floors down, a modest studio layout with a loft. Heavy drapes covered the windows. There were absolutely no feminine touches to the place, although it was clean enough.

She crossed to the drapes, still coughing softly. "You like green?"

"On sale when I got my first long-term piloting gig."

"They go nicely with the carpeting."

He took a glass from a cabinet over the small stove. "That came with the place. Brown wouldn't have been my first choice."

"It hides dirt nicely."

The faucet grumbled as he filled the glass. "I'm not sure you really want to hide dirt, do you?"

She took the glass from him. The water looked clear enough, but it had a definite metallic taste. Or maybe that was the smoke? She finished the drink off and handed him the glass. "Thanks. So. I've seen how the winners live."

"If you meant that sarcastically, you're wrong. I'm successful."

"I'm not sure how I meant it. Other than you mentioned clothes?"

"I did." He scurried into his bedroom, squeezing between the bed and a wall separating the sleeping space from the kitchen. A moment later, he returned with two hangers that held dull, white, almost shapeless cloth. "This is a *mykla*."

"*Mykla?*"

"We've evolved our own dialect here. It means 'common clothes.'" He pulled one outfit from its hangar. "The material is cheap, it breathes well, and it wicks away water. Most people save up to buy an ultraviolet resistant suit for the summer. These are basic."

What he handed her amounted to a baggy jacket and loose pants. Zippers could be used to lengthen the sleeves and legs. Straps on the ankles and wrists could tighten the material there. "Is this...clean?"

"Cleaner than anything you'll see down there."

She sniffed it and caught a hint of…detergent? "If it's safe to move around down there, why the wall?"

"It's safe if you look like you belong. Otherwise, there can be trouble."

"Such as?"

"Murder. Rape."

Her stomach knotted. "That doesn't sound safe at all."

"You'll fit in fine. Anyway, I always have a sidearm with me." He showed her the inside of his *mykla* jacket, which had a holster sewn in. A white, shiny plastic weapon rested inside the holster.

"Is that real?"

"Six shots. 12mm. Disposable."

"Okay. Is that *legal?*"

"I'm cleared for it. Unfortunately, anyone inside these walls is legally cleared to kill anyone outside these walls."

"That's…"

He winced. "I know. The bathroom's back there, near the entry."

She let herself in and locked the door. There was a hook on the inside of the door with a hanger. She undressed slowly, listening in between pulling off her jacket and pants: quiet. When she was down to her underwear, she checked the medicine cabinet. There were no surprises, although she did cock an eyebrow at the presence of a fertility suppressant dispenser. Most men in Kedraalian space took their own sperm suppressant pills, just to be safe. Perhaps Gulmar women had some reason not to count on that.

The *mykla* material was surprisingly soft and despite it feeling thick was actually light. She had to unzip the legs and sleeves fully to cover her wrists and ankles, but the clothes fit. She twisted and stretched to test everything and was satisfied.

Thiessen stood in the small living space, pulling on dull, orange shoes. He'd set a second pair out for her. It was the same concept: sturdy, simple, and adjustable. "What d'you think?"

"Comfortable. A lot more comfortable than my uniform."

"We're not much for painted-on clothing down there."

"I don't care for tight clothes, actually, but we're encouraged to have our uniforms tailored—"

"I wasn't judging, Captain."

She smiled, realizing how ridiculous it must seem to become defensive over clothes. "Do we fly there?"

The Gulmar pilot chuckled. "That would shatter the illusion."

He led her back out to the elevator, then tapped the bottom key. When well-dressed people got on, they frowned and edged into the corners, away from the two of them.

In the basement, expensive and stylish vehicles sparkled beneath bright white lights. Orange dust piled around columns and walls, but the vehicles were immaculate.

At least those vehicles visible from the elevator.

Thiessen escorted her past those vehicles, going deeper until the lights were dim and the parking spaces mostly empty. Finally, he pointed ahead, where a large, white, dust-coated, and scraped bus stood. It looked like it could hold ten or twelve passengers.

Benson stopped. "Does that even work?"

"I've rebuilt the engine a few times and rewired it. It may not look like much, but it works. And it fits right in."

"You really know how to—" She stopped herself. She'd nearly said *show a girl a good time*. It was humor meant for someone she knew, and it might not even be appropriate on Radetta. "I hope it's not offensive to say you really know how to live it up."

"That's a compliment. Thanks."

He pried the door open, scraped a boot through orange sediment collected on the steps, then let her aboard before settling in front of her in the driver's seat. The interior had the same sulfuric smell as the air on the roof, but there was also the stench of body odor. Rather than harnesses, the passenger seats had belts. Those were stained, the buckles rusty and scraped. Surprisingly, when he powered the vehicle on, the engine hummed softly. The drive was even more surprising: smooth and responsive.

Once on the street, the ochre fog was once again thick. The vehicle's wipers kicked on almost immediately, squeaking and streaking across the windshield. Thiessen seemed unaffected, merging into traffic and speeding along until they were at the giant gate, where he was waved through by a squinting guard.

The Gulmar pilot craned his neck enough to call over his shoulder. "Normally, I take some people with me when I go out."

"Friends?"

"Sure. Day laborers and live-in assistants and the like. Folks like to visit relatives."

"Oh. That adds to authenticity?"

"Mostly it's just nice to have people to talk to."

"That guard gave you a look."

"A lot of people like to forget where they come from. You get inside the walls, it's easy to buy into the resentment and propaganda."

Benson sat back. The road outside the city was mostly clear, and the bus was managing a good speed. "Do you miss home?"

"No." He straightened in his seat. "I miss family."

"They can't move inside the wall?"

"They don't have the skills to get a job."

"But you did?"

"I got lucky. I was a natural with engines and motors. There were opportunities with the Haidakura, and I took them. That got me piloting training eventually, then I was able to return here."

Corporate-owned cities, continents, and planets. It was crazy. "Has there ever been any attempt to change the balance of power?"

"Overthrow the Gulmar Conglomerate?" He leaned forward in his seat. "I guess the Haidakura could try something like that, if they wanted. They run most of the security operations. But they have seats on the board of directors, so they share power already. Maybe the Norvus Group and Takeshi Companies could try something. I can't see them doing that, though. They're all making money the way things are right now."

And that was all that mattered, apparently.

Through the grimy windshield, the outskirts of the slums came into view. The road became pitted, forcing Thiessen to slow down. A minute later, they were through the outskirts of the place, rocking as the wheels fell into holes or rolled over bumps. People dressed in *mykla* wandered around, sometimes stopping to glance at the vehicle.

There were no glares, though. Everyone just seemed curious.

People coming home from work. Family.

Thiessen drove with confidence, taking turns onto unlabeled streets, waving at people, and finally pulling into an open lot where three other buses were parked. He unbuckled and descended the steps to push the door open.

A bearded young man with stained and crooked teeth approached, head tilted sideways. "Floyd, zatyou?"

The pilot hurried over to the bearded man and extended a hand, apparently unconcerned with the dirt caking his nails and palms. "Hey! You still have 202 running?"

The bearded man squinted at Benson, then jerked his head toward the bus farthest from theirs. "The regulator short."

"I should have some time off this weekend. You want me to give it a look?"

"Yeahyeah."

Thiessen caught the other man squinting at Benson again and smiled. "Pretty, huh?"

"Yeahyeah."

"I'm taking her to see Gillian."

"Uh." The bearded man's head bowed. "Say hi, huh."

"Will do."

Benson waited until the other man had returned to the side of the building adjoining the parking area, then fell in beside the Gulmar pilot. "What was that about?"

"Gillian's my sister. Ramon used to be sweet on her."

"Why'd you call me...pretty?"

Thiessen shrugged. "You are. It's just guy talk. Sorry."

"Is he trouble?"

"Ramon?" The pilot glanced back over his shoulder. "No. He's just like other people: curious. And lonely."

"I thought you said there were a lot of...pretty women."

"Out here? Not really. The pretty ones find work inside the wall."

Work. *Sex* work. She wanted to pick up the pace, but she wasn't sure where they were going. The assortment of rusty and cracked cargo containers, shacks, mud huts, and small modular buildings seemed like a maze of repeating patterns. Even the people they passed looked the same: sad, tired, worn down.

Thiessen turned toward one of the mud huts. "This won't take long."

It was a tight space, maybe half the size of his apartment. Inside, the intensity of body odor was only overcome by sickness. The place was all one room, with a bed of blankets in each corner. In the center was a small space for a stove and some preparation materials: banged-up pots, pans, and clay bowls. Buzzing came from everywhere, and the occasional black shape darted in and out of the open windows, which had been fashioned from clear plastic sheets.

Benson coughed. "Sorry. That exhaust."

The pilot nodded, distracted. He headed to the bed across from the door and to the right, where a spindly, greasy-haired woman slept. She was wrinkled, her eyes sunken. Something moved to Benson's left: a small, dark-eyed baby naked except for a stained diaper. Darker than Thiessen, with a head of beautiful brown curls, it had been hidden in the shadows, or maybe it had been covered by some of the bedding. Now it watched her.

"This is Gillian." Thiessen's voice snapped Benson out of the moment. He had helped the older woman up.

He'd said sister, but the woman looked old enough to be his mother. Her outfit was tattered and stained and couldn't do a thing to hide her bony body. Benson swallowed. "Nice to meet you."

The woman smiled, exposing a few teeth and lots of gaps. She shuffled over to the baby and lifted it with some effort, then headed out through the open door. The baby never took its eyes off Benson until Gillian disappeared around another shack.

Thiessen cleared his throat. "I gave her some money."

Where would someone start with money? Food? Clothes? There wasn't even running water. "You're close?"

"Family. But Lori, she's my little darling."

"The baby?"

He nodded. "She has a heart defect. I'm trying to save up for surgery."

Was this all an exercise to soften up a diplomat, to make her weak when it came time to negotiate? The Gulmar had a well-earned reputation for manipulating people's emotions. It was amazing to see how malleable even educated, skeptical people were when the marketer knew their craft.

Benson swallowed. "I'm sorry to hear that."

"Don't be. She's one of the lucky ones. No one here can afford medicine or even visiting a doctor. A lot of kids won't make it to fifteen."

"You mind me asking why you would even bother having kids if that's the case?"

"It's sort of encouraged. We're a labor force, potentially."

"With all the robotics and automation, there are still jobs?"

"Humans can be a lot cheaper than robots. It's just about how you treat them. C'mon, I want you to meet Mills."

"Mills?"

Thiessen stepped back onto the street, then turned left. "My brother."

They passed more shacks and boxes until Benson was completely turned around. If she lost track of her host, she wasn't getting out of the place. Fortunately, it wasn't long before he crossed the street and entered a somewhat large building.

Inside, there were rickety chairs and tables and a bar that looked like it had been taken from a junk pile. Two men—bent, big—were slumped at the bar. One of them twisted around, cast a red eye at Thiessen, then swatted the other on the shoulder.

The other man turned, revealing someone nearly as old as Gillian. There might have been some shared features between the three, but Benson couldn't see it.

After a second, the pilot patted Benson on the back. "Mills, this is Benson."

The older man screwed up his eyes. "What kinda name is that?"

"She's from a different planet."

Mills grunted. "Never a good thing, being from somewhere else." He brushed greasy, thinning hair from his brow with a hand that was missing its pinky and a slice of flesh below.

Benson pushed back the onset of a headache. "Nice to meet you."

The older man twisted back around and stared into the chipped and puckered mirror behind the bar, studying her. "You an executive or something?"

"Mili—" She straightened. "Security."

"Yeah, figured as much. That's the easy way to rise up, ain't it, Big Brother?"

He's the younger brother? Benson shook her head. "I don't know that I've ever heard anyone describe security as easy."

"It's not like loading and unloading. Working the docks."

"That's—" She cleared her throat. "—hard work."

"Damn straight. It's how a man gets recognized. It's how you move up."

"What, um, what sort of job do you have your eye on? When you move up, I mean."

Mills turned around again, a shot glass squeezed between his remaining digits. "Gonna have one of those towers myself one day. Run a business."

"Run a—" Benson caught the smirk on Thiessen's face. He knew this routine.

"Figure the Gulmar family lose people every year." Mills stared out through the open door. "One day, they'll need someone like me—hard worker, determined."

"And you'll get...promoted?"

"Run a business! Live like a king! Why not? Look at everyone else. Lazy and undisciplined, listening to those damned Moskav spies. Fuck 'em!"

Thiessen nodded. "I gave Gillian some money. She's going to buy Lori some medicine."

"Yeah." Mills slumped and then turned back around. "Give her money."

"Maybe you could check in on her?"

The hand missing a finger came up, waving them away. "Sure. Doesn't deserve it. Never worked a day in her life."

"Thanks."

"You just remember where you came from, Big Brother. Everyone's wise to your games now."

Thiessen's eyes widened. He pushed past Benson and hurried into the street, breathing hard. She waited until they were some distance away, moving quickly, then moved closer. "A real charmer."

"Isn't he."

"What about your parents?"

"People don't live to an old age here."

"Oh. He said there are spies."

"Some. Not many."

"Moskav spies?"

"Among others. The one thing the executive committee'll spend money on is rooting out spies. People will sell out family for the kind of money being offered for reward."

"So there are other spies?"

The pilot arched a brow at her. "Azoren, Kedraalian... You do know we're competitors, right? You have spies here, and we have spies in Kedraalian space."

"Okay. But how would the Azoren get spies embedded here?"

Thiessen snorted. "You think there's a big difference between their beliefs and ours?"

"I-I'd always thought so."

He picked up the pace even more. "Yeah, well, I'm not so sure."

The parking area with the buses came into view, but the pilot didn't slow down. Benson's *mykla* felt hot and heavy, the dirt rising from the street choking. "Floyd, can we slow down?"

"We're almost there."

"I'm having a hard time breathing."

He slowed, but his lips were twisted down angrily. "We need to hurry back."

"What's the rush? I thought you wanted to show me the real city."

"You've seen enough, haven't you?"

Benson glanced around as they entered the parking area. There were small clusters of men moving toward them, not quite matching their speed but following. Other people moved away from the men, melting into alleys or structures.

She tapped the pilot's shoulder. "We're being followed."

"I know."

He sped up again, coming to a stop at the bus and waving her up the steps.

The men following them hurried into the area and made a beeline toward the bus. Thiessen unzipped his top and pulled out the pistol, flashing it over his head. "Time to head back home, fellas."

That froze the men in place, except for a big one with wild hair. He stepped forward, pointing a beefy finger at the bus. "Gonna want her."

"Nope."

"Gonna want her, *Floyd*."

Benson recoiled. These men knew him!

"Go home." Thiessen pointed the pistol at the speaker. "Now. Last chance."

The big man moved closer. "Think we'll be taking—"

Thiessen aimed at the other man's leg and fired. The shot was like a thunderclap. Instantly, the man collapsed, clutching his leg. Blood slipped between his thick fingers.

"Get him out of here!" The pilot pointed the gun at the others.

They dragged the groaning man away, and Thiessen rushed onto the bus, sealing it up and pulling out more aggressively than was probably safe. They darted down one road and then another, and a few minutes later they were headed toward the edge of the slums. Something cracked against one of the windows: a muddy rock. The glass was spiderwebbed.

The pilot barely glanced at it. "Sorry about that."

Benson's heart pounded. "Was that—"

"Normal? No. Spies stirred them up, I guess. You saw what you needed to see. That's what matters."

"It's terrible."

"The lifestyle? It's not that bad. Not if everyone lived the same, at least."

"Wouldn't it be better if everyone lived a nicer life?"

"Sure. You think that's going to happen? You think the people behind the wall have any interest in making things better for everyone?"

Benson tightened her seatbelt. "What next?"

"A meeting with the executive committee." Thiessen pulled a small tablet from his jacket. "They'll be ready for us in a little while. Time to see if you understand us after all."

Benson sniffed at the fabric of the *mykla*, remembering the filth and misery. Did she understand the people of the city?

Perhaps. Maybe she understood them more than the executives.

She was going to have to figure them all out soon enough, though. Negotiations were just around the corner.

16

Benson scratched at her arm, imagining she could still feel the slimy water from Thiessen's shower on her flesh. Despite soap and a nice perfume he'd let her use, she couldn't shake the faint sulfuric smell that had gotten under her skin and onto her tongue. The slickness felt and tasted alien, like she needed to scrub her mouth with a brush. She was going to need a full medical workup from Dietrich once she got back to the *Valor*. Parasites, bacteria…she'd been exposed to *something*, she was sure.

Thiessen turned in the shuttle pilot seat to regard her. "You going to be all right? I could ask for a delay."

"Hm?"

The engines thrummed, and the orange smoke swirled, but they hadn't lifted off yet. "You look like you're gonna throw up."

"It's just the water."

"They'll have alcohol in the boardroom. That washes away a lot."

"That sounds good, actually."

"Okay." He pulled back on the controls, and the engines revved higher. Before long, they were out of the smoke, above the city, and headed toward the towers. "It's pretty this time of day."

It was—the sun starting its downward fall, the sky taking on the colors of the exhaust plumes and a deep coral. Lights were slowly coming to life along the rooftops, flickering like torches in the haze. Even the towers took on an impressive, majestic air, rising like platinum spires topped by huge bowls of fire.

Thiessen set down on the rooftop pad, and Benson realized there were actually other pads. Maybe ten shuttles of much more impressive design rested on other sections of the three towers. Each shuttle was emblazoned with the Gulmar Union flag along with other symbols.

Corporate logos.

The young man who'd met them before was engaged with an older man when Benson stepped out of the elevator. Unlike the executive assistant, the older man was hunched, skinny, anemic. His pale, blue eyes bugged out as they twitched in her direction. His thin lips parted in a sickly smile that exposed crooked teeth.

Thiessen leaned close to her ear. "Ambassador Anders Manshaus."

She turned away from the old man. "They've invited the Azoren ambassador?"

"It's an executive committee meeting."

"The Azoren ordered a Haidakura executive kidnapping. They were trying to steal your defense system codes."

"That's what you're trying to convince them of. He's doing the opposite."

A faint odor of cleaning chemicals brought Benson around as the scrape of shoes reached her ear. Manshaus came to a stop too close to her, still smiling. He brushed back wispy, blond hair streaked white. "Captain Faith Benson?"

She shivered. "Ambassador Manshaus. I'm sorry for not recognizing you."

He bowed, which emphasized the appearance of having caved in on himself. "Does the Kedraalian Republic seek to normalize relations with those who scorned it?"

"I'm sure the Republic would welcome healthy relations with everyone once peace becomes an accepted goal."

"The Azoren Federation has ever sought a unified peace."

"I'll be sure to convey that to the prime minister."

"Ah, and how is Minister Zenawi?" There was a mischievous gleam to the old man's eyes.

Of course he knew about the transition of power. Did he know Zenawi's coalition was on the verge of collapse? Were the Azoren behind any of the efforts to destabilize the Kedraalian government?

The executive assistant cleared his throat. "Captain Benson? Ambassador Manshaus?" The young man combined a wave and a bow, then headed toward the glass wall at the end of the hallways.

Thiessen didn't move.

Benson hovered, unsure whether she should rush after the young man or stay with the pilot. "You're not going in?"

"Not for an executive committee meeting like this, no."

"Will they have a militar—a security representative?"

Manshaus chortled. "Security is an operating expense. The directors watch the bottom line with the intensity of a hawk, Captain." The ambassador shuffled after the young man.

Thiessen didn't seem bothered in the least. "I'll wait for you."

Benson followed the Azoren diplomat through the glass doors and did her best not to react to the sight of the people filling the conference room. They were the same group of youthful-looking husks that had been waiting outside when the first meeting with Trang had concluded so abruptly. Now those people stood in little clusters, softly chatting, munching on plates of food served from an impressive table at the far end of the room, oblivious to the diplomats. The spread probably cost more than a family in the slums made in a lifetime.

Benson was rooted in place. She didn't have much of a stomach for pomp and circumstance, but being ignored...

An older man in one of the clusters seemed to take note of her and the ambassador, then turned back to his three comrades. The four of them drifted over, smiling convincingly. They all appeared older than the rest of the executives, and there was a weariness in their eyes that seemed reflected in their clothes, which lacked some of the stylish accents of their comrades. The woman among the four wore a skirt that reached mid-shin, hiding thick calves that lacked the shapely toning flashed by the other women. None of the elderly executives flashed the sort of jewelry their comrades favored.

The man who'd spotted Benson seemed to be the apparent leader of the group. He had thick brown hair creeping back in a high widow's peak and the sort of waxen skin that seemed to highlight his stubble, which sparkled silver in the conference room light. "Ambassador. Captain."

Manshaus bowed. "Mr. Cartwright. How has the transition been to the new defense grid?"

"Excellent. Thank you."

"If the Azoren Federation can in any way provide assistance, do not hesitate to call upon us."

"You know we won't."

Cartwright's dark eyes sparkled as he looked up at Benson. "I understand you arrived just this morning, Captain." His breath was stale, his teeth more yellow than the others.

"I did."

"What do you think of Voelker?"

"Oh, I haven't had enough time to appreciate a place like this, I'm afraid."

A rumbling shook the executive's chest. "That's a very diplomatic thing for a military officer to say, now isn't it? I mean, it's a terrifying sight, don't you think? Have you seen the slums?"

The other three executives frowned for a moment, then they put on cold smiles.

Benson knew the man's words were a trap or a test but couldn't get a sense of his intent. "Actually, Mr. Cartwright, the truly terrifying sight was finding the remnants of your fleet waiting for us."

Manshaus's big eyes narrowed. "There has been an incident with Security Fleet One?"

Cartwright coughed. "I'm surprised you haven't seen the official report, Anders."

"Was it made available?"

The four older executives exchanged a look, but before they could say anything more, a pleasant chime played from speakers embedded in the walls, and Leona Trang moved to the head of the table.

She clasped her hands in front of her. "We should begin."

Beautiful and stylish executives bustled past, one of them pointing to a seat closer to Trang's. Benson caught a glimpse of the Azoren diplomat scurrying behind the executive director, then took the indicated seat. Manshaus dropped into the chair opposite.

Trang pulled her chair in closer and waved to the Azoren and Kedraalian guests. "We've had a chance to review the latest data. Now it's time to discuss our alternatives. Captain Benson, perhaps you wouldn't mind presenting the message you brought from Prime Minister Zenawi?"

In front of the ambassador. No one had said that would happen, but if Trang wanted to operate that way…

"Thank you." Benson turned toward the other executives. "You've been briefed on the threat the Kedraalian government perceives in the Azoren Federation."

Manshaus's bushy eyebrows arched.

Benson set her hands on her lap, out of sight, hoping to hide their shaking. "I'm afraid the latest event shows us that threat has been eclipsed by that presented by the Khanate."

The Azoren ambassador held a finger up. "If I might, Captain?"

"I haven't presented the case of the Kedraalian government yet."

"This is true. Yet you have already spoken of my government. I would seek the opportunity to provide clarity."

"All right." Benson squeezed her hands tight.

The old man straightened in his chair, and the ever-present toothy smile broadened into something a little warmer. "As the fine colleagues of the Gulmar Union know, it is the position of the Azoren Federation that we should all seek solutions to problems before matters escalate to—" He wrinkled his face in disgust. "—violence. Whatever unfortunate circumstances have led to the instability and tumult facing the noble but misguided Kedraalian Republic that was founded so many years ago to provide hope for our people, there is no justification for lashing out and projecting fault upon those of us who bristled against the yoke of totalitarian intolerance and thus rightly demanded our freedom."

Heat flashed through Benson. Intolerance? Projecting fault? Manshaus was engaging in the most pathetic and amateurish political ploy of stealing the words of an opponent to hijack the message. It was a ridiculous and petty approach that should have been below the station of a diplomat, and it was wasting the time of people who would obviously see through—

Trang nodded somberly. "We're well aware of the Kedraalian affinity for war, Ambassador."

Benson leaned forward. "What?"

"No one is going to forget that your government fired the first shots when citizens demanded liberty, Captain."

"Wait. Stop. This isn't going to help anyone. Ambassador Manshaus, my point—"

"Captain!" Trang leaned back in her seat. "I realize that in the military, you're used to having authority, but this is my boardroom, and this is my meeting."

"I appreciate that. But I get the sense you don't understand the sort of threat you're up against."

"Are you making a threat? Will your task force attack us?"

"I'm referring to the Khanate. You've seen the data we recovered from what little survived of your ships. They obliterated your fleet. They destroyed two of my ships."

"We'll have our security experts analyze the data."

"Please do. But I want to save you time, because there's a lot more at stake than you seem to grasp."

"Don't condescend, Captain. I really am quite capable, thank you."

Benson turned to Manshaus. "I'm sure you've seen the report."

The old diplomat's eyes flew wide. "What report could you possibly—?"

"We don't have time for this. The ships you attacked Kedraal with? They wouldn't have stood a chance against this Khanate fleet."

"Are you saying we committed attacks against the Kedraalian Republic?"

A groan slipped from Benson. "Don't you all understand? This is an existential threat! The Khanate has a history. They're genocidal on a scale beyond even the Azoren!"

Manshaus gasped and bowed his head. "I must protest this language."

"Executive Director Trang, bring in your security experts. Bring in Captain Thiessen. Have them look at the data."

Trang closed her eyes, and her face tightened. "Captain Benson—"

"These people are radicals! They're ideological lunatics! They've killed hundreds of thousands, and that was when they had a backwards military. That fleet they have is—"

"Captain!"

Benson's nails dug into the palms of her hands. "Time matters. Alarms should be ringing right now."

Someone coughed farther down the table: the old man, Cartwright. "Leona, the data *was* pretty clear. The fleet was destroyed within minutes."

Trang's lips stretched into a thin smile. "Thank you, Gordon."

"We know there were spies aboard. Bombs detonated."

"So you said."

"What the captain is saying is sound. For whatever reason, the Khanate chose to attack us first, but if the fleet they've put into space is as capable as she's said, then everyone is at risk." Cartwright wagged a finger at Manshaus. "Even the Azoren, Anders. I'm sure your spies have had a chance to brief you about this by now."

Manshaus shook his head again. "Spies? Such claims are hurtful."

The theater and absurdity of it all had Benson's gut twisting. She was no longer concerned about the slickness on her tongue, but she did need a drink. How could these people look at hard data—*irrefutable data!*—and not act? "Executive Director Trang, I've been given substantial leeway in my role as negotiator. The task force I have at my disposal is capable, but I don't believe it's ideal to stand against this Khanate fleet."

"So you want us to spend the millions of credits it would take to activate our second fleet to aid you? We're facing scrutiny in our budgeting this year. It would be cheaper to simply pay off whatever demands they have."

Challenging the idea that the electorate might somehow vote out their leadership—that the electoral system even had the capability to support a change in power—wasn't the right approach. Then again, there didn't seem to be any approach at all. Perhaps the Gulmar leadership were simply looking to position themselves to absorb as little risk as possible, but it felt like they didn't comprehend the gravity of the threat. The idea of hiring their military—their security forces outright…?

Benson stood. "There's no value in spending any more time on this."

For a second, Trang's eyelids fluttered: She hadn't expected that. "Captain—"

"Excuse me, Executive Director. I believe what you're looking for and what the Republic is offering are too far apart to be of value. Ambassador Manshaus, perhaps the Azoren would be open to discussions about an alliance against a threat of this magnitude."

Cartwright's head swiveled, and he shook his finger at Benson. "You hear that? If you needed proof that the Haidakura should be handling these negotiations, that's it right there!"

The soft chime sounded again, and Trang pushed to her feet. "I believe it's time for a break."

Murmurs ran through the executives, who seemed caught up in their own debates.

Trang motioned toward the door. "Captain."

Benson spun on a heel and hurried out, stopping a few meters beyond the door at Trang's voice. "Captain! A moment."

There was no haste in the executive director's stride, but the fact that she was exiting the boardroom while her team debated what had been said spoke volumes. Behind her, the Azoren diplomatic doddered, bugged-out eyes latched onto the two women.

At the end of the hallway, Thiessen stood straight, lips compressed.

Storming away wasn't an option, so Benson drew up. "Yes?"

Trang stopped. "I'll see if I can arrange a contract for you to take back to your parliament."

"A…contract?"

"Activating the fleet will be a significant economic blow. I'm not even sure we can create a popular enough narrative to support it. It would be easier if the ships were fully automated, but that's even more expensive."

"You want me to take a contract proposal back to the prime minister…?"

"Our security forces don't work for free."

"They're meant to defend you."

The smile on Manshaus's face spread wider as the two argued. He truly was a malevolent soul.

Trang glanced over her shoulder at the closed glass door. Her executives were arguing back there, possibly considering ousting her. "Take it or leave it, Captain."

"Transmit it to the *Valor*, please."

"We'll need to iron out the details. I'll see if I can reach consensus on a steering committee to develop the parameters of the framework."

Committee. Parameters. Framework. "How long do you expect that to take?"

"Given the criticality of the matter, the committee should be able to come together within a week or two."

"A…week?"

"Or two."

"The Khanate fleet is out there! They could strike anytime, anywhere."

"So you've said. It was interesting meeting you, Captain."

The executive director turned, nodded at the ambassador, then reentered the conference room.

Manshaus laughed and clapped his hands together. "Brilliant maneuvering!"

Benson spun around and strode to Thiessen, who glared at the glass wall. He bowed slightly toward the Azoren diplomat, who had trailed behind Benson. "Ambassador."

"Captain Thiessen. You are well?"

"I'm not sure yet." The pilot tilted his head toward Benson. "What happened?"

"I suppose I'm on hold, waiting for a *contract proposal* that I'm expected to transport back to Kedraal for further deliberations." She sighed. "Did the galaxy go mad?"

The ambassador pinched his chin. "Some might say it did long ago."

"By creating inferior humans? Is that right?"

"You assume a monolithic fervency for uncomfortable doctrine among my people that I assure you does not exist."

"You're a diplomat. Are you trying to tell me that the Azoren would—"

"Captain…" Manshaus deployed his toothy smile. "Do you seriously believe that my assignment holds the prestige of, say, your own? The Supreme Leader holds diplomacy in quite low regard, I can assure you."

"But he values spies."

The hunched diplomat coughed. "We all do."

"Not me."

"You should. The value of a well-established spy network can never be overstated."

Thiessen waved to the elevator. "Sounds like we've been dismissed."

"Indeed we have." The diplomat's eyebrows fluttered. "Might I have a ride with you? Perhaps to discuss further the idea broached in the conference?"

"Idea?"

Benson slumped. "If your government won't activate your fleet, seeking an alliance with the Azoren might be our only choice."

"You'd do that?" The pilot sounded hurt.

"We have a fleet out there that could strike anywhere. It could be heading for Kedraalian space right now."

Manshaus grunted. "Or Azoren space, yes. I have made such a point already."

"So you are a spy."

"Me? No." He chuckled dryly. "I am too old for that. But I do know a few."

Thiessen slapped the elevator button, then shoved his hands in his pockets. It was an uncomfortable ride to the roof, with even the ambassador keeping his head down until they reached the shuttle.

The old man stepped back with a raspy hack. "I could talk to the captain later, if you would prefer, Captain Thiessen?"

"No. I'm just trying to figure this all out." The Gulmar captain opened the shuttle and climbed inside. He dropped into the pilot seat and studied the skyline, which had darkened. "This is the way they operate. Everything takes time, and they have to work out the costs."

Benson buckled in. "I understand that. Government always moves slowly. Except when survival is at risk."

Thiessen grumbled beneath his breath, then powered the shuttle on and sealed the door. They lifted off, and below them, the city looked like a lake reflecting stars. Benson's breath caught at the surprising beauty. Just as Thiessen had said, winds were blowing the pollution beyond the walls, revealing what could only be described as a remarkable design.

Then the lights on the buildings winked out, plunging the city into a frightening darkness.

"What—?" Benson searched around for any sign of an emergency.

Thiessen searched his console. "It's out: power, navigation, security."

The Azoren diplomat huffed. "Your infrastructure within the walls is admirable. This seems highly unlikely."

Lights streaked down from the heavens, plunging toward the city. Benson pointed at the glowing contrails with horror. "Missiles."

There were more than missiles: Khanate fighter craft.

They plunged through the atmosphere at terrible speed, glowing hot in the black of approaching night. Then they rammed into the Gulmar Towers, one after the other.

Fire blossomed like a miniature star forming in the heart of the towers.

War had come to the Gulmar Union.

17

McLeod swirled a spoon in the steaming mix of aromatic spices and herbal powders he'd taken to drinking since resuscitation. The honey-laced vapor floated through his office, mixing with the fragrance of cleaning oils coming off his heavy wooden desk. Fresh-scrubbed and rested, with a stomach full of nutrient-filled soup, Stiles was content to sip cool water as the colonel's wall display spat out a correlated summary of the data taken from the secret Ravens base. She'd seen the raw data pull: more than eighty petabytes compressed. It was an impressive haul, but the summary report didn't show any conclusive takeaways.

The colonel sipped his milky brew. "Maybe twenty more arrests. Twice as many people we can put under surveillance, assuming we can get the funding."

Stiles swallowed. "They're trying to cut our funding again?"

"This isn't the Ravens and Owls. Prime Minister Zenawi's in trouble."

"Representative Benson?"

McLeod sipped his tea. "The impossible appears to be possible. My contacts within parliament say she's close to forming a coalition. Zenawi hasn't come through on his promises, and it looks like things are getting worse on Dramora, not better."

"Could that be the work of one of the dark agencies?"

"I'm starting to believe *anything* is possible."

"They seemed earnest when they talked about their mission."

"Destroying the factions that broke off?"

"I think these organizations go back longer than we realize."

Steam rose around the older man's face. "There will always be shadows."

"When we broke off from Earth, how were people selected?"

"Candidates were ranked based on a lot of criteria: computer-driven intelligence and emotional scoring systems; education; experience; health; age; troublesome genetic markers."

"That sounds...problematic."

"But necessary. Unfortunately, the organization that ran the selection program had its own agenda."

"I hadn't heard about that."

The newly appointed director of counter-intelligence bowed his head. "It's an embarrassing oversight no one openly talks about."

"History is history, isn't it?"

"If only that were true. History is the interpretation of events in the eyes of the victor. For now, the sane claim that title, so the truth's been largely...forgotten. By most."

"Would I be able to hear that truth?"

McLeod took a long drink of the warm brew and set the cup on his desktop. "How much do you know about Earth?"

"Home of the human species. Wiped out by ecological disasters."

"Destroyed by greed and excess, but it's not necessarily wiped out. Pollution, wholesale devastation from extracting natural resources, a climate that became inhospitable... But there are still by most estimates a few billion people there."

"Living?"

"If you want to call it that. They're really only one pandemic or lunatic's nuclear salvo away from their final breath. By all accounts, those were the irredeemable. Unfortunately, the dispersion on the data of what qualified as redeemable appears to have been...off."

"The organization that ran the selection program?"

"A Norwegian-owned data analysis firm named for a group of islands off the west coast of the European continent. They were supposed to be unaffiliated with any of the crazy fringe groups so prevalent at the time, but someone didn't dig deep enough, or someone behind the Diaspora movement had an agenda of their own. Whichever it was, the Azoren Corporation let through thousands of people with problematic psychological profiles."

"Azoren? *The* Azoren?"

"They take their name from the corporation, which might explain why some of us are reluctant to believe this was a simple computer error."

Stiles took a long pull from her water container. "You think it's possible the Owls and Ravens were involved in this?"

"It seems more likely they're a reaction to it." He pointed to the summary report on the display. "Most of the people we've identified come from families that opposed the Diaspora Movement. They would've been content to leave everyone on Earth."

"Are they all powerful families like the Patels?"

"That's the most influential one."

"Then it makes sense to continue to focus on them."

McLeod drummed his fingers on his desktop. "Ultimately, I think they're just pawns. The real agenda runs deeper."

"Deeper than eliminating these dangerous ideologues?"

"When you remove the people who were forced into the populations of these radical movements, there really aren't that many people to eliminate, are there?"

"The Ravens seem to believe in guilt by association."

"A lot of these people were from families who fled Earth the second they could. They were victims of cultural persecution or other forms of trouble. They weren't what you'd consider typical followers."

"Then removing the organizational leaders should be enough."

The colonel rubbed where Gadreau had shot him. "Ideology is like a carcinogen. Even healthy people can succumb with sufficient exposure."

"That sounds like the Ravens' thinking."

"I'm not advocating for war, Lieutenant—I'm trying to prevent it."

Stiles rubbed her thumb along the smooth surface of the water container. There were times to talk and times to listen. Serving under

McLeod meant mostly listening. The man had been resuscitated despite rumored dangerous political affiliations and intrigues, then he'd been promoted. He was smart, resourceful, and without a doubt connected.

But she was having a hard time seeing the line that separated his views from the Ravens. "What about the Khanate threat?"

McLeod turned back to the display. "I'm still curious why we haven't found more about this threat."

"You don't think it's real?"

"Oh, this Dev Rai was certainly real enough. Apparently, SAID missed him."

"Does that make him an edge case, someone we shouldn't be concerned about?"

"Hardly. If anything, I'm more concerned about this Khanate threat than the Azoren or Moskav."

"I thought the Khanate had been crushed."

"And that doesn't concern you? We had some early successes against them, and by all accounts, the Azoren and Moskav finished the job. Yet this Dev Rai infiltrated Azoren and Gulmar organizations. That medallion was authentic. He had to have been senior in the Khanate organization—a trusted spy. Somehow, no one noticed him."

"So they could be anywhere?"

"Only the Azoren have notions of a singular ideal for our species. Gulmar, Khanate, and Moskav spies could be anyone. We have a good idea of who's spying for the Gulmar, and the Moskav are fairly crude in their methods."

"Have we heard anything back from the *Valor*, sir?"

"Not for a couple more weeks, assuming they get the Fold Space transmission."

Stiles pulled her data tablet out and downloaded the summary report. She had hundreds of queries of her own running against the captured data, but those queries were in the queue, waiting for approval. Without the filtered data, the summary report was her best look into the Ravens as the GSA now understood them.

Names from the report seemed to support the idea that the Ravens organization was made up of old families. Along with the Patels, she recognized the Aguayo, Janikowski, Morrison, Walker, and Xander families.

She powered the tablet back down. "What about the Owls, Colonel?"

The corner of the colonel's mouth turned down in a perplexed frown. "I don't think we've made any progress on them."

"Could they be a splinter group?"

"I think they're both splinter groups. The question is: What did they splinter from? They're obviously of different minds, but I'm not sure on what."

"Could the names answer that?"

"We've tried that angle. What separates the two birds? Where were they regionally on Earth? What history do they share? Nothing obvious jumps out."

"But you have studied them."

"We have. The leading theories point to the differences. Ravens are problem solvers. Owls are hunters. Ravens can be clever. Owls can be patient."

"Both came to the stars?"

"With some success. My understanding is that we lost too many species to ever fully understand them as they used to be. I'm not sure we can learn anything from studying them here, but we have videos available online."

"Thank you." Hunters. Problem solvers. "They sound like they both served distinct roles, but neither sounds like an organization that *leads*."

"No." McLeod leaned back in his chair. "Do you have a theory, Lieutenant?"

"If they were part of a larger organization, and they had separate roles, I think those roles might help define the organization."

The colonel stared off into space, then he nodded. "So what would this organization look like?"

"To need a patient group of hunters and another group of clever problem solvers, the organization would need an enemy or more broadly an objective."

"That's not helpful, Lieutenant."

"What sort of objective requires hunters and problem solvers?"

"Too broad. We've pursued that angle and had no success."

"But the problem solvers tried to eliminate me, sir. It sounded like they might have been behind the elimination of my family."

"I see. Since your…family was designed to help the GSA with its more *sensitive* jobs—"

"We were a problem. That means that this other organization would have to run counter to at least some of the GSA mandates."

"Since the Genesis program started as a means to further military efficiency, that might help refine the shape of this theoretical organization. Are you sure the Ravens were behind this?"

"They bragged about it. It sounded sincere."

"That adds some clarity." McLeod picked up his cup and swirled the spoon around again. "I'll pass that along to the team running this research."

Stiles squeezed the water container until her knuckles were white. "The Genesis program, sir?"

"Yes?"

"There isn't much data on it."

"Some things are best kept a secret."

"But you know about it?"

"Some." He looked up from his cup. "About Gen 3."

"Why did they stop with us? We may be peak human, but they could have created something more."

"You asked about the budget cuts before, whether it was Owls or Ravens."

"They brought the program to an end?"

"That's what it looks like, although I've never heard a clear answer on that. I know some of the scientists quit. Genetic engineering comes dangerously close to Azoren eugenics. Their Golden Child program apparently took off shortly after ours was shut down."

"Spies."

"It would explain a good deal."

"And the Gen 1 and Gen 2? Why is there so little data about them?"

"Gen 1 was a disaster. It almost ended the program before it started."

"A disease?"

"You could say that. From what I understand, the researchers started with the idea that you proposed: Take the human ideal and add in more."

"More as in adding non-human DNA?"

"Animal, maybe even alien. No official records exist, at least not that I can access."

"More human than human?"

"They called it Icarus after shutting it down."

"Icarus?"

"An old Earth tale about hubris."

"What about Gen 2? Was it more successful?"

"No one will ever know. The lead scientist behind that project disappeared. Rumor is, the samples remaining in the lab all failed to take when implanted."

"They had human mothers?"

"Volunteers. Mostly, it was infertile women who were given treatments in exchange for carrying these embryos."

"That's sad." Stiles looked away and blinked back a tear.

"That was more than three decades ago."

"But those women. Did they know they might lose these children?"

"I don't know."

"Did they know they were carrying…a Genesis?"

"Don't feel bad about your creation, Lieutenant. You're a human, whether you were born from a woman or an artificial womb. Your DNA is the same as anyone else's. It's just scrubbed of the vulnerabilities and flaws most of us have."

"And tweaked."

"Over millennia, we've given up some of the more beneficial traits our ancestors had. You're still human."

"Not in the eyes of these Ravens."

The colonel finished off his drink and returned the cup to his desk with a clatter of spoon and ceramic. "These Owls and Ravens have the exact same sort of commitment to their cause that separates you from average people. They don't see you as an inferior but as a challenge to their own mission. That's why they want to kill you, not because you're something inhuman."

"I won't let that drive me away from my objective, Colonel."

"Good." He pushed up from his chair and paced, his gait still a little awkward despite months of rehab. "Nothing we took out of that Ravens site has changed our situation. These secret organizations pose a threat to the Kedraalian government."

"They do."

McLeod smiled. "I don't think we have what it takes to change our approach."

"Then we focus on the Patels?"

"For now. Until someone breaks under questioning."

Stiles shivered at the memory of the freezing room. Her mind could block out pain in the moment, and she could transport her thinking to a completely different level, but the body remembered. "Will they be shown the sort of humane treatment I wasn't?"

The colonel scraped to a stop. "We can't become them."

"Because we're human."

"We are." He turned back to the display. "Are you ready for the next level?"

"The Patels?"

"You have carte blanche."

She snapped straight, nearly knocking her seat over. "I'll take them down, Colonel."

"Try to keep the damage to a minimum, Lieutenant." He bowed his head. "Maybe one of them will be the puzzle piece we're missing."

"Yes, sir." She took a step.

"Brianna?"

"Sir?"

"A little more caution, please. We can't lose you."

"I'll try."

Stiles hurried from his office, already assembling a list of things she needed to do before departing for the next leg of her investigation. Her body would heal quickly enough, especially now that she had access to the sort of treatment, nutrients, and rest she needed. Her mind was a different problem.

Not far from the room she had inside the GSA compound was a

sensory deprivation tank. No one else used it, so it became almost like a private pool for her. She let herself into the lab, peeled off her uniform, and slipped into the helmet that would monitor her vitals. A few moments later, she was floating in the thick fluid, and drifting off to sleep.

There was data to absorb—on the Ravens and Owls, on the Azoren and Khanate, and on humans. Data also needed to be purged: the damage done by her captors.

She set her mind to both tasks and to the future.

18

———

Data whipped past almost too fast for Satrap to absorb it, applying a pressure against his brain that felt as real as a punch, carrying with it an electric buzz louder than the rocket roar. Sweat collected under his arms and on his chest. The shuttle dedicated to his use—almost a small frigate, really—was amply accommodated, but his body had its needs, and stuffed in with the Jakkara and Ikhama, those needs weren't being met.

Night pushed in on the ship, but it was an incomplete darkness, broken by the fires of hatred. Satrap squeezed his eyes shut and triggered a drip of fluids that would moisten his parched throat. He'd tasted the fluids once, long ago, just to know what was going into him. They were sweet, like a diluted, floral honey.

You are in the data, not squeezed among soldiers and old Ikhama.

His mind cleared enough to make more sense of the digital flows.

Imagery filled his awareness: still shots of buildings falling in on themselves to be swallowed by fiery smoke; short videos of gray shapes running through the darkened streets—Gulmar citizens; sensor-enhanced input showing weapons fire tearing through structures and people alike.

The towers were down. The leadership had fallen. His plan was a success.

Rumbling brought him back to the now, where the shuttle hovered over a darkened rooftop. Fighter craft circled outside, the remote controllers seeking targets for those strapped inside the cockpits to destroy.

So many buildings were gone already: the towers, the reactor; the apartment buildings that were home to the highborn and powerful.

Without meaning to, Satrap returned his attention to the imagery.

It was the sensor-enhanced images that made it the worst. In many other images and videos, the Gulmar were indistinct, less than true data points. The sensors removed any doubt of what was happening. People were being torn to pieces. They were being buried beneath smoldering rubble. They were being burned alive.

He activated another drip, this one to dull the pain in his mind.

A new data feed: Captain Zohar was connecting from the *Might of the Khan.*

Satrap accepted. "Glory and power to our Khan, Captain."

Zohar frowned. "You mock the quest to bring about purity and justice."

"It isn't mockery but fatigue. Travel is a strain on my body. My limbs swell, and my joints burn."

"Only Satrap may bear witness to Great Khan how complete is the victory."

"Another blessing among the infinite."

"What has Ikhama seen?"

The old woman stared into a wide display anchored to an arm that connected to the shuttle ceiling. She had brought the display down to just above her thighs once they were into the atmosphere, and she hadn't looked up since. It was the same data feed Satrap was receiving but stripped down to video.

Satrap's stomach lurched as another of the fighter craft launched itself into a building that his systems identified as a Gulmar Conglomerate research facility. Sixty stories high, constructed with the arrogance only known to the truly successful—the initial impact took out three floors. While that wave of energy was still radiating out, the explosives packed into the rear of the fighter detonated.

Strained support beams disintegrated, and the upper floors lifted away from the lower ones, rising and collapsing in on themselves. Then, in a giant fireball, everything fell down. Waves of debris and superheated dust rolled out from the bottom of the falling building.

Another of the fighter craft dropped into the valley between the towers bracketing the main thoroughfare and accelerated toward the giant gate that had started to close at the first sign of the attack. Vehicles and pedestrians clogged that exit. There would be thousands there at this hour, citizens from the slums returning to their pathetic homes for a short night of sleep, breathing in the pollution and disease spilling out of the city proper.

The fighter plowed into a large bus meters short of the half-closed gate.

Close enough.

An explosion thundered. Fire slithered and climbed. The giant gates were torn off their hinges and slammed back.

How many innocents had been on the bus? In the vehicles? Running away?

War is a mad dog snapping and snarling. It cares not whom it hurts. It serves only itself. Take care that when you raise your sword, you strike at your target. Take greater care that your target is one who has struck at you.

Those had been the words of the Great and Holy Khan, his admonition against war.

One who has struck at you. It meant someone capable of defending themselves, never civilians. The Ikhama no longer interpreted it that way, but Satrap had seen the original context and the other parables around the writing, none of which had made it into the final text.

Age and disease had stolen much of the Great and Holy Khan's mind by the time his work was collected and published for all to absorb. Bitterness had stolen the words of wisdom. Thousands and thousands of the Khan's followers had been butchered without the ability to defend themselves, and that had contributed to the old man's collapse.

Zohar cleared his throat. "The video feeds come through now."

"Fire like the purifying touch of the sun. Do you think our Great and Holy Khan would be proud of us, Zohar?"

"I believe we fight back when pushed into a corner."

Ikhama looked up from her display. "You speak to Captain Zohar?"

Satrap bowed his head. "Would you as well?"

Her attention jumped back to the display for a moment, and a hint of sadness touched her face. "I would."

It was nothing for Satrap to establish the connection—nothing but a nauseating certainty that she would insert herself into the discussion as the word of the current Great Kahn. "Captain Zohar, Ikhama joins us."

The woman sucked in a breath. "Death can be troubling when seen with such clarity."

They were words Satrap hadn't expected. He closed his eyes to focus on the data exclusively. "A city with millions squeezed into a small space. No defenses stand against us."

"I saw a small shuttle flying for the starport."

Zohar grumbled over the scrape of fingernail on display. "The video lag is troubling. Where is this happening?"

"On the west side of the city." She exhaled with ghostly quiet.

"I will inform the landing teams to be aware of possible defense craft."

Satrap reviewed the data to be sure. "It's a civilian shuttle. It poses no threat."

Ikhama's head rocked back and forth. "*A robe might serve as warmth against the cold night, or it might serve as protection against sun and sand. A robe might act to reveal the curve of a lip before a kiss, or it might hide the edge of a blade meant to seek your heart.*"

"I have seen the shuttle signals. *It poses no threat.*"

Zohar sighed. "Threat or not, the assault on the starport begins soon. The Gulmar fighter aircraft have already been wiped from the skies. This shuttle will be destroyed as surely as every other ship or person found there."

Satrap waved away the words, an action only he could see. "The last of the critical buildings within the city wall has fallen. Fires will do the rest."

"Fire and the work of our people. Look."

After a few seconds, the captain's message came through: video of people moving within the city against the flow of traffic. Citizens headed toward low-value buildings that still stood.

Even as Satrap processed the video, more explosions lit the city below.

Of course. Many spies would have survived the first attacks. They would have been positioned for their deadly work, regardless of what could only be terrifying chaos.

The old woman bowed and muttered a prayer.

Satrap couldn't see what had provoked the reaction at first, then his attention was drawn to video from some of the reconnaissance shuttles that had now moved out to the slums. Within the heart of the maze of tumbledown shacks, large groups had gathered around fires to dance and cheer.

Downtrodden. Forgotten. Desperate.

Did they care at all for those who had lost relatives inside the city? Did they care at all for those whose miserable lives were now shattered?

It would be hard to care for anyone when there was only misery.

Zohar highlighted the area where the celebrations were in full swing. "Do we wish to alert these people to the incoming missiles?"

On the choppy, grainy video, the celebrants weren't mothers and children; they weren't fathers and laborers. They were vague shapes caught up in the joy of watching their oppressors collapse. Nothing guaranteed they were even Khanate resources.

"Let the missiles fall, Captain."

"What if these are our agents?"

"Unlikely. Where are the explosions that should lay low the slums? Blood should run in the streets already, if our agents were in place."

Ikhama's head came up. *"When you set the foundation for your home, you dig a trench for water to come in. You dig another trench to take away waste. Remember the danger of poison and set far apart the one from the other."*

Golden fire trailed from the heavens—missile exhaust. The deadly weapons were heading toward the slums.

A trench to drain away the poisonous waste.

Satrap switched his attention to the starport for a moment. Shuttles were landing there now, and data flowed in.

Gunfire. Unexpected resistance. Casualties.

The shuttles were lifting off again. Some were taking heavy fire.

Images: armored vehicles, soldiers with heavy weapons.

More aircraft were now scrambling from the starport. The shuttles were vulnerable.

"Captain Zohar." Satrap identified the problem areas. "We have the potential for a breakout."

"We have a sizable force engaging—"

"That sizable force is being crushed. Allocate missiles to the area."

"The intent was to try to capture aircraft. This was *your* plan."

"A plan that was based upon defective data. Fire salvos at the starport."

Zohar left the connection open as he engaged with the captains from the rest of the fleet. Precious seconds ticked by as the shuttles continued their fight with the unexpected Gulmar warriors.

Satrap reviewed the intelligence he'd been given on the city, searching for the starport.

Capable of supporting as many as forty defensive craft. Guarded by a small force of security personnel. Potentially a rally point for fleet operations, with the capacity to manage vessels as large as gunships and other small orbital craft.

There was nothing about a defense force capable of engaging—*destroying!*—a modest-sized strike team. Yet two shuttles were down now, and three others were seriously damaged. The ground assault teams were in shambles, with many reporting casualties.

Something had changed. Spies had failed.

Ikhama clasped her bony hands in front of her. "*Strike the cur when it growls. Strike the cur when it whimpers. Strike the cur when it bows its head. Only by striking the cur does it understand what awaits should it trouble you.*"

"The cur has already troubled me, Ikhama. We've lost security personnel."

"They go on to serve in our Great and Holy Khan's army as he readies to bring the light of the stars to the darkness of filth and decay."

Columns of fire rose in the distance, as missiles landed among the buildings of the slums.

"We've already brought as much light as these people will ever know."

"Blood shed from our brothers and sisters calls for fire."

In the video feed from the reconnaissance aircraft, the circle of fire expanded out from the center of the slum. Buildings burned or crumbled. There were no dancers. Few people even stood.

Satrap grunted and disconnected from the data flow for a moment and rubbed his eyes. There was no removing the data impression, though.

The old woman shook her head. "Do not mourn the infidel, Satrap."

"War is between soldiers."

"When they attacked our people during the rebellion, they killed indiscriminately."

"*These* people did? They weren't even born then. They've spent their lives living right there. What threat do they represent?"

"Their people killed ours."

"So we should be murderous dogs like them?"

"Vengeance is either taken or not. When it is not, the cycle of injustice continues forever. Innocents died in our homes."

To remind her that it was usually the result of the Khanate's cowardly soldiers using the innocent as shields would only draw out more of the old woman's nonsensical rambling. And, after all, he had been the one to plan out the complete destruction of the city. The fireballs, the fighter craft, the demolitions work: He had architected it all.

Create a plan to appease the drooling madman holding all the power or die. The choice had been easy enough.

But living with the results of the plan?

Satrap tapped the shoulder of the Jakkara captain. "Fly us to the slums. Captain Zohar, the starport situation must be resolved within ten minutes."

"Missiles are away, Satrap." The captain's voice sounded strained.

"The others understand that casualties are a part of war."

"They do, and yet they question how the clear victory promised in this assault could so easily vaporize."

Data flowed in again: a few vehicles still moved along the road leading to the slum...until his personal shuttle opened fire, destroying them; deadly smoke hung over the mishmash of buildings; the fire spread as quickly as people could move; inside the walls of the city, nothing would be standing by dawn.

"This is victory at an unprecedented scale, Captain. We have crushed the Gulmar center of power."

"I am not the one your plan has soured."

Of course not. Zohar's forces had largely been deployed as security for the fleet. The others would have seen this and understood its necessity, but they would have resented it nonetheless. It was the destructive embrace of competition and jockeying for attention that the Khan nurtured despite all evidence of its ruinous nature.

Below Satrap's shuttle, the last of the slums faded. To the west, the night grew bright again as the starport erupted in flames.

He tapped the Jakkara captain's shoulder again. "The starport."

The bodyguard bowed, and the shuttle maneuvered sharply, pushing Satrap back in his seat. He rubbed his thighs, but the pain didn't lessen. None of the pain would lessen for him. Ever. Not until death.

Once more the data flowed in as the fires from the missile strikes registered. Hangars, the control tower, the communications systems—all gone. Nothing could have survived the sort of devastation the sensors were picking up.

There was satisfaction in that, at least.

Satrap flipped through the various data feeds one last time.

No unidentified shuttle flew through the sky. None could have survived the damage his fleet had dealt to the area.

"Captain Zohar, please inform the fleet that our mission here is complete. Prepare the fleet to maneuver to the Gulmar Second Fleet once I've returned to the *Might of the Khan*."

"I will do as you command."

Malice and resentment. Nothing seemed good enough to satisfy the captain.

Perhaps destroying the last of the Gulmar space force would change that.

19

The horizon spun—one second fire, the next a darkening sky from which the fire slid down. Or maybe it was the fire that created the near-black sky. Benson wasn't sure. From the instant the Khanate fighter craft had plowed into the Gulmar Conglomerate towers, everything had descended into chaos.

It was here. The attack she'd feared against Kedraal. But it wasn't the Azoren, and the attack was destroying Voelker.

What about the task force? Were they far enough out to avoid detection?

Thiessen grunted over the whine of the engines and twisted the flight controls again. "They're firing on civilians!"

Benson's harness dug into her as they flipped. "We need to get out."

The pilot glanced at the control console, which flared red. "I know."

From the smaller second row of seats, Ambassador Manshaus's squeaky voice barely rose above the engines. "I have a specialized radio in my apartment."

"If your apartment's not already on fire, it will be soon."

"It will take but a moment for me to radio the diplomatic command—"

"You wouldn't make it, and we're not setting down long enough to be a target." Thiessen shot a questioning glance at Benson: *Are we?*

She shook her head. "How far away is the Second Fleet?"

"Maybe six hours at full burn. Not in this shuttle, though."

"We need to radio the *Valor*."

"Same problem: Not in this shuttle. It's built for atmospheric work. Top range on the radio system is a few hundred kilometers. You want something built to transmit to a starship, we need to get to a security facility."

Something shot past them and crashed into the front of a building: another fighter. Glass and concrete blew out of warping walls, then a concussive wave hammered the shuttle.

Thiessen growled as he jerked on the flight controls. "This isn't a combat craft."

Fire curled from the building like a giant serpent. A dark cloud of smoke rolled outward as the floors above the impact point began to fall in on themselves, then on the floors beneath.

Manshaus's medicine-heavy breath hit Benson. "Savages. We should have destroyed them when we had the chance."

The words sent a chill down her back. Wholesale slaughter like what she was seeing all around her was nauseating, terrifying, inhuman. But what Manshaus was saying sounded exactly the same. "After the rebellion, our expeditionary fleet crippled theirs."

"Yes. It was a gift appreciated by the Supreme Leader, Captain. But the distraction lasted too long, and we pulled out while they lived still."

"They shouldn't be able to field a fleet like this. They were crushed."

"Like bugs—unless annihilated, they will return."

"Thank you, Ambassador, but these aren't bugs. They're human beings."

"Human beings susceptible to fanatical zeal." The little man was almost shaking; his voice was almost a shout. He sat back. "They are a danger to all humans."

"Because everyone else is rational and peaceful. I get it." Benson saw the corners of Thiessen's mouth shoot upward in a smile. He didn't seem to be onboard with the idea of genocide, either, even with his own people being targeted. "Can you get us to a security facility?"

The shuttle leveled off a few meters shy of a building being raked by weapons fire that gouged away the facade in fiery chunks. The Gulmar pilot banked and dove, leveling off again just above the roofs of vehicles lining the broad avenue to the main gate. In the glow of raging fires and explosions, passengers gawked up at the speeding aircraft.

We need to save them. We need to save this planet! Benson ducked in her seat when another aircraft sped past overhead: another Khanate fighter.

Headed toward the gate.

She pointed at it, but Thiessen was already pulling back on the controls.

He gritted his teeth. "I see it."

The shuttle climbed back to rooftop level and twisted away from the gate, now heading west, over the city. Around them, more weapons fire tore into building tops. Sections of rooftop collapsed inward. In some areas, fire spiked up from the holes.

Benson squeezed her eyes shut. "They're using white phosphorous rounds."

"Being burned alive or crushed in a collapsing building—there's no good way to die."

"Those are civilians—"

Thiessen shook his head. "You think they care if a railgun round turns them into a fine mist? Dead is dead, and they're all going to be dead when this is over."

He pushed the aircraft hard, banking once they were over the wall and dropping back to fly just above the shadowy surface of the land. After a moment, the shuttle's exterior lights turned off, and the windshield took on a black-and-green hue: night-vision.

They passed over the cleared land in seconds and the green-black shape of treetops came into view.

The shuttle climbed just above the obstacles.

Once again, Manshaus leaned forward, breathing his sickly air. "Now where do we go? Is outrunning an invading fleet a real desire?"

Benson glared at the little man, who was turned toward the pilot. "Ambassador, are you suicidal?"

He turned to her. "Not to my knowledge, no."

"Then what would you propose we do?"

"My radio—"

"Your spying device won't help us here."

"It was heavily encrypted and not detectable, Captain."

Thiessen snorted. "Do you seriously believe that the executive director didn't know about your Fold Space transmitter?"

Manshaus leaned back. "Nothing was ever said."

"What would that have accomplished?"

"A curtailment of my spying, yes?"

"Unless you knew what she wanted you to know."

The old man grumbled softly.

Benson pointed to a clearing. "Is that the starport?"

In answer, the pilot's eyes narrowed, and his grin widened. "We can get a better vehicle there."

"The Khanate has air superiority."

"I didn't say aircraft."

Dark shapes moved inside the walled compound. "Do those security forces know we're coming?"

"It wouldn't matter. I can't pay their fees."

"So we just fly in?"

"They know what's happening in Voelker."

"And they care?"

Thiessen's grin disappeared. "They come from the slums, just like me."

"What if the Khanate doesn't attack the slums?"

"They will. The ambassador is right: The Khanate forces are savages. It's one thing to ambush a military force. It's another to have spies aboard to perform sabotage. Doing that to a city filled with civilians…?"

Benson almost brought up the Azoren attack on Kedraalian space, but Thiessen wasn't going to be swayed by something his own people hadn't done. And if she was honest with herself, she understood the point being made: The actions of one group against the Khanate didn't justify their actions against another group.

But what she couldn't get past was how they'd even been able to do what they did. At the academy, extensive time had been dedicated to the war against the Khanate. Their behavior during the rebellion was heinous, even compared to the Azoren. Terrorism and criminal brutality were well documented. Some had argued to parliament that it wasn't enough to merely cripple the Khanate interstellar capabilities, but calmer heads had prevailed.

The shuttle slowed, then dropped hard against the tarmac beside one of the hangars. Thiessen popped his harness buckle while the aircraft was still rocking on its gear. "Hurry."

Benson unbuckled as the exit hatch opened. Bright searchlights played across the tarmac to the north. She helped Manshaus out of his seat and out the open hatch, then she hopped out and moved the old man aside to give Thiessen room to get out.

Once he was on the ground, the pilot pointed to a door on the hangar front. "Through there."

He darted for the door, pulling up to type in a code and press a hand against a biometric device. The door popped open, and he waved for them to follow. Lights flashed on inside, revealing not the main hangar, but the inside of a large garage. There were three vehicles: low, angular, armored, with large, bulbous tires. About six meters long and every centimeter a flat black, they seemed to suck in the light.

"An armored personnel carrier?" Benson didn't know how else to describe it.

The pilot jogged to the closest of the vehicles. "Sure. But not quite."

"I doubt it can withstand the sort of weapons they're using."

"It won't have to." A hatch popped open, revealing a two-seat front cabin. The pilot waved toward the rear, where another hatch opened. "Ambassador, you'll need to come in from back there."

Benson had to pull herself up into the passenger compartment seat, which reminded her of a fighter pilot seat: sturdy, stiff, heavy. The harness was well-padded and the belts thick. "Do I want to know what this is?"

"Like you said, an APC." Thiessen chortled as he strapped in.

The hatch closed, and the interior went dark, then the console woke, bathing them in a pale, red light. Instrumentation glowed, and steering wheels extended on thick columns. Dangling beneath the wheels: bands of black plastic about five centimeters tall.

Thiessen slid his on over his head, then slid thin strips of plastic down over his eyes. "You'll want to be wired in."

Benson pulled the band from the steering wheel. The plastic went over her head easily, adjusting on its own to a comfortable tightness. She had to turn it slightly to get the strip to align with her eyes. "Heads-up display?"

"Everything's wireless."

AR-data fed into the strip, which turned opaque. Now Benson had a better sense of the console. When she turned her head, her vision was filled with crisp displays. "Nice. It's still not going to help against aircraft."

"It's not meant for combat."

A soft whine filled the cabin as the motors came online, then the vehicle vibrated up through her spine. "Is that the—"

"Power train. Ambassador, are you buckled in?"

"Yes. It feels very snug."

"All right."

A button lit on the console in Benson's AR: a door slid shut behind her. The front cab was sealed off from the rear.

Manshaus was cut off from them.

Something rumbled at the end of the room opposite where they'd entered, and the vehicle shot forward, its tires chirping on the concrete floor as Thiessen turned sharply. The acceleration was breathtaking given the size of the vehicle. Then again, the thing didn't *feel* massive or cumbersome.

As they picked up speed, Benson realized the rumble she'd heard had been a larger door opening on the far end of the garage. The APC burst through that door and onto the concrete that ran from the hangars to the administrative buildings and control tower.

Benson straightened in her seat. "Um. Those paramilitary APCs are headed toward us."

"They're headed toward the hangar." Thiessen nudged the vehicle to the left.

"We're between them and the hangar, so..."

The pilot accelerated. "They're using night-vision, same as we are. The difference is, this thing isn't reflective at all, and just in case they have infrared, the signature is close to ambient."

They passed between two of the APCs, which continued on toward the hangar.

Stealth technology. It seemed close to what the Azoren had, maybe even more refined. A few seconds later, they approached a gate, which opened just ahead of them.

After they sped through, Benson leaned toward the Gulmar pilot. "Is this stolen technology?"

He chuckled. "All technology is stolen." He didn't whisper as she had.

"From the Azoren?"

"Well, some of it. Keep in mind that they use us to refine some of their manufacturing work. They've been trying to automate everything they can, but the prototypes and sometimes the entire assembly process comes here."

"You build weapons for your enemies?"

"That's…complicated." Thiessen sighed. "Most of the executives don't really see anyone else as an enemy. Not as a military enemy, at least. So, we end up building prototypes or manufacturing weapons systems for pretty much anyone who pays."

"They just ignore history?"

"What little education I received seemed to focus on business more than history, Captain. When people like Leona Trang talked strategy, it was always about maximizing profits. They were angrier at the Kedraalian Republic for all the taxes and fees and regulations than at the Azoren or Moskav."

Benson squeezed her eyes shut. "She thought she could just buy her way out of war."

"Yeah, well, maybe she changed her mind there at the end."

The vehicle sped through the night, easily moving at fifty kilometers an hour over open terrain. Benson's seat shook slightly, but there were no other indications they were tearing across a broken surface. "I'm sorry about all of this."

Thiessen was silent for a moment. "You asked me about the Second Fleet."

"Is that where we're going—someplace that can warn them?"

"There's no one to warn."

Benson twisted against the harness. "What?"

"I told you before: the security forces are kept at minimal manning to save money."

"Are you saying you've got a fleet in space without even a skeleton crew?"

"Ships don't need a skeleton crew. We send folks up once a quarter to run diagnostics and check everything. Automated systems maintain positioning."

"What about training? Discipline?"

"We're what you'd consider reserves. Funding an actual call-up of the crews requires executive committee authorization."

"You don't *have* an executive committee, Floyd."

"I know."

"So what's the plan?"

"I don't know."

"Where are we going?"

"Banicafin. It's about two hundred kilometers south."

"I don't think I've heard of it."

"It's sort of a rival city. Three of the second-tier corporations have headquarters there. One of the factories there produced the tires for this."

"Wonderful. Will they have a radio I can use to contact my task force?"

"Yes. But I don't think they'll approve."

"Of me calling the *Valor*?"

"Or of calling up the reserves for the Second Fleet."

Pain blossomed above Benson's eyes. She ground a knuckle against her forehead, just above the plastic AR band. "They have to understand that you're at war. Your capital city is being blown up *right now*."

"Not *their* capital city. They didn't have seats on the executive committee."

"This isn't happening."

"Don't act like that's crazy."

"Our parliament has procedures and traditions and all sorts of crazy stuff. I get that, and it drives me nuts when it drags progress to a stop. But this?"

"We do things differently; that's all."

"Floyd, if you don't have an executive director or executive committee, who's in charge? How do things get done?"

Silence filled the cabin. "The different corporations are going to have to call executives in for an unscheduled meeting, I guess. They'll have to appoint new leadership."

"How long will that take?"

"It shouldn't be more than a couple months."

"Months?"

"People will have to fly in from other planets."

"If you don't get that fleet operational, there won't be a planet for these executives to fly to."

The console lit up in Benson's AR view. "What's that?"

Thiessen flipped through several screens. "They've bombed the starport. It's gone."

Benson bowed her head. She didn't know how to feel about someone blowing up the security people who'd extracted "fees" from her own shuttle. If the starport was destroyed, it seemed likely the entire city would be similarly targeted, including the slums. Thiessen had probably figured that out on his own.

After a few more minutes, her seat quit shaking. They were on a road, picking up speed.

She realized a window had popped up tracking their estimated arrival time: ninety-one minutes. She swiped a hand through the air until she had an idea how the AR interface worked, then highlighted the destination on her HUD. "Is that Banicafin?"

"Close to it."

"Some sort of security checkpoint?"

"Another starport. Smaller. Everything in Banicafin is smaller."

"Is there a transmitter there I can use?"

"And a shuttle."

"Will we need to get approval before I make the call?"

"We'll... No."

She settled in her seat, trying to find a comfortable position. The cushion was hard, but she eventually found a way to lean against the harness that allowed her to drift off a little.

And then they were braking, and something crashed against the shell of the vehicle.

Benson looked around, but the AR console didn't show any systems alarming. "What was that? What happened?"

"We're here. At the starport." Thiessen sounded irritated.

No dark shapes moved inside the compound. "Where are the security forces?"

"They don't have any here. Their budget doesn't really allow for it."

A small cluster of long and low black shapes came into view: hangars. The APC came to a stop at the base of a tall building: the control tower. After a second, the AR system powered down. Benson took her headband off just as Thiessen popped open a panel beneath the console.

He pulled out two big pistols and holsters and handed one of each to her. "Viper machine pistol. Fully automatic. Twenty-round magazine. One reload."

The weapon had some heft to it. "You think there might be saboteurs here?"

"Maybe." He didn't sound convincing. Before she could ask another question, he popped the hatches and the panel separating them from the Azoren ambassador. "Ambassador Manshaus, if you could stay here, we won't be long."

"Oh?" The old man sounded weak, his breathing raspy.

"We're going to make a call."

"Yes. I see. I will remain here."

Thiessen climbed out; Benson followed. His security code was apparently enough to gain access to the control tower, which powered on as they entered. A lift door opened as they approached, which meant either the area still had power or the building had good reserves. On the top floor, they exited into a hallway with two doors off of it. He led her through the one opposite the lift.

It was the control tower proper.

The pilot settled in a chair and fiddled with some controls. "I haven't really done this before."

Benson took the seat to his right. "Can I help?"

"Can you?"

Radio systems were similar in design, apparently, because she found a familiar control panel in less than a minute. She flipped a couple switches, and the system powered on. Headsets hung from hooks along the width of the console. She helped herself to the newest of the devices and slid that over her ear. To her left, Thiessen was doing the same.

Benson programmed in the frequency for her ship, synchronized her communicator, then waited.

But Thiessen was doing something else. He was already chatting with someone while he tapped furiously. It was as if he'd forgotten what they'd come to the control tower to do.

Fine. We can chat later. Benson connected to the *Valor*. "*Valor*, this is Benson. Do you copy?"

Nuñez's voice was on the connection almost immediately. "Captain Benson?"

"Yes. Lieutenant, sorry for using an unconventional channel—"

"I can't believe— Just a moment, Captain. Commander Chopra for you."

Chopra's voice nearly drowned out the lieutenant's. "Captain? You're alive!"

Benson smiled. "I am. How's the task force?"

"Out from the planet. Considerably. The Khanate fleet—"

"Yes. They wiped out Voelker."

"Wiped out?"

"It was burning to the ground when we escaped."

"Oh. That's terrible."

"It is. Commander, we're going to need to make a run for you. Can you send me a rendezvous point?"

"Of course, of course! When…?"

"Soon. Maybe three hours."

A message came through on her communicator. She decompressed it. "Coordinates received. I see the point and time."

"They're maintaining a tight grouping. We should be clear for that rendezvous."

"Good."

"Will we be making top speed for Kedraalian space, Captain?"

"No. Not immediately."

Thiessen shot her an intense glare, then stood. "We'll need escort out to the fleet."

Benson covered her mic. "What?"

"My personnel. I recalled them. The ones I could reach."

"The executives in Banicafin approved?"

"No. They told me I'm not authorized to assume security operations command in the absence of an executive committee."

"But they understand what's going on?"

"They do. They're scrambling local security personnel to get aircraft into the airspace over the city."

"With a fleet in the sky? Do they understand—?"

"Remember, I'm the one who isn't capable."

Benson sank in on herself and uncovered her mic. "Commander, things just became a little more complicated."

"Oh?"

"We're going to need escort for more shuttles."

"More shuttles? There will be more than just you?"

"There will. And they'll need escort to their destination."

"Where is that, Captain?"

She glanced at Thiessen, who typed in a set of coordinates for her. "I'll transmit the destination once we're in space, Commander. Please have everyone ready. This mission must succeed, or we'll lose our Gulmar allies. And maybe the war."

20

The Sutton building was the tallest on the continent of Platino. In the relatively small city of South Croy, the structure easily towered over everything else. It had taken Stiles nearly an hour to gain entry through the roof, then it had taken another hour to make her way down the elevator shafts and stairwells undetected. Now she was winded and sweaty, her replacement shadowsuit barely at half power trying to keep up with her exertions. The technology made her nearly invisible, and her steps were as quiet as a mouse, but that hadn't prevented the Ravens from catching her before. She wasn't about to let her guard down again.

At the intersection of two long hallways, the security guard she'd been tailing came to a stop and turned around quickly, as if he'd heard something behind him.

Stiles pressed tight against the door into the electrical room and held her breath.

Something squeaked behind her, and the guard laughed.

A wrinkled and stooped man pushing a wheeled bucket with the end of a mop came to a stop a few meters short of her position and waved at the guard. "Nearly done, Gencio."

The guard shook his head and exhaled, loosening the tight-fitting shirt that covered his thick chest. "With that stale mop head, why bother with floor cleaner? I could smell you before I heard you."

"I change it once a week. Cost savings."

"Typical management."

The guard turned left at the intersection, and the janitor followed, stopping just beyond the turn to crank up a device mounted to his hip. Crashing metal and pounding drums filled the sub-basement halls, then the old man started singing.

Painfully.

He pushed the sloshing bucket into the hallway before pulling the mop head from the filmy gray water, which he splashed over the dark tiles.

Beyond the slick puddle of water now being dragged across the floor by the distracted janitor, the guard disappeared.

That was where Stiles needed to be.

She sprinted toward the janitor, who didn't look up from his labor, then jumped at the last second. She landed on her hands just beyond the water, tucked into a ball, and rolled, coming to a stop where the hallway turned right.

A door was closing meters beyond the turn. Beside the door, the label read: Special Projects Storage.

She sprinted, but the door closed before she could reach it.

The metallic beat and off-key singing grew louder. If she stayed in front of the door, the janitor would bump into her.

Stiles jumped to the ceiling and clamped on with the suction filaments on her gloves and knee pads. It would burn through battery power quicker than she liked, but there weren't any other options. She needed to get through the door, and hacking it would take too long and risk too much. The whole point of following the security guards around had been to minimize the risk of detection. She wasn't about to risk that now.

Seconds passed, then a minute, and the janitor finally came around the corner, hips swaying to his own singing. In his wake, the filmy water beaded on the black tiles.

A minute after he passed below, the door opened again, and the guard she'd been following stepped out, groaning and pinching his nose as he delicately navigated the wet floor.

Stiles let her knees take her full weight and stretched to catch the door before it closed fully, keeping it open with a finger.

When the guard was out of sight, she curled her fingers over the top of the door and dropped from the ceiling, slowly bringing her legs down so that they didn't slam into the door. Her muscles burned, but neither of the two men noticed her as she slipped into the Special Projects Storage room.

Her first priority was to take out the two cameras within. One was on the wall just above the door, the other was on the glass wall opposite, each about twenty centimeters off from the other.

Stiles connected to the devices and triggered firmware downloads, taking them offline. Now she had ten minutes or more.

The data from the Ravens facility had eventually produced something meaningful, starting with connections between the Patels and Dramoran rebels. Some of those connections were tenuous and would prove useless in a courtroom situation, but others…

Computer systems hummed and flashed in the dark depths of the underground secure room beyond the glass wall. A keypad and biometric reader were to the right of the door in the center of that wall. Three desks with terminals were off to her right.

Terminals.

She settled in front of the closest, which showed a generic system prompt, and pulled a slender, rectangular computing tablet from a thigh pouch. The device was a flat black until she pulled a glove off and ran a finger over the hard plastic surface.

Buttons flashed on the front: hacking tools, recording tools, a limited AI.

The hacking button opened a suite of applications options, software she was still learning after the latest updates to the system. According to what she'd uncovered in her research into the Sutton building occupants, the corporations running research operations preferred a very specific set of solutions for security. It was a respectable solution provider and the software was up to date, but there were also vulnerabilities.

After a few false starts, the hacking software finally breached the outer security layer, and the terminal offered a login prompt that looked quite different from the one that had first showed.

Stiles pulled a small, gray device shaped like a clip from another hip pouch and slid that over the tablet. The ID prompt field filled, then the password field did the same.

Then the terminal showed a plain interface screen with a few windows.

She tapped one of the windows, then another, then the last. It was in that one that she found what she was looking for: a series of folder icons. One was labeled Off-World Mineral Research.

OWMR.

That was the project funded by the Patel family through several layers of shell businesses, and the amounts being funneled through those businesses was impressive. OWMR had to be more than just the asteroid mining operation it was advertised to be.

She launched a download operation to her tablet.

At best, she was looking at eight minutes. Tight.

Colonel McLeod's data analysts could tear into the data when she handed it over, but Stiles was trained for pattern recognition, for intuiting things.

While the download ran, she fired off a series of queries.

Unfortunately, searching through the OWMR records didn't return the sort of data that backed the assumption that the project was anything more than advertised. One after the other, the queries returned nothing but asteroid mining data: mineral content, location, cost estimates to extract meaningful quantities, equipment rental, shipping costs, refinement costs.

Searching for and exploiting asteroids wasn't cheap, but the Patels had spent billions of credits in the last few decades through the shell companies compared to a couple hundred million credits in revenue. That wasn't how a family with holdings in the tens of billions stayed wealthy.

It wasn't fake data, either. There were video and image files showing the probes and even robot mining operations. Ships were dedicated for weeks to the extraction sites, some breaking the asteroids up, others hauling the chunks of rock to space stations for ore extraction before carrying the ore to other facilities for final processing. Every step of the process was recorded, along with the costs.

The Patel mining business really was that inefficient.

Could that be why they operated through so many layers—to hide their incompetence?

No. Samir had been if not brilliant then at least clever and resourceful.

What else, then? If they weren't incompetent, how could they lose so much money in what was generally seen as a sure thing? Mining asteroids was mostly automated, something that had limited costs once you were operational and knew what you were doing, yet...

Yet...

Stiles went back to one of the more recent records and loaded up the entire operation from start to finish, rounding everything up to kilo-credits.

Acquiring data on potential asteroids from a firm that did surveys: 25 KCr.

The amount seemed curious, and a quick check showed the bids made by competitors. No one else had bid even half that.

Next came the vessel used to haul the robotic mining gear out: 10 KCr.

That seemed about right, although a little on the high end. The insurance rate accounted for that. For some reason, the coverage was costly.

After that, the ore hauler: 100 KCr.

That seemed impossibly high. The vessels were large but rugged and didn't cost anywhere near as much to rent as luxury yachts, merchant ships, or other private vessels. A typical ore hauler required a small crew to oversee all the robot work. The actual containers used to haul the mined materials were modular, easily added on or not. They could accommodate anywhere from a few tons to thousands of tons.

So where did the expense come from?

Drilling down deeper, Stiles found at least a part of the problem: the insurance again.

Insurance actuarial tables were attached to the report. The region of space in question was simply more expensive than others—nearly ten times so.

It didn't take long to find the reason embedded in the tables: piracy.

Stiles opened an older report. The same sort of strange data cropped up: paying too much for survey data; paying premium rates on insurance.

And something she'd missed before: taking far more cargo containers than needed.

Why would the ore haulers carry around useless containers?

Stiles searched through some of the folders that hadn't caught her eye previously. These were purely operational data: salaries, basic expenses, revenue, and other transactions. It was just operational data, the sort of thing any business needed to look legitimate, nothing of val—

She reopened a folder she'd quickly closed: Miscellaneous Revenue.

Something about the numbers seemed odd. Line after line of kilocredits being received from insurance companies.

Payments coming in?

There were links buried in the lines. She clicked.

Piracy. Apparently one of the most notorious pirates: Lev Goldman. The mining companies were making back most of their investments through insurance payouts. Each payout raised the rates for the company, but when the rates became too high or the insurer wouldn't cover the mining operation, another company took over.

So that was the reason for the shell companies.

But why spend so much money to exploit insurance companies? Why not simply avoid the areas known for piracy? It wasn't like the operations weren't generating revenue legitimately.

Stiles blinked at the realization of what she was seeing: *The ships hit by pirates were still delivering ore!*

Hadn't anyone noticed that?

The pirates weren't stealing ore; they were stealing empty cargo containers.

What were the Patels up to? Why carry empty containers into space…?

She reviewed the list of company names behind the mining operations. There were eleven. There had been twelve companies in the network of shell companies uncovered.

Somehow, the twelfth had avoided involvement in the asteroid mining operations.

Guiding Star Shipping.

There were records for the company in the OWMR folder, but the activities were unimpressive. Guiding Star Shipping seemed to haul cargo from starport to warehouse or warehouse to starport. It was comfortably profitable doing conventional work, unlike the other shell companies.

There were no obvious connections beyond being in the OWMR folder.

Stiles searched the business operations, tracking back to initial formation, locations, and personnel. It was actually the oldest and largest of the companies, with a presence on every occupied planet in the Republic. Everything about it looked legitimate, including the connections to multiple corporations, which used Guiding Star as their exclusive shipping company. Even the military had contracts with Guiding Star.

Legitimate. With government contracts. Military contracts.

To haul what?

Everything, apparently. Invoices she opened ranged from equipment transfers to personal belongings being shipped from one military facility to another. The shipping company was ubiquitous, unremarkable, probably completely forgettable.

Stiles leaned in closer to the terminal. She'd been poking through data for seven minutes. The download was nearly done, and the camera firmware updates were closing in on completion. All she'd found was a group of poorly run asteroid mining companies and one profitable shipping company. There were no obvious connections and nothing outrageously criminal, unless the GSA wanted to make a case around what might be insurance fraud.

But this had to be the link she was looking for. She was missing something…

She entered a query to compare the shipping company operations to the mining operations: Did they ever move in the same circles?

Data came back. Lots of data.

Everywhere the ore haulers launched from, Guiding Star Shipping operated out of. In fact, the shipping company delivered shipping containers to the orbital launch facilities for the ore haulers to load up. Or at least it delivered *some* of the containers. Most containers were kept up in space.

Why would the ore haulers have empty shipping containers sent up from planetside? That was another inefficiency.

The tablet flashed: *Download complete.*

She had seconds before the camera firmware finished. Time enough for one more query, this one about the cost of the cargo container launch. Did they match the cost of an empty container?

Seconds ticked by. The cameras were cycling through the final step of the upgrade.

Stiles needed to go. She slid her glove back on and readied the tablet to sever the connection to the system. The colonel's experts would have to tear the data apart—

The query came back.

There were costs listed for empty cargo containers being sent into space, and they didn't match at all to the costs of the containers sent up by Guiding Star. It was as expensive sending up full containers as the supposedly empty containers.

Which meant the company wasn't sending up empty containers but loaded ones.

She disconnected, slid the tablet and credential clip back into their pouches, then pushed the door open to check the hallway: empty.

Now mostly dry, the dark tile was still slick beneath her, forcing her to move with extra caution. Her audio sensors picked up the janitor's singing somewhere off to her left, out of sight. The shadowsuit was at thirty-two percent power—just enough.

Rather than wait for a guard to follow around again, she headed for the stairwell and transmitted the janitor's credentials into the card reader. He would have to answer to security when he finished his work in the sub-basement and tried to exit a second time.

Once she reached the second floor, she exited and made her way to the elevators. The whole way up to the top floor, she tried to puzzle out what she'd stumbled across. Obviously, the Patels were shipping something illegally, and they were using their asteroid mining operations to hide that. What would a notorious pirate like Lev Goldman want from the Patels?

It was something she wasn't going to get an answer for anytime soon.

No one had ever managed to get inside Goldman's operation—not and live.

The elevator opened on the top floor, and Stiles retraced her way to the roof, clearing her trail behind her. No one was going to know she'd penetrated the building this time. She'd taken every possible precaution—

Three forms stepped from cover behind the air-conditioning units. They wore sealed helmets and had assault carbines trained on her.

One of the forms stepped away from the others, barrel centered on Stiles's chest. "Lieutenant Stiles, please place one hand on your head and use the other to very, very slowly pull your tablet from your thigh pouch."

Tablet! They knew somehow. "Who do you work for?"

"The tablet, Lieutenant."

She put her hand on her head, as directed, then lowered her other to the thigh pouch that held her tablet.

And a flashbang grenade.

As if reading her mind, the speaker clucked his tongue against his teeth. "Don't try the flashbang. We're not amateurs."

Her fingers slipped over to the tablet. It didn't really matter if they shot her over trying to toss the weapon at them or not. She was surprised they were letting her live long enough to pull the tablet out. Perhaps they considered the contents too valuable to risk shooting her.

She pulled the device out and held it up. "I could toss this off the roof."

"Not really. If you move your arm in any way other than how I tell you to, we'll shoot you." The speaker moved closer—foot edging forward, stopping, other foot dragging. He was centered on her chest and wasn't wavering in the least. "I want you to very slowly lower the tablet to the rooftop."

"You have access to GSA systems. You have people inside—"

"The tablet, Lieutenant. Very. Slowly."

She squatted, still keeping her hand on her head. If she'd brought a firearm, she could've dropped flat and risked the shootout. No matter how fast or accurate they were, she would be faster and more accurate. But there were three, and they were armored, and they had some sort of system that could see through the suit's stealth capabilities. Her only choice at the moment was cooperation. "I'm setting the tablet down."

"Very good. Now step back, Lieutenant." The speaker didn't move or say anything more, but one of the other forms—this one feminine—hurried forward with the same sort of caution the speaker had shown.

Then the form stumbled and fell face down on the rooftop.

Stiles froze. There had been a soft pop, a flash of light…

The speaker twisted around, scanning the rooftop behind him.

Another soft pop, another instantaneous flash of light, and the one still leaning against the air conditioning unit fell to the rooftop.

The speaker must have seen something, because he fired—a short burst.

Then he fell onto his back, and his weapon clattered at his side.

Stiles tumbled toward the carbine, trying to keep the source of the gunfire in sight, hoping to get to the weapon before—

Something stomped on the carbine as she reached for it, and a second later, a shape resolved in the dark: an athletic man in a black suit not so different from hers. He had a pistol of some sort leveled at her brow.

"Don't move, Brianna."

The voice! "Darien?"

The man pulled his mask off with his free hand, revealing a face like hers but more masculine. There were a couple scars on his cheek, and the stern glare he fixed on her said he had seen far too much to be fooled by anything she did. "You're getting sloppy."

"I—"

"Get the tablet, if you want to live."

21

As much as the Great and Mighty Khan wrote in the Khan Kabal about the glory of the light of the Guiding Star that would one day be home to his followers, he probably had no idea of the sort of heat of such a place. Looking at the golden glow of Voelker with naked eyes, Satrap understood the hellish fire at a star's core. His shuttle's hull registered that sort of heat in the land below. Bodies would be rapidly turned to ash in those flames.

Our welcome home, as the scripture said.

How could the outrageous contradictions and illogical writings be seen as anything other than the failures and imperfections of a human mind? Yet here they were, the blessed heralds of the Khan, bringing peace and purity to the universe. Ikhama's droning voice repeated prayers and exaltations, but she couldn't silence the screams of the dying that dominated Satrap's imagination.

He closed his eyes, sucked in the smells of his Jakkara and the conditioned air within his personal shuttle, then focused on the data stream. In the face of such devastation, he had no right to complain about the stuffy air or the cables and lines pinching his skin when the spacecraft maneuvered too hard. For kilometers in all directions, no structure stood. If any had survived the assault, they would be broken and fleeing into the wilds of the planet. It was the same as death.

Zohar requested a connection, which Satrap welcomed for once. "What is it, Captain?"

"Your shuttle returns already?"

"We've completed a final flyover of the area. Nothing remains."

"Voelker is but one city. The plan was to destroy all three major population points."

Nausea tugged at Satrap. "How long before the next wave of fighters are ready to launch?"

"A little less than twelve hours."

"Without fighters, the work would be long and tedious, perhaps even dangerous."

"The fleet looks upon the deeds of its satrap for guidance."

"Does the fleet not feel the joy of victory? We have destroyed our enemy."

"Perhaps the lack of challenge has left an empty feeling for them."

"What of the shuttles we lost? The security teams?"

"War is a thirsty beast. Your captains seek greater opposition."

"There will be tests without end before long. Have the other captains study the results of our work here today. It is unlikely we will ever see such…uncontested battle again."

The captain disconnected, apparently disgusted by the idea that the assault against undefended cities might be delayed. There were missiles yet to be fired, after all.

Satrap collapsed in on himself, his energy long ago depleted. "Ikhama, if you could give us all a respite from your prayers, it would be appreciated."

Her old eyes held surprising energy as she considered him. "Yes."

After a moment, the captain of the Jakkara turned to consider Satrap but said nothing.

Undying loyalty had its value.

The shuttle climbed, and without the prayers, the pilot's chatter crept into Satrap's awareness. They had an escort of gunships from the carriers, and no enemy aircraft remained in the sky for at least a hundred kilometers in any direction, yet there was an undeniable anxiety in the pilot's voice.

Danger came in many forms beyond immediate military danger. A good pilot was probably sensitive to things beyond obvious threats in the data stream, but Satrap contented himself studying what he had available to him.

No obvious military or natural dangers seemed close by. The shuttle systems all showed well into the green.

Then what?

At the moment Satrap was ready to connect to the pilot to determine the cause of concern, Zohar connected again. Was this related to the anxiety? Satrap accepted the connection. "You have new information, Captain Zohar?"

"Sensors have detected multiple launches to the south of Voelker."

"Launches? Weapons systems?"

"The shapes are consistent with spacecraft or aircraft."

"Defensive forces we weren't informed of?"

"It is possible. The profiles look more like shuttles."

"Shuttles? Not gunships?"

"Far too small. I will send you the tracking data."

After a few seconds, the signals were integrated with the shuttle sensors. They were indeed Gulmar shuttles. To what purpose? "Ninety-six?"

"At the moment, but they continue to launch in waves."

"Shuttles."

"As I said."

"Yes, as you said. But it makes no sense."

"If you were to redirect your force to the south, you could intercept the main group."

The fleet commander tensed. Zohar recommending tactics wasn't new, but the tone was…troubling. Satrap sent a message to the pilot to adjust the shuttle's course to maneuver away from the Gulmar shuttle signals. "We are en route to the *Might of the Khan*. For now, it is enough for you to track these shuttles."

"We could launch missiles at them."

"Unless they fly together tightly packed, that seems a bad idea."

"It is best to destroy them."

"Without knowing their intent? No. Track them."

"Our carrier captains are…impatient to see this problem resolved."

Once again, Zohar's tone was troubling. Had something happened among the captains once their fleet commander took his personal shuttle to the front line? Now the pilot's anxiety made more sense.

Satrap sent another message to the pilot: *Separate from our escort. Take an indirect route to the* Might of the Khan. "Captain Zohar, perhaps you are right. I have no need of escort now. Have the carrier captains send their gunships after these Gulmar shuttles."

"I will convey your suggestion—"

"It is not a suggestion."

"—to the others. Excuse me."

With that, the connection was terminated.

The captain of the Jakkara unbuckled and squeezed from his seat, heading aft. His fellows watched, necks craning, eyes squinting. At a signal from him, they sealed their suits and turned their attention to the man they were committed to protecting.

Was something going on Satrap had missed? Had a mutiny been enacted without telltale communications through the data stream?

What was there to do when your body was broken and frail?

"My Satrap." The Jakkara captain had returned, and in his hands was an armored environmental suit, modified to accommodate the wires, tubes, and lines of the life support system. "I beg your forgiveness, but our pilot voices concern about the conditions we fly in. It is best if you were protected should something go wrong."

So, at least the Jakkara weren't part of whatever conspiracy was underway. One of the more senior soldiers helped Ikhama from her harness and led her aft.

Satrap nodded, then went limp as the leader of the bodyguards began putting the suit on, starting with the boots. They were huge, big enough to comfortably fit the swollen and misshapen things that could no longer support the weight of Satrap's wrecked body. Getting the leg pieces around the bony legs and the sagging, atrophied muscles that had once been more than capable of traversing the palace grounds was a little more of a challenge. The helmet was the worst, and it was still being sealed when the soldier who'd helped Ikhama returned without her.

The Jakkara captain nodded to the other man, and the two of them lifted Satrap from his seat.

He gasped. "What is happening?"

"Communications with the escort vessels has become unreliable. This leads to erratic maneuvers and other problems best compensated for by placing you and Ikhama in the escape module."

"A mutiny? They have initiated a mutiny?"

The two men carrying Satrap glanced at each other, then bowed their heads. At the back of the shuttle, steps led down to a small compartment. Ikhama sat there, hunched against a harness. They strapped Satrap in across from her, reconnecting cables and tubes that had been disconnected for the move.

"My Satrap?" The captain squatted until he was looking his charge in the eyes. "All that can be done to protect you will be done."

"Your...voice is strong. Thank you."

After patting Satrap on the shoulder, the two men retreated up the steps and dropped a metal door into place with a heavy *clang*.

Instantly, the data feed resumed. The escort gunships hadn't veered off as he'd instructed. In fact, they were in what looked like a clear pursuit of Satrap's shuttle. In all his planning, Satrap had never considered a mutiny a realistic threat. His protectors were too powerful, his value as a tactician and strategist too high. Yet—

Zohar connected. "Satrap? Are you there?"

"Alive still, yes."

"Hm. You should know that things have changed."

"I'm quite aware of the *change*, thank you."

"Not of this, I would imagine."

Another data stream came through the connection. It was the feed from the fleet, but facing out from the planet now. Numerous signals were on the screen: enemy signals.

Satrap blinked at the largest one. "Is that the *Valor*?"

"It is the Kedraalian task force. They move to intercept us."

"To attack?"

"Since we detected their approach, they have maneuvered to place themselves between the Gulmar shuttles and our ships."

"Did the frigates have any luck with their searches for the Gulmar fleet?"

"None. But the Kedraalian task force has several Gulmar gunships with it."

"The Second Gulmar Fleet has six destroyers and two cruisers, Zohar. You will not be able to confuse the signals for gunships."

"Then we have not found the missing fleet."

Unless… A smile slipped across Satrap's face. "Actually, we have."

"Your shuttle has found something our signals ships have failed to detect?"

"My mind has seen the unseen. Those Gulmar shuttles—they head for the fleet."

Zohar hissed, then went silent for several heartbeats. "We should accept the challenge presented by the Kedraalians."

"Have you forgotten that we're hours out from having fighters again?"

"Our fleet has no need for fighters. The Kedraalians are weak."

Satrap shook his head, then muted the connection and opened his environment suit visor. "Ikhama?"

The old woman struggled with her visor for a moment, then slid the thick plastic shield up. *"In moments where maelstroms threaten, the Earth provides shelter. Trust in the embrace of the land for strength and guidance."*

"If you've forgotten, we're in space right now. Nothing protects us but the armor of these suits and this shuttle."

"It is the trust you miss. Whether metal or stone, we have been embraced."

"We are being hunted down like dogs."

"Weakness in others draws out the strength of the warrior. The blade draws blood the same from opponents strong and feeble, but the blood of the brave comes with greater effort."

"This is no time for ridiculous parables and meaningless prattle. We are dead if this mutiny succeeds."

"You are protected by the Jakkara."

"The Jakkara are bodyguards. This betrayal comes from the fleet!"

"It was the wisdom of the Khan that crafted this fleet." The old woman rocked against the harness that held her tight.

"Speak to these captains. Remind them that I am our Khan's chosen Satrap."

"How is one to remind the flower of its scent or the bee of its sting? It is in the nature of things to know what they are. Ask not for the universe to remember you but remember yourself."

Satrap clenched his jaw. Not only had he been saddled with traitors as captains, but he had been given a senile and delusional priestess. "I remember who I am."

Zohar gasped. "A shuttle breaks from the others. Satrap? You hear?"

"I hear—" Satrap unmuted. "I hear you. Where does it go?"

"To the task force. It is a special shuttle."

"They are all special. If you had been more focused on the Gulmar threat instead of killing your commander—"

"I have taken no action against you."

"You have done nothing to stand for me, either."

"My forces were diminished following your orders before, or did you forget that?"

Satrap slammed the back of his helmet against the compartment wall hard enough to see spots. He closed his eyes and focused on the data stream coming from the *Might of the Khan*. In that flow of data, the Gulmar gunships embedded inside the Kedraalian task force were now peeling off and pursuing the Gulmar shuttles.

No. Not pursuing. Following.

"Zohar, those Gulmar shuttles will take you to the fleet."

"Why would we pursue them when we can fight the Kedraalians?"

"Think! Why would the fleet have not been in orbit? The Gulmar frequently defund their security forces to save money."

The captain snorted. "That is false intelligence! Our spies were weak!"

"No. It is the way of these people to see their military as an expense. They do not appreciate the threats they face."

"It is a trap to pursue them."

When Satrap glanced at Ikhama, she looked away.

But there was confusion in her eyes. How could her doctrine be so useless while she still embraced it?

And yet, what she said was true. If Satrap failed to support his fleet engaging the Kedraalians, he would be ruled a heretic and the mutiny would prove justified. It didn't matter if the fleet failed. What mattered was that they fought! That engagement, though, couldn't be won. They were without fighters to harry the weakest ships and to force the enemy into a defensive posture.

He had no choice. "Zohar, tell the captains to engage."

"They have been preparing as much already." The man's gloating smile was almost audible.

"Remember, though, that I advised against this."

"No one will forget."

Without supporting the mutineers, Zohar stood to gain the greatest advantage once it came time to contest for the title of satrap. It was a disgusting truth that left Satrap feeling weak.

All he could do was watch the data stream as his fleet began its brutish maneuvers, the work of unimaginative and overconfident captains bent on proving themselves the best candidate to replace the doomed fleet commander.

No fighters launched from the aircraft carriers, and many of their gunships were still trailing their commander's shuttle, which left only missiles and heavy mounted weapons—lasers, mostly. The lack of fighters rendered the frigates less effective as well. Even the cruisers—oversized signals ships—were out of their element. There was no coordination, no concentration of firepower to bring down shields. Instead, everything devolved into wild engagements where individual Khanate ships tried to fire on individual Kedraalian vessels.

While that pointless exercise occupied his captains, the Kedraalian ships did exactly what they'd done before: broke into computer-driven random maneuvers. Then they focused fire on isolated ships, quickly breaching shields and inflicting serious damage.

One of the frigates disappeared from the data stream. A cruiser flared to red from serious damage.

Minutes dragged on.

A message came from the Jakkara captain: *The gunships have locked on.*

Satrap's eyes flew wide as the shuttle shuddered. They'd been hit. Explosions and fire—

"Ikhama! Your visor!" He slammed his own visor down a second before the shuddering intensified.

Something groaned overhead, then he was slammed against the wall.

Acceleration! The escape module had launched.

He remained pinned against the wall, and it felt like the needles that carried his life fluids might tear free of his flesh.

They spun wildly. The metal of the compartment warped as something hit it but didn't quite penetrate.

Satrap swallowed, fighting back nausea.

Another frigate disappeared from the data stream, and the *Might of the Khan* dipped toward amber.

"Ikhama!" Satrap wanted—needed—to squeeze the harness but couldn't. "These captains who worship your notion of strength have set the fleet on a course to destruction. They have ordered their Ikhama assassinated. Our mission is close to its end with little to show for it."

The old woman seemed to nod. "*In darkness, the faintest fire blinds as easily as it informs.*"

A deafening *clang* rumbled through the hull as another warp twisted the escape module.

Satrap squeezed his hands into small, ineffective fists. If there were the power within him to use them, he would. "Please! We will *die* out here if you don't stop them!"

"It is not the Khan's will." That was a whisper, but a moment later, she connected to all the officers. "*From the heavens come rain and fire. The fire is the light of our Guiding Star. The rain is the tears of the dead.*"

One of the captains muttered, "*Show us the path.*"

"*Footsteps are all that remains of the traveler now gone to the stars.*"

"*Show us the path.*" It was the same captain.

"*Not every flower bears fruit. Not every fruit bears flesh to be eaten.*"

"*There is poison, even in paradise.*" Other captains had joined in.

"This battle is poison. Satrap has said as much and speaks with the wisdom of our Khan."

"*Spit out the poison.*" That was Zohar and only Zohar.

Ikhama's voice trembled. "We must seek a time and place to strike. This is not it. Rescue the satrap. Salvage the work of the Khan."

"Ikhama has spoken." Zohar's voice was a growl. "Disengage from the Kedraalian force. Leave the escape module unmolested. I will rescue our leaders and we will regroup at Rendezvous Point 3."

Satrap counted the seconds, but his fleet didn't pull back from the Kedraalians. The two forces continued to exchange fire.

Then one of the carriers flashed amber, and the ships started breaking off. Kedraalian ships pursued the wounded carrier, pushing its status deeper into amber.

A heavy, metallic clang preceded the escape module coming to a sudden halt that threw Satrap against his harness. A groan slipped out, but only he heard it. He had been muted since Ikhama had begun her sermon.

It felt as if something pulled the module through space—faster and faster.

Minutes sped by, and the Kedraalians abandoned their pursuit.

Gravity returned to the escape capsule, and Satrap found himself breathing hard. The exertion of space was taking its toll.

Metal clanked on metal overhead, then the warped panel was yanked free. One of Zohar's security officers—a young man with wide lips twisted in a wicked snarl—dropped into the capsule. He trained his weapon first on Ikhama, then on Satrap.

The captain stuck his head in through the open top. "Satrap. How fortunate you survived. Please take our leader to his cabin and be sure that no one disturbs him."

Satrap was too weak to resist the rough efforts of the scowling security officer. Doing so would only have given the man a reason to swat his commander or maybe to shoot him.

As the officer dragged Satrap from the module and casually tossed him onto a cart, it seemed likely his survival was but a respite.

What lay ahead? He was sure it wasn't anything pleasant.

22

———————

No rocket existed that was powerful enough to push the old, battered Gulmar shuttle faster toward Benson's fleet. At full thrust, she was pressed against the padding of the co-pilot seat, her breathing labored and loud in her head, louder than the rumble of the rocket coming through the spacecraft body. She would have accepted worse to get to the *Valor*.

Thiessen leaned forward, face strained, eyes darting across the console. It was relatively cool in the shuttle, but he was sweating. His cologne wafted from the top of his open environment suit, mixing with the stale smell of the old vessel. "I should be with my people."

Heat shot through Benson. She dug the tip of a thumb into the padding poking out of the bottom of her seat. "I understand. If we want to send a signal to your…government, I need you aboard the *Valor*."

"I'm the only one who knows how to lead our fleet."

"It won't be long. When we get to my ship, we need to call the people putting your emergency government together to show that we're aligned."

The Gulmar captain glanced back at Manshaus, who was fully sealed inside his environment suit, clinging to the harness holding him to his seat. He would have stayed on Radetta, if not for Benson's orders to accompany them. The Azoren diplomat was too valuable to leave behind.

Thiessen smirked. "Aligned and fully supported by our allies?"

"Optics matter." Benson looked away.

"So we show the new leadership that we have the momentum."

"It should work in our favor when negotiations start."

"It's too late now to back out."

She turned just enough to see Thiessen out of the corner of her eye. "Are you having second thoughts?"

"It wouldn't matter if I did. We all made a commitment when we launched."

Does he understand the importance of my plan?

Before she could form a question, red light flashed from the console, and he tapped command keys in response. "Those Khanate ships won't leave well enough alone."

Benson leaned forward enough to see the sensor display. "Missiles?"

"And lasers. And railguns. And everything else they have."

"They were firing on my task force earlier."

"Well, now they want to add us to the mix."

Thrusters fired, changing the shuttle vector and pushing her to the right. "They're just covering their retreat."

"It doesn't look like your ships were giving serious pursuit."

"There might be damage to deal with. Maybe rescues."

He squinted at the console. "Good call."

Another maneuvering thruster fire, and Benson was shoved to the opposite side of her seat. "How old are these harnesses?"

"Old. Sorry about that. I didn't feel right taking one of the newer shuttles, not with us going where there was protection."

"Not even the Khanate would pursue a lone shuttle."

"Why pursue when they can—" He stabbed at the console, and the shuttle maneuvered again. "At least they're too far away to manage solid lock-on, but those missiles are going to be a problem."

Even though the console's sensors were ancient, Benson could make out the incoming weapons. Eight were headed toward her own ships, but three were coming toward the shuttle. "How long?"

"Almost ten minutes, assuming I'm dumb enough to let them hit us."

"ETA to the *Valor*?"

"That's where the math gets ugly. Close to twelve minutes."

"They'll provide cover."

"They've got problems of their own. Like, six of those other missiles."

"Dinesh knows what he's doing."

"That's your… What are you—fleet commander? How many officers do you have under your command?"

"Two hundred. Unless we lost more people."

Thiessen bowed his head and looked away. "We owe you."

"No. We—"

"Your task force saved our fleet. Maybe you saved the Union."

"We did what was necessary."

He turned back to study her. "Why? We're at half strength now. We don't really offer much help, not if you really think about it. You might as well let the bastards finish us off and head back to Kedraalian space to get ready for them."

"We're stronger together. And you said you're the masters of manufacturing. It shouldn't take long to turn out new ships. The *Valor* was built in less than a year."

"A year, huh? I saw the scans of it. A ship like that would take five years to assemble and twice as long to fund."

"Robotic manufacturing. Fully staffing up. Running around the clock."

"Too expensive."

"You'd be surprised how things change when you're attacked."

"Not here. Not when all that matters is profits and losses."

"That kind of thinking…"

"I'm telling you, it's how they view the universe. Anyone who gets in the way of their money is the enemy."

"Not us. We're here to help."

"Well, you're the only ones, then."

"Maybe." She glanced back at the seat behind them, where the Azoren ambassador seemed to be glued into place. "Or maybe we can find allies once everyone understands the stakes."

Thiessen snorted. "The Azoren are just another flavor of poison."

"Sometimes, poison can be used for good."

"Remind me never to try your cooking."

Static hissed in Benson's ear: Shuttle-441. One of hers. She accepted, and the identifier flipped from the shuttle to Lieutenant Tsipras, the ranking Marine with Halliwell down. "Lieutenant Tsipras, this is Captain Benson. Go ahead."

"Good to hear your voice, Captain." The connection still had static on it, lending a masculine tone to the Marine's voice. "We've come to escort you to the *Valor*."

"Thanks. We've got missiles incoming."

"Saw that, ma'am." The static dropped to a manageable level.

Benson pointed to the console in front of her. "Can I—?"

Thiessen tapped a few command keys, and the display in front of her blacked out. She sent the connection to the screen, revealing a grainy image of the other woman. Light brown hair framed a long face with a strong nose. The lieutenant was barely halfway through her twenties, but there was a tiredness around her dark eyes.

Having to assume Halliwell's command probably wasn't helping. "How're you holding up, Lieutenant?"

"All right, ma'am. I just think of Nikolaos and how he's keeping everything under control."

"That's the way to do it."

The Gulmar captain pursed his lips.

"One moment, Lieutenant." Benson muted her connection to Tsipras and turned to Thiessen. "You have a question?"

"Not really. It just sounds odd."

"What sounds odd?"

"Nikolaos?"

"Her husband. They have two children waiting for gene therapy. It's a big drain on the whole family, but when the opportunity for such a prestigious assignment came up, Nikolaos blessed Danae pursuing it."

"Danae?" Thiessen nodded at the lieutenant's image on the console. "You know her name, her husband's name, her family?"

"We're all family. That's how you survive in the military."

"I barely know my crew."

"I'm sorry to hear that."

"It's the nature of the job. Every time we're mobilized, a lot of my people change."

"Burnout?"

"Sometimes. Mostly, it's based on who responds to the offered contracts. If you've found another job, it's hard to just drop that and spend six weeks or half a year in space for probably half what you're making with dirt under your feet."

"Your leadership should know better."

"The executives? They couldn't care less. We're commodities."

"That's probably the worst description I've ever heard for a military professional."

The Gulmar fleet commander smirked. "I'm not about to argue against that."

Tsipras sent a ping; Benson accepted. "Something new, Lieutenant?"

"Five minutes out. We've got missiles inbound."

"We're tracking them."

"Sounds like things got ugly down there."

"I'll be glad to be back aboard, that's for certain."

"No doubt. I don't know if you've heard anything more, but Clive's stable."

Thiessen cocked his head at the name. "Clive?"

Benson muted her connection. "My Marine commander. He was injured in an earlier engagement."

"I'm sorry to hear that."

Benson thought she caught a strange tone in Thiessen's voice but didn't think he would be upset about the lack of formality in talking about her officers. She filed that away to address with him later, then came off mute. "Lieutenant, we've also got the Azoren ambassador aboard."

"How…fortunate, ma'am."

"We may need to reach out to them."

"I hadn't thought of that, Captain. Would you be interested in a relay of the *Valor*'s data? I think our connection can handle it."

"Please."

The Marine's image was replaced with the data feed from the task force. Weapons tracking, simulations of the retreating ships, timers, damage reports. The Gulmar captain seemed impressed.

Then a strange pall passed over his face.

Benson leaned back. "What's wrong?"

"Nothing. It's just—"

The data feed from Tsipras's shuttle died. There wasn't even the previous static, just the silence of a dead connection.

"Lieutenant Tsipras?" Benson tried another channel to no avail. "The shuttle's comms—"

Thiessen pointed to the console. "Something's wrong. They're not accelerating anymore."

"Did they get hit?"

"Not likely. The only thing they'd have to worry about is those missiles."

"And those are still minutes out. Then…what? Wait! I'm getting something." Benson switched to her communicator's internal systems. There was a request from Tsipras. "Lieutenant? What happened?"

"Bomb." The Marine's voice sounded far away. "I've got six people down."

"How?"

"—don't know—" Now the audio wasn't just faint but choppy. Then it was gone again.

Benson shook her head. "She must be using her own communicator to ride on the shuttle radio system. Her battery won't last pushing a system like that."

Thiessen's fingers hovered over the control console. "What happened?"

"She said a bomb took out six of her people."

"Khanate—like with our fleet."

"We had people on alert, Marines posted to watch critical systems."

"The bombs could have been placed before you left Kedraal."

"I—I should have had bomb sniffers go through everything." Before she could wallow in self-pity, Tsipras connected again.

"Captain?"

"I hear you."

"Battery's low. Our systems are out. Sorry, ma'am. Not much of an escort."

Thiessen signaled for Benson to mute, then shared his console display to hers. "Those missiles have lock-on."

Two of the missiles were headed straight for Tsipras's vessel. Benson massaged her forehead with the palm of her hand. "Can we get to them in time?"

"In time?"

"To get them out."

"That's a tight window."

"I've served on a search-and-rescue vessel. We can do this."

The Gulmar captain cracked his knuckles. "We can try."

Benson unmuted. "Lieutenant, we're coming to you."

"You can't put yourself at risk, ma'am."

"We're not. Have your people prepare for egress."

"Copy that, Captain."

"Have everyone seal up. Conserve your battery."

"Tsipras out."

When the shuttle adjusted course, Thiessen frowned. "We'll need to take some risks. If those Khanate ships figure out they can take some shots at us..."

The enemy was still in full retreat, as far as Benson could tell. "I think it's just those missiles now."

"Let's hope so."

Minutes passed, and the missiles closed. It was going to be close, but tight windows were a part of rescue operations.

Benson sealed her helmet and unbuckled her harness, then headed aft.

When Manshaus looked up, she gave him her best calming smile. He went back to his anxious clinging to the harness.

At the airlock, she searched around for a moment, then connected to the Gulmar captain. "We'll be pulling the wounded aboard first. These cargo strap hooks back here are the only place I can see for people to tie into."

"All right. Thirty-eight seconds. Grab a handhold. Maneuvering."

After cycling the airlock, she stepped inside and depressurized it.

Through the porthole, the other shuttle was a faint shape speeding against the curtain of black. Benson grabbed a couple handholds and braced herself a second before the maneuvers to match the other vessel's movement began.

Their airlock aligned to 441's airlock, and the maneuvering stopped.

They had two minutes and twelve seconds to get the Marines off the shuttle.

Benson deployed the umbilical to the other craft. A seal couldn't be made without risk of altering the shuttle's course, so she pulled two cables from the airlock wall and latched one to her suit, then headed into the far-too-flimsy frame. The two spacecraft were five meters apart.

At the end of the umbilical, she reached for the 441's hull. There were hooks for the cable, but to get to them, she would have to extend beyond the protection of the umbilical. It was one of the scarier operations she'd trained for.

You're connected. Stay calm.

Thiessen's voice was in her ear. "Hold on. I'm almost there. I can help."

For some reason, irritation flared up at the back of her mind. He didn't mean anything by it, but...

She extended, then pushed off with the tips of her toes, cable hand extended...

And missed.

The Gulmar captain gasped. "Captain Benson!"

"I'm fine." As she drifted past the hook, her free hand caught it.

She pulled herself back and hooked the cable in, then maneuvered herself to open the shuttle airlock. "Lieutenant Tsipras?"

"Here, Captain." The audio was stronger but distorted.

"We've opened the outer airlock." Benson waved for Thiessen to extend the umbilical. When it touched the skin of the Marine shuttle, she hauled hard on the cable until the umbilical could be clamped into place.

Thiessen was in the umbilical, squatting. "Less than a minute, Captain."

"I know." Her upper body ached from the exertion and tension, but when the inner airlock hatch opened, the sensation became inconsequential. Marines stood just inside the wounded shuttle, carrying wounded.

Benson waved them past, then spotted Tsipras at the back. The lieutenant was nearly as tall and much more muscular. She pushed her people ahead of her. "Let's go!"

Although trained for space combat, the Marines were carrying wounded into a tight, uncertain space.

They weren't going to make it.

Benson waved Tsipras forward. "Lieutenant, we need to abandon ship."

The Marine officer nodded. "Coming, Captain. We have to get our people—"

Light flashed like a star inside the shuttle: another bomb!

Tsipras grunted, then floated forward. Blood misted in atmosphere as it escaped from gashes in her environment suit.

Benson grabbed the wounded officer's arm and hauled her into the umbilical.

The Gulmar captain squeezed past the Marines and grabbed the lieutenant's other arm, pushing Benson ahead. "The missile!"

No sooner had he said that than another bright flash lit the shuttle interior. This time, the wounded vehicle twisted, impacted by larger chunks of shrapnel. With the vector change, the umbilical was wrenched and contorted, shifting the Gulmar shuttle as well.

Thiessen grunted, then his grip on Tsipras slipped. "I'm hit."

Benson grabbed his hand and dragged the two wounded people after her, careful of the jagged edges of the umbilical frame. Marines met her at the airlock, taking the wounded and strapping them to the cargo hooks.

She sealed the airlock and ejected the umbilical, then staggered toward the pilot seat. Now that she had a connection into the shuttle's control console, she switched to her own communicator riding through the shuttle comms. "*Valor*, this is Benson. Do you read?"

Chopra took the connection. "We read you, Captain. We lost 441."

"Bombs took the systems out. We've got wounded."

"We'll scramble another shuttle—"

"Negative. This is a lot like one of the shuttles I trained with years ago. I'm on my way. Have the medical team ready. If you could get this last missile off of us, that would be appreciated."

"Working on it, Captain."

"Benson out."

It only took a moment to refamiliarize herself with the controls. Once that was done, she had them moving at full acceleration away from the last missile. She was so focused on the piloting, she almost didn't see the missile disappear from the sensors.

At least one thing had gone right.

Just as she'd requested, medical teams were waiting aboard the *Valor*. Kohn and Dietrich were there with medical technicians and nurses, mentor and student still bickering.

Benson made her way over, listening in on Dietrich's scolding as the two men examined Tsipras. "You're forgetting that she suffered these wounds in space. Look closer at her vitals. Look at her blood pressure."

Sweat beaded on Kohn's forehead. "I did. It's dangerously low. She's—"

"I'm not interested in another misdiagnosis, Ensign Kohn. You were wrong about Halliwell; now you've nearly killed this woman." The surgeon waved one of the nurses over and rattled off a series of directions, then waved a medical technician over. "The two of you get the lieutenant prepped immediately."

Kohn seemed about to buckle. "Sorry, Doctor. I'll help with the prep."

"Please."

Dietrich hurried over to the other wounded Marines, quickly determining that two were dead and giving instructions to his staff for the others.

Benson hung back as he examined Thiessen. "Does it look serious?"

The doctor didn't turn from his examinations. "Shrapnel. A head wound like this— Why didn't you treat it immediately? He's lost a good deal of blood."

"We were a little busy trying to get everyone back to the *Valor*."

"Well, that haste may have cost him his life." After medical techs set the Gulmar captain onto a gurney and wheeled him away, Dietrich pulled his gory gloves off. "At some point, all this violence has to come to an end."

It was enough to stun Benson. She had to rush after the doctor, barely squeezing into the lift as he headed to the medical center. "He's important."

Dietrich frowned. "Everyone's important, Captain."

"More important than most. He's the only one of the Gulmar with a hint of how to run their security forces."

"You mean he's the only way we'll have more bloodshed?"

"Ernie, you know better than that. Without someone to stand against them, the Khanate will take their bloodthirsty brand of warfare to the stars."

"Did I miss something? I thought they already had."

"No one will be safe."

"Wasn't that your argument about the Azoren?"

"And it was true. It still is."

"How convenient for the warrior to always have enemies who threaten the peace they swear to protect." Dietrich exited the lift at a brisk pace.

Benson wasn't sure she had the strength to argue anymore, but she followed. "Can you at least go easy on Ensign Kohn?"

"I *am* going easy. He's taking too many risks."

"You said in your recommendation that was what made him valuable."

The doctor arched an eyebrow at her, then stormed into the medical center. "He needs to learn and to be conventional before worrying about being unconventional."

She stayed on his tail. "That's funny."

"I'm afraid I don't have time to understand your concept of humor—"

"Oh, it's nothing. It's just you sound a lot like Chief Parkinson now."

Dietrich came to a stop. "There isn't an iota of humor in that sort of nonsense."

"Isn't there? Or maybe it's sad that you two have more in common than I realized. Excuse me, I need to talk to the chief now."

A burly male nurse rushed over to Dietrich as Benson turned away, distracting her enough that she nearly walked straight into Grier.

"Captain!" The sergeant hooked an arm around Benson and pulled her away from the surgical area with a little more force than was probably necessary.

"Sergeant Grier. I was on my way to see Chief Parkinson."

"I think it can wait, ma'am."

Benson tensed. "Did something happen to—"

"Clive's stable. But he's not in any shape to do anything, and I heard over the radio that Lieutenant Tsipras is dead."

"She's badly wounded."

"That's great, but she was the last officer we had on her feet."

"What about Lieutenant Kong?"

"Her shuttle took a railgun round. Her whole team is out of commission for now."

"Lieutenant Hardinaj?"

"He got caught in a blast on the *Seattle*."

"A blast? A bomb?"

The muscular Marine shrugged. "They're saying it was loose ordnance."

"Do you believe that?"

"No. But they don't have any video of the area where the explosion happened. It was ordnance storage, so it's possible. It could've been a lot worse."

"Have you heard of a munitions accident since you joined the Marines, Sergeant?"

"Aboard a ship? No, ma'am. But—"

"But nothing. We have saboteurs aboard our ships."

Grier winced. "Unless we can get Clive on his feet soon, we're running without officers, and Commander Dietrich said Clive's not going anywhere anytime soon."

"We should be thankful he's alive."

"I am. That doesn't change things, though. Everyone's yelling at me now."

"That's how command works. When someone goes down, the next in line steps up."

"I get that, ma'am. Like I said, we don't have a next in line."

"*You* are the next in line. Step up."

"Me?" All the strength seemed to drain from the sergeant. "I'm not ready for something like this!"

"You have to be ready for it. We need you."

Muscles bunched along the young woman's neck. "I..."

"If you can't do this, tell me. Find another NCO who can."

Grier bowed her head. "I've got it, Captain."

"Good." Benson set a hand on the shorter woman's thick shoulder. "I need someone I can trust."

That seemed to bolster the sergeant, who straightened and smiled. "Clive should be able to receive visitors soon."

"We'll talk to him when he can. For now, I need you to have your Marines organize bomb sniffing teams to search the ships."

"We're already stretched too thin!"

"I know. I'm heading down to talk to Chief Parkinson now. I'm pretty sure he should be able to do something with our drones to help out."

"Good luck getting anything useful out of him."

"Don't give up on him yet."

Benson headed out of the medical center, but she was bothered by what she'd seen on Grier's face: a smirk. Apparently, the sergeant *had* given up on Parkinson, which was a bad development. The task force needed someone with the chief's skills.

Yet…

The thought was still gnawing at Benson when she stepped into the engineer's office, which had the familiar signatures of heat and ozone from overworked equipment. He had a VR helmet on and didn't respond to her immediately. Instead, his head turned away, and he leaned forward in his chair. A display on his desktop flickered to life, flashing a wireframe of a ship corridor that quickly transformed into a gray, walled passageway.

He chuckled and pointed at something only he could see. "Got it!"

She scuffed closer to him, annoyed. "Chief?"

"Shit!" He pulled the helmet off. "I didn't hear you!"

"What's this?" At his confused look, she pointed at the display.

"Oh. It's data from the Gulmar black box. I've been rebuilding things—"

"Well, stop."

"Stop? You told me—"

"Things are falling apart, in case you haven't noticed."

"I'm doing everything I can." His voice dipped toward a whine.

"We need more, Chief. There were bombs aboard Shuttle-441."

"Bombs? What happened to your Marines?"

"I didn't think to have them search for bombs that might already be in place."

Parkinson rubbed the back of his neck. "I guess that was a mistake."

She leaned in closer. "I'm correcting that now."

"Well, you don't need me for that, do you?"

"What can your drones do? We don't have the Marines to search every ship stem to stern."

The engineer rolled his eyes. "What else are they going to do?"

"Chief—" She leaned in closer still. "—Lieutenant Hardinaj was caught in an explosion aboard the *Seattle*."

The little man straightened in his chair. "I heard."

"They're saying it was loose ordnance."

"It happens."

"We need to be sure it really was." She leaned against his desk.

His eyes went from her face to the hand on his desk. "What do you want me to do?"

"Pull all the video down."

"From the *Seattle*?"

"You can't access it?"

"Sure. I mean, I should be able to."

"Good. Check it. We have to know exactly what happened."

"What about this Gulmar black box research?"

"Work on that, too."

"When am I supposed to get any sleep?"

"You don't look all that stressed, Chief."

"That's not fair!"

Heat rolled through Benson, and before she realized what she was doing, she had grabbed Parkinson by the front of his jumpsuit. "We're at war, Parkinson! While you sit in your safe little office, people are dying!"

"Hey!" He tugged at her wrist. "This is assault!"

Benson let go and backed away. "Sorry."

His face trembled in fear and pain. "You can't just grab someone like that."

There was more to his reaction than just resentment, she realized. His psychological profile was consistent with someone equally full of themselves and insecure. He had gone from big fish in a little pond before joining the military to just another bright mind in a sea full of stars and hadn't adjusted well at all.

But she needed him, and she'd overstepped her bounds. "I really am sorry, Chief." She sagged. "And I really do need you. The task force does."

He smoothed his jumpsuit. "Well, sure."

"We're all being pushed too hard, and that's not going to change until we can put this Khanate threat down."

"I get that."

"Good. Help us out. Okay? Give me something to pull everyone together."

The engineer glanced at the display and frowned. "I—I thought I was."

"You're doing good work." She stepped back, sucked in a breath, and did her best to smile. "When this is over, I'll be sure that work is acknowledged."

"Yeah?" Parkinson straightened. "Good."

Benson turned but froze when he grabbed her by the wrist.

"Hey, and—" The engineer released her and stood straight. "—don't worry about, y'know…grabbing me. That's just between us." He smiled awkwardly.

"Thanks, Chief."

She sped out, scolding herself for slipping up. Maybe Parkinson hadn't meant anything by the display and contact, or maybe he had. Either way, she'd left herself vulnerable at a time where that couldn't happen. Everyone needed her to be her best. It wasn't just her life on the line.

It was the fate of the Republic.

23

Ambassador Manshaus reminded Benson of a mouse, with his big eyes darting around, and his face constantly twitching. Even his movement was soft like a rodent scurrying, easily lost in the whisper of the air recyclers. Although he constantly muttered praise about the *Valor*'s design and aesthetics and about the care the crew showed to keep the deck and bulkheads scuff-free, she noticed from the start that he was always peering down passageways she declined to show him or listening at hatches that weren't meant for anyone outside the crew.

As they came to a stop outside the cabin that had been assigned to him, he offered up his toothy smile. "It is with no small sense of shame that I have to admit that your ship would be the envy of the Azoren Navy, Captain. I have been aboard several of our finest vessels, and never have known air so clean and cool."

Despite knowing better, a tingle of satisfaction ran down her back. "Thank you, Ambassador. We are proud of it."

"I assume such a…new vessel must contain the latest technology."

"Technology advances too quickly for any ship to truly be said to have the latest."

"It is the greatest threat that persistently faces any military."

"I know some people who would argue that the greatest threat facing any military is the lack of oversight and the growth of complacency in monitoring the relations between military leadership and the industries surrounding it."

"This sounds like a politician's belief. Do you share it?"

"No. It's hard to ignore the smoke clouding the atmosphere on Radetta when you talk about the greatest threat facing a military."

"It is the enemy, yes?"

"The enemy who wants to completely obliterate you." She bent closer to him. "By sending a fleet to attack civilians, for instance."

Manshaus froze for a moment, mouth agape. "Yes. Terrible."

"In an undeclared war, you might say it's unforgivable."

"Many things are exactly so." The diplomat bowed his head. "Not every action of a nation reflects the will of its people, though."

"I agree. Would that sort of disagreement reflect a small minority, though?"

The man's big eyes jumped around, then he shook his head. "Politics within the Federation has a complexity that can be off-putting. There is but one voice of power, and for the rest of us to manage a collective whisper is a miracle."

"That's somewhat true everywhere. The complexity of humans, I mean."

"Animals who make art and argue philosophy. Complicated is the correct description." The little man coughed. "This politician who voiced the idea that the military's ties to industry are the greatest threat, would it happen to be a member of Parliament who shares a name with you, hm?"

"You do your job too well to need to ask that question."

"Yet I have done that very thing. How rude of me."

"My mother has been consistent and outspoken for decades. It's all part of her legacy."

"Uncompromising and incorruptible. There are worse titles in life."

"You could also say pigheaded and overbearing."

"A harsh characterization of a politician, it seems."

"If the characterization fits…"

"Yes, well, should your mother ever need some assistance in her work, you now know how to contact me, Captain."

Benson's back stiffened. "Excuse me?"

"You have done the Azoren a favor."

"Rescuing you? That's just being human. Maybe your people have forgotten—"

"Please. The insult is unworthy of you. I mean by my words that should you ever need, perhaps evidence that might eliminate a rival by forcing that rival to step down—"

"My mother would never engage in anything so unethical."

"And what about you, Captain?"

"No, thank you. In any honorable and decent society, working with an enemy to fabricate such dirt would rightly destroy a person's career—politician or officer."

Manshaus bowed. "Nonetheless, the offer remains."

Benson waited until the little man's hatch had closed, then shivered. He represented so much that was wrong with politicians, yet there was also a sincerity about him when he spoke about the possibility that the Azoren people might not be as supportive of their Supreme Leader as many assumed.

Her communicator sent a tickling sensation into the headset now anchored on her left ear, then the device chimed. "Staff meeting, fifteen minutes, deck three, conference room three hundred."

The leadership team meeting! She'd almost forgotten.

She hurried to the lift and took it to the third level. A quick check confirmed that Grier and Parkinson were en route. Benson waited for them in the passageway. They exited separate lifts not even a second apart.

"If you two wouldn't mind?" The captain pointed to the passageway that would take them to the conference room.

Grier's eyes widened, then she sucked in a deep breath, leaned forward, and marched ahead.

Parkinson's face twitched from smirk to frown as he fell in beside Benson. "She looks scared."

Annoyance plucked at Benson's calm. "This is new for her."

"Sure. Marines like to keep things physical and simple."

"Chief, I don't think there's a lot of value in that line of thought."

His cheeks sunk in. "I was just trying to make conversation."

The Marine sergeant was waiting for them outside the conference room, shoulders squared. "There are some people inside already, ma'am."

"Commanders Chopra and Tuleyev, probably. We still have a few minutes."

Grier adjusted her gray uniform shirt. "I could just pass the update on to you."

"The rest of the leadership team needs to hear the update."

"But—"

"It's best they have the chance to ask you questions."

That hit the sergeant like a punch to the gut. "Yes, ma'am."

Parkinson chuckled. "They take a crap just like we do, Sergeant."

"Thanks, Chief. That really helped." The muscular Marine's voice was flat.

Benson smoothed her uniform sleeves. "It's going to be pretty straightforward for both of you: Provide an update when I call on you, and answer any questions to the best of your ability. That's it."

Grier chewed on her lip. "I'll do my best."

"That's all we can ask of you."

The hatch opened when presented with the captain's credentials, revealing a modest conference room with a clear, plastic table less than two meters long running the width of the room. Chopra and Tuleyev rose from chairs that rode on gimbals beneath the floor. Benson waved for them to take their seats, then did the same herself. Grier and Parkinson sat to the left of the other officers.

Once everyone was seated, the table flickered and turned into a display, revealing the captains of the remaining ships and the senior pilots from each shuttle contingent.

Benson folded her hands on the table in front of her. "Thank you, everyone. I want to keep this short and sweet. I've reviewed your morning status reports. Do we have any updates?"

One of the shuttle pilots—a lieutenant commander from the *Seattle* who could have been a Marine—raised a beefy hand. His bronze skin seemed almost sunburned. "Captain?"

"Go ahead, Commander Funes."

"How long before our shuttles are cleared for service?"

"I'll let Chief Parkinson answer that." Benson nodded at the engineer.

Parkinson puffed out his chest. "You've probably already heard that I've taken your drones offline."

The captain of the *Seattle* grumbled so softly, her words were lost in the audio pickup. Benson let it go and indicated the engineer should continue.

"Anyway—" Parkinson flashed an annoyed smile. "—I've been reprogramming everything. I've also had your staff install new sensors."

Once again, the *Seattle*'s commander grumbled, but this time, she ran stubby fingers through the short, white curls that barely covered her scalp. "My engineers had to delay critical repairs to do that work, Chief. Chief Taylor's furious. I'd appreciate you running that sort of thing through me next time."

Benson cleared her throat. "I asked Chief Parkinson to prioritize this work, Commander Karras."

"I'm sorry. I must have missed the communication about that, Captain."

"I'll do a better job coordinating this in the future. For now, my focus is on getting this completed."

The *Seattle* commander leaned in toward her camera. "What is 'this,' exactly?"

Benson nodded to her engineer. "Chief?"

Parkinson laced his fingers together and twiddled his thumbs absently. "We're going to free up some of your people by automating the bomb search."

Karras rolled her eyes. "Bomb search? You took personnel from—"

Benson held up a finger. "Commander, if I could explain?"

The older woman sat back in her chair, puffy cheeks red. "If you would, Captain."

"We're still not sure what happened to Lieutenant Hardinaj—" Benson glanced at Parkinson, who shook his head slightly. "—but want to be sure we eliminate any chance the explosion that killed him was the work of a saboteur."

"Saboteurs would have already struck by now, wouldn't they?"

"I believe the work of Sergeant Grier's Marines has kept a lid on the threat so far."

Grier stiffened when the eyes of the officers on the tabletop turned to her.

Benson waited a moment, then cleared her throat again. "It's possible the bombs aboard Shuttle-441 were planted just before it launched, but it seems more likely they were from some point earlier. Our failure to check the shuttles put two Marines in cold sleep, and Lieutenant Tsipras is touch and go. We can't afford any further losses of such valuable personnel."

Tuleyev shrugged his shoulders, pulling his coat tight over his gut. "Our best hope now would be that no Khanate boarding parties attack, yes? Our Marines have no real leadership."

The Marine sergeant's eyelids fluttered, and she swallowed, but she didn't look the commander in the eye.

Good. Benson closed her eyes to collect her thoughts. "Commander Chopra, what about your assessment of the Gulmar situation?"

Chopra beamed, bright teeth showing. "I'm happy to report that things on that front aren't that bad."

"We all look forward to good news."

"It is. The ship design is older but solid. I was allowed aboard two ships—destroyers by designation—and was pleasantly surprised."

Tuleyev stuck a pinky in an ear and twisted the digit. His face creased in concentration. "And what of the crew and ship condition?"

"The crew members I met were enthusiastic, perhaps even hopeful."

"Hopeful." Tuleyev inspected the tip of his finger. "This wins battles?"

"Of course not. But these aren't just gunships. They have destroyers."

"So you said. And cruisers. *Real* cruisers?"

"Well, they don't have modern armor, but the weapons systems are good enough, and they have missiles. With the proper coordination, we easily outgun the Khanate fleet."

"And how does this *coordination* work with an entirely different Navy?"

Benson fixed her gaze on Tuleyev. "That's the problem we face right now, Commander. Floyd Thiessen is the captain of that force, and he's still in intensive care."

Her second-in-command shook a finger at her XO. "What about Dinesh here?"

"I don't think the Gulmar crew would be open to the idea of allowing a Kedraalian commander to run their operation. But I'm more concerned about their…leadership."

Tuleyev's lips twisted. "The report said there is no leadership."

"They're working on it. There's an accelerated executive search committee process underway."

"Staying here, that is folly." The portly commander glanced at the tabletop display. "Leave them to fight these Khanate ships. We return to Kedraalian space and wait for the enemy there. Fighting to defend another power…?"

Benson exhaled slowly. "Actually, Commander Chopra's assessment gives me confidence that holding here is the better approach."

"Such a decision should fall to the prime minister."

"He specifically gave me exactly that sort of decision-making authority, Commander."

"For such a junior officer, this is too much."

"In case you forgot, Alexander, I *am* a captain."

"And you are very inexperienced."

"I've had more combat command experience than anyone in this task force."

"Commanding an outdated fleet staffed by volunteers and people pressed into service? I think your experience is unlikely to be of help."

"Actually, that describes nicely the task force we took into Azoren space."

Tuleyev waved her words off. "These ships have no armor and no capacity to defend themselves."

Parkinson turned his chair around to face Tuleyev. "Actually, I'm nearly done analyzing the black box we took from the Gulmar ship."

"There! See? More proof they are not worth the effort! Their main fleet—"

"That ship had the same technology aboard it that the *Pandora* had."

Benson did her best to conceal her surprise. "The Gulmar ships had advanced shadow technology?"

"A couple generations old, but it was there, yeah."

Tuleyev threw his hands up. "Useless! It did them no good."

The senior engineer stroked his chin. "Saboteurs took everything down before the ambush. No technology in the universe can save you from people you can't trust."

"And these people—these Gulmar—they cannot be trusted."

Benson caught the nods of the other captains on the tabletop display. They weren't interested in protecting the Gulmar. Mistrust made sense. The corporations had turned against the Kedraalian Republic when the rebellion began. But... "We need allies. The Gulmar are our best chance at stopping this fleet."

Tuleyev tugged on his jowls. "We cannot defeat this Khanate fleet."

"We don't have to defeat them. If we punch them in the nose again, if we show them they can't count on spies and saboteurs, they'll have to change their strategy."

The portly commander's face reddened. "These people, they do not change anything."

"They've changed their tactics. They've changed their philosophy about being a naval power."

"And that, that is exactly what should concern us. Never have they had officers and scientists to build such a military. How is it possible they do this now?"

Benson thought back to the way Thiessen had reacted at the images of the Khanate ships and to what he'd said about manufacturing things for anyone and everyone. "They had help."

"The Khanate, they are monsters. They slaughter any who will not change to their way. Who would help such people?"

"I don't know. Maybe it's stolen technology? Maybe they—"

Tuleyev slammed a hand down on the tabletop. "It is a crime! A treason! What they did during the war, to help them to rise to such a level now? Treason! As bad as helping the Azoren!"

"I understand. That's not our concern at the moment. Stopping them here: That's our concern."

"Feh! It is only a delay. Victory for them will come through attrition."

"Then we have to seek out even more allies."

A deep, throaty laugh bubbled out of the commander. "From where? Who is there but the five powers? You would go to the Moskav? They have no fleet."

"No. We need a fleet."

"That leaves only the Azoren. You would go to them?"

Sweat dampened Benson's palms. "We have an Azoren diplomat aboard the *Valor*. He already has shown an interest in seeing the Khanate broken."

"Yes! The Khanate today, then a knife in our back and we are next!"

"Commander Tuleyev, the reality facing us is exactly as you said: We can't defeat this Khanate fleet alone, and it's unlikely the Gulmar fleet will be enough to win the day, either. What would you propose we do?"

The old commander looked away. "This is a problem for the prime minister."

"Because we can't handle it, or because returning to Kedraalian space without trying to stop this Khanate fleet would be a failure for me?"

A smile drew the corners of the commander's lips up. "Such a selfish viewpoint."

"You're damn right it is. Is it yours?"

Tuleyev stood, towering over the table. "There is no questioning my loyalties, Captain. If you will excuse me."

She let him exit the conference room, then turned back to the tabletop display. "That concludes our meeting for now, everyone. Thank you."

Chopra didn't wait for her signal to kill the connection. He glanced at Grier and Parkinson, then back at Benson. "This presents a problem, Captain."

"It could. I've been keeping everyone in the chain of command informed of what's going on. I won't make a move toward the Azoren without approval. Not unless I have no choice."

"Getting this Captain Thiessen back on his feet would seem to be a priority."

Benson pushed up from her seat. "I guess that's reason enough to check in on Commander Dietrich to get an update." She smiled at Grier and Parkinson. "Thank you, both."

Grier licked her lips. "Sorry you took the hit for my lack of leadership, ma'am."

"You're doing fine. And if we can find proof it was the work of a saboteur, I think everyone will settle down a little."

Parkinson scuffed past Chopra to stop at the hatch and turn back to Benson. "I'll get on the video next."

"Please let me know if you find anything."

Before the hatch could close, Chopra and Grier shuffled out, whispering.

Saboteurs, spies, inexplicable technology and weapons transfers, officers more interested in advancing their careers than doing the smart thing... How much had the intelligence agencies known about what Benson's task force was heading into?

It was something she would have to dig into when she returned to Republic space.

If she lived long enough.

24

———————

The dinner hour was long past when Benson's stomach rumbled beneath her gym T-shirt. She groaned and pushed back from her desk, staring at thighs that seemed to soften right before her eyes. Where was the time going? She rubbed her aching neck and glared at the command tablet glowing on the desktop. Status reports, medical reports, supply reports—her hours were spent reviewing, questioning, and correcting rather than...*leading!*

She laughed at herself. Logistics and administration were a large part of leadership.

Her tongue was dry against the roof of her mouth, and her breath was terrible. She brushed her teeth and washed her face with cold water, then considered stretching out for a nap before seeing Commander Tuleyev off, but seeing the pillow Halliwell slept on made her chest ache. Touching the material, feeling its smoothness beneath her fingers—

A soft vibration from her communicator made her jump. It was Grier. "Is everything okay, Sergeant?"

"Not really, ma'am. Would it be okay if I swung by to have one of those long chats you and Clive have?"

Benson blushed, then she realized the young Marine probably had no idea just how far outside acceptable behavior her commanders were operating. It wasn't innocence. Grier knew they were intimate, but it probably was a stretch for most people to think the task force commander would risk so much for...

For what? That was a question Benson hadn't sought to answer recently. She needed to. One day.

She pulled her hand back from the pillow. "Meet me outside the Officer's Mess hatch in five minutes."

"Officer's Mess, ma'am? I'm—"

"Five minutes."

Benson disconnected and switched from her gym outfit to her jumpsuit. The highly tailored uniforms were getting uncomfortably snug, something she needed to work on.

Later. The Khanate situation took priority for now.

The passageways were mostly empty, with shift change completed and those off-duty grabbing some precious shuteye. She should be doing the same, but Tuleyev had insisted on staying aboard the *Valor* to go over tactics and operations with Chopra. And, of course, protocol required her to see the old man off with a salute and a smile.

Outside the mess hatch, exactly as ordered, stood Grier in her uniform. She looked sleepy and anxious, but there wasn't a hint of softness in her thick shoulders and arms. She wasn't making excuses, not like her captain.

I'll change things around. Tomorrow.

The sergeant straightened. "Ma'am. Sorry for the trouble—"

Benson shook her head. "No trouble at all." She punched in the code to gain access to the mess, then waved the younger woman through, noting the heat and faint scent of perspiration coming off of her. "Just coming from the gym?"

"Half an hour on the weights. I—I needed to work off some stress."

The captain directed her acting Marine commander to a table near the food preparation area. "I just told myself I was going to have to do something myself. I'm letting this all get to me." Benson patted her gut.

"You look great for someone your age." Grier winced. "Ma'am."

"Thanks. You hungry?"

"No one's working, are they?"

"I know the boss." Benson slipped into the kitchen and opened one of the chillers. "Fresh-frozen fruit? Vegetable treats?"

"I could use some fiber, actually."

"Vegetable treats it is. Your choice of Rutabaga and Turnip on Pulped Beet, Kale and Spinach Delight, or Carrot and Zucchini Pasta Without Pasta."

"Oh. The carrots thing, I guess."

Benson took out a packet of the carrot mix and a rutabaga mix for herself. While they heated in the cooker, she took plates and spoons from a tray. Grier set those out on a table while Benson brewed coffee. A few minutes later, they were seated across from each other with steaming food and drink.

Grier shoved a scoop of carrot and squash into her mouth and chewed with gusto. "Wow. I never realized how good it was to be an officer."

The sarcasm drew a welcome chuckle from Benson. "Clive didn't tell you?"

"We don't really get to talk much anymore, y'know? I mean, other than work and all. He's really worried about being too friendly with his team leader."

"Yes." The earthy tartness seemed to drain from the rutabaga into Benson's mouth. "Fraternization can be troublesome."

"Nah. I checked. The last case anyone was prosecuted was decades ago."

"It can still derail your career."

The Marine slurped her coffee. "He's worth it, right?"

Benson inhaled her own coffee, then took a long sip, enjoying the experience and buying time before answering. "Everyone is worth it."

"Ew. You just made me think of Parkinson. No thanks."

"I mean everyone in the crew is worth the risks involved in what we do."

"Oh. Not getting tangled in the sheets?"

"Not necessarily, no." It was impossible to tell whether Grier was playing a game or not. "What's troubling you?"

"You mean besides looking like an idiot in that meeting this morning?"

"You did fine."

"Not like Clive would've. I've watched him, y'know. He's so smooth."

"He's been through training, and he has experience."

"Yeah. I wish I could have his experience, y'know?" The sergeant winked.

"Have you talked to him?"

"About—?"

"Your feelings for him."

Grier's face went rigid, then all the humor faded from her eyes, and she stared down into her cup. "Nah. I mean, I can't. Not since, well, you two..."

"Clive's a grown man. You should talk to him."

The sergeant put her cup down and dropped her hands—thick, muscular hands—out of sight. "I—I don't like competing when there's no chance of winning."

Benson took another long sip, then she sat back, heart racing at Grier's openness. "You have a fun personality."

"Yeah, that's what guys say, right? Life of the party."

"I don't own him. Our relationship is...complicated."

"All the fighting, right? Everyone kind of knows you ride him pretty hard about his Marines."

"We—" The crew really thought their relationship was professional. That was a huge relief. "I think he demands as much of me as I do of him."

"Well, you're doing great. You were doing great on the *Pandora*. The captain was okay, but he started going crazy there at the end. You kept it all together."

"Thank you, but it wasn't just me. I think we all pulled together."

"A captain is only as good as the crew, right?"

"Right."

"So, um, yeah. What the hell's up with Chief Parkinson, then? Why'd you bring him along?"

"Because he's good."

"He's a tool, though."

Benson grinned. "He's improving."

"If you say so, Captain."

"People like him have to work hard at change."

"A ship like the *Valor*? You could've found someone lower maintenance."

"Everyone has flaws. Parkinson just suffers from a desperate need for constant acknowledgement."

"Mommy didn't hug him enough, right?"

"Actually, she might not have. But the bigger problem was where he came from."

"What's so bad about Varudin?"

"He's from Lowell."

"Lowell? Is that someplace outside the capital?"

"It's a little town on the primary continent on Rungier."

"Rungier? Like, rustic backwoods and mountains Rungier?"

Benson finished off the vegetable paste she'd been toying with. It was surprisingly tasty. "Lowell was a farming and mining town. He was head of his class there his entire life. According to his records, he was insufferable there, too."

"So he says he's from Varudin to hide that?"

"And to make himself feel important. He's had to seek counseling."

"For lying?"

"For his needs—acknowledgment, attention. Commander Martinez didn't help with the way he enabled instead of correcting."

"Oh. Friction I didn't even know about."

"Chief Parkinson resents Ensign Kohn because of what he represents: someone with even greater potential."

"*That* friction I knew about. It's still screwed up."

"We're complicated organisms. You'll learn that the more experience you gain as a leader."

"Or maybe I don't have to do this much longer? I mean, if Clive's up soon."

"You're still a sergeant. With our wartime footing, the promotion backlog is going to be cleared up. In a year or two, you'll be looking at another stripe."

"Sorry if that doesn't excite me."

"It should. Part of being a professional is progress."

Grier pushed back from the table. "I'll keep that in mind, ma'am."

Benson stood. "Thank you for the chat."

"I can get the plates and cups."

"I'll show you the way." The captain took her own silverware and plates to the kitchen and set them in a machine. Once the other items were inside, she sealed the machine up and turned it on. "One of the things I insisted on learning about the *Valor* was how the kitchen works."

Tension seemed to ease from the Marine's body as they passed through the dining area, and once they were in the passageway, she actually smiled and waved.

Her question about Halliwell had actually left Benson thinking. She headed for the medical center to check on the Marine lieutenant and on Thiessen.

The place was dark, a nurse and med-tech sitting in a monitoring room, eyes glued to the bank of displays lit with the vitals of their patients. When Benson approached the hatch, it slid open, and the two people stood, adjusting their blue scrubs.

"Captain Benson." The nurse—a burly, bronze-skinned man with surprisingly pale eyes—seemed to hover between taking a step toward her and standing at attention. "We weren't expecting a visit."

"I was hoping to chat with the doctor on duty." Benson saw a look of concern flash across the young med-tech's cute face. "Is that going to be a problem?"

"No, ma'am." The med-tech's big eyes didn't do much to hide her concern, though. "Ensign Kohn is in the doctors' room."

Benson waved for the young woman to lead the way, trying to figure out what about the woman seemed *off*. When she let herself into the office where Kohn was stretched out on a bunk sleeping, realization began to creep in. The young woman's gentle shake of Kohn's shoulder confirmed it—her caramel skin and dark hair, her body type… She could easily fill in as Stiles for someone still aching from losing the GSA spy.

Kohn's head came up, and he took the med-tech's hand. "What's—?" She glanced at Benson, and Kohn let go, then cleared his throat. "Captain, is everything okay?"

"Fine. I needed to talk to you."

"Okay."

After a second, the med-tech let herself out of the office, and Benson scuffed over to the bunk while the doctor-in-training sat up and rubbed his eyes. "You still sure you want to be a doctor, Ensign?"

"Sometimes, I'm not so sure."

"Is it the hours or the stress?"

He pulled sneakers on and stood. "The stress can be a lot."

"The life-or-death decisions, or is it a certain cranky mentor?"

Kohn glanced around, as if expecting someone might be hiding in the small cabin. "I'd rather not say."

"I can ask him to ease up."

"That won't help."

"Does it help to know he does it because he sees potential in you?"

"I guess." Kohn sagged. "Is that what you came by to talk about?"

"I was wondering how bad things were with Captain Thiessen and Lieutenant Halliwell."

"Clive's doing better. I think he could be released to duty in a few days."

"And our Gulmar patient?"

The doctor's shoulders slumped even more. "That's tough."

"I was hoping for something more reassuring. Is he dying?"

"No. He's stable. The problem is with the wound. Shrapnel pierced his skull, and it's putting pressure on the fluid sac around his brain. We're concerned it might pierce the membrane."

"That's it? I thought he'd lost a lot of blood."

"He's fine now. The shrapnel's the real problem."

"Can't you just pull it out?"

"Well, Ernie—Doctor Dietrich—is worried about the sensitivity of the operation. He insists it should be handled at a real hospital."

"He designed the specifics of this facility—"

"Oh, we have the equipment and training to do it here. I think *I* could do it with a robotic assist. The problem is we could lose power or gravity during the operation. Or maybe there's an explosion close enough that it affects the surgery area. Any of that at the right moment could be deadly."

"But you think you could do it?"

"Well, yeah. I mean, the risk of something like that happening isn't very high. The surgery is only a few hours, and we have redundancies. Plus we're positioned—"

"We need Floyd, Chuck."

Once again, the ensign's eyes darted around. "For what?"

Benson sighed. "To lead his fleet and to give the Gulmar a leader. Those Gulmar ships won't get involved without his command."

"I thought the Khanate fleet fled."

"They could return at any time."

"Oh." Kohn licked his lips. "Then maybe the surgery would be a bad idea."

"What if we did it now?"

"Now? Without Dr. Dietrich?"

"You said he wouldn't approve."

"Um…"

Benson set a hand on the ensign's arm. "You'd be following orders I gave."

"Are you?"

"Am I what?"

"Ordering me."

Could she? "If I have to. Floyd could be the difference between turning the Gulmar into meaningful allies or losing them completely. That fleet of his isn't much use without someone of his experience commanding it. They're waiting for his word to even get involved."

"I—I'll need to get another nurse and med-tech to help me."

"You seemed pretty content with your petty officer. Cunningham?"

"Gia? Um—" Kohn's face turned a deep red. "Oh."

"Be discreet and professional."

"I…" Kohn nodded. "I'll get some people down here and have the captain prepped. Are you sure about this, ma'am?"

"I don't think we have much choice, unfortunately."

"All right."

Benson's communicator vibrated. "I'll leave you to your work. I have duties of my own to attend to."

Tuleyev was waiting for her outside the hangar bay, arms crossed behind his back, chatting with a Marine corporal assigned to guard the area.

The Marine—a young, pale woman who could use some of Grier's gym routine—gave a relieved smile. "Excuse me, sir. I need to get back to my patrol."

Eyebrows arched, the captain of the *Lyon* watched her go.

Benson did her best to ignore the older man's leering gaze. "How was your visit, Commander?"

"I must admit, I am more impressed by the *Valor* now than before."

"Did you and Dinesh have a fruitful session?"

"He is a very capable officer."

"That's good to hear." She extended a hand. "Your visit can only improve the performance of our task force."

He hesitated, then shook her hand. "About the task force?"

"Yes?"

"Your role as a diplomat—you were jesting before?"

"Jesting?"

"Reaching out to the Azoren? This cannot be."

Her body tensed; she tried to calm herself. They didn't need a big fight after making progress patching things up. "It's something the prime minister and I discussed back on Kedraal."

"Allying ourselves with these animals?"

"Not specifically, no. At the time, we discussed the possibility of reaching out to the Moskav if the Gulmar came through with their end of the deal."

"Ah! The Moskav are not the animals these racial purity monsters are."

"Unfortunately, the Moskav don't have a fleet. Using them to help in a ground war would have been fine. If it gets to that point with the Khanate, perhaps we could still reach out to them."

"The Moskav will never cooperate with the Azoren. If we align ourselves with those devils, it will mean never seeing the Moskav as allies."

"It's a risk we'll have to take."

"But the Moskav, they have broken the Azoren on the ground. This is the ally we need! This is who can strike against the Khanate with no fear."

"Unless the Moskav soldiers can get themselves into space, they won't do us any good, Alexander."

Tuleyev shook his head and turned away. "Such a thing is unconscionable."

"I know you have problems with the Azoren. We all do."

"What the Khanate did after the rebellion—barbaric! But what the Azoren did *during* the rebellion?" He spun around and glowered. "These are not humans."

"The Moskav have a bloody history, too."

"Against themselves. Against the Azoren and Khanate. Their struggle against us was civil as war allows."

"We don't have a choice. The Khanate fleet is a threat we never expected to see. It presents problems on so many levels, I firmly believe the prime minister and the parliament would accept the compromise of a temporary alliance with the Azoren."

Tuleyev bowed his head. "In this matter, Captain Benson, we will not agree."

"I was hoping you might understand my position."

"That cannot be. It is my belief that you are taking great liberties with your interpretation of just how much latitude the prime minister's assignment as diplomat grants you."

"Actually, what I'm doing is *exactly* what the prime minister demanded of me."

"For your sake, I can hope this is true. Also, I would hope you received more than a handshake and a smile from a politician. You are putting yourself at great risk, and that is something politicians do not do."

He turned sharply and passed through the hangar bay hatch, striding stiffly to his shuttle. Benson remained glued to the hatch porthole until the shuttle was away, then headed back to her cabin on shaking legs. The whole time she cleaned up for bed, she couldn't stop thinking through her meetings with Prime Minister Zenawi.

There were recordings. There were documents. She had been cautious about the wording of her orders. She'd consulted her seniors. She'd talked with her mother, painful as that was.

But there was nothing that guaranteed she wouldn't be the scapegoat should everything go wrong.

Was that the inevitable part of command?

The thought that she might be a simple pawn in the war playing out now kept her awake, tossing and turning. She'd made enemies. There were people who would cheer her fall when it came, but would they do that at the expense of the Kedraalian Republic? It didn't seem possible.

Finally, that logic sank in. What she was dealing with was an existential crisis. The Azoren fleet that had tried to destroy Kedraal was so much scrap. It had been deadly and had come close, but it must have been a terrible expense, and losing it had to have put the Azoren Federation in a bind. They would be suing for peace once she brought her task force and even a handful of Gulmar destroyers into Azoren space.

She was doing the right thing! Anyone would be able to see that!

Peace replaced the swirling doubts, and she started to drift off.

But she woke almost instantly to the shrill, piercing tone of the general quarters alarm.

Her communicator chirped as she grabbed it from her desktop. "This is Benson. What's going on?"

"Captain!" The voice was one of the second shift crew.

"Go ahead."

"There's been an explosion on deck three."

The medical center! "Casualties?"

"Damage control teams are on the way. Ma'am, the Khanate fleet—"

Static hissed, and the lights winked out.

And all doubts about the Azoren alliance disappeared.

Her task force was under attack, and the enemy was among them.

25

———————

No cabin was big enough to squeeze Stiles and Caville into, and the modest honeymoon suite he'd purchased aboard the *Vole* certainly wasn't meant to provide space. His annoying music—deep bass and drums with simple spoken rhymes—played just loud enough for her ears to pick it up. She had demanded the small foldout "emergency" bunk, which had probably been intended to deal with the inevitable marital squabbles. He had taken the larger "honeymoon" bunk, which he had refused to make each morning.

Typical.

And probably something he'd done to annoy her—like keeping the cabin thermostat locked onto a chilly 16° Celsius—same as when they were young. Then, it might be stealing someone else's milk or not brushing his teeth or…

Something.

The two of them had been at each other's throats for as far back as she could recall. Even their trainers had been reluctant to let them spar, fearing they might cripple each other despite their proven durability.

She stared at him from her bunk, noting the way muscles rippled beneath his golden skin as he pulled his nightshirt on. Their differences extended beyond the greater testosterone produced by the male body and the other aspects of his male physiology. He had always been more aggressive, quicker to anger, louder, and more reckless.

Even the pheromones he gave off—a scent stronger than the inoffensive shipboard soap—were different.

He seemed to sense her attention, spinning suddenly and glaring at her. "What?"

"Would it be so hard for you to stop with your man scent?"

Her brother snorted. "Jealous?"

"That I don't smell like a locker room?"

"Your nose is too sensitive."

"It's saved my life multiple times. Anyway, you don't need your scent. Our looks were coded to be enough to give us all the edge we need."

"You know how many women I've been propositioned by since we left Kedraal?"

"I know how many you've slept with."

"Like I said: jealous."

"If my mission called for me to have sex, I would have sex."

He plopped onto the honeymoon bunk. "So what is your mission, anyway?"

"You already know, or you wouldn't have been at the Sutton building."

"I know you're tracking down information on the Patel family. GSA wants to cut them out of operations, right?"

"They're a problem."

"Sure." He stretched out on the bed, pulling a data tablet from the foldout nightstand where he'd set his valuables. His fingers danced across the tablet surface with a masculine grace that was both brutish and hypnotic. "You found Kusno Saripado. So, you're plugging holes."

"You know about him?"

Caville shrugged. "Senior manager of Analysis & Reporting, Counter-Espionage Directorate. Compromised by the GSA about twenty years ago."

"Compromised? Really? You don't sound like someone loyal to the agency."

"Are we loyal to the agency or to the Republic?"

She pushed up on an elbow, letting the blanket slip down her bare arm.

The chill was nothing compared to what the Ravens had put her through. "I don't know, Darien: Who are *you* loyal to?"

His eyes narrowed. "We have the same conditioning, the same background."

"That's not an answer."

"You think I'm a traitor now?"

"I haven't seen you in six years. You were supposedly dead."

"And I thought you were dead. That makes us even."

"Not quite. You knew I was going to be at the Sutton building. If I were dead—"

The corner of his mouth ticked up. "Past tense, Sis. Obviously, I found out you were alive."

"And you came after me why?"

"You were stomping around in my territory."

She threw off the covers and pressed her back against the bulkhead, feeling goosebumps rise on her arms. Switching from sleeveless T-shirt and underwear to sweats would have been more comfortable, but it also would have been giving him a small victory. That wasn't happening. "*Your* territory? You want me to share information on my assignment, but you won't talk about yours?"

"I just did: You were stomping on *my* territory."

"So, you protect the Patels?"

"You'd be dead if that were the case."

"Like those people you shot on the roof?"

"I don't know. Why don't you tell me who they were?"

"You—" *He didn't know.* She kept her eyes from showing surprise with a little effort. "They were part of the group protecting the Patel family."

"Wrong."

"Then you knew them?"

"Nope. I know who they weren't, though."

"Can you at least tell me that?"

"Who they weren't?" He smirked. "Sure. They weren't part of the Patel organization. And they weren't SAID or CED."

"You're leaving something off."

"It's good to see some of your training stuck."

"Meaning what?"

"Meaning you were sloppy and nearly got yourself killed by a small group of humans. You should have seen them coming."

"Should I? They had gear that could detect my shadowsuit. They weren't on the rooftop when I went in. They didn't follow me all day while I staked the place out. They weren't on the building's security network. Even we have limits."

"Speak for yourself. I clocked them before you entered the building."

"You were watching me. That's completely different. Shadowing someone from a distance is easier than trying to root out surveillance."

"Like I said: sloppy. They were just human."

"You keep saying that." She pushed off from the bunk and crossed to the thermostat, bumping it up two degrees. "How sloppy were they, though? By coming after me in *your* territory and you not knowing who they were, exactly how is it that *you* weren't the sloppy one?"

He came up behind her and stretched for the thermostat, but she blocked him with her body. When he tried to shove her aside, she drove an elbow into his solar plexus and punched him in the jaw.

Almost.

His arm blocked her fist, and he backed into a fighting stance. "You think you can take me? Seriously?"

No amount of training could make him sound convincing. His breath had been knocked out of him. She had caught him off-guard, and he was hurting at that moment.

But he wasn't her assignment, either. She strutted past him, now the one smirking, and climbed back onto her bunk. "You're trying to avoid answering. Again."

Caville relaxed. "How about this: We play a game."

"Since when did you like games?"

"I didn't say I would enjoy it."

"What are the rules?"

"One: No lies." He dropped back onto his bed. "Two: We take turns sharing one piece of information. Three: The second one of us figures out what the other is doing, we reveal that guess, and the other person has to answer yes or no."

"All right. Change to the second rule: We take turns asking each other one piece of information."

He tried to hide his annoyance at that but a quick frown was there and gone. "I'll start."

"Flip a coin."

"Why? That's wasteful."

"Flip it."

"Fine." He grabbed his data tablet and held it up. "Display side is heads. You call."

The device spun in the air over the covers—

"Tails."

—then landed with a soft thud…back of the device up.

Her brother's face contorted, and he snatched the tablet up. For a second, it looked like he might throw it against the floor.

Same sore loser as when he was a kid.

She leaned against the bulkhead and brought her knees up to rest her chin on them. "Are you still working for the GSA?"

"That's a stupid question."

"Yes or no, honest answer—your rules."

"Okay. Yes." He pointed the device at her. "My turn. Are you trying to kill Sajid Patel?"

"No."

"You can't lie. That's the rule."

"I'm not lying."

"It's in your face, Sis, plain as day."

"It's not a lie. I'm not trying to kill him."

Caville tapped the tablet against his muscular leg. "Fine. But you're not being completely honest."

"You asked a crappy question. That's not my fault. Second question: Are you working for the Patels?"

"Nope."

"Now you're lying."

"No more than you are about killing Sajid."

"All right. I'll clarify my answer if you clarify yours."

"Deal. You go first."

"I'm not trying to kill Sajid Patel, but I am trying to kill *one* of the Patels."

"Okay." Caville rocked back and forth on his bed, tablet pressed against his chin. "Interesting. I think I'm ready to guess."

"You're not going to clarify your answer first?"

"My answer came to a question you asked after giving a bad answer."

Stiles groaned inwardly. He could sometimes be almost clever. "What's your guess?"

"You're trying to stop the Dramoran Independence Movement."

"Bad guess."

"Lying! You're lying again!"

"Stopping the Dramoran radicals is a side benefit of my mission, not the primary objective."

Once again, he tapped his chin with the edge of the tablet. "Fine."

"You owe me a clarification of your mission: Are you working for the Patels?"

"Not directly."

"That's not clarification."

"I work for them, but I'm undercover." He was being honest, or at least he was being as honest as their job ever allowed.

"Okay. You guessed and were wrong. Third question: Are you working for Lev Goldman?"

Caville froze. "How did you find out that name?"

"Why does that matter?"

He spun around and pulled his pistol from the nightstand. "I'm going to ask you one more time: How did you find out about Lev Goldman?"

"His name was in the data I stole from the Sutton building sub-basement."

The pistol didn't budge from the center of her chest. It wouldn't likely be a lethal shot, not given how quickly she could move if she twisted away, but her brother was equally fast or close to it. He would pull the trigger before she could twist away completely, and she would be hit. And she would bleed. And he would have the advantage he needed to defeat her in combat.

So she sat very still. "Darien?"

"You shouldn't know that name. That complicates things."

"You're working for him?"

"The same way I'm working for the Patels. No one else is supposed to know."

"Except Kusno Saripado?"

Caville's eyes drifted away, but he nodded. "You're becoming a real problem."

"You're a mole within the CED."

His eyes came back to her. "I've been watching over Saripado for six years."

"Because of his ties to the Patels?"

Her brother nodded. "And to Goldman."

"Goldman's a spy. He's an SAID asset."

"He's…SAID?"

"Deep cover. They're behind a big operation. Worth billions of credits."

"I see." The way Caville shifted…he knew.

"Have you ever heard of—" Stiles froze when Caville's eyes narrowed. "You okay?"

"Have I heard of who?"

"Nothing."

"Too late for that." He waved the gunpoint at her to encourage her. "Who?"

"Well—" She needed to pull off the impossible, to fool someone as gifted as she was at sensing lies. Her intent to ask about Ravens and Owls was premature, placing trust in Caville without justification. He could be compromised. "Have you heard of Colonel Avis McLeod?"

"GSA? Sure. That wasn't what you were going to ask."

"No. But if you didn't know him, the question wouldn't make sense."

Caville studied her with a hot gaze. "Okay. And the question is…?"

"He had a relationship with Samir Patel. Something that went a long way back. Colonel McLeod won't talk about it, but I heard he had a history of some sort of troublesome behavior."

"McLeod? He has a background in philosophy and other crap, which never looks good in our field."

"He had to cut some sort of deal to be resuscitated."

Caville's eyes widened slightly. "He died?"

"Taking down some double agents."

"Well, I've heard he's got some sort of kink. He's had his clearance yanked a few times, but he always gets it back."

Stiles scrutinized the man who was supposed to be her twin brother; his aim never wavered. "How did he make it so high up if he's a suspect in anything questionable?"

Caville shrugged. "Family. He comes from money. Not Patel money, but their families have connections."

"Can I trust him?"

"In our line of work, you don't trust anyone!"

"I have to trust *someone*. Now he's running the operation I'm on, and every time I start to make progress, I run into someone like those people you killed on the rooftop."

That drew an energetic nod from her brother. "Or people like me, right?"

"Yes."

"So McLeod has you looking to gun down one of the Patels? Is that it?"

"I killed Samir."

"Okay. Impressive. I'm surprised you're still alive, to be honest. He was heavily modified."

"It was close."

"And now you need to take the head off the snake? Is that it?"

"One strike is all I get, so it needs to count."

"Well, you don't want to waste that on Sajid. He's a drunk who chases whores. He cut his empire up and delegated it to his kids and grandkids."

"So, who would you recommend I target?"

"The mother—Devanshi."

"But not until you let me go, I gather."

Caville put the pistol back on the nightstand. "You're not a prisoner."

"I can leave anytime I want."

"If you can make your way through Fold Space, yup."

"And once we arrive wherever this ship is going—"

He gave her a heavy dose of side-eye. "You know where it's going. I'm not an idiot. You've been inside the ship's systems at least twice by now."

"Four times, but yes. Once we reach Dramora, what happens?"

"That's entirely up to you. I needed you to leave the Patels alone long enough for me to get to my next objective. Getting you aboard the *Vole* accomplished that."

"So, tomorrow morning, we just say…goodbye?"

"If you'd like. However, I have a proposal."

The strange facial expressions—conflicted and annoyed—that had been messing with him began making sense. He needed something from her. "I'm listening."

"Devanshi Patel is meeting with Lev Goldman in three days."

"What? Where?"

"In orbit around Dramora."

"You brought me out here— Wait. Were you at the Sutton building to *kill* me?"

"I was there to stop whoever was messing around with the Patel operations. I didn't know it was you, but it sure sounded like it might be. If it hadn't been, I would've killed the troublemaker."

"Even if it was another GSA operative?"

"Brianna, what I'm doing is bigger than you think."

She crossed her arms over her chest. "Working for an SAID asset posing as a pirate? No, wait. Working for a CED double-agent? Or is it working for one of the wealthiest merchant families in the Republic?"

"It's all three, and they're all involved in an ugly mess that could drag the Republic down."

"Then we kill them. The two of us working together, no one could stop us."

"This one time, violence isn't the answer."

"I never thought I'd hear those words from you."

"You did. So, are you interested?"

"I'm listening."

"Good. But I'll warn you, you may not like it."

26

Without the life-sustaining feeds properly supplying him, Satrap was weak and helpless. His atrophied limbs trembled whether he kept them stretched out or curled against him. His breathing was a loud wheeze thick with a cloying medicinal smell that was fading far too quickly. When his heart beat, it was a thready, irregular thud in his ears.

It was the sound of dying.

Betrayal had brought him this low. Only his loyal Jakkara had even kept him alive. Him and the old woman, the Ikhama.

For how long?

At least they had been given a new lease on life, such as it was, abandoned in his cabin aboard the *Might of the Khan*.

Satrap blinked sweat from his eyes and read the message again: *All praise to the glory of the Great and Holy Khan! Strike at the appointed hour! At my next signal, the Kedraalian task force will be defenseless!*

The message had been sent to his connection, same as the message sent just before the attack on the Gulmar fleet. Only the senior spies among the various militaries knew of his private address, and they would only transmit before taking acts that would expose them to great risk, possibly death.

Yet here the message was.

Ikhama pulled her robes up at her waist and groaned. She looked every bit as bad off as Satrap felt. *"Like wind through the valley, preceding the charge of the cavalry..."* She pressed a hand to her face. "Satrap, I can barely breathe."

"The heat in this room is worse than any animal should bare."

"A heat meant for punishment."

"Yes. To break us."

"As a child, I wandered the desert. Did you know this?"

"No. We—"

"The attention of the Khan's people, the way they sought what might please his eye. *In beauty is the delight of a thousand songs. It is the will...the will of... It is the will of the stars...*"

"It is the will of the stars that the most holy should know all delights."

"A terrible thing to learn when you are but a child with a pleasant aspect."

"Or a child with a bright and inquisitive mind."

"My prayers, my thoughts—nothing is my own. No words come when I summon them."

Satrap rubbed the aching joints that had been ruined by the Khan so long ago. "We don't need the parables right now. We need to convince Zohar that he must keep us alive to succeed."

"He has cast aside his own life, throwing in with thieves and brigands. When walking through the peace of the valley..." She sighed. "May the Great and Holy Khan guide me to my place in the stars."

"You live still. Remember that."

"Without the words of wisdom, what value do I have?"

"Your mind is your own. That is more important than any words you've memorized."

"Heresy."

"Truth. Religions fear free thought. Accept this loosening of the yoke."

"As a shepherd guides his flock, so do the rays of the guiding stars..."

"So do the rays of the guiding stars bring the people of the Great and Holy Khan to his side when they fall." He wiped sweat from his face. "Listen to me: We are not dead yet."

"Soon."

"You feel the maneuvering? The acceleration that tests your heart?"

"And breath."

"That can mean only one thing: Zohar took my suggestion to attack again now that the fighters are ready to launch."

"Combat only hastens our death. The blade rises and falls with no concern..."

"For the weak or poor." Satrap flinched at his ability to recall scripture he loathed so deeply. "Ikhama, listen to me. Please!"

Her breathing was even louder than his, although it was dry and tremulous rather than his wet and strained sounds. She was leaning against the corner opposite him, a ghostly white shape that might have been a spirit. "I listen still."

"Do you understand that Zohar did as I suggested?"

After some unsteady breaths, she made a soft noise. Then another. "Yes."

"He understands that I have insight beyond the tactical and strategic training he lacks."

"You have ever been..."

"The Khan's favored and hated. I know."

"Favored and..." She gasped. "What he did to you. What has become of them?"

"Our Khans? They were all monsters, at least by the time they finally became too much for the universe to tolerate any longer."

"Heresy." Her breathing stopped.

"Ikhama!"

One dry rasp followed another. "I live."

"Do *not* give in to the pain! I need you!"

"I...live."

"Zohar launches the attack. We have returned to engage the Kedraalians. For the moment, he trusts me."

"Clever and wicked..."

"It isn't wicked. What I do doesn't merely keep us alive a while longer. If it proves true, it gives us a chance to destroy the Kedraalian task force."

"Such death and destruction. How could one so filled with hatred of the Khans be so effective fulfilling their will?"

Satrap hesitated. It was a question he had trouble answering to his own satisfaction when he was left to himself. Death—whether efficient and swift or slow and painful—was still death. Should there be satisfaction in producing what he so despised as the sick obsession of his people? "We strike against the military. These are warriors who know the risks of what they do."

"*Treasure and lies are but swords in hidden scabbards.*"

"Yes. But I have a question for you."

"The one who knows so much has a question for the one who knows only—"

"—only parables. I know it sounds impossible. Listen, please. The message I conveyed to Zohar? This idea to attack?"

"Yes?"

"One of our saboteurs lives still aboard one of the Kedraalian ships. I received the message that they stand ready to strike soon."

"The precious children of savage, godless beasts."

"They are still our brothers and sisters. And this one seems ready to cripple the task force."

For several long seconds, the old woman gasped and groaned. "You told Zohar this?"

"No. I simply fed his bloodlust when the data rolled in through the limited access I have that the fighters were complete. I gave him the assurance he needed to pursue his own desires."

"He would expend these pilots when worrying about his own son…"

"It's the race among these captains to prove one is more bloodthirsty than another. Rouhani makes the contest suicidal. Even Zohar's family is cast aside. He fears for his life."

"They all do."

"No. Some have embraced the death aspect of this strange cult."

"Heresy."

"Stop saying what you don't believe. This is your chosen life no more than it is mine."

Ikhama uttered unintelligible sounds, then there was only her labored breathing.

"The fleet attacks under Zohar's guidance."

"He wished to replace you."

"Yes, but there is no unanimity. His orders are challenged at every turn."

"Do any demand your return?"

"We would be dead already if that were the case. The only thing these thankless traitors have ever agreed upon is the need to remove whoever commands them. Now Zohar understands this."

"How do we survive this, Satrap? I am too old to fight."

"There is an advantage: This saboteur."

The old woman muttered.

With some effort, Satrap pushed up on an elbow. "What?"

"I lack your tactical thinking. What advantage is this?"

"What if this spy is compromised? What if the Kedraalians await our attack?"

"Still, the advantage eludes me."

"No. That isn't the advantage. That is the risk. The advantage comes if the spy isn't compromised. At that point, we have the edge in recommending when to strike. But to appreciate the advantage, we have to acknowledge the risk."

"That this is…a trap?"

"Yes. The Kedraalians have been completely unlike the Gulmar. They have been quick to adapt. Or maybe they have seen through our ways and have found out our spies."

"The risk is death, then."

"Damage to the fleet, certainly. And there is where we gain: Even in risk, we have opportunity."

Ikhama's breathing seemed to grow easier, as if the discussion might be distraction enough to take her mind off the miserable heat. "Zohar is left vulnerable if the fleet suffers damage."

"And if we succeed, my value is proven again."

"This seems more dangerous than rewarding."

"Bold plans always are."

"Hm." She coughed. "What would you do should you regain command?"

"Break the Kedraalians, then break the Gulmar fleet."

"Then destroy the Gulmar worlds?"

"No. Without a fleet, they are no threat."

"But there are swords waiting to taste blood in conquest."

Satrap winced. "That is not my concern."

"Content yourself with the blood of warriors."

"Such was my charter. I cannot anger the Khan by doing as commanded."

"Yet look at us. Your decision has angered your subordinates, and they would kill us soon enough."

"A victory changes that."

"Did the victory against the Gulmar city of sin appease your subordinates?"

"It…should have."

"For someone so clever, you have yet to understand those you would lead."

"But if we destroy these threats, then proceed into Azoren space and crush them, I *can* regain command. I simply need to choose my approach and time things perfectly."

Satrap's communicator buzzed; he accepted the connection request without even realizing it was Zohar. "Yes?"

The captain's face was strained. "There are problems."

A trap? "There is little I can do to help you, isolated as I am."

"Help me, and the isolation can be reduced."

"I see no value in such a proposition, Captain."

"Remember, Satrap—you have no Jakkara to protect you now."

"Access to the full data stream. If you would ask my help, I would have full knowledge of what transpires in *my* fleet."

Zohar grumbled, but the full data stream flowed again. Bright lines of intelligence flowed into the processors and memory embedded in Satrap's skull. Digital representations of his fleet—their locations and disposition—tickled the optical sensors that were now the most important part of his eyes.

It was like a drink for a dying man in the desert wastes.

Satrap's lips trembled as the data filled the empty spaces within him. "Why has the fleet split in half?"

"There are fools among us."

"Rouhani."

"He would bypass the Kedraalians and seek out the Gulmar fleet we were told would be in orbit here."

"The shuttle group that flew up from Radetta."

"So goes the argument."

"The Gulmar fleet will be as easily dispatched as its sister fleet once you've disposed of the greater threat."

Zohar nodded enthusiastically. "This is the obvious answer!"

"But they won't listen to you."

"They threaten mutiny and favor Rouhani's inept plan!"

The captain's indignity was a rich and tasty feast for Satrap's amusement. "How preposterous."

"Yes! They propose destroying my ship and removing two problems at once."

"How quickly the snake bites its tail."

Zohar's image froze on a face clenched in fury.

Ikhama smirked. "You quote the parables, Satrap."

He muted. "Our Kahn stole wisdom. Sometimes it survived his corruption."

The old woman rested her chin on her chest. "Heresy."

As abruptly as it had frozen, Zohar's image became animated again. "What do you propose to keep Rouhani and his traitor captains in line?"

It was hard for someone lying on the floor, sweating and gasping, to appear nonchalant, but Satrap did what he could. "They became your problem once Ikhama and I lost the protection of the Jakkara."

"The others wanted you dead. You owe your life to me."

"I should feel more grateful. I cannot imagine why I don't."

Zohar disconnected.

Ikhama rasped and shuddered. "Strategic thinking?"

"Manipulation." Satrap touched fingers to his damp forehead. "He needs us more than we need him."

"What transpires?"

"There has been a mutiny within the mutiny. Half the fleet apparently has thrown in with Rouhani and feels the need to seek out the missing Gulmar fleet and eradicate it. The rest have currently thrown in with

Zohar. More splintering might be imminent based on communications chatter."

"The constant competition you curse."

"Done well, competition can produce elite leaders. Under the Khan's haphazard guidance, promoting the idea that blood grants strength, all we have is a manic spiral of cutthroat—" The communicator vibrated again. "Zohar wishes to speak to me once more."

Zohar's face seemed even more stressed than before. "I have given you access to the data stream, as you asked."

"You have. I see things are close to fracturing more."

"The *Desert Sands* would attack Radetta and finish the two next largest cities."

"Serving no purpose whatsoever."

"I…agree."

"You have the Kedraalian task force at a disadvantage. They seem to be doing nothing but defensive maneuvers and reacting rather than counter-attacking."

"As you said they would."

Satrap fought back a smug smile. "This satrap of yours must be quite knowledgeable in the ways of war."

"He must." Zohar flashed teeth. "Will he show more of this?"

"I would have my quarters restored to a survivable environment. And my fluids and medicines must be restored as well."

"I will see what I can do. Satrap."

The fleet commander chuckled as the connection died. "Ikhama?"

"Yes?"

"Do you remember the risk and advantage we discussed?"

"My breathing troubles me so. I fear the light I see when I open my eyes is the Guiding Star calling me."

"Put that belief aside. It won't be long before we have the comfort of my—"

The hatch to the compartment opened, and six of Zohar's soldiers moved in, sour frowns twisting their faces. Cool air rushed in from the passageway. Sweat chilled on Satrap's face, and he was quickly shivering.

He searched around his bed for the tubes and cables, then with their assistance slowly reconnected the critical ones that drained away poisons and filled him with nutrients and drugs. Straps came out of the wall and wrapped around him, securing him against the ship's maneuvering thrusters. In seconds, he was breathing easier, and the pain was drifting away.

Zohar's men slipped out from the cabin, some of them looking ashamed rather than angry.

Ikhama got to her knees and crawled to the small refrigerator that had been sealed when they'd returned, where she pulled out a container of nutrient-rich fluid. She opened that and quickly drained it, then tried to assume the prostrate position expected of her in her superior's presence.

Satrap waved a hand lazily. "Stop. I need your attention."

"I am…attentive." She settled on her butt.

"It won't be long, then Zohar will connect again. The fleet has squandered this opportunity. If this spy is truly one of ours, we have one last chance."

"To strike when the Kedraalians are crippled?"

"And to do so as a fleet. It would position us for the next phase."

"The Gulmar."

"Their fleet, yes. Then on to the Azoren."

The old woman fanned herself. "You have this puzzled out. You don't need me."

"I will need your wisdom and grace."

"For what?"

"To—" The communicator vibrated. "Zohar. Are you prepared to guide him?"

"I will do what I can."

Satrap accepted the connection, then he opened the cabin's radio system fully. "Captain Zohar, I've joined Ikhama to our chat."

Zohar's teeth clacked together. "Ikhama. You are rested?"

"The serenity of the moon reflecting on the waters touches deep within the soul, freeing the pure soul from dark moments that fester into weakness and doubt."

"Good." A cold smile was there and gone, then the captain's attention was on Satrap. "We are now close to seeing other ships join the *Desert*

Sands in the attack against Radetta. The fleet cannot hold if this division transpires."

"Captain Zohar, I have a proposal for you."

"To bring the fleet together again?"

"And to have that fleet see things through to success."

"I am listening."

"Of course. The unfortunate matter of my Jakkara dying and my shuttle being destroyed must be set aside."

"A very wise thing."

"However, the mistreatment suffered by Ikhama—it must come down to a troublesome soldier?"

"Perhaps—" Zohar's eyes drifted off. "I have a lieutenant who is overzealous and inclined to pursue his own ambitions. He could be punished to show this is unacceptable."

"Good. Then with my return to command, we have one objective."

"Command is contingent on exhibiting competence."

Ikhama cleared her throat. "*When the wind speaks the commands of the heavens, even the mountains in their solidity must in time give ear. It is from the heavens that lightning and fire and rain are born, and stone is worn down over millennia.*"

A twitch bunched up Zohar's cheek. "Satrap? Your objective?"

"The fleet must come together to focus on the Kedraalian task force."

The captain snorted. "You will have to do better than that to resume command."

"When I told you that the time to attack the Kedraalians was now, did you doubt me?"

"The fighter craft were ready. Pilots were begging for a chance to die in the name of the Khan."

"So now I tell you that the time is imminent for us to strike the Kedraalian ships, and you must believe."

"Why? The other captains will do no such thing."

"If I say so, and you echo it, and Ikhama has blessed it?"

Zohar shook his head. "Not enough."

"Then what if I told you a spy from one of the Kedraalian ships has contacted me and will soon signal? At that signal, the task force will be defenseless, and the easy victory we need to appease our impatient brothers will be at hand."

"This is a truth you speak?"

"It is."

The captain rubbed his chin. "Crushing an enemy has a way of healing wounds."

"You speak with a wisdom of your own, Captain."

Zohar smiled. "A moment, Satrap." The captain stared off beyond the camera's eye, then turned back. "The other captains are connected in through me. My fellow captains, can you hear me?"

A dozen different voices grumbled and shouted over each other. The rest of the ships' commanders remained silent.

Then Rouhani's voice was there, clear and loud. "Your time as fleet commander has come to an end!"

Zohar clapped softly. "Thank you, Captain Rouhani."

Satrap's hatch opened, and two of Zohar's soldiers stepped in. One was a lieutenant—tall and angular, with a dark sneer. They pointed heavy shotguns at Satrap and Ikhama.

On the connection, Zohar continued. "You will be pleased to know that our Satrap has agreed to accept an advisory role."

Rouhani laughed. The captains grumbled and growled at each other and Zohar.

Once more, Zohar clapped. "Thank you. In his advisory role, Satrap has given us a plan to consider. He has staked his life on this plan's success. I accept his guidance after hearing the guidance of our Ikhama."

"What is this plan, Zohar?" Rouhani sounded like he was chewing glass.

"We must come together and strike against the Kedraalian ships—"

"They are weak and run rather than fight."

"Our Satrap assures me that when he speaks the word, the Kedraalian ships will be helpless. We can slaughter them, perhaps even send some of our security teams across to butcher their sailors and claim their ships as our own. Could this planet offer such rewards?"

The other captains mumbled among themselves. In the data stream, the ships that had been maneuvering away stopped.

Rouhani finally silenced the others. "We will wait for your signal."

Zohar bowed. "This is good."

"If you are wrong—"

"Oh, rest assured—" Zohar glowered at Satrap. "—there can be only one outcome should this not go as described."

Satrap tried to smile at the lieutenant and his shotgun.

Risks and advantages.

It had seemed so sure a proposition, but now it seemed ridiculous. The captain had outwitted Satrap, and win or lose, he was a dead man.

27

———————

With power out and no artificial gravity, the *Valor*'s stairways were jammed with people pulling themselves along the rails to move between decks. Benson kept her eyes focused on the steps and wall so that she wouldn't be blinded by an errant flashlight. There was only the rustle of skin and cloth on metal and the whispers of anxious sailors.

At the entry to the third deck, she pivoted to look up and down the stairs. "The atmosphere won't go stale for several hours, people, and the reactor has so many safeguards built into it, it's almost impossible for radiation release. If you're on a damage control team, get to your stations. If you're not, go to your cabin and stay ready for updates."

"Yes, ma'am." That was the reply from several folks above and below her.

Good. Her crew was as good as available—sailors with high marks and recommendations. They had training for emergencies exactly like the one facing the *Valor*.

Then again, panic was gnawing at her. The ship was blind. It wasn't accelerating or maneuvering anymore. It didn't have shields or weapons. It didn't have active countermeasures running. Simply launching or taking in shuttles would require expert piloting and risky extra-vehicular activities.

That made them easy targets, and the bridge communication had indicated the Khanate...

What? Were they closing? Were they attacking?

Benson pulled herself along the passageway, heart pounding. There were hundreds of lives at risk, people counting on *her*. The entire task force would be at risk if the *Valor* went down.

She stopped at the entry to engineering, which had been locked open. Inside, people hovered in front of lockers, pulling on hazardous environment suits. Parkinson was already dressed in one—a dull gray with black gloves and boots in the emergency lights. He tapped a young woman on the shoulder. "Take McDonald, Johnston, and Simmons to the reactor. See if you can find where the break is."

"Chief?" Benson skipped along the deck, guiding herself using the lockers.

He turned. "Captain? Shouldn't you be on the bridge?"

"Commander Chopra's on his way there with his crew."

"Well—" Parkinson squeezed his helmet against his hip. "We've got this under control. We'll have power restored in no time."

"You know where the bomb went off?"

"Bomb? Power was taken out using some sort of blocking device."

"A what?"

"Something shunted everything into an overload. We've got breakers popped on three decks."

"Not a bomb?"

"I heard someone say there was an explosion near the medical center, but—" His eyes widened. "You okay?"

She swallowed and fought against the rising panic. "I—I'm trying to—"

"There's a munitions storage area up there. Maybe something blew up in there."

"We..." The engineers were listening, watching. "Could you show me the area you're talking about, Chief? In your office?"

"Huh? Sure..."

He led the way, twisting to look at her over his shoulder a few times, clearly confused. At least he managed to keep his questions to himself while still among his staff.

Once through the hatch, he powered on a battery pack. Another already glowed under his desk. "Can't risk losing some of my critical systems even for a second."

"Chief, that was a terrorist operation."

"Terrorist? The blast?"

"The blast and this shunt you're talking about."

"The block? No way. That's a design element."

"What do you—?"

"You don't reroute power like this with a couple snips and laying down some cabling of your own. Someone screwed around with wiring when the ship was being built."

"That's impossible. Most of the construction was done by robots."

"Robots can be hacked. And humans can sneak into a robot construction area pretty easily."

"Access to the shipyard was restricted. All the engineers and laborers were cleared."

Parkinson snorted. "Yeah, well, obviously it wasn't restricted enough."

He pulled himself into his chair, which carried even more of his scent without all the hardware running. The display on his desktop showed a wireframe of the ship, which he quickly drilled down into at a speed that she couldn't keep up with.

"Chief..."

"I know. Just a second. Here. See this? Reactor? These are the junction boxes the cabling goes through. Into this distributor, right? Then each deck gets a feed through multiple channels for redundancy. Like here. See?" He indicated a spot where a thick line split into two, then dragged along that line to where it split again. Then again. "Never a single point of failure."

"Okay."

"But somewhere, someone set up a mechanism to allow them to introduce a short. Probably a few physical switches here and there, and all that power gets dumped to ground, and you pop the breakers." He tugged on his soul patch. "See?"

"Not the bomb?"

"It doesn't have to be a bomb to be sabotage. This is worse, actually."

"How so?"

"If that was a bomb, it didn't take anything out. Nothing serious, at least. We're going to be hours finding what happened with this electrical problem."

"We don't have hours, Chief. We're dead in space right now."

"So? Atmosphere will be—"

"The Khanate fleet is back."

"What?" He almost launched himself out of his seat. "Why didn't someone say that?"

"Word's getting out slowly. Communicators might be able to transmit the length of the ship, but if people are sealed inside their cabins or—" She rapped knuckles against the heavy bulkhead at the back of his office.

"All right. All right." He pinched his bottom lip. "So, we don't worry about getting *everything* back up and fixing the problem. We focus on vital systems. I'll tell the team what to do."

"Good." As he moved past, she caught his shoulder. "Wait. There's no way this *just* happened right before the Khanate fleet arrived. Not by chance."

"That's sort of obvious, isn't it?"

"What's the implication of that, though?"

"Well, they obviously have some sort of…communication— Shit!"

"Exactly. Our saboteurs must have the ability to coordinate with each other and with the fleet."

"Using the ship comms?"

Benson pointed back to the display showing the *Valor*'s power cabling. "If these people could sabotage ship design, wouldn't it make sense to embed their own comms gear as well?"

"Or bring it on with their personal belongings or in cargo."

"If we want to stop these saboteurs, finding this communication mechanism needs to be a priority, too."

"We don't have the people—"

"Everyone's stretched thin. I understand that. That doesn't change a thing."

Parkinson sighed dramatically. "I'll come up with *something*."

"Thanks, Chief." She could feel one of his dramatic turns coming, so she kicked past him. "I need to get to the medical center. Keep me updated."

Zero gravity movement was something she qualified on annually, so moving through the passageways became easier with each transition from deck to deck and from compartment to compartment. She found her way to the medical center easily enough using the light from others' flashlights and the cold white of the emergency lighting.

Her heart sank at the activity within. The same cold white lit the surgical bay interior. There were two surgeries underway, and a third body lay on the final surgery table—prepared but abandoned.

Dead.

Despite the horrible wounds and gore, the body was recognizable: the young Marine corporal who'd been talking with Tuleyev earlier.

The cute med-tech whom Kohn appeared to be involved with—Petty Officer Cunningham—came out of the surgical bay, pulling her mask down. "Captain? Dr. Dietrich…" The young woman glanced back into the room where it was now clear that Dietrich was overseeing both surgeries. "He's…"

"How's Floyd? Um, the Gulmar captain?"

"A-alive. Dr. Dietrich is…upset."

"I understand. Who's the other wounded person?" Maybe it was time to encourage Dietrich to take a little break. Even if he turned to the bottle for relief, that was better than tearing everyone else down.

"Chief Petty Officer McTiernan. She was wounded in the blast, like the…corporal."

"Did the Marine's resuscitation ring work?"

"It should. We'll put her in cold sleep after we clean her body up."

McTiernan. The name didn't set off any alarms. Benson would have to do some research. Should the petty officer have been in the area of the blast? "Did either McTiernan or the corporal have a necklace?"

"A—" The petty officer's brow wrinkled. "I'll check."

"With a medallion."

The young woman nodded, then headed back through the airlock. She searched the Marine's ruined corpse, then moved to McTiernan's. After a moment, the medical technician shook her head, then she froze. She pulled something from the corpse and returned to the airlock, holding it up.

A Khanate medallion!

Benson waved the med-tech out. "How long will your reserve power work?"

"Eight hours. With a normal load."

Benson pressed against the glass wall. The robot assistant was offline, and Dietrich was splitting his attention between the two tables. When he was at Thiessen's table, he seemed to spend as much time yelling at Kohn as helping.

He's losing sight of the objective.

She went to the intercom panel and activated the link into the bay. "Commander Dietrich—"

His head came up, and despite the surgical mask, the fury on his face came through. "Captain Benson! Was there something *else* you needed to break?"

"I need you to focus your efforts on Captain Thiessen."

Dietrich pointed a gory instrument at her. "This is *my* department, Captain! I will not have you come in here and—"

"This is a strategic priority. The success of this mission—"

The doctor stomped back to the other surgical table. "A life is a life."

"Not when millions of other lives are at stake."

His pale eyes flashed at her. "This woman won't survive cold sleep without my intervention."

"Then she dies, Commander." Benson swallowed. There was no way to *know* whether or not McTiernan was a saboteur. She could have been doing her job when the explosion happened. But the medallion... "Save Captain Thiessen."

Dietrich shot across the room, eyes wide, hands extended to stop him when he reached the glass wall. "If you hadn't countermanded my orders, this choice wouldn't be necessary!"

"We need Captain Thiessen—"

"I know damned well what you need, and I'm telling you—!"

"Commander Dietrich, this is something we can discuss in private." Her communicator vibrated. "Excuse me."

She pushed away from the glass, keeping Dietrich in her peripheral vision until he returned to Thiessen's table.

The person calling her was a Marine, a private Benson didn't recognize. "Private Dominguez?"

"Yes, ma'am. Sorry to bother you, Captain, but I responded to a distress signal up here in Officer Country."

"Is anyone hurt?"

"Not hurt, ma'am, but the Azoren ambassador was in a panic."

The explosion and power going out. Manshaus knew everything there was to know about the Gulmar fleet being destroyed. It made sense he would panic. "Tell him we have things under control."

"I did, ma'am. He was demanding to see you."

"I'm making the rounds. He's on my list to visit. Keep an eye on him." It would be unprofessional to tell the Marine to babysit the diplomat, although it sounded like that was what was needed.

"Will do, Captain."

Benson got a glimpse of Kohn's pained expression, then left. If he survived Parkinson, Martinez, and now Dietrich, there wouldn't be much worse to overcome in even the bumpiest career. How a kid from a more advantaged status could have so much trouble believing in himself was beyond her—

She groaned at that thought. Her situation was no different.

The Marines on the bridge were on full alert, turning with clattering weapons as she skimmed into the silent bridge. They relaxed a little at her smile, then she pushed along to the command station, waving for Chopra to stay there. There were only two emergency lights, but that was enough when combined with the dull glow coming from the battery-powered consoles.

An anxious frown twisted the executive officer's face. "Still flying blind, Captain."

"At least the air hasn't gotten too stuffy yet."

"It won't be long. But there's a little good news."

"I could use some."

"We have a shuttle launched and should have some communicator concentrators deployed soon."

"A relay to the task force?"

"Exactly."

The hum of the displays grew louder, and images flickered across them: tactical data from the shuttle. Her task force was maneuvering as expected—green squares tracing across the black of space. Surprisingly, the Khanate force had broken into three groups, this time with no clear sense about them.

She pointed to the closest of the three Khanate groups. "Any idea what's going on?"

"An error, perhaps?"

"I don't think so." She moved closer to the big display, which was operating in low-power mode. The video was lower resolution, the details minimal. It was what the shuttle pilots had to work with, which was enough, but… "We get spoiled easily."

"Hm?"

"The video. All the details we come to rely upon. We get spoiled."

"Ah. We do."

Nuñez glanced at Benson for a moment, hesitated, then twisted around to Chopra. "Commander Tuleyev would like to speak to you, sir."

The XO waved Benson to the raised command platform, then tapped the console panel. "Commander Tuleyev, this is Commander Chopra. Captain Benson just joined us on the bridge."

Benson pulled herself up to Chopra's level. "How are things, Alexander?"

"It is not good, Captain."

She signaled for Chopra to take over, and he cleared his throat. "We have only limited data on the task force at this point, Commander. Could you fill us in on the problems facing you?"

"You went silent. We were ready to abandon the *Valor*."

"We can't defend ourselves at the moment."

"And the task force is badly outnumbered without you. I could save everyone by putting the Gulmar fleet between us and the Khanate ships."

Benson's jaw squeezed tight. The idea was as practical as it was cowardly.

Chopra ran a hand over his bald scalp. "We were damaged by saboteurs, but we should be online soon."

"What is *soon*? This enemy captain has split his forces. I do not know what he plans. It could be a feint. Perhaps they try to get behind us before resuming coordinated operations."

Benson tapped the mute button. "Ask him if they know we're offline."

Chopra's eyes widened. "The Khanate fleet? They can't know, or they would have attacked."

"Ask him. It might keep him from abandoning us."

"I—" The XO sighed. "Commander Tuleyev, it doesn't appear the Khanate ships realize we're offline. Can you determine anything with your systems?"

"We have yet to crack their communications encryption."

"But they haven't maneuvered toward us. They must not know."

The other commander grumbled softly. "So it would seem. Knowing you were inoperative, they would be launching a serious attack against us all."

"If you keep the task force between the Khanate fleet and us, they might not be able to notice our condition."

"Yes. I see this."

"You could always break away—to preserve the task force—if things change."

"It is my primary objective to salvage the Republic's greatest asset."

"A very good objective."

"Hm."

Grier pushed through the bridge entry, stopping long enough to chat with the two Marines on guard, then grabbing a rail not far from the command station. She looked panicked but held her position, chewing on her bottom lip.

Benson muted the command console again. "Keep talking him through this, Dinesh."

"I will."

She guided herself to Grier, whose eyes went to the hatch. Benson leaned in close. "What's wrong?"

"It's Clive. I went by the medical center. They're talking about putting him in cold sleep."

"What? Why? He was stable."

"He still needs all the equipment, though, and they're using up a lot of power right now."

Dietrich. Even if he wasn't being petty, it came across that way. "We should have power restored soon."

"But if they put him in cold sleep, he might not come out of it."

"He's going to be okay."

"They've already resuscitated him once—"

"Sergeant Grier, listen to me."

"We can't lose Clive, ma'am! We—"

"Sergeant! You need to get your head into this."

Grier blinked. "I—"

"We have saboteurs aboard the *Valor*. We have ships out there that could attack us at any moment."

"But..."

Benson's stomach twisted at the desperate look in the other woman's eyes. "This is bigger than Clive."

Tears started in the corner of the sergeant's eyes.

Parkinson's ID showed on Benson's communicator just as it vibrated. "Hold on one second, Sergeant Grier." When Grier nodded, Benson turned away. "Tell me something good, Chief."

"Well, sort of. I just found out about this shuttle flying alongside us outside the hangar bay."

"We're in communications with the task force now."

"I see that. And so I powered on one of my critical systems and used that to connect into one of the signals ships to monitor task force comms."

"Searching for that signal?"

"Yup. And guess what just happened?"

"Another signal?"

"Another—" He exhaled dramatically. "A signal *burst*."

"A burst? What was in it?"

"I don't know yet. It's encrypted."

Of course it was encrypted. "We need to know, Chief."

"I *know*. I'm working on it."

"Thanks. This is good news. Can you tell where it came from?"

"Oh. That's the part you're going to love: the *Lyon*!"

Tuleyev's ship? "Excellent work, Chief."

Benson glanced over at Chopra, who had turned toward her. He signaled that he was muted, then leaned closer to her. "You have something about the *Lyon*, Captain?"

"A possible problem. *Big* problem."

"Should I tell Alexander?"

"In a moment." Benson turned back to Grier. "Have your sergeant on the *Lyon* lock everything down."

Grier winced, then pulled herself back toward the hatch.

But she was talking to someone. That was a start.

Benson dragged herself back to Chopra. "I'm taking Sergeant Grier over to the *Lyon*."

The XO gulped. "That won't go over well."

"I know. Tell him we're coming over."

"Perhaps you should."

"You two seem to have a pretty good relationship."

"I—" Chopra sagged. He took the console off mute and connected Benson in. "Alexander?"

"Yes?"

"Captain Benson needs to come over to your ship. She—"

"What? No! The *Lyon* is my vessel! She must stay aboard the flagship."

"Alexander, it's a matter of security."

"Then have her tell me what the matter is. I will deal with it myself."

Benson shook her head.

Chopra's breathing seemed labored. "Alexander, she isn't asking. I'm simply telling you what's happening. She's on her way to the hangar bay now. Please alter your defensive maneuvers to bring the *Lyon* closer to the *Valor*."

"She is not fit for command, Dinesh! I will see her removed when we return to Kedraal! I—"

The XO killed Benson's connection and muted himself. "I'm sorry, Captain."

"Have a pilot meet us in the hangar bay. You might want to warn Alexander that I'm not in the mood for any nonsense."

"Yes. Of course."

Grier was outside the bridge, head down. "This isn't going to go over well, ma'am."

"What now?"

"Commander Tuleyev has been trying to bully my Marines around."

"That's going to stop."

"I understand. But that's what I was saying about Clive. He wouldn't put up with this sort of shit." Grier winced. "Sorry."

Benson chuckled. "He wouldn't have. And now it's up to you to do the same."

"He's a *commander*."

"And I'm his boss, and you work for me."

It seemed by the way Grier loosened up on the way to the hangar bay that the message was sinking in. It was an ugly spot, having a convoluted chain of command, but it was necessary for the mission, especially in light of the saboteurs. Halliwell would have had it just as bad; he simply would have hit his limit with someone like Tuleyev earlier.

There was a shuttle waiting for them; they launched without hesitation. As they pulled on their environment suits, Grier's face twisted, running from fear to anger. "I think this Tuleyev's up to something, ma'am."

"That's what I'm worried about."

"Trying to tell my Marines what to do…"

"He's used to them reporting to him. That's the normal structure."

"Well, I'm used to having an officer running things."

"Things are strange right now."

"Strange as fu—" The sergeant's voice dropped off. "Sorry."

"I'm not some fragile soul."

Grier smirked. "No kidding."

A tone chimed on the intercom, and the pilot twisted around slightly. He pointed port. "*Lyon*, one minute, Captain. She's coming our way fast."

Tuleyev had followed orders, at least. That was something.

The shuttle began maneuvering, and before long, the belly of the cruiser filled the front screen. A couple minutes later, they were inside. As they settled onto the hangar floor, Benson's communicator vibrated. It wasn't Tuleyev but Chopra. More trouble? "Go ahead, Dinesh."

"Captain! Khanate fighter craft incoming!"

"Which ship are they targeting?"

"The *Valor*, Captain! They're coming for us!"

28

Far beneath the rented shuttle, Dramora slowly spun, an ugly, brown ball with gray clouds that filled the view screen. In the claustrophobic cabin of the rented shuttle, Stiles felt locked into the dreadful planet's gravity well. Of course, she knew better. She and Caville weren't going to be dragged down to the planet any more than the planet was truly a clump of mud. Huge storms created a haze that obscured some of the oceans, that was all. But the planet wasn't one of the prettiest in human space, whether in orbit above or on the surface below. Large swathes were sandy desert that smelled sulfuric and vile, a stench that clung to the shuttle interior. What mattered more was that Dramora was mineral rich, and there was money to be made. Millions had flocked to the eight continents as a result.

Caville's snort rose above the rattle and hum of the shuttle systems. "Your loathing is showing."

"It's not loathing. You can't loathe a planet."

He stretched in the pilot seat. "But you can loathe an idea?"

"An ideology that's toxic to human survival? Absolutely."

"Then you loathe what this place represents."

"Unfettered greed?" She shrugged, then she tapped the environmental control panel, bumping the temperature up two degrees. "Anything without reasonable limits is destructive. That's part of Republic philosophy."

"The people who settled this world worked hard to make it human compatible."

"So that they could strip-mine mountains and poison valleys."

"They're repairing the damage."

"Where it's proving too toxic not to. When groundwater becomes lethal—"

"You shouldn't stay on Dramora, Sis. They would hate you."

Stiles pulled off her gloves and twisted her hands around in the pale light coming from the control panel. "I don't match their ideal. Neither do you."

"They're not Azoren."

"Half of them want to be."

"They don't know what they want. They've been fed so much propaganda, they can't tell good from bad."

"Whose fault is that? Finding truth isn't so hard."

"Now you believe in an absolute truth?" The young man shook his head.

"Have you turned away from science and logic?"

"Not everything is that easy."

"When they strip-mined, did it or did it not poison the groundwater? Did it or did it not cause significant change to the ecosystem for kilometers around? That's science."

"It is. But it ignores the economic benefits realized by those efforts. Thousands became wealthy from that mining."

"Thousands? Including the people who did the work?"

"Success is never evenly distributed."

Stiles glared at the ugly planet. "And that's worth destroying the world?"

"It's not destroyed. People still live there. People still *move* there."

"For the promise of wealth. That attracts a certain type of person."

Caville ran a sensor check, then sat back in his seat. "You think the struggle with Dramora is purely about wealth and natural resources?"

"Those play a part."

"That's simplistic. If that were all that's at play, they could easily root out the troublemakers."

"What—kill them?"

He shrugged. "If it's all about the resources."

"That's not a good solution. It's how the other nations work."

"It's not a necessary solution, because the problem with Dramora isn't about resources or wealth. Resources can be found everywhere. The galaxy has systems full of dead rocks we can mine with no risk to human life. If we even need to go that route. We can fabricate almost anything now from simple base components."

"But these people won't abandon their mining."

"Because the disagreement is about control. The people down there want to prove they can do what they want, and the people in Parliament want to prove that *they* have the power to dictate how things are done."

It would be easy to point out the flaws in her brother's argument, but at the core, he was right. Letting Dramora choose its own destiny—which might include joining the Azoren Federation—was losing control of a key Republic asset. It wasn't just the billions of credits in trade that the planet represented but the millions of people. Taking those out of the Republic would be devastating, whether by virtue of giving the planet independence or allowing it to join a twisted, murderous enemy.

Still—

Caville leaned forward. "About time."

A sharp chirp cycled from the console, warning about an approaching object. The sensors showed an angular design—a ship about the size of a corvette, like the fleet's gunships. It was closing quickly from sunward.

Stiles regulated her breathing. "This is Goldman's ship?"

"The *Ollie*."

"It looks like a fairly new design."

"Wait until you get a look at it."

The radio chimed: a challenge. Caville accepted. "This is Caville."

Static hissing answered, then the connection went silent. "What is your destination, Dramora Shuttle-592?"

"McFarlane Tower."

Stiles tensed. That was Caville's code. It had to be.

"Prepare to dock, Dramora Shuttle-592."

Caville's fingers danced across the console, bringing systems to life. "Awaiting clearance."

The other ship decelerated, and within minutes had come to a stop maybe a kilometer away. After that, the clearance signal was sent, and the shuttle began its own acceleration. Her brother's piloting was nimble and controlled.

As they closed, Caville glanced at her. "Remember what we agreed to."

"Don't challenge Goldman. You and I go back several years."

"You're former military."

"I can handle a gun."

"And you know your way around a ship."

"Medic, mechanic, sensors—what do you need?"

"Good." Her brother's smile was cool and sincere. "Patience. Wait for things to come to you—just like I said."

They docked portside and to the rear, suited up the rest of the way, grabbed their gear, and transferred through an umbilical to the *Ollie*. Once through the airlock, they found themselves in a spacious hangar that had been arranged by someone who knew what they were doing. Crates were stacked three high, strapped against each other and the deck, with gaps between them wide enough for other crates to be maneuvered through.

In between the airlock and those crates, four men with shotguns were spread in an arc behind a fifth man. Dark hair, a cybernetic eye that could pass for human if not for the glow coming from the iris, and scars on his arms that indicated other enhancements gave the man a dangerous, weathered look.

Goldman.

He rolled his thick neck and advanced toward Caville. "Prostitute, Darien? You know better than that."

"Actually, she's looking for a job."

Goldman turned toward Stiles. "You are, huh? What can you do?"

"I spent a few years in the Navy."

"There are thousands of bodies floating in space who could have said that…if they were alive."

"I can handle a weapon. I know my way around a ship. I'm a decent medic."

"You are, huh?" Goldman pointed to one of his crew—a broad man with olive skin, a big nose, and dark, bloodshot eyes. "What can you tell me about Theo, huh?"

"He's ugly."

Theo snarled and took a clumsy step toward Stiles. "Who the fuck—?"

Stiles lowered her bag to the deck. "And hungover. I can smell him from here."

"I'll show you ugly." The olive-skinned man brought his shotgun up for a buttstroke.

Which she easily avoided. She punched him in the gut, hooked a leg behind him, and sent him to the deck with a shove, taking away his shotgun in the process. Without missing a beat, she ejected the shells so that they clattered all around the fallen man's head. When the weapon was empty, she handed it to Goldman without looking at him. "He's also clumsy."

The pirate chuckled. "All right. So she's capable. I'm still not interested."

Caville helped Theo up. "She's trustworthy."

Goldman handed the glaring pirate his shotgun. "Pick up your ammo."

Caville stepped around the squatting pirate who was grunting as he scooped the shells up. "I'll stake my reputation on her."

The pirate chief looked Stiles up and down again. "All right. You'll make half what Darien here makes. If you don't like that, you're welcome to take the shuttle back down dirtside."

Stiles made a hard heel turn for the airlock. "Fuck you."

"Seventy-five percent."

She stopped and glowered at the pirate. "I don't give out discounts to people I don't know. Full price."

"You better be as good as advertised."

"And you better have the money."

A smile spread across Goldman's face. "I have plenty of money, Miss—"

"Brianna Stiles."

"Theo will show you to your quarters, Brianna. Darien, if you have a moment, we need to talk."

Stiles grabbed her bag and fell in behind the staggering man. When they reached steps that led up, he glanced over his shoulder at her. She narrowed her eyes. "You don't want me to hurt you, Theo."

He grunted, then led her up to a passageway sealed off from the rest of the ship by an airlock. Hatches lined both sides. "Your place is at the end, starboard side, next to the head."

The hatch opened as he neared it. Inside were two sets of bunks, lockers, and a sink. Faint traces of perfume mixed with stronger hints of alcohol. She set her bags down and checked the lockers—empty. The first two bunks she flipped down didn't have linens.

"I get the whole place to myself?"

"We lost some people in the last operation." Theo wiped the back of his hand across his mouth. "Best not to get attached."

"Thanks."

He stepped out, and the hatch sealed behind him. She tested to be sure she hadn't been locked in, then checked to be sure she could lock it from the inside.

As she was unpacking, the faintest tremor ran through the deck. It was probably the shuttle returning to Dramora on autopilot. A couple minutes later, another tremor ran through the deck.

Another ship docking?

She opened the hatch to her room and listened. The passageway was silent. "Hello?"

Nothing.

Someone else must have connected to the *Ollie*.

She hurried to the hatch that let out onto the landing and the stairs, but the hatch didn't open.

There had to be another way out—a maintenance hatch or a second exit. Stiles retraced her path down the passageway, pausing before each hatch to see if any of the others were unlocked like hers. Of course they weren't.

Except for the bathroom. It opened with a grinding clank, revealing a well-used shower, two stalls, and two urinals. Everything was grimy and worn.

More importantly, there was a maintenance access panel in the floor, beside the overflow drain.

How big would the crawlspace be? Would it lead to other crawlspaces?

She returned to her cabin, grabbed a flashlight and a multitool she'd picked up while on Dramora, and then squatted beside the access panel, unscrewing the fasteners as quickly as she could.

The crawlspace was spacious as maintenance areas went—a meter deep and probably twice that to a side. Plumbing and cabling took up a lot of space, but there was another access panel in the deck, and when she popped that, she smiled: A ladder led down to a larger maintenance area.

After pulling the two panels closed behind her, she got a feel for the larger maintenance area. It had even more plumbing and cabling along with ducts. All of those ran into stencil-labeled wall connectors: AD1, AD2, PC1, PC2, PC3, RP1, SC1, and SC2. Atmosphere ducts, power cabling, recycling pipes, and system cabling. This had to be a major junction area for the forward section of the vessel.

And it had to have another—

She spotted the hatch around a bend, nearly hidden. Rather than electronic, the controls were mechanical. There was no listening through something so heavy, so she focused on opening it as quietly as she could.

Light came through the narrow gap. And voices. Off to her left.

The cargo bay.

She opened the hatch wider and found herself looking onto a passageway. To the left, she thought she spotted the stairs she'd taken up to the crew quarters. To the right, it looked like an engineering station.

Stiles slipped out from the compartment and closed the hatch behind her, then padded to the stairs. If she poked her head out just enough, she could see people standing near the spot where she and Theo had shared their moment. Goldman and Caville were there. There were also two hard-looking men with deep gold skin and black hair. They wore armored environment suits and had pistols holstered beneath their shoulders. Between them stood an older woman with graying hair and even darker skin. She had a pronounced nose and a mole on her cheek that made her easy to identify: Devanshi Patel.

But there were other voices besides hers.

Stiles dropped to her belly and crawled out until she could see almost the entire entry to the cargo bay. To Devanshi Patel's left, another three people in black armor were doing their best to look casual and nothing at all like special operators.

Ravens.

They had to be.

Beyond them all, Theo and the rest of Goldman's men were loading crates from the airlock.

The Patel matron's attention focused on those men. "It would take too long to go through the usual process, so we've adjusted the books to make it look like this shipment will go out next week."

Goldman followed her attention. "It's all so automated now, we should be fine."

They were breaking routine. For what? Something was special about the cargo, something that made it time-sensitive.

Brianna slithered back under the stairs and worked her way around the cargo area, moving through shadows and stopping completely when Goldman's men came back from where they were securing the crates.

It was a compartment she hadn't noticed before.

The way was clear to it at the moment, so she darted from cover and ran to the hatch. It was another physical rather than electronic mechanism, but it had an electronic lock attached. And the hatch was sealed, obviously.

She slid her tablet from a leg pocket and had the device try the lock. Seconds passed, with her constantly looking back down the row of piled-high crates. Finally, the lock popped. It was far too loud for her taste, but no shouts of alarm went up when she opened the hatch.

Inside, the newly delivered crates were secured to hooks on the bulkheads and deck. There were no markings, nothing to indicate origin or destination. She scanned for radio identifiers and found nothing.

Upon closer inspection, she found that each crate had seals along with a sophisticated locking mechanism. Defeating the lock was a big enough problem on its own. The seals?

If she opened a crate, they'd know. Darien's cover would be blown.

Assuming he truly was undercover. It was just as possible he'd been turned and was playing her, using her in some elaborate scheme to compromise the GSA.

But that seemed unlikely.

Still, she had to know what was in the crates.

Patience. Wait for things to come to you.

She had the tablet scan the lock of a crate that was only stacked on top of one other.

The tablet's hacking interface returned a warning: *No known interface.*

Great. She would have to let a more detailed hack run, which meant leaving the device attached to the crate.

There were a few options to speed the process up; she worked her way through those. The first was to prioritize checking against government and military systems. In addition to that, she launched a series of device pings to test for possible manufacturer codes to exploit. Finally, she told the tablet to favor time over battery efficiency.

While the device worked through the initial set of options she'd given it, Stiles returned to the hatch. If she strained, she could still make out the Patel woman and Goldman. The Ravens weren't very talkative.

At least until one of them or one of Devanshi Patel's bodyguards said something about another guest arriving soon.

That was the last thing Stiles needed.

Her tablet pinged her communicator with a surprising notice: A government protocol had been identified in the security device. She hurried back to the crate. Identifying the protocol wasn't going to provide a solution immediately, but it was progress.

The hatch handle clacked loudly behind her.

Stiles dimmed the tablet screen and slid behind one of the taller stacks of crates.

Someone reeking of alcohol stumbled inside, breathing through his mouth.

Theo. It had to be.

She got small. As much as she would enjoy punching the pirate a few times, she couldn't afford to give herself away.

The tablet sent her a message: *Security mechanism solution discovered. Force solution or Abort? Force solution in 10 seconds.*

She pulled her communicator out but froze. Theo was moving closer, neck craning toward the tablet. If she responded to the prompt from the device, the front display would light up in acknowledgment. He would see it.

Force solution or Abort? Force solution in 4 seconds.

Theo's foul breathing was loud. His warmth was close; his boots were soft scrapes on the deck.

Force solution or Abort? Force solution in 1 second.

"Hey, now—" The pirate was just around the crates from Stiles.

The same shudder through the decks that she'd felt earlier ran through them now.

Theo growled. "What?" He was on his communicator. "All right. I'm coming."

He shuffled back out, wheezing, laying down his whisky stench, shutting the hatch behind him.

Stiles ran to the tablet, but the screen was already lit.

Solution forced. Security breached.

It was just the lock. There was still the seal to contend with. No one might ever notice the lock being compromised if she didn't break the seal.

But could she really lose the opportunity to know what was going on?

Those were Ravens. Devanshi Patel was involved.

Stiles pulled the multitool and carefully sliced through the seal.

Inside the crate, there were circuits. Modules. Advanced technology.

Shadow technology.

It was the same sort she'd used on the *Pandora*. Not the most current, but it was as good as what anyone else had.

They were smuggling advanced technology—weapons—to…

What was their destination? Were they giving away tech to the Azoren? The Moskav? The Gulmar?

She sealed the crate back up and did what she could to make the seal look intact. Anyone who paid it close attention would see the cut, but to a casual observer, it might be missed.

The way was clear back to the stairs except for one man—one of Goldman's pirates. He was focused on something else.

Stiles hurried back to the stairs and listened to be sure no one had noticed her.

Then she froze.

There was a new voice, one she'd heard before.

Stiles belly-crawled to where she could see everyone talking.

A woman with dark skin but pale brown eyes now stood next to Goldman. She was one of Prime Minister Mengitsu Zenawi's top aides: Denise Gallo. Stiles had noted the woman when doing background research on the prime minister.

Gallo set a hand on Goldman's beefy forearm. "My people will release the last of the hostages with this delivery."

The pirate captain smiled. "What about your cover?"

"It's no use anymore. Zenawi's coalition is crumbling. He'll be out of power in a month."

"You moving on?"

"Actually, I was hoping to stay aboard your ship."

"Heading home, then?"

The woman pulled away and bowed her head. "It's long past time I returned to Azh Shivan."

Azh Shivan? That was the Khanate home world! Goldman and Patel were trading weapons for hostages the Khanate held?

Stiles had to get word back to Colonel McLeod!

Something scraped behind her. She twisted around and found herself looking down the barrel of a shotgun. Theo's shotgun.

"Hey! Lev! Got something back here!" The drunken brute's mouth split into a grin, exposing crooked teeth. "I thought you was supposed to be in your cabin, Missy. What say we move around nice and slow and have a little talk with the boss, hm?"

She readied herself for a leap but froze when the ugly brute shook his head slightly.

He pushed the shotgun barrel a little closer. "Get up. Or I spray that pretty face of yours across the deck."

The pirate was ready. Nothing she could do would be fast enough.

There were no other options but surrender.

29

Even in quarters meant to keep Satrap alive and in relative peace, the needles in his arms itched, and the medicine on his tongue provided nothing but a cool, metallic respite from his nervous salivating. Shifting around to get a glimpse of Ikhama was a challenge with the weight of his robes bearing him down. Her trembling glances said that she suffered the same as him.

It was Zohar's machinations that made things so unbearable. Not the machinations themselves but missing them. Satrap was always thinking about where his opponents would step not then but several moments—days—later.

Somehow, he had missed the captain's move.

How does one miss a usurpation, a mutiny?

Zohar's security team offered nothing but cool threat, guns not quite leveled but ready. When they shifted, their armor creaked.

They weren't without stress; it was thick in the air.

Anxiety. Waiting for the order.

"Kill them." It would probably be as inglorious as that.

No prayers. No salutations. The roar of boarding shotguns, the spatter of brains against the bulkhead—an instant of agony come and gone, taking with it life.

Someone reached out to Satrap's communicator: Zohar. There was nothing to do but swallow. "How may I help you, Captain?"

"You see the data feeds."

"I do."

"As I told you, this won't last much longer, with or without your promised signal."

That supposition was readily supported by the data. Red triangles showed the much smaller Kedraalian force. They were doing nothing that could be described as a serious attempt at repelling the assault. Two of the largest ships didn't even seem to be firing. In the empty vastness of space, even with lock-on, the odds of hitting another ship engaging in defensive maneuvers were slim, but a shot not fired was a shot guaranteed not to hit.

The Kedraalians were already failing, thanks to the saboteur. Without another signal, Satrap had no leverage or value.

He drew a deep breath. "Your tactics and leadership will no doubt lead to your elevation, Zohar."

"If there were justice, yes. Then again, I should have been satrap."

"I cannot pretend to know the wisdom of our Khan."

"Wisdom." A low, contemptuous snort slid from the captain. "I wanted to let you know that this was not done with malice."

"The mutiny?"

"The correcting of our organizational structure. There were elements beyond our Khan's control."

"Careful, Captain—you drift toward blasphemy."

"Do not attempt to unnerve me. I contacted you to let you know the time is coming. Your promise has failed to come to fruition. Make your peace. Let the old woman know the same. We will not make a grand display of this. If there were a way to avoid it, I would."

"Regret about murder softens the pain of death and calms my soul."

Zohar's face tightened, then he disconnected.

Ikhama brushed her hands over the fabric of her robe. "Perhaps there are better things to do than to antagonize the one who holds the sword dangled over your neck."

"It is entirely possible." Satrap slumped slightly. "I apologize."

"You expected a different reaction?"

"The captain is in a precarious position. The assault has an advantage at the moment, but the saboteur has yet to confirm the enemy is powerless."

"This could all be a ruse?"

"It could. Or our saboteur may be dead."

While the data feed showed extreme promise, it could only show what it could detect. The Kedraalians had a superior form of the same technology given to the Khanate by its questionable allies. Still, everything showed a battle going unimaginably well. At the rate things were unfolding, it was likely Zohar and his allies might find victory despite throwing aside the only person from the Khanate who truly understood space naval warfare tactics and strategy.

And it was yet possible that value might be shown.

"Ikhama, is it wrong to value our own lives over the good of the Khanate?"

"Your words are spoken with malice, Satrap. Only the Khan matters."

"Not malice. I'm not sure of the exact feeling. Amusement."

"*As strikes the sword, so strikes the Khan.*"

"Will your last breath be spent on such useless quotes?"

The old woman nodded toward one of the shotguns. "You will know soon enough."

"Or maybe not so soon. There is a folly to what they've committed themselves to."

"Folly?"

"Zohar apparently has failed to note the way his fellow captains have maneuvered. Or perhaps he trusts their loyalty now."

"It *is* folly to trust a peer."

"Only in our inefficient structure but yes. And now that trust or inattentiveness has led to missing the way the *Divine Wind* maneuvers. Despite agreeing to rejoin the fleet, Captain Rouhani takes a small force farther out than can be adequately defended. It would seem he has noticed the vulnerability of the largest of the Kedraalian ships."

"This *Valor* we were assured would be ours to destroy?"

"The same."

"Then blessed be the Khan."

"Yes. Blessed be. Except, if the saboteur has failed, that small group of ships will hardly be sufficient to destroy a ship of that size."

"The fighters could do so."

"If all of them struck, certainly. But if the ship has shields…"

"Then you must warn them."

"I have. In this matter Rouhani has committed himself. The question is: Can we leverage this with our dear Captain Zohar?"

"I understand." The old woman's focus remained on the weapon pointed at her.

"Let me see if our benefactor might be willing to hear me out." Satrap sent a text message to Zohar: *Captain Rouhani fails to follow the course you gave. Would you be interested in discussing how this might be to your advantage?*

Then Satrap left an open channel to the captain.

Almost immediately, Zohar sent a connection to that open channel. "What do you mean, Satrap?"

"Your voice is welcome, Zohar."

"Do not waste my time. What did you mean?"

"About Rouhani or about the advantage to be gained?"

Zohar's bottom lip jutted out. "The advantage. I cannot control Rouhani."

"Well, it was *your* plan to re-assemble into a single fleet and press the attack on the Kedraalians."

"It was."

"And it would seem Rouhani has decided to steal some of the glory of that plan."

"Yes." Zohar's eyes narrowed—he understood Satrap's true meaning. "I will come to you personally."

"I welcome the visit."

Satrap smiled at the assassins watching him and Ikhama with cool resolve. They were not to blame. He was no better: a killer who could simply claim he was only following orders.

He turned to the old woman. "We will have a visitor soon."

"I enjoy visitors. The universe is large enough to share." Some of the tension left her body.

A few minutes later, Zohar strode up to the cabin entry and huddled with the assassins. After a moment, they departed, leaving only the captain.

Each small victory increased the odds of survival. Satrap smiled.

Zohar stepped into the cabin; the hatch sealed behind him. He slumped against the bulkhead and pressed a hand to his face. "These betrayals and lies, Satrap—"

"The machinations meant to winnow the weak instead leave us all weaker."

"Yes. It is all so draining, but I have no other choice but to do this."

"Survival. You know that is all I have sought for myself."

"You are strange. You ascended through a different path."

Satrap touched the array of medical devices that barely kept him alive. "It's hardly a convenient path."

"Certainly, it isn't desirable. Now, about this advantage—tell me."

The hunger in his eyes... He enjoys the competition with his peers, even if he truly does hate it as well. "If Rouhani were to fail while trying to execute your strategy, perhaps it was your strategy that was at fault." Satrap winced as a burning pain ran through his legs. Would his ruined body never cease its betrayal? He needed focus at this delicate moment if he were to manipulate the man who had stolen not just the fleet but his superior's strategy.

"Satrap?"

"I'm sorry. It's just the pain that sometimes flares up."

"I see." Zohar flashed an embarrassed smile at the priestess. "I do apologize for making the two of you so uncomfortable."

Ikhama bowed her head. *"Suffering is life as life is divinity."*

"Only through suffering may we know the path to the stars." The captain bowed.

Finally, the pain subsided enough for Satrap to let out a shuddering breath. "As I was saying, Captain, a failure executing any version of your plan would see you lose face before your...peers."

"I did not need your words to know this. This was your wisdom?"

"Obviously not. But the advantage I spoke of?"

"Yes—the advantage." Zohar pushed off from the wall. "Quit delaying!"

"First, show your rivals a victory. Show them you cannot be second-guessed."

"How? Rouhani has primary control over the fighters."

"With proper access, I can override this."

"And destroy our ship? No."

"I have no interest in killing myself, Zohar."

The captain leaned back and stroked his chin. "I trust you in this."

"Then restore my full capabilities and privileges as you did my access to the data stream."

"And you will do what, exactly?"

"The quick success that shows your wisdom: Destroy one of their smaller ships. A destroyer." Satrap indicated the destroyer in the data feed that was farthest from the *Valor*. "You have enough ships under your command yet to do this with the fighters under your command."

"And this quick success comes with other benefits beyond showing we can eliminate a destroyer without Rouhani and his ships?"

"Rouhani makes the assumption that the ship he targets is helpless."

"And you are not so sure?"

"We have heard nothing more from the saboteur. It could be a ruse. It could all have been a ruse from the start."

"Then the *Divine Wind* and the captains who've thrown in with Rouhani are at risk?"

"No ship is irreplaceable. Were I to send a message to our glorious Khan requesting reinforcements, they would be sent to me as soon as ready."

"Were *you*."

"Survival is all I seek, Captain. Ikhama and I are not like you."

The old woman dipped her head for a moment. "Service to our Khan is our path."

Zohar grunted. "I couldn't care less about Rouhani. His ship, though…"

"It will be replaced."

"My command will be weakened, regardless."

"Will it?" Satrap stroked the cables and tubes that ran into his body. "Imagine an ally who is willing to work with you, Zohar. You as the effective leader of the fleet, that ally as your consultant, as you described previously. When the war ends, my duty is complete. A new satrap must be named for the next phase. What might the words of such an ally mean to our Khan when we return?"

The captain paced between his two erstwhile prisoners, then pulled out a data pad and tapped on it. He put the device away and sighed. "I have returned full access to you. Can you wrest the fighters away from Rouhani?"

Satrap closed his eyes, seeing the fleet data fully now, feeling the security systems of the fleet, immersing himself into it all. At this point, he could see the enemy ships as more than red triangles, the weapons fire as more than short flashes followed by longer readouts of the limited effectiveness. Every data point grated on him, reminding him of just how incompetent his captains were. Despite being "unified" under Zohar, the fleet ships were showing no cohesion, no coordination. They fired wherever they wished, without any hint of discipline.

But Zohar was the only one who exhibited a scintilla of competence and perhaps…mercy?

So Satrap pushed through the data until he was into the secure communications running from one ship to another. There were messages between Rouhani and his fellow rebellious captains, and there were connections from Rouhani to some of the captains supposedly loyal to Zohar.

Finally, there were packets running from the *Divine Wind* to the fighters.

Did the pilots know what target they were being hurled at by their remote controller? Did they care?

Most likely, they were caught in the fervor of prayer to the glory of the khan.

To override Rouhani's commands meant first cracking the encryption keys he was using. That should have been a significant task. Any captain worth his title would have used the most robust methods available. Certainly, Satrap had done everything he could to secure his own ship and the Jakkara against hacking.

But Rouhani?

Satrap broke through on the second try, using default configurations provided by the ship builders.

Once inside the *Divine Wind*'s command systems, it was only a matter of resetting keys, changing out encryption configurations, and securing the root privileges against the troublesome captain's crew.

And making a backup of the old configuration. Satrap kept that ready in hot swap, timed to return as the master configuration if he failed to signal every fifteen minutes.

Safety against treachery. Zohar had shown once already who he was.

There were other traps that could be laid, of course, but those would take time. For now, Satrap had to be focused on immediate benefits.

He transferred control to Zohar's bridge, then returned basic command of the *Divine Wind* to Rouhani.

"It is done, Zohar." Satrap eased back on his bed.

"The fighters are under my command?"

"And headed for the destroyer I indicated."

"And Rouhani?"

"It won't be long before he realizes what I've done."

Zohar sneered. "What *I* have done."

A faint tingle ran through Satrap, as if he'd suddenly forgotten something important. "What…?" His privileged access! Zohar had taken it away again!

"I fear I have misled you to a degree."

The hatch opened, and the captain crossed to where the two assassins now stood, shotguns once more pointed down.

Satrap's heart stuttered. "But we—"

Zohar turned just beyond the opening. "Not we—*I*. This is *my* fleet to run."

"You—"

"I know enough now. And when Rouhani connects to me to vent over my theft of the fighters, why, I guess I must tell him the truth about your momentary betrayal and how it has forced me to use the fighters effectively… To attack the *Valor* myself."

"With my execution the price to be paid."

"If it wasn't a certainty before, it must be now. Excuse me."

"Why?"

"Because I had to. As you say, it's survival."

What was the belief taught among the officers? *Those who aren't being promoted are slowly dying.* It *was* a matter of survival. Satrap should have expected the betrayal. "My offer of assistance stands."

"I know. And I feel terrible about what must be done to the two of you."

Satrap caught a glimpse of the priestess making a sign to ask for forgiveness. "Ikhama doesn't need to suffer my fate."

"The two of you are connected."

"Would any protest if we were simply set adrift in a shuttle or sent to the planet below?"

"There must be proof of resolution. For solidarity."

And to appease the bloodthirsty savages in command. "How?"

"How? How will you die?" Zohar shrugged. "Work it out between you. Something fast and painless, preferably. I harbor no hatred and despise unnecessary suffering."

Was it real or imagined that pity hung in the eyes of the two security men for just a moment as their captain strode away?

Satrap clenched his teeth tight and pinched the loose flesh of his legs. Once again, he had been fooled by the captain.

Except that wasn't true.

Once again, the captain had failed to understand the offer being made. The Kedraalian task force wasn't so helpless as Zohar and the others thought. Its tactics reflected what might be chaos or a rift of some sort, but that could all be part of the plan. The task force had shown remarkable resiliency to date.

And now—

Satrap's communicator connection vibrated: The saboteur!

The bomb has been placed. At my next signal, the Kedraalian task force will be yours to destroy. To the glory of the Khanate!

Was it a deception? Another layer in some complex plan?

That was unlikely. The message had originated from a Kedraalian ship. It had been sent directly to him, same as the messages from the Gulmar fleet.

After so long, the saboteur was about to render the enemy vulnerable.

But who could be turned to? Who would spare him his life in exchange for this opportunity at sure victory?

Or was it better to let the fleet face defeat?

Satrap glanced at the old priestess. She wouldn't offer anything more than ridiculous parables and desperation.

He would have to find the answer himself. Soon.

30

Benson couldn't budge from her shuttle seat. Her breathing was shallow yet filled her awareness, the sound panicked. And why wouldn't she be? Everything was spinning out of control. If she pushed out of her seat, she was going to be slammed against a wall. Or she would fall to the deck.

She would definitely fall. Anyone could see that. Fall and fail.

What do I do?

Beyond the airlock, the *Lyon* hangar bay awaited. Somewhere in the ship—Tuleyev's ship—someone had transmitted an encoded message, and shortly after that, the Khanate suicide fighter craft had turned toward the crippled *Valor*. The best bet at breaking the fighter assault was crippling the signals ship remotely controlling the fighters.

Finding a potential saboteur was as important as stopping the fighters, but the only person she could trust was…

She pushed her harness up with shaking hands. "Sergeant Grier."

"Ma'am?"

"Call Chief Parkinson. Tell him to find which of those Khanate ships is controlling the fighters. Then take that ship out, like you did the other one."

Grier's eyes widened. "We got lucky, ma'am."

"Then we need to get lucky again. If they take the *Valor* out, this task force won't last."

"We'll have to pull Marines off guard duty and from multiple ships."

"Do it. These are *your* Marines now, Sergeant."

"Yes, ma'am." The muscular woman licked her lips. "Hey—"

Benson nearly staggered as she stood. "We don't have much time—"

With a quick flourish, the Marine unbuckled her pistol belt and held it out. "That's Clive's. I'm not really comfortable wearing it anyway."

The belt and weapon felt almost flimsy. "I don't need—"

"Maybe you do. You don't know who you can trust, right?"

"Thank you."

"Luck, Captain!"

At the airlock, Benson turned. "You don't need luck, Sergeant. You're good enough to do this."

Benson's boots clomped hollowly against the deck. Tuleyev hadn't sent anyone to escort her. Was that a good or bad sign? There were so many unknowns at the moment, and his true loyalty was one of them.

She rushed to the hatch and let herself into the passageway beyond.

A young Marine private stood there, weapon at the ready, dangerous looking in his armor. His dark eyes were like Grier's when she heard about the mission to attack the enemy signals ship: wide. Sweat beaded above his thin upper lip. "Captain? I-I'm your escort. Private Gao." He squared his shoulders, maybe to convince himself he was ready for this.

"Is this Commander Tuleyev's idea?"

"H-he wants to be sure you're protected."

"I can protect myself, Private." She slipped the weapons belt over her hip, wincing at how tight it felt.

"It's the commander's orders, ma'am."

The kid was barely old enough to shave. He was a pawn in Tuleyev's game, meant to impede her search. Was it petty nonsense, or was there more to the commander's decision? "All right, Private Gao. I'll need you to keep up."

"Yes, ma'am. Would you like a tour?"

She pointed to the flashing lights reflecting off the passageway and deck. "We're in the middle of a general quarters situation."

"Yes, ma'am."

Benson's communicator vibrated: Parkinson. "Go ahead, Chief."

"Just had a call from Sergeant Grier."

"We've got fighter aircraft headed toward the *Valor*, Chief. Stopping those is our priority."

The engineer groaned. "Wonderful. You want this data burst information?"

"You decrypted it?"

"As much as it can be. The second one, at least."

"Second—"

"Our saboteur's been busy."

"What did you find?"

"Garbage. Or at least I thought it was at first. Then I realized it's the control codes to the shadow sensors."

"Control codes?" Benson held a finger up to signal for the Marine to wait a moment. "What's that mean?"

"The sensors filter out our ships' signals when they scan for stealth tech. Each vessel has a control code. We all show up registered green—"

"In the sensor output. All right, I get it. So this signal burst—"

"Sent whoever it was meant for all of our codes."

"Meaning the enemy ships can spoof our signals, turn from red to green?"

"If their equipment's close enough to ours, they should be able to. I'm pretty sure it is."

"Can we change codes?"

"Sure. We've all got different code sets. It needs to be coordinated, though. In case you forgot, we're offline."

"How long before power's restored?"

"A few more minutes, assuming we found all the design problems."

"I'll have Commander Chopra get things prepared. Do you have an idea where the signal originated?"

"A ballpark idea. If you'd let me focus on this—"

"Chief, if those fighters reach the *Valor*, you won't be able to help anyone."

"I know, I know. Okay, so head to deck three."

"That's it? An entire deck?"

"Well, I can keep running the search from this end and forward it to you…"

"Please do."

"It would be quicker for me to actually commit—"

"Chief—"

"I know, I know. I'm off to save the *Valor*, then."

Parkinson's voice was replaced by a strange series of beeps and buzzes: data from the search process.

Benson sent the signal to her command tablet and strapped that to her forearm, then she turned to the Marine. "Private…?"

"Gao, ma'am."

"Take me to deck three."

The young man set off for the lifts at a jog, and she followed. On the ride up, she studied the tablet display, which seemed to be working its way aft from the forward area of the ship. It had already eliminated the front quarter of the vessel.

"Is that…?" Gao was looking at the display.

"A possible saboteur."

"Commander Tuleyev didn't sound—"

The lift hatch opened, and the Marine stepped out, frowning when she stuck her head out after him. He waved at another Marine down at the other end of the passageway before jerking his head for Benson to follow. "All clear, Captain."

Benson pointed to the other Marine. "We could probably cut our search time—"

"Commander Tuleyev said you'd have to talk to him for any changes, Captain."

They weren't going anywhere without a sense of where to search, anyway. She connected to Tuleyev. "Commander Tuleyev."

It was easy to imagine the old man glaring at her voice. "Captain. Welcome aboard the *Lyon*."

"I'm sorry for breaching protocol, but we've whittled down the likely—"

"The enemy has shifted its tactical positioning. Were you aware of this?"

"The *Valor*'s sensors were offline when I left."

"They have now two clear forces. Before there were three, then one. Now, as I said, two."

"And they've sent their fighters against the *Valor*."

"You should abandon ship. Even the *Valor* cannot withstand such an assault."

"Or we could work together—as the task force was designed to do—to protect the *Valor*." Benson squeezed her eyes shut. A painful pressure was building above and behind her eyes. "Commander, this engagement isn't lost. If I can find the saboteur, we take away a potential threat."

"This is a goose chase. There is no saboteur."

"Two distinct signals have been transmitted from your ship, Commander."

"Yet it is your ship that has no power. It is obvious where the saboteur was."

"There's more than one." She stifled a groan; the young Marine looked away, head down. "Commander Tuleyev—Alexander—we have a shared mission. We need to cooperate."

Tuleyev harrumphed. "That is not known. We focus on what we know."

Benson killed the connection. This was his ship. The only way she was going to get him to budge was by having a face-to-face showdown, which would have ugly repercussions. Replacing him in the middle of a battle would do irreparable damage.

The search on her tablet seemed to be frozen. "Private, what's up there, on the starboard side?"

"Engineering, ma'am."

Of course. The *Lyon* was similar in layout to the *Valor* but smaller. "We need to check that compartment out."

Relief spread across the private's face. He jogged ahead and stood at the hatch, gun hanging low.

Once Benson reached the door, she pointed to the weapon. "Might want to be ready for trouble."

"Oh." The Marine adjusted his grip. "Ready, ma'am."

Benson tried her credentials, but the hatch didn't open. "Private Gao?"

He entered his credentials, then frowned. "Locked, Captain."

"Can you override it?"

The young man pulled out a small security tablet and pressed that against the lock mechanism. "I'll need Commander Tuleyev's approval."

"What about Sergeant Grier's approval? She's your commander right now."

"Well…" Gao blinked. "I—"

"I'll get her on the line." Benson connected to Grier. "Sergeant Grier?"

"What's up, Captain?"

"I need you to authorize Private Gao here with a security override for the engineering section on the *Lyon*."

"No shit? The saboteur's in there?"

"I can't think of a good reason to lock the hatch otherwise."

"Well, I think I've got this security stuff figured out. Tell Gao to try now."

The captain nodded, and the Marine tapped through a sequence of screens on his tablet until there was a soft flash on the security control panel.

Gao grinned and stepped back. "That did it."

Benson tensed. "We're headed in, Sergeant."

"We are, too." Her signal chittered and squeaked because of the distance.

"Stay safe." Benson disconnected, then pressed the key to open the hatch.

A young woman in a blood-stained engineering jumpsuit with petty officer insignia stumbled toward the opening out of the darkened compartment, eyes darting around. Dark curls were matted to her plain, puffy face by blood and sweat. "Help." She glanced back over her shoulder with a whimper.

Gao stepped between the two women. "What's going on?"

"Chief Tucci."

Benson pulled Halliwell's pistol and pushed past the woman. "Where?"

"In her office." The young engineer pointed toward the back of the engineering compartment. "She…"

"Private Gao, let the commander know we've got a problem."

"Ma'am—"

"Stay here. Both of you." Benson made sure the safety was off, then headed into the darkened depths. She tried to turn on lights but had no luck.

Tucci. It wasn't a name that stood out. She was one of Parkinson's junior peers. If he knew her, he'd never said anything about her. At least she hadn't filed a complaint against the chief. That probably indicated they didn't know each other well at all.

Feeling along the bulkhead, Benson found a flashlight and took it from its mount, then powered the device on. There was blood on the deck and scattered tools. The blood grew more noticeable as she drew closer to the chief's office, which was open and dark.

"Chief Tucci?" Benson braced the flashlight on top of the pistol barrel.

She jumped to the other side of the open hatch.

There were bodies inside on the floor. Bloody bodies. Nothing moved.

If the office was laid out like Parkinson's, the desk would be to the left, along with computing gear and a small worktable. There would be a couple lockers on the right side, and tools, along with whatever gear had been brought into the space for inspection or work. The best hiding place would be there, among whatever was piled up on the right.

Benson hopped through the hatch and squatted, running the flashlight beam across the stacked gear.

Tucci would have to be about Parkinson's size to hide completely. Benson groused at herself for not remembering Tucci. She'd left the engineering teams to Parkinson both to try to make him feel a little more secure and because she had spent so much time trying to deal with the fragile egos of captains like Tuleyev. Mostly Tuleyev.

A quick check confirmed the three people on the deck were dead. Their jumpsuits were bloodier than the young engineer survivor, and there were multiple wounds on each.

With the flashlight beam still focused on the probable hiding space, Benson worked her way to the wall opposite the hatch. "Chief Tucci?"

Nothing.

"Chief, this doesn't have to end in—"

Lights winked and flashed in the flashlight beam. No Tucci, but there was a big device spread out across the deck. A device with a timer and lots of black cases with wires connecting them.

A bomb.

Benson connected to Tuleyev. "Commander Tuleyev, about that problem..."

"Captain Benson—" The older man huffed. "I am—"

"Listen to me! There's a bomb in your engineering bay, and three of your engineers are dead. I can't find Chief Tucci—"

A loud groan brought Benson around, followed a moment later by the sound of something dropping to the deck. It had come from out in the main engineering compartment.

She stepped back out through the hatch and searched around the crowded space. Gao and the young engineer weren't in the passageway. "Private Gao?"

Her light ran over something on the floor.

Gao. Blood gushed from a neck wound.

The young engineer stepped from the dark, face drenched in sweat, the Marine's weapon in her hands. She had the barrel pointed at Benson. "Glory and honor to the Khan."

Benson had a decent chance of hitting the young woman at the relatively short range. "Put the weapon down."

"You can't shoot me, Captain. I'm wired to the bomb."

"I don't want to shoot you. Petty Officer...?" *Why didn't I check?*

"My name doesn't matter. All that matters is the peace of the afterlife, to stand in the warmth of the Guiding Star and to walk beside the Khan—"

"There's plenty to live for in this world."

"All that I live for now is to see you and your people suffer while you wait for the inevitable explosion and the launch of the mighty—"

Her voice was lost in the boom of a gun.

Tuleyev stood in the compartment hatchway. "Captain Benson, you are well?"

Benson dashed to where the engineer had collapsed, gurgling blood. "There's a dead-man switch on her!"

"A…" The commander bolted into the engineering bay. "The bomb?"

"Tucci's office." Benson unzipped the young woman's jumpsuit as the commander continued past her. There were no cuts in the material, just blood. The victims' blood. It was a missed detail that cost Gao his life. A velcro-secured vest with flashing lights covered the engineer's T-shirt.

The petty officer's eyes widened. She tried to say something but only managed to gag on her own blood.

Despite the moment, Benson felt pity. "I'm sorry it had to end this way."

One of the young woman's hands came up—bloody, shaking. She tugged at a necklace hanging from her throat and mouthed words Benson couldn't make out.

She rested the woman's head on the deck and connected to Parkinson. "Chief?"

"Busy!" It sounded like gear clattering around in the background.

"We've got a bomb on the *Lyon*. It's in the engineering bay."

"Yeah, well, have Lana help you with it. She's good at tearing things apart."

"Was that Chief Tucci's name?"

"Was—?" Parkinson gulped. "She's dead?"

"Killed by the saboteur. She was an engineer on Chief—on Lana's team."

"Shit." The clatter and rattle of equipment stopped. "Okay. Okay."

"We've got a bomb and a dead-man switch." Benson pulled her command tablet out and recorded video of the vest. "You getting the switch?"

"Yeah. Ugh. Okay, that's not a simple configuration."

"Can we undo it? She's dying."

"Um." Parkinson's voice disappeared in more clattering. "It's not wired, right? It's a radio signal of some sort?"

Benson ran her flashlight over the dying woman. "No wires coming off of her."

"Great. So, I need full access to your command tablet."

"I can't—"

"You want to stop that bomb?"

"Hold on." The captain ran through the security interface until she was at the root access approval prompt. "Connect to it."

A connection request flashed on the screen as the young woman's eyes grew even larger. Her mouth opened, and blood trailed down her cheeks.

She was seconds away from death.

Benson approved the connection request.

The tablet interface zipped through until Parkinson had it at a command level she'd never seen before. Text strings sped across a window, then the engineering bay lights came on. Equipment buzzed and hummed.

Tuleyev stumbled out of the chief's office. "Captain, what is going on?"

"Chief Parkinson's trying to prevent that bomb from detonating."

"From…" The commander's eyes narrowed. "You have given him access to your tablet?"

"I trust my chief."

A grunt was the only response Tuleyev managed, but he studied the tablet over her shoulder.

Then the petty officer let out a wet gasp and went rigid.

"Chief?" Benson felt for a pulse in the engineer's throat. It was fading.

"A few more seconds…" Parkinson was typing wildly, sometimes backing up and retyping. "Can you give her CPR?"

"With this vest on?"

"Shit." More typing leapt onto the tablet screen.

Tuleyev whispered something under his breath, then cleared his throat. "The bomb has several dozen kilograms of high-yield explosives. We could survive if we move—"

The petty officer's faint pulse disappeared completely.

But the bomb didn't detonate.

Benson swallowed. "She's dead, Chief."

"And I captured the signal from her switch. You need to get some engineers in there *now*, Captain. I'll have power restored on the *Valor* in a few more seconds, but Sergeant Grier needs me to foil those Khanate systems if she's going to get her Marines in close enough."

"Thank you, Chief."

Parkinson disconnected, leaving Benson confounded about how to deal with him.

Like Tuleyev.

She holstered Halliwell's pistol and clasped her hands to hide the shaking.

The commander stepped away, hunched over, speaking with enough volume for her to hear him calling for his engineers. After a short discussion, he straightened and returned to Benson's side. Her legs trembled, and sweat dampened her T-shirt.

Tuleyev cleared his throat. "It would seem, Captain, that I owe you an apology. When Private Gao called, I came as quickly as possible."

"Let's worry about apologies *after* we deal with the Khanate fleet."

"A wise decision." The old man turned, stopped, and waved her ahead. "After you, Captain."

It was a minor protocol, something Benson never really concerned herself with, but it was an effort Tuleyev was making. That meant a lot.

She headed out, smiling. Maybe people *could* change.

Stiles couldn't meet Caville's glare. He was right to be furious. She'd put everything at risk and slipped up in her urgency to kill Devanshi Patel. Now, the Genesis siblings stood with their hands raised in a cargo compartment grown stiflingly hot thanks to the deadly pirates and soldiers circled around and considering what to do with the two of them.

When Stiles examined the weapons pointed at her, she noted that they weren't pretty show pieces. Nicked, scraped, and hanging from worn and stained straps that probably smelled like they'd been drawn from a cauldron of gore and sweat—these were deadly tools of the trade.

And the people holding those tools were well versed in murder.

Goldman swung his pistol like a pendulum at his side, his features stretched tight as he squinted at the older Genesis child. "Care to explain, Darien?"

Caville's shoulders slumped. "You wouldn't understand."

"Try me."

One of the Ravens—a burly, gray-haired man with a scarred face—waved his weapon at Stiles. "I think I've seen her before."

His partner, who was younger and whose deep brown skin was smooth, stepped closer. "Yeah. Yeah! She's GSA."

The pirate captain froze. "You're sure?"

"She—" The younger Raven leaned in toward Stiles. "—looks like someone—"

Stiles straightened. "I work for Kusno Saripado."

Goldman pointed his pistol at her forehead. "Nope."

"Last year, the Directorate started an investigation into Khanate influence in Prime Minister Zenawi's cabinet. Kusno caught wind of the GSA starting to poke around because she—" Stiles glared at the prime minister's aide. "—started getting sloppy, focusing on recruiting more Khanate spies than making sure the weapons-for-hostages deal went through."

Gallo snorted. "That's a lie."

"Is it?" Stiles pointed at the Khanate spy. "Kusno recruited me to make sure she disappeared before she could give up anything critical."

The pirate captain's pistol barrel drifted. "You're GSA?"

"I *was*, same as Darien. That's where we met."

"And what were you supposed to do with Miss Gallo?"

"What do you think? There're more options to erasing people than the Silence Centers."

The older Raven made a deep sound in his chest.

Goldman tilted his head toward Caville. "Were you in on this?"

"No."

"But you're former GSA?"

"I told you I worked in intelligence."

"Sure, but I thought you were an SAID contractor."

Caville's face remained perfectly calm. "Among other things. And what I told you was true. She's good."

"Except for trying to kill Denise."

Stiles cleared her throat. "I needed to make sure she was heading back to Khanate space permanently. So long as she disappears, Kusno doesn't care about the details."

The pirate captain's cheek ticked upward, and his pistol drifted back to Stiles's forehead. "You still lied to me."

"Did I? When she's dropped off on Azh Shivan, my contract is up."

"Still a lie."

"Fine. Then send me back to Dramora. My job is still complete once she leaves Republic space."

"Sorry, but you know too much." Goldman flipped his pistol so that he held the barrel and the grip was pointed toward Caville. "And I need a test of loyalty from Darien."

Stiles's brother chuckled. "No thanks."

"You refuse to kill her?"

"I shoot her, then Theo blows my head off. You think I betrayed you. I can't do anything to change your mind."

"Kill her, and I have no reason to doubt you."

Caville glared at Theo. "You even think of shooting me, you're dead."

The ugly man flashed a yellow grin. "Try it."

"Let me see the pistol." The Genesis agent took the weapon, never looking up as he ejected the magazine and checked the ammunition, then glancing down the barrel.

There were no words that could be said to prevent the execution. It was purely taking the best option of an array of terrible options. The two of them were in too bad a position to take down so many capable and ready killers.

Stiles had screwed up. She'd gotten sloppy.

If her brother truly was deep undercover and not compromised, then whatever mission he was on was more important than her life. She could only hope he was being truthful and was still working in the Republic's interest.

He slapped the magazine back into place, shifted slightly to keep Theo in sight, then pressed the weapon against the side of Stiles's head. "Tough luck, Brianna." His voice cracked just enough that she caught it.

"I—"

An explosion, an instant of pain, a flash of light—

31

———————

The data flow—

Satrap hunched forward, eyes closed, head jerking to keep up with all of the changes. There were so many.

Red triangles had moved deep toward the fleet, passing the frigates and fighters, then those triangles had…disappeared. How? The Kedraalian force was diminished. The grand, red symbol for the *Valor* had been dead for minutes. Without the flagship, they should be caught up in chaos, leaderless.

But the enemy had persevered, and now that grand symbol was flickering.

He set his back against the bulkhead with a pained gasp. With a thought, he upped the pain medication and activated drains that had fallen behind, leaving his gut bloated and his sinuses backing up until a foul, salty taste filled his head. "Ikhama?"

The old woman had been rocking for nearly a minute, her voice a drone of prayers and parables and nonsense that filled the cabin.

"Ikhama!"

She stopped. "Satrap speaks. Has our Khan touched you?"

"In more ways that I wish to remember. This, however, is a different matter—one relevant to our survival."

"Our fate has been set. *Fight not the winds, but follow where they might—*"

"Stop it. Listen!" With a stretch of his neck, Satrap could make out the two assassins just beyond the hatchway. They were paying no attention. He waved her closer. "Something has changed."

A surprising clarity settled on her face as she crawled to his side. "And what is that?"

Satrap bowed his head. "Offer me a prayer of forgiveness."

"*From the heavens shine the light of divinity, the Guiding Star, the home of our Great and Glorious Khan—*"

"That is enough. Just nod now."

"You blaspheme yet again."

"More weight on the scale against my trip to some ridiculous star I have no wish to see. Listen now. Earlier, I turned control of the fighters over to Zohar and made the *Might of the Khan* the active signals ship, but it was only for a short while. Now he and Rouhani fight one another for the right to send those pilots to their deaths against the enemy command ship. While they squabble and bicker, several small enemy craft flew past our outlying ships, then disappeared."

"And these smaller ships that disappeared—they have gone unnoticed?"

"I would have missed them myself had I not been deep into the data stream."

"They come for us?"

"Do you remember in our first engagement? There were ships we could not see until they had boarded. It cost us a ship—the *True Light of the Way.*"

"Yes. A tragic loss."

"Not really. It was the main signals ship, Ikhama. Do you understand?"

The clarity that had surprised him before registered the meaning. "Rouhani's *Divine Wind* is the controlling signals ship now?"

"It is. And were something to happen to it, control would fall back to us."

Her lips curled into a slight smile. "Would Captain Zohar turn to his satrap in the face of such a threat?"

"At the least, he would have no time to waste on executions."

"Satrap has long been a clever schemer."

"This is good fortune rather than planning. And there is more."

"Of good or ill?"

"That is hard to say." Satrap projected the relevant data to the wall display. "Look. Do you see the largest of the red symbols?"

She squinted and leaned toward the display. "Yes."

"The *Valor*. It is maneuvering again. For minutes, it was moving in a straight line, and there were indications it was without power."

"And now the enemy flees?"

"They have no reason to. We are the ones at risk. If those are Marines come to board Rouhani's ship, we will be at a disadvantage staying here."

"This is more than a moment to gloat in unison."

"It is. I want to live, Ikhama. I assume you do as well."

"If that is the Khan's will." Her eyes twinkled with mischievous humor.

"Then I intend to make one last bid to regain power over Zohar. Are you with me?"

"We have spoken before about the will of our great and glorious leader. Only the strongest should rise."

"I haven't Zohar's strength or numbers now. Work with me."

"Know your followers if you wish to lead. *The mind grants strength as mighty as the thews.*"

Only someone who has never known infirmity would write such garbage. Satrap bowed. "May it be so." He waved her back to her place at the other wall.

Once again, he closed his eyes and dove into the data stream. Green and red ship symbols darted about in the digital representation of the space battlefield. In the vast distance, the Gulmar capital of Radetta hung —a pathetic prize.

He marked where he'd earlier estimated the Gulmar shuttles had headed to. That would be where the second fleet was hidden. If it were ready, it would have joined the current battle. Combined, the two naval forces were too great to stand against, at least at the moment.

That message would be critical to get across to Zohar.

But everything would depend on what the Kedraalian stealth ships were doing, assuming they weren't ghost signals to begin with. If they were coming for Zohar's ship, everything else was moot. Attack the *Divine Wind*, though, and...

Satrap settled back in his bunk for a moment, focusing on the slow dance of the battle until the truth revealed itself.

With Rouhani now firmly in control of the fighters, the frigates and remote-controlled vessels were making full speed toward the *Valor*. Now that Satrap was safely removed from conducting the strategic maneuvering of the fleet himself, he had the opportunity to watch the data from a different perspective. So it was that he spotted the subtle maneuvering of the rest of the enemy task force. Their cruisers weren't pursuing the fighters but slowly inserting themselves between the frigates and the rest of his—Zohar's—ships.

Had the *Valor* been a lure all along? That was beyond bold. It was reckless.

Yet there it was: Zohar had allowed Rouhani to drift away from the other cruisers, and now, even if the stealth ships weren't real, the *Divine Wind* was exposed and vulnerable.

Satrap detected an incoming signal. It was Zohar rather than the saboteur. "Captain Zohar, how may I assist you?"

"You gave Rouhani control of the fighters!"

"No. If you had given me a moment longer to explain, I would have told you that to maintain control of the fighters, I would need to stay logged in—"

"I should have you killed!"

"If you might spare me a moment longer, Captain, there is something you should know."

"More lies about your saboteur? I don't care about this!"

"Unfortunately, I believe the saboteur has failed."

The two assassins moved into the cabin, weapons shifting.

Zohar snorted. "You are riddled with failure, Satrap."

Before the opportunity could pass, Satrap raised his hands in supplication. "The *Valor* has returned to full operation."

Although the captain didn't reply, the assassins lowered their shotguns. They glanced at each other, then fell back beyond the hatchway. Spots danced in Satrap's vision, and he found himself struggling to breathe. His personal data stream warned of dangerous blood pressure and toxicity, and what it couldn't fully perceive—the aches in his ruined joints—nearly rendered the rest irrelevant.

He needed to be strong. He needed to be firm. And merciless. It was the only way to stand up to his captains.

Finally, Zohar sighed. "I see now that the Kedraalian flagship maneuvers again."

"That is only the first of the changes to our situation."

"*Our* situation? Satrap, the respite you've gained is momentary."

"Then valuable information will go with me to the Guiding Star."

"I am conducting a battle here. I have no time for—"

Satrap pointed to Ikhama and hooked her into the connection. "What would happen to you, Zohar, if you were found to be responsible for executing the appointed satrap of a fleet that subsequently suffered an ignominious defeat—assuming you survived?"

The old woman brushed her robe across her communicator microphone, sending a gentle scratching sound over the connection. "Captain, although my value to the fleet has already been served, perhaps a small parable would be acceptable."

Zohar said nothing.

At Satrap's nod, the priestess squared her narrow shoulders and thrust out her wrinkled jaw. "*Drive the enemy before you. Strike down the weak. Find joy in the wailing of their women. And when those above you fail to seize such opportunities, strike them down and take their power as yours. But be sure of your path, for failure is the most certain way to destruction before our Khan.*"

After a second, the captain disconnected, and the assassins returned to the compartment.

Why? What doesn't he see? How can he hope to survive now?

One of the assassins pressed the barrel of his weapon against Satrap's brow, pinning his head against the wall. His personal data stream fired off warning after warning about his vitals. A terrible shudder ran through him, and his teeth chattered.

Then the pressure of the barrel was removed.

The captain connected again. "Rouhani's ship is under attack."

"Kedraalian—" Satrap swallowed and tried to catch his breath. "Kedraalian Marines?"

"You knew this?"

"I tried to warn you." The small red signals were mere wisps on the skin of the *Divine Wind*. "They are the least of your concern."

Zohar made a video connection. He, too, quivered, but his face was red with rage. "You conspire to drag me down."

"I offered you an alliance, a chance to command the fleet in all but title."

"This is something I have done my entire career—lead but allow others the glory."

"You hold against me the decisions of our Khan." Satrap glanced up at the assassin, who still held his weapon at the ready. It was hard to sound confident and assertive with death so close, but that was exactly what the moment demanded. "I have an offer, Zohar, but the terms are not so favorable as they were before."

"I could have you killed at any time."

"No. You will hear me out, and you will grant my demands, or you will die—today or when you return to Azh Shivan."

The captain's eyes drew down to narrow slits. "You have one minute."

Satrap sent the data he'd been focused on to Zohar's station. "Do you see what I've highlighted here?"

"The Kedraalian force?"

"And Rouhani's cruiser. And the frigates. Note the location of the Kedraalian ships?"

"All right."

"Now see what they have done." Satrap sent the historical data, which showed the drift in the Kedraalian ships' movements. "Do you see how they have positioned themselves to block off not just the frigates but the *Divine Wind*?"

Zohar's face grew dark. "I see."

"You have seized command of *my* fleet. You have threatened to kill me. Now the fleet stands on the edge of obliteration."

"And you have a solution to prevent this."

"There is one opportunity for the two of us to escape this battle alive and to turn a loss into a chance to extend our service to our great and glorious Khan."

The captain stroked a thumb and forefinger over his eyebrows. "And your demands?"

"Send half of your security team to my cabin. Do so immediately. They have five minutes to arrive."

"Half of my—"

"Five minutes, Zohar." Satrap disconnected just as vomit rushed up to splash against the back of his throat. He swallowed the thick fluid back down.

It would be obvious if the captain refused the offer: The two assassins would step forward and finish what they had started a few moments before.

But they stood like trees, jaws clenched.

Waiting.

And after a couple minutes, the first of their comrades arrived, weapons at the ready, flush from rushing. More followed, and Satrap counted them, comparing their numbers to the duty roster Zohar maintained. There were twenty-two squeezed into the cabin now, plus the two who had been sent to kill their rightful superiors. That made them dangerous and loyal soldiers in Zohar's eyes.

Satrap reconnected to the captain. "Twenty-two out of forty-three. This is a good first step, Zohar."

"And now you—"

"I'm not done yet." Satrap snapped his fingers. "Ikhama, the oath of the Jakkara."

The old woman's eyes fluttered. *"In service to my Khan. In service to the Satrap appointed to be the Khan in war. My life is no longer my own. My loyalty is to none but my Satrap as blessed by our Guiding Star. To fail in service to my Satrap is to fail not just my family but my Khan."*

Satrap bowed his head toward the newcomers. "Kneel. Take this oath."

Zohar let out a strained gasp. "They are my—"

"They *were* your security forces."

"I will have no one to stand against the other captains!"

"They will be sending me twenty-two of their soldiers as well. Free these men from your oath, Zohar. Do so now."

The captain's breathing became loud over the connection. "You are no longer in service to my family or me."

As one, the soldiers dropped to a knee.

But Satrap pointed for the two assassins to rise and move away from the newcomers, then he nodded for his new Jakkara to repeat their oath, which they did.

"Good. Rise." When they were standing again, he waved a hand at the two assassins. "Take them to the nearest airlock and throw them into the void."

Before the two assassins could bring their weapons up in defense, they were overpowered. Four of the freshly appointed Jakkara roughly bore the two men out, shaken by their screams but still showing resolve.

It was the weakness of the fanatic and the blind adherence to beliefs. Satrap had allowed his disdain for such idiocy to blind him to the power it provided.

That had nearly cost him his life.

He waved two of the senior men forward. "Take half of your team into the Jakkara quarters. Switch to your new uniforms and weapons, then return so that the rest can do the same. Henceforth, you will allow no one to threaten or risk my life. Is that understood?"

The two men bowed deeply.

They were his now.

Satrap took a deep breath, truly relieved and feeling protected for the first time since his previous bodyguards had been killed. "Captain Zohar."

A stern, angry glare looked back from the display. "And now my fate?"

"You know that already, at least as far as I'm concerned. You are my senior captain."

Some of the anger slipped away from Zohar's sharp features. "And the fleet?"

"As my senior captain, would you agree that retreat is our only option?"

"I—"

"A situation brought on by the failures of Captain Rouhani?"

"Well—" Zohar's eyes drifted to something off to his right.

Satrap tensed, then he realized it was the airlock alarm as the two assassins—Zohar's two most reliable soldiers—that had distracted him. "Captain, if we retreat now, we take with us the bulk of the fleet. We have an opportunity to resupply and seek out our next objective. It is not a failure doing so. The *Divine Wind* and the *True Light of the Way* can be replaced."

The captain shook his head. "Retreat is for the weak."

More red triangles appeared on the battlefield from where Satrap had guessed the Gulmar fleet must be hidden. "Zohar, check your sensors."

Zohar glanced off to his left. His jaw dropped, and his shoulders sagged. "You are correct, Satrap. A retreat is necessary."

"Good. Return full access to all systems to me immediately, then prepare to speak to Captain Rouhani."

The full control that had been stolen from Satrap was returned. He immediately issued a string of commands to protect himself from that control being seized again. When he was done, Zohar looked back from the screen, slumped and blinking rapidly.

Several of the Jakkara returned in their new uniforms, relieving those who hadn't yet changed. Satrap smiled. In imminent defeat, he might yet find victory. This was more than luck—it was what the khan had seen in him, what Ikhama had spoken of.

I am a capable commander, better than the rest. "Captain, the *Divine Wind?*"

Zohar contacted Rouhani over the shared connection. "Captain Rouhani."

The other man's head darted about. His lips twisted. "Zohar! They have Marines in my passageways! Explosions gut my ship! My security forces are repelled!"

Satrap did his best to bow his chest. "Captain Rouhani."

Now Rouhani's eyes widened. "Satrap? You live?"

"For now. Unfortunately, you have put the fleet in a dangerous position, forcing a change in strategy and an embarrassing need to flee."

"I cannot flee. These Marines have damaged my reactor! My engines—"

"This is your time to serve the Khanate with honor, Captain."

Rouhani's jaw dropped. "But my ship—!"

"Any loss in war is unfortunate. Remember the value of bravery and discipline. For the glory of our Khan!"

The captain of the *Divine Wind* stiffened, then bowed. "For our Khanate."

"You have control of the fighters. See that they find their path to the Guiding Star." Satrap killed the connection. "Captain Zohar, alert the rest of the fleet to the order to retreat. Have them meet at Rally Point 4. Inform them that any ship that fails to comply immediately will be considered compromised and will be destroyed."

"My Satrap." Zohar bowed deeply, then disconnected.

Satrap slumped and squeezed his eyes shut. Already, the results of his actions were apparent in the data stream.

The fleet was accelerating away from the Kedraalians.

His captains were again chattering, asking what was going on and what had brought this change about.

Damage continued to pile up for the *Divine Wind*.

Soon enough, Satrap would send out the command to provide soldiers for his bodyguards—perhaps at the rally point. Once again, he would have the single largest protective force at his disposal. This time, he wouldn't allow anyone to take that protection away. His assignment had come from the khan and had been resisted for years.

No more.

It was fight or die, and Satrap had come closer to death than he had ever wanted. From this point forward, he would be the ideal fleet commander until the mission was over and his freedom had been won.

And woe to the enemies of the Khanate.

32

Aboard the *Valor*, there wasn't so much a sense of jubilation at the Khanate fleet retreat as there was a collective sigh of relief. Benson took it all in from the bridge, standing behind Chopra as he chatted with his team about their performance during the tense moments. She had changed back into the constricting dress whites to get out of her soiled jumpsuit, so she wasn't as comfortable as the others. They deserved the break from formality. No one had performed without fault—that was an unrealistic expectation with so new a ship and crew. There were, however, far more positives to acknowledge than negatives.

She stepped back and let the light from the giant display wash over her. "Commander Chopra, the conn is yours."

Her XO turned and smiled. "You heading out for the call, Captain?"

"No keeping our Gulmar friends waiting."

"We'll remain vigilant." He returned to his conversation with the crew.

Alone in the quiet passageways on the way down to the medical center, her mind drifted to the vastness of space where the enemy had retreated for now. That place could be dark, but it also could hold amazing beauty and light. Stars such as the one in the Radetta system provided proof that the universe was more than shadow.

When Benson entered the outer section of the medical facility, she sucked in the smells—chemicals and medicine. She was surprised by the sight of Captain Floyd Thiessen. He was now dressed in the crisp, no-nonsense sea-gray of the Gulmar Navy, shuffling stiffly across the space between the beds lining the compartment. Ensign Kohn had one of the Gulmar officer's arms over a shoulder, while the cute nurse who had replaced Stiles in the ensign's life had the other arm.

Thiessen's head came around, and he smiled at Benson. He directed his guides to lead him to her, then shooed them away once he stood before her. "Ready for duty, as ordered."

Benson caught a glimpse of movement in the recovery area behind the Gulmar officer: Grier. The sergeant stood beside Halliwell's bed, throwing her arms in the air and twisting around, then ducking and bringing up an imaginary rifle.

The Gulmar captain followed Benson's look. "Oh. The Marine sergeant and her tales about the attack on the Khanate fleet."

"It's a good story."

"Yeah, well, I think she's mostly interested in talking with the other Marine. He's a good-looking guy."

"He—" Benson swallowed, then smiled. "You ready for the call?"

"The executive search committee wouldn't dream of me missing a meeting."

"I thought we'd set you up to take it at your bed, but if you're up for it, there's a small conference room down the way."

The Gulmar officer extended a hand. "I'll need assistance."

His weight was a welcome pressure against her, and his warmth was equally welcome. "Are you always the sort to show up for the last minute rescue?"

"My fleet showing up? Or is that a question about my stamina and timing?"

"Neither. I'm trying to gauge what sort of ally you represent."

There was a mirthful lightness to his smile that abruptly disappeared. "Your doctors brought me around once they had power. The charming one—"

"Commander Dietrich."

"That one. He told me I needed to bring my fleet to bear. So I made a call. I'm sure I sounded pathetic with all the drugs I had in me."

"What matters is our allies saved the day."

"I'm not sure I'll be an ally for long, Captain Benson."

"Faith, please. At least while we're like this."

He chuckled, but it was an anxious sound. "I'm serious."

She helped him through the conference room hatch and into a seat, then she tugged the hem of her jacket until everything felt right again. As the display came to life, she settled in the chair beside him, wondering if there was a slight whiff of cologne under the boring smell of soap and freshly printed uniform. What sort of cologne did a man who grew up in the slums but rose to part-time fleet captain wear? It seemed like something sweet and herbal.

Thiessen's face creased, but he turned from her to the display where a timer was counting down. "One minute, five seconds. You know they'll be late."

"In the military, it's a show of authority. If a senior officer is prompt, there's a worry it signals that he or she isn't important enough. At least that's what some of them think."

"Some things are universal, then." He glanced at his quivering hand, then balled it into a fist.

"You worry this committee will sever the proposed alliance?"

"Sever?" He snorted. "It was never officially signed."

"So they'll seek the means to escape it?"

"They had the opportunity to throw in with your government when you offered what looked like a pretty lopsided deal and didn't. Now they know what's out there, threatening us."

The counter dropped to ten seconds, then proceeded to zero—right on time.

Benson straightened. "Well, that's surprising. Let's come back to the worst-case scenario analysis after the meeting."

"My point is that you need to be ready for that worst case."

The display scrambled into a billion dazzling colors, then those collapsed into an unfamiliar symbol that must have belonged to one of the other corporations besides Gulmar. After several seconds of what seemed to be branding video, the display resolved into another ostentatious conference room filled with an assortment of beautiful people in outrageously expensive clothing.

A young-looking, dark-haired woman with a high forehead sat at the head of the table, smiling stiffly. "Hello. Is this Captain Faith Benson?"

"Of the Kedraalian ship *Valor*." Benson leaned toward Thiessen. "I'm here with Captain Floyd Thiessen, captain of your second fleet."

That shattered the smile. "Actually, we have no need of Mr. Thiessen's presence in this meeting."

Without meaning to, Benson jerked forward. "What?"

"We have yet to agree upon the wording, Captain Benson, but you should receive a formal request for the arrest of Mr. Thiessen by close of business today."

"Arrest?"

"Sadly, yes."

Benson caught the stiffness in the other officer's posture. He must have expected something like this. Why hadn't he said anything? "Excuse me, Miss—?"

"Elle Baumeier. I'm the head of the search committee."

"Well, Miss Baumeier, your search committee wouldn't even be around right now if not for the captain's quick and deliberate actions."

"That doesn't change anything."

"It needs to. You were all minutes away from being turned into ash."

Baumeier blinked rapidly, and the same forced smile reappeared. "Captain Benson, does your military have laws?"

"Yes."

"And do those laws clarify the limits of your roles? Because ours do. Mr. Thiessen operated well outside the limits of his position when he scrambled his crew. He went even further outside the limits of his position by having the fleet move into position to engage the Khanate ships."

"I would assume that even for your government, command officers are provided some leeway in the execution of their duties, Miss Baumeier."

"Mr. Thiessen wasn't acting in his capacity as an officer. Even if he were, we don't expect our security forces to operate independently of their rulers."

"So you plan to charge him with what?"

"This is a matter for the new leadership group, not for the Republic's representative. I will remind you: You're just a negotiator, not an ally."

Thiessen winced. "I would hope the charges don't extend to other personnel."

The executive frowned. "That's also a matter for the new leadership."

Benson muted the connection. "Floyd, I'm going to need you to trust me on where I'm taking this."

"I'm a little short on trust right now."

"I think this will work." Benson did her best to smile, which grew in strength when he gave a resigned nod.

She took the connection off mute. "Miss Baumeier, I assume you've had the opportunity to review the analysis of the Khanate engagement that I provided?"

"We're still going through the detail—"

"Let me provide a summary for you: Radetta should be a lifeless husk."

The executive leaned closer to her camera. "Excuse me, Captain?"

"The Khanate fleet not only has more firepower than your two fleets combined, they have shadow technology we still haven't quite cracked. Your ships obviously have inadequate systems to even manage what we—"

"That's quite enough—"

"—managed. Yet Captain Thiessen was able to not only get enough personnel into space before the subsequent wave of attacks could—"

Baumeier jumped to her feet. "That will be—"

"Don't think you can order me around, Miss Baumeier. You hold a temporary position on a committee that will search for someone who will be nothing more than a spokesperson for a group of allied corporations."

"You have no right—"

"Stop. Right now." Benson pressed a knuckle against her forehead. "I want you to ask yourself: What's stopping me from finishing what the Khanate started?"

The young executive's jaw dropped. "Threats are hardly responsible negotiation tactics."

"It's not a threat. I'm pointing out what should be obvious to you: You have *nothing* defending you. Arrest Captain Thiessen and his crews, and your last fleet doesn't even have anyone to crew it."

"These are ships that are largely automated. We can train new crews inside of a year."

"And you think the Khanate will wait a year to return to finish the job?"

Baumeier folded her arms over her chest. "The Republic came to us seeking allies, Captain. Are you rescinding that offer?"

"What value do you present to the Kedraalian Republic if you can't field a fleet?"

"That hardly sounds like the words of an ally."

"We're not allies, remember? I believe you said I was just a negotiator?"

Heads turned around to the youthful executive. She glanced around the table, mouth working without speaking.

Except she was—she'd muted her end. Then the connection closed.

Benson exhaled, then turned to Thiessen. "Before you—"

"Hell." Thiessen ran a shaking hand over his face. "I'm trying to back your move here, but you're sounding pretty crazy."

"I'm speaking the truth: We're not allies."

"Yeah, that sounds opportunistic to someone who just lost his home."

"Sorry. It's the hard truth. We came here seeking people who could help us. If she cripples her fleet, she removes any value as an ally. An ally has to contribute *something* to—"

The connection to the search committee resumed. Baumeier had returned to her seat. "Captain Benson?"

Benson tried to seem as relaxed as the other woman. "Yes?"

"We would like to initiate negotiations with you immediately. Would you be available to come down to meet with us next week?"

"No, actually."

"No?"

"We can begin today, if you'd like. However, you should know that any negotiations are going to have preconditions."

"Pre—?" Baumeier raised her chin slightly. "Such as?"

"First, you must have a standing security force. Without that, you don't interest us."

"We…" The executive cleared her throat. "That takes time."

"Second, you must have a proven, competent officer leading that security force. Captain Floyd Thiessen represents the only competent senior officer I've met in your security force to date, so if you want to expedite negotiations, I would recommend appointing him interim security chief."

"That's not—"

Benson held up a hand. "You *do* know what preconditions are, don't you, Ms. Baumeier?"

The executive's face pinched, adding years to her appearance. "Are there any others?"

"I could have reinforcements en route to Radetta with a single call. That could place a small task force in orbit around your planet capable of detecting the enemy fleet. Combined with elements of your Second Fleet, you would have an effective defense. However, I would expect you to contribute part of your fleet to the war against the Khanate. Once again, my preference would be to have that force led by Captain Thiessen."

"And is there anything *else*?"

"Along with fully funding your security forces, you will need to begin constructing ships to replace your lost fleet and to start training crews. And I don't want to hear about the costs and your concerns for profit. I think it should be quite obvious by now that the Republic is shouldering the bulk of the economic burden in this matter. All we ask of you is to show a little interest in your own survival."

Baumeier drummed fingers on the tabletop before her. "And you intend to pursue this Khanate fleet with this joint task force?"

"I think we'll need to seek out allies first."

The young executive perked up. "*That* we can agree with. And here's where we would assert our own precondition: Our allies in this joint endeavor will be the Azoren."

Benson flinched. It was a fair demand, and there weren't really any other options. She'd been coming to grips with that for days. "I would like to hold our first meeting in four hours, Ms. Baumeier."

"We'll be wrapping for the day—"

"Then a working dinner seems ideal." Benson stood. "We'll have the

Azoren ambassador with us, so please plan to have him at the table as well. Captain Benson out."

She killed the connection.

Thiessen stared at the black display. "I never thought I'd see the day where someone was more cold-blooded than a Gulmar executive."

"Cold-blooded?" She bent down to help him to his feet. "I prefer to think of it as practical."

He grunted as he got his balance. "Is this something you learned from your mother?"

"In a way, I guess." She threw his arm over her shoulder. "It's time we pay Ambassador Manshaus a visit. We have some negotiations to attend to, and I think he's going to want to be part of those."

Caville's head felt heavy, as if it were sinking deep into his pillow. The look on Stiles's face—the pained acceptance of her fate—gnawed at him. They'd been competitors since childhood, but in a way, they'd also been friends.

And now she was gone from his life.

The hatch to his small compartment opened, and the lights flickered on. Dark gray walls, scuffed and stained, drew the light in. They were just another reminder of the conditions he had come to call home in the years since accepting the mission he was sure would be his last.

Goldman stepped in, two bottles of beer held high. "Is it too early for a peace offering?"

Caville spun around on his butt, setting his socked feet on the deck. Like him, the captain was down to casual clothes now that they were underway. "It's never too early for brews."

The pirate sat down at the foot of the bed and offered one of the beers. "I'm sorry you had to kill her. You know my rules about spies."

"You're a spy."

"That's how I know not to trust them. I mean, I trust you. You've proved yourself. You did it again today."

"Yeah." The drink was cold, with a heavy hops undertone that lingered.

Goldman rubbed condensation from the brown glass of his bottle. "You were close to her?"

"We worked a couple tough jobs. You know how that is."

"Sure. They're all tough."

"Some are worse than others. There aren't a lot of people like Brianna."

"That was classy, paying Devanshi to take her body down to Dramora."

"Brianna would have wanted that."

"She was from there?"

"No. I think she just assigned some sort of meaning to it."

"Did you love her?"

Memories bubbled up: their childhood; the intense competition; and the times where they actually tried to hurt each other. "In a way, I guess."

"And you didn't know she was trying to kill Denise?"

"It's the shadows, Lev. You never know the real truth until a second before the bullet hits."

"Fair enough. But you know the mission now, right?"

"I know it. Rescue the hostages, or all these years of kowtowing to the Khanate mean nothing."

"It has to mean something. Billions of credits have been spent on this."

"And when we're done with them?"

The pirate captain finished off his beer, then belched. "I don't know. We're not paid to think about that, are we?"

Caville drained his bottle. "We aren't."

"Don't make it sound like the end of the universe." Goldman collected Caville's empty bottle. "Get some rest. We've got a lot of work to do before we drop the goods off. You might want to see if you can repair trust with Denise. She was pretty rattled by this whole thing."

"Hard to believe a Khanate spy has never seen a corpse before."

"I think it was more the idea that someone had come so close to killing her."

"How unfortunate."

Goldman stopped at the hatch. "They're still our partners in this."

"They are. I get it."

For a few seconds, the pirate captain just stared, then he chuckled. "Go pull your magic on Denise. She's pretty enough, you'll be over your heart-break in no time. Who know—maybe you can convert her."

Caville waited until the hatch closed again, then he pushed up from the bunk. The idea had some merit. Getting close to the Khanate spy had a lot of potential upsides, and using his abilities to seduce her certainly would put him in a good position once they landed on Azh Shivan.

And what he had to accomplish there... That would take a lot more pain away.

But he had to survive until then.

And there were a lot of shadows to pass through on the way.

ACKNOWLEDGMENTS

Shadow Talk is the fourth chapter of **The War in Shadow**. This chapter is once again a combination of space opera and military science fiction, something I really enjoy and hope I can convey to readers.

The historical influences on *Shadow Talk* may not be obvious, but they draw from many sources, the greatest being the ugly work around the Iran rebellion (including the Iran-Contra scandal).

If you are enjoying this series, I hope you'll consider posting a review of the books and letting friends know about it. Word of mouth and reviews are pure gold.

For updates on new releases and news on other series, please visit my website and sign up for my mailing list at:

http://www.p-r-adams.com

ABOUT THE AUTHOR

I was born and raised in Tampa, Florida. I joined the Air Force, and my career took me from coast to coast before depositing me in the St. Louis, Missouri area for several years. After a tour in Korea and a short return to the St. Louis area, I retired and moved to the greater Denver, Colorado metropolitan area.

I write speculative fiction, mostly science fiction and fantasy. My favorite writers over the years have been Robert E. Howard, Philip K. Dick, Roger Zelazny, and Michael Crichton.

Social Media:
www.p-r-adams.com
pradams_author@comcast.net

www.ingramcontent.com/pod-product-compliance
Lightning Source LLC
Chambersburg PA
CBHW070821190726
48292CB00006B/2075